Praise for Council of Peacocks

"You dive into this world and feel for once
someone has not re-told the same story
with just a different colouring."

- CHRISTOPH FISCHER,
author of *The Three Nations Trilogy*.

"The Council of Peacocks has it all: epic
battles, conspiracy theories, romance, and
a great story line. The first page will suck
you into a complex and unpredictable,
page-turning plot."

- TIFFANY HUSON

"This is precisely the kind of book I
enjoy reading. It hits all the buttons: Epic battles,
...moments of self-discovery, ...tales
of heroes and villains, and of course there's loads of
angst ridden teenagers with badass
paranormal/psychokinesis abilities."

- TRAVIS LUEDKE,
Author of *The Nightlife Series*

Works by M Joseph Murphy

ACTIVATION SERIES
Council of Peacocks
Beyond the Black Sea
Terra Incognita (Coming 2015)

SWORD OF KASSANDRA SERIES
A Fallen Hero Rises
Demons of DunDegore (Coming Sept 2014)

Council of Peacocks

Book One: Activation Series

M Joseph Murphy

Council of Peacocks

Cover design by M Joseph Murphy
M Joseph Murphy's Official Website: mjosephmurphy.info

First electronic Edition: July 2013
First Paperback Edition: June 2014

"The risks of too much knowledge are far greater than the menace of too little. With knowledge comes responsibility and power – two things for which the race is not yet ready."
Alice Bailey, *Initiation, Human and Solar*

"To Paradise, the Arabs say, Satan could never find the way. Until the peacock led him in."
Charles Godfrey Leland, *The Peacock*

To Rob Welch.
Council of Peacocks would never have
seen the light of day without you.

Chapter One

Wisdom fell fifty feet and landed face-first on concrete. His skull bounced off the sidewalk twice. Then he lay still. He kept his eyes closed. Each breath brought stabbing pain. At least three ribs were broken. Probably more. Still, it was over: the Djinn was dead.

Nearby, a little girl screamed.

He blinked repeatedly, forcing his eyes to focus. Misty shapes solidified and he realized he was no longer in the underground fortress of the Council. Cold mist fell on his face. The air rumbled with the sound of rushing water. He realized where he was.

"Niagara Falls? How the hell...?"

He pushed himself up on weak arms and looked around. Snow-covered ice blanketed everything. Spray from the waterfall froze on the faces and jackets of the crowd of tourists gathered around him. They stared at him, repulsed. Looking down, he saw why. It was impossible to tell where tattered flesh ended and tattered suit began: both were the same shade of red. Fortunately, aside from the ribs, nothing seemed to be broken. It was small consolation. Everything had gone so wrong.

Well, not everything.

"I won," he said. The Djinn was dead and the Council defeated. His back muscles spasmed as he forced himself to his feet. "Any idea what the date is? Don't worry, I won't bite."

A woman with overly-bleached blond hair took off running before he finished speaking. Two men in their early twenties stared at him and took a collective step back.

"Jesus, I said I wouldn't bite." Wisdom stretched his arms, groaning as tattered muscles and tendons slipped back into place. "Now tell me what day it is before I change my mind about the biting thing."

"Is there a problem here?"

He turned to face a thick-armed police officer with a graying crew cut.

"There won't be a problem if someone tells me what the bloody date is." Wisdom spoke through clenched jaws. "Did they outlaw common courtesy while I was away?"

"You've been away, eh?" The police officer scratched his jaw and stared openly at Wisdom. Then he exhaled slowly, an internal conversation flashing across his face. "You're in pretty rough shape there. Maybe it would be best if you come with me."

Wisdom clenched his fists; orange fire flared in his eyes.

The police officer rose off the ground two feet, clutching his throat as if being choked by invisible hands.

"Maybe," Wisdom said, "it would be best if you just answered the damn question."

"It's January 15th!"

"Four months," he said. "We fought for four months? That definitely explains why I'm exhausted." Wisdom smiled down at the young girl who had shouted the date and relaxed his fists. The police officer dropped, reaching for his gun even as he struggled back to his feet.

"This is tiresome." Wisdom waved his hand and the man stopped moving.

Everyone within seven hundred feet stopped moving.

A hush fell on Queen Victoria Park. The only sound was the rush of the Niagara River racing over the escarpment to slam against the rocks below. Some things even Wisdom's power couldn't stop. He walked up wide stone steps toward the nearest hotel.

Something moved at the edge of the temporal distortion. He turned slowly toward it. Near the entrance to an alleyway, behind a hot dog stand, a glint of gold flashed. Just a speck of light. He tried to focus on whatever was moving in the shadows, but the harder he concentrated, the more the image blurred.

"I'm seeing things," he said. "Must be more drained than I thought." He rubbed his eyes and walked away from the mystery.

Each step was painful. Shoeless, his raw, open flesh and exposed bones left a trail of bloody footprints behind him. Snow crunched underfoot, the sound echoing back from parked cars and storefronts. Past the edge of his displaced time, children pulled at parents' hands, urging them into arcades and haunted houses.

"Hasn't changed much," he said under his breath. "Haven't been here in years. Still the same flashy lights and gaudy tourist traps. Looks like I'm not the only thing keeping this city stuck in time."

He slipped through the revolving doors of a hotel. People in winter coats scattered. Two heavily-muscled men in crisp white security uniforms marched toward him, clubs in hand. A balding man behind the front desk reached for the phone.

"Put that down." The concierge went rigid and did as he was told.

Then Wisdom turned to the security guards. "And you two, go home. Consider this a spa day." The stern intimidation on each guard's face was replaced by vacant numbness. In unison, they nodded and walked out the front door.

Wisdom sighed and limped the rest of the way to the front desk.

"Now. Please. Give me the best room you have. And I don't care if it's occupied. Just give me the key. I'll take care of anyone in the room. Also, I want clothes." Wisdom reached over the counter for a pen and pad of paper. Blood dripped from his forearms onto a pile of credit card receipts behind the counter. "These are my measurements. Charge everything to my room. And send up food, too. One of everything on the menu."

The front desk clerk nodded slowly, the same vacant look on his face. He programmed a keycard and handed it to Wisdom.

"Thank you." Wisdom bowed his head. Keycard in

hand, he went to the bank of elevators on the other side of the lobby. People stared at him and talked amongst themselves, but no one else approached him. At the elevators, he pushed the button and waited. And waited. He grunted and pushed the button several more times.

"I can kill a Djinn yet, despite all my power, I'm stuck waiting on elevators. My life is brimful of subtext." While the car descended, he studied his reflection in the mirrored walls, finally seeing the extent of his injuries. He was a large man, nearly seven feet tall, with thick, well-developed muscles. His skin was normally dark brown, the color of wet dirt. It was impossible to tell in his current state. Large chunks of his flesh were missing, revealing wet gristle and bone. His black eyes glowed reddish-orange, adding an extra element of menace. "I look like day-old road kill."

Eventually, the elevator arrived. Mercifully, the other guests let him ride up alone. He rode to the 16th floor and found the room listed on the keycard. It was a two-story presidential suite complete with whirlpool. Thankfully, it was unoccupied.

He headed straight for the bathroom. He pulled off the remnants of his clothes, careful not to pull away flesh. They fell in wet piles on the tiled floor.

"I pity the bastard who has to clean this up," he said as he turned on the shower. "Speaking of poor bastards, I wonder what happened to the Anomalies. Did Elaine get them out? I should call Echo." He shook the thought away. Whatever had happened to the Anomalies, he was in no shape to deal with it now. He'd been gone for four months. A few more days wouldn't change anything. All that mattered was Echo, and he felt certain she was fine. She was a survivor.

He stepped under the water, hissing in pain. Loose pieces of flesh flapped under the spray. The shower quickly filled with blood. He thought of biting his lip to brace against screaming but decided against it. In his current state, it might come off. He leaned against the shower wall and stayed under the water until it ran cool. Then he turned the taps off and stood on shaky knees.

Looking at the pools of blood covering the floor, Wisdom grunted. To get back he would have step through the mess he'd made. He waved his hand and the blood disappeared. Then, so as not to make his actions futile, he cauterized his wounds by will. The exertion was regrettable. He fell to his knees for a moment until his strength returned.

"Guess I'd better not attempt to heal myself just yet. It'll probably take at least a week before I'm back to my old self. I can't risk heading to one of my offices either, not before I know what I'm heading into. The Council may be defeated but they have allies."

Pushing himself back to his feet, he walked to the king-sized bed and slipped beneath the covers. He turned on the TV, flipping channels until he found an infomercial about a complex food processor. Completely engrossed, he watched for several minutes.

"What the hell am I doing?" Embarrassed, he changed the channel. "I haven't cooked my own meals in decades." He surfed for a few more minutes. Then he landed on CNN. What he saw made him feel much colder than the snow and ice outside.

Greece.

Wolf Blitzer sat on an overly-lit set constructed atop the White Tower in Thessaloniki. The night sky sporadically exploded in blasts of light and sound. But it was the man in the chair next to Wolf that concerned Wisdom.

"I'm here with Propates," Wolf said into the camera. "He's the leader of the Council of Peacocks who, as we speak, continues to challenge the Greek government for sovereignty over the area. This is the twenty-third day of the occupation. Casualties have been extremely one-sided. Hundreds confirmed dead. Despite their best efforts, the Greeks have yet to win a single skirmish. The U.N. remains uncommitted, with no other country willing to commit. Earlier today, we were contacted by Propates. He wants the

Greeks to 'stop fighting a war they cannot win' – his words. Propates, you claim your once-secret organization has found a way to forcibly evolve humans. Some feel statements like this prove you're a little, how shall I say..."

"Nuts?" Propates smiled at Wolf and winked at the camera. He was darkly handsome with an olive complexion and short-cropped black hair. His eyes were a shade of bluish-green that hinted of the ocean: the color of peacock feathers. "I'll tell you what's nuts, Wolf. It's completely insane for people to see what me and the other Council members are capable of doing and continue to delude themselves."

Wisdom clenched his fists, tearing at the sheets. His concentration flickered. Blood leaked from his wounds.

Propates turned back to Wolf. "There are hundreds of Council members around the world. Thirteen of us walked into Athens. We tore the city apart. Thirteen. I believe it was your network that showed the first images. And then there are my angels, the Edimmu. You can probably see some of them flying behind us right now. We have tens of thousands. This war is already won. To pretend it's not, that, my friend, is truly insane."

Wolf swallowed visibly, his complexion pale despite the heavy makeup. "We have reports today, as I'm sure you've heard, from the Vatican."

"Oh, yes. I've heard."

"They declared you are Satan and that the Last Days are here."

"I suppose I should be flattered." Propates turned to the camera again. "But I'm not. Whether you call him Argus or Melek Taus, Christians have vilified my God for centuries. They're right about one thing. These definitely are the last days of the old regime. Big changes are coming. If the Pope has anything else to say, I'd be more than happy to pop on over to Rome for a private conversation."

Wisdom shook his head. "Propates, what the hell are you doing?"

"Well, well, well." On the screen, Propates slowly sat back in his chair and looked fully into the camera. "Wolf, I'm afraid I have to leave. I just got a message from an old friend."

With a burst of bright light, the camera flickered and the TV screen filled with static.

Wisdom jumped out of bed. He waved his hand, calling up the thin threads of his power. White sheets leapt off the bed and coiled around his body. They twisted and mutated around from their original form into a blood-red three-piece suit. Fear threatened to overwhelm him. He thought of running but shook the thought away. He couldn't let Propates see how weak he was.

Darkness dripped like syrup down the walls, filling the room like a pool. Within moments the hotel room was flooded with shadow. He saw the face first. It surfaced from the murk, eyes and smile bright sparks. Then Propates stepped forward and he was fully in the hotel room. Behind him, there were hints of movement in the shadows. Propates had not come alone.

"Well, Wisdom, I was beginning to wonder when your father would tire of torturing you."

Momentary doubt crossed Wisdom's mind. He shook it away. "Your ignorance is tiring. Once again, you prove how little you know, Propates. My father didn't torture me. He wanted to drag me back to the Kaz. We fought. Then I killed him."

"Really? Shame. Considering the deal we worked out."

Doubt returned and settled firmly in Wisdom's mind.

"You see, Wisdom, you're the arrogant one. That's not an insult. It's just the truth. You think you're so smart, but you've never been able to see the 'Big Picture.' You always focus on the individual pieces, not how they mingle together. Did you wonder *why* your father chose now to come get you? Of course not. That would require forethought. Or maybe you just underestimated me. I'm not the Roman peasant I used to be. I outplayed you. This is check and mate.

Concede."

"Send all the Edimmu after me you want." Wisdom took a step forward. He hid how much his knees trembled, but just barely.

Propates sneered and looked over his shoulder. "I didn't bring Edimmu. These are your precious Anomalies. You still don't get it, do you? Echo did, in the end. And I'm afraid I do mean it was the end for her. You see, unlike you, she was an intellectual threat. So I tossed her into a volcano."

Wisdom took another step forward. This time his knees didn't tremble in the least.

"Relax, Wisdom." The movement from the shadows behind Propates increased. "I'm not here to fight. The Council has big plans for this planet. You could still be part of it. You and I working together just like old times. Don't you see what we've already accomplished?"

"Spell it out for me." Wisdom's head pounded, his face flush with anger. "After all, I'm too stupid to see the big picture, right?"

Propates walked over to a burgundy chair by the window and, with a quiet chuckle, sat down. "I really have you to thank. What you did to me and Echo was the inspiration for the project. We perfected the process of Eyeness. It took longer than expected, but the results are remarkable. Just imagine the forced evolution of the human race, the things we could be capable of. So much untapped power. We used your Anomalies, but I'm afraid you may not recognize them anymore. The process does put the body through a few changes."

Wisdom held his hand up. With a grunt, he pushed the shadows away. They retreated like soiled water flowing down the drain. The strain opened up several of his old wounds but he felt little of the pain. He was alone with Propates.

"Congratulations." Wisdom wiped blood from his lip. "You've won. Touché and all that. I can't believe I didn't see this coming. Really, I can't. I guess you're right. I did underestimate you. Fortunately for me, you've made two mistakes."

"Really? And what would they be?" Propates beamed, the smile on his face showing no trace of fear.

"First, never make deals with my father. Djinn can't be trusted. You see, if he really wanted you to succeed, he would have let you in on a little secret. Your second mistake. Remember the portals I can make? The ones that let me travel around the world? The ones I taught you and Echo how to make so long ago?" Wisdom leaned forward and lowered his voice. Now it was his turn to smile. "I didn't teach you everything."

"What are you getting at, Wisdom?" Doubt flickered across Propates' face.

"Come now. You pride yourself on how smart you are. I could give you a hint, but from the look on your face, I think you've worked it out."

Propates was on his feet moving toward Wisdom.

Wisdom's eyes flashed bright orange. With a flick of the wrist he sent Propates flying; he crashed through the reinforced windows and fell to the streets below.

"See you soon," Wisdom said. Then he opened a portal and traveled back through time.

Chapter Two

July 30th

Driving down the dirt road, Josh removed his sunglasses when the sun dropped below the tall pines. They had left Ottawa only two hours ago but this felt like an alien world: pristine and pure. Beside him, his girlfriend, Jan, admired the tree-covered mountains of the Laurentians. The six of them were going to the cabin Jan's parents owned on Lac Manitou. The SUV was filled with enough food and alcohol to tide them over for the three weeks they planned to spend in the woods. Jan's parents had paid for all of it. Money was no object as long as Jan spent it somewhere else.

"Jesus! You drive like an old woman. We should have been there, like, five hours ago."

"What are you? Twelve?" Josh glanced in the rearview mirror at his best friend. Brian was a thick-necked brute with hazel eyes and short brown hair. On a good day, he verged on charming. Today was not one of those days. "Just chill and have another drink?"

"Way ahead of you." Brian smiled and sipped vodka from a Tim Hortons' cup. "It's not the same, though. These cups make the vodka taste like ass."

Josh shook his head. "And yet you still drink it. Says volumes about you. Since I'm an old lady, did you wanna drive for a bit? Oh wait. You can't. Someone lost their license because they were stupid enough to drive drunk."

"Correction." Rebecca, Brian's girlfriend since 10th grade, looked up from her cell phone. Her long, curly brown hair was pulled away from her face to deal with the heat. She sat directly behind Jan. "Someone was stupid enough to get *caught* drinking and driving. I'm sure he's learned his lesson. Does anyone else have service? My phone just died."

"Maybe it's a sign to put your phone away." Matt stopped making out with his new girlfriend, Tonia, and leaned forward from the back row of seats. "And for the record, Brian's not really the learning type. Anyone know exactly how many times he's smashed his car into the garage? Anyone? 'Cause, you know, I can't."

"Twice." Brian turned around in his seat and faced Matt. "I did that twice. And it's not like I broke the garage. Bunch of puritans, that's what you are."

Josh reached over and squeezed Jan's hand. She smiled and squeezed back. Then his smile slipped as he remembered the problems back home. For the last six months, his parents' fighting was on a whole new level. Mom accused Dad of having an affair. Dad claimed it was only work that took him away from home. Considering what Dad did, it was feasible.

"You're doing it again." Jan put a hand on his neck and massaged the tension away. She was nearly the physical antithesis of Josh. Every feature on her face hinted at prestige and class. Josh's features were soft and boyish, almost feminine. She kept her black hair in a short bob; his was a thick, blond tangle. The only attribute they shared in common was their light blue eyes. "We agreed no wallowing until we return to civilization, remember?"

Josh turned to her and smiled. "Sorry. Thanks for noticing."

"Not like you're hard to read, Mr. Wilkinson." She released his hand and checked her cell. "You're easily the worst liar I've ever met, which is just fine by me. I have no signal either, Becka. Must be a dead zone."

"Is there coverage at the cabin?" Tonia said as she checked her phone. "My parents will freak if they can't contact me."

"Unfortunately, there is." Jan put her phone away. "We're supposed to be getting away from all this crap. Otherwise, what's the point in camping?"

Moments later, Josh reached down and turned up the music.

"Hey, what's up?" Jan asked. "Don't like my singing?"

"Were you singing?" He pretended to wince as Jan slapped him.

"You know I was. You always do that – turn up the music when I'm singing."

"Really? Must be a coincidence. I just love this song."

Brian kicked the back of Josh's chair. "Since when do you like One Direction, man? Just tell her the truth. No? Fine, then I will. Every time you sing, Josh gets so blinded by his love for you that he just can't drive straight. That's why he's turning up the music."

"Oh please." Matt threw a book at Brian's head. It missed and hit Josh.

"Come on guys! Trying to drive here." Josh yelled into the rear-view mirror. The horseplay wouldn't normally bother him. Maybe Jan was right. Maybe he was letting things back home get to him.

"Oh yeah," Rebecca said as she grabbed Brian's cup. "All this traffic makes it really dangerous. What do you think you'd hit? A moose?"

"Either that or a tree." Josh brushed his sweat-damp hair from his forehead. "I'm not trying to be a buzz kill. Just stop the flying shrapnel, okay?"

Josh turned off onto a road marked with a hand-painted sign. On one side of the road, he caught glimpses of the lake. The trees pushed in further on the road, blocking out even more light.

"Do people actually live up here?" Tonia pushed her glasses back into place and stared out the windows at tall pine trees on either side of the road. "We haven't seen a car or house since we left that creepy gas station."

"What's the matter?" Matt put his arm around Tonia and passed her a wine cooler. "Afraid this is going to turn out to be a little Québécois *Chainsaw Massacre* thing? Of course people live here. And not the crazy hillbilly type. The guy in the cottage next to ours has a helicopter pad. Tons of celebrities and millionaires buy places out here. You couldn't ask for a safer place. Or maybe," he said leaning forward, fingers curled into claws. "Maybe there are cannibal fur traders just waiting in the woods to…"

The front two tires blew out. With a loud hiss and pop, the SUV swerved off the road.

A sudden rush of adrenaline negated Josh's exhaustion. He fought with the steering wheel to get the SUV back on the asphalt. He knew it was a losing battle even before they hit the tree. Luckily, everyone was wearing their seatbelts. Aside from the burn of the seatbelts against their chests, there were no injuries. The vehicle, however, was totaled. The front end was wrapped firmly around an evergreen.

"Damn." Matt's voice was quiet.

The engine sputtered and died. The wind blew through the trees; birds called out from unseen places. Josh turned off the ignition. He looked over his shoulder at Brian and Matt. Without a word, the men got out of the vehicle to inspect the damage.

"This can't be happening," Matt held his head with both hands. He looked up and down the street. There was still no sign of other cars.

"Your dad is so going to kill you." Brian walked to the front of the SUV and stared at the crunched metal. Slowly and repeatedly, he shook his head.

"How bad is it?" Jan got out of the vehicle, rubbing her chest where the seatbelt had hit.

"Get back in the car," Josh said. He inhaled deeply and knelt to inspect the tires. When he stood, he held two foot-long shards of metal. They were black and tapered, shaped like long feathers. On the wide end was an etching of a peacock.

Matt knelt down and inspected the front tires on the passenger side. "Crap. There's some over here, too."

Jan stared at the daggers still stuck in the passenger-side tire. "It's possible they were just lying in the road."

Josh gave her a very steady look. Then he turned to study the woods.

"Crap." Brian's eyes went wide. "Rebecca, stay in the

car." He surveyed the woods on the other side of the road.

Matt looked at Tonia and just shook his head.

"Pull those things out," Josh said. "You're going to need them."

"Stop, Josh. You're freaking me out." Brian's eyes were red.

"Good. We need to be scared. They've done this before. If we don't think straight, we're as good as dead."

"What about you, Josh?" Matt asked. "You're smaller than either of us."

"There's not enough for all of us," Josh said. "I can take care of myself."

"But...?" Matt said.

"Let it go." Brian took one of the daggers, all the while staring at Josh.

"Oh? Had many encounters with crazed woodmen who trap tourists?"

"Not exactly. Let's just say I have a few secrets. We don't have time for this. This is the point in the movies when the disposable teens split up."

"And the body count starts." Matt went pale as soon as he realized what he had just said. He backed up until his shoulders were firmly against the side of the SUV. Tonia knocked on the window and he whirled around. Opening the side door, he passed a shard to each of the women. "We probably won't need these. Just to be safe." Matt smiled. It was thin and unconvincing.

"Safe?" Tonia pressed a hand against her stomach, repulsed as she took the blade.

"We can't stay here," Jan walked over to Josh and grabbed his arm. "We're sitting ducks. They're probably watching us right now. What if they have guns?"

Josh kissed her on the cheek. "If they had guns they probably would've shot the tires out."

"You'd have to be a pretty good shot to hit the tires of a moving car." Jan studied the metal in her hands. "Sharp objects on the road make for better odds."

Rebecca stepped out of the car, blade in hand. "Don't you think we're, like, overreacting or something? Maybe these things just fell off a truck or something."

"Shut up." Josh held up his hand and whispered the word. It was enough to quiet everyone. He walked up the road, eyes down.

"Wait up!" Jan raced after him. "Where are you going? You know we shouldn't split up."

"They shouldn't have gone into the tires like that."

"What do you mean?"

Josh stopped and turned to her. "Sharp pieces of metal lying in the road would tear a hole in the tread. They wouldn't get stuck in like that."

Jan shook her head for a moment. Then she nodded and folded her arms across her chest. "They went in the side of the tires."

Josh nodded. "I doubt they'd be in the sides if we ran over them. Help me look. If someone threw them, there could be others lying around."

Brian walked over from the SUV. "What's going on here, Josh?"

"I don't know."

"Is this like the last time?"

Josh stopped. "What last time? What are you talking about?"

Brian opened his mouth, then sighed and looked at the ground. "Never mind."

"No sign of any others," Jan said.

Josh wiped the sweat from his forehead. "Means they must be really good shots. Didn't miss once."

Brian stiffened and his eyes went wide. "Either that or they ran up to the road and got them back already."

Josh looked at his best friend and his girlfriend.

Jan started to back up. "We should get back."

Josh nodded.

They all walked quickly back to the SUV.

"Are we going?" Rebecca asked.

"We stay," Brian took her in his arms and kissed the top of her head. "It's not much, but the vehicle is the only cover we have. That and the trees. Besides, it's not impossible that another car could drive by. I'm not holding my breath, but it could happen. In theory."

Josh reached into the car to grab his sunglasses. "Why did we take this way again?"

Jan rolled her eyes. "You wanted to try a different route than last year. See new scenery."

"Looks like you got your wish." Rebecca shook her dagger at Josh.

"Yikes." Josh bit his lip and winced. "Sorry. Let's try to get this off the tree." He opened the front passenger door, stepped inside and reached over the wheel. He turned the key a quarter turn until he heard the steering wheel unlock. Then he put the gear in neutral and slid back out. "Tonia, take the wheel. Everyone else, come help. The way it's lodged, we're going to need you."

Within seconds, Tonia was craning her neck to look out the rear window while the other five pushed on the front of the car.

She never saw what hit her.

"Jesus Christ!" Brian screamed as the driver's side window exploded. Glass fragments blasted everywhere. Instinctively, everyone covered their faces and closed their eyes.

Josh dropped to the ground. He pulled the others by their shorts and beltlines until all were lying flat in the underbrush. Matt wheezed, an asthmatic sound. His body went through a steady string of spasms. As he stared into nothing, his lips worked their way around Tonia's name.

"Stay." Josh gripped Jan's shoulder, making it an order rather than a plea. He crawled on his stomach toward the road; each breath was hot and painful. "Please don't be dead," he whispered to himself. He hoped it'd been a rock, a bird, anything but another of those shards. A shard would mean blood and death. He got off his stomach when he reached the road, using the SUV for protection. He opened the passenger door as quietly as he could and peeked inside at Tonia's body.

"Blood and death." Her neck was twisted at an unnatural angle. The impact had snapped her spine. A six-inch black blade – identical to the ones in the tires – had slammed into the lower left section of her skull. A part of him, a dark part that spoke to him more often than he wanted to admit, told him to take the shard out of her head. It was a weapon and he was going to need it. One thought of Matt and he knew he couldn't do it.

He climbed into the SUV and pushed Tonia's body back up in the driver's seat. He crouched down near the floor and used her body as cover. He wasn't a big man. Her body wouldn't have been much protection for Matt or Brian.

Josh moved to roll down the driver's side window. When his fingers touched glass fragments on the window control, he realized what he was doing. There was no window anymore.

"Brian," he said as calmly as he could.

After a moment he heard a very quiet answer. "Is she…?"

"Not now. Keep Matt down. Don't let him see this. I want you all to stay on your knees but try to push the van backwards. I'll steer."

"Are you crazy?" Jan said. "You'll be killed."

"Not. Now. I'm okay. Don't think about what I'm doing. Just focus on pushing this thing backwards. Do it now."

He didn't expect it to work. The four of them, even Matt, were on their knees pushing the vehicle off the tree. The SUV shuddered, then, unexpectedly, pushed forcefully off the tree.

"Stay down," he said out the window. "Use the trees for protection. We know where they are now." He lied for their peace of mind more than anything. Panic would get someone else killed. He turned the key in the ignition. The engine sputtered and complained. "I need a miracle now. Right now. Come on."

The engine sparked into life. He was in the middle of breathing a sigh of relief when he saw movement out of the corner of his eye. He looked into the woods. Three dark shadows raced toward them.

Josh yelled out the window. "Get in! Now!" Maybe it was something in his voice or some sound they heard from the woods, but they all followed his lead. Still crouched over, they raced through the side doors. Josh didn't wait for the doors to close before he drove off.

Chapter Three

For several minutes they drove in silence. Jan sat behind the driver's seat constantly watching the woods. Brian sat beside her drinking vodka from the bottle. In the back row Matt sobbed, head in hands. Rebecca sat beside him, her hand on his knees.

"Please," Matt said. "You're hurting her. Stop for a second. Let me get her."

Jan touched Josh's back. "Let them move the body, Josh. You can drive better if you're the only body in the seat."

It was difficult for Josh to drive with Tonia's body in the driver's seat. He had to twist his own body at awkward angles to reach the gas pedal. His instinct told him to keep driving. Eventually they would hit a town or something. Still, he gave in to the pleas from Matt and the others.

"I'll stop up ahead at the crossroads," he said. It was the safest place he'd seen so far. There was a hundred yards of clearing between the vehicle and the edge of the woods. Once he reached it, he hit the brakes. He put it in park but kept the motor running.

He got out as Brian and Matt moved Tonia's body to the back seat. Jan went to him and they embraced.

"How are you so calm?" Jan pulled back and looked into his eyes.

Josh looked away. "I'm just in survival mode. We shouldn't stay here long. They have vehicles."

"We can't be far from the cabin." Jan took out her cell again and tapped the screen. "This is really weird. There are cell towers everywhere. I've never had service interruption up here."

"They could be jamming it."

"Are you serious? Is that possible?"

"We need to get going." Josh put an arm around her and pushed her back toward the van. "We'll call my dad from the cabin."

"Your dad? Shouldn't we call the police?"

Josh spat and smacked his head. "I'll explain later."

As soon as the front seat was clear he started driving again. He did not wait until Tonia's body was secure. No one complained. From the wide-eyed expressions on their faces, Josh suspected his level of composure scared them as much as anything else. He wanted to explain to them why he was handling this so well, but knew he couldn't. His dad had sworn him to secrecy.

He was tempted to go as fast as the SUV could take him, but the flat tires made steering unpredictable. The sound of rims scraping against the road was eerie and deafening. They needed to move quickly; no one would have a problem tracking them.

Brian came forward and spoke to Jan. "Can we switch spots?"

Jan looked at Brian curiously then slipped past him to sit beside Rebecca. He drank more vodka and stared openly at Josh.

The longer the stare continued, the more uncomfortable Josh became.

"What's up, Bri?"

"Did you catch a look at them?"

Josh nodded. "Just shadows. Three of them. They look big."

"Did they look human?"

"What?" Josh glared at his friend. "Of course they looked human. What are you talking about?"

"I remember, Josh. We've never talked about it but I do. Remember the bush party?"

"There were a lot of bush parties." A series of images flashed through his mind, but Josh couldn't place any of them.

"Not like this one." Brian stared out the window. "Grade 10, after the football game. A gang crashed it and beat the hell out of Tommy Delonki. Remember? He died a few days later?"

Josh nodded slowly. "Sorta. What does that have to do with me?"

Brian let out a snort. He coughed a little and then let out a long slow breath. "Either you think I'm a moron or you honestly don't remember. I've struggled for years with those memories. They can't be real but I remember them. I guess if you found a way to block it all out you're the lucky one."

Josh shifted uncomfortably in his seat. He looked in the rear-view mirror to see if anyone else was listening. Matt was staring straight ahead; Jan still held his hand. Rebecca was draping a blanket over Tonia's body.

"Bri, I'm not really sure what you're talking about. I barely knew Tommy Delonki. I think we had a few classes together but that's it."

"You really don't remember?" Brian turned in his chair to face him. "Tommy was your next-door neighbor. You were best friends until high school. Ring a bell? That night, at the party, you and I were doing shots when Tommy came racing out of the dark. He was all cut up and bruised wearing only a pair of jogging pants. No shoes or socks."

"How drunk are you, man? Are you taking those pills again?" Josh was beyond uncomfortable now. None of this was even vaguely familiar. How could he forget someone who'd been his best friend?

Brian hit him in the arm. Hard. "No! I'm not drunk and I haven't used those pills for years. I'll have you know the only reason I was ever on those pills is because of that night. If you don't believe me, ask Matt. He was there, too. He can also vouch for Tommy being your neighbor. You're the one with amnesia, so don't talk down to me!"

Everyone stared at them now. Brian's voice became increasingly louder as he went on. Josh looked over at him. Brian's face was red and his veins were bulging, but the redness had gone from his eyes. Whatever else he was, Brian was not drunk.

"I'm sorry," Josh said as he rubbed the back of his neck. "I don't remember him being my neighbor, or my friend. What happened?"

"How can you not remember that party?" Rebecca slid forward and handed Brian a Diet Pepsi. "I wasn't even there and I've heard about it. Weren't there, like, twenty or thirty black guys in green tracksuits or something?"

"I heard they brought guns," Matt said. Josh was surprised to hear him speak. His voice sounded far away, like he was talking in his sleep. "I remember seeing them. Sort of. They looked eight feet tall. And he was your friend, Josh. You used to skateboard with him until he had that knee surgery."

Knee surgery. For some reason that rang a bell. A memory flashed through Josh's mind: going to the hospital with a skateboard signed by everyone in his class. He could see himself giving it to a thin-boned pale boy he recognized as Tommy Delonki. His head started to hurt.

"How can I not remember him?"

"Good question." Brian cleared his throat and sank back into the passenger seat, facing forward. "I'll never forget. Tommy ran out of the woods. He bolted past everyone and went straight to you. You saw him and dropped your drink just as he collapsed. You put a hand on his cheek, like he was a lover or something, and Tommy just starts crying. *'They came back for me,'* he said. And you? You didn't ask him what he was talking about. You stood up and said *'I warned them.'* Then you grabbed a log off the bloody bonfire and started off into the woods."

"I ran into the woods with a flaming log?"

"Nuh uh. You didn't run. You walked. Gave me the damned creeps. Sobered me up, too. That's why I followed you. I saw what you did to them."

"What did I do to them?" Josh stared at his hands on the steering wheel. They were shaking.

"You killed them." Brian took a sip of his Pepsi.

"I what?"

Jan leaned forward. "What the hell are you talking about, Brian?"

"I saw it. And so did a few others. Only nothing ever happened. And I mean there must have been like twenty people around. But we never talked about it. No one went to the police. How could we? See, those guys, they weren't black guys. They had...."

Suddenly the image came back to Josh very clearly.

"They had wings."

***

No one spoke for a while.

It was just as well. Josh had a lot to process. Although he couldn't recall the events leading up to the deaths, he could clearly see himself at the party now. He heard the whirl of air and the crackle of burning embers as he swung the log. He could see his hands bashing heads, setting green wings on fire. He also remembered how expected it was. It didn't seem strange to him at the time. He knew who they were, knew what Tommy meant by *'They've come back for me.'* Now it was all a mystery.

Brian finally broke the silence.

"Is that what you were talking about?" Brian's eyes glazed over. "Back there, after the crash, you said 'I've got a few secrets'. Was that what you were talking about?"

Josh shook his head. "No. Not even close. I think we need to be clear about something. Those people in the woods back there were human. They didn't have wings or tails and they weren't eight feet tall. I didn't see their faces but they were definitely human. Doesn't make them any less dangerous. He looked in the rear-view mirror. Tonia's body bounced limply beneath the blanket. Someone had put a seatbelt across her chest to keep her upright. "Madmen are a different kind of monster. They'll use tricks, guerrilla tactics. You just never know what to expect."

"What if..." Rebecca stopped and cleared her throat. "I mean, when I think of wings, I think of angels."

"What are you talking about?" Brian shot her a look over his shoulder.

Josh felt blood rush to his face.

"I'm just saying," Rebecca sank back into her seat, pushing herself as far away from Josh as she could. "What if those things you killed were angels? Maybe this is some sort of revenge. Maybe…"

Brian turned around. "Don't!"

"I know he's your friend but how can you not see this?"

"Rebecca, you're trying in a not-so-subtle way to say this is all Josh's fault. So enough of the angel crap. If it wasn't for Josh we'd probably all be dead now."

Matt sank back into his seat, too. "Or we'd be at the cottage."

Josh felt like she had kicked him in the gut. His body went stiff, his eyes very focused on the road.

There was a long stretch of silence again before Brian continued the conversation.

"So what was it, then? What was your big secret?"

Once again, Josh felt he could breathe.

"Damn. My dad's going to kill me. If anyone deserves the truth, it's you guys. You know how my dad owns that garage downtown?"

"Yeah," Brian said. "I've picked you up there a few times. You worked there during the summer in high school."

Josh nodded while Brian talked. "It's a front. You ever heard of CSIS?"

"That show on CBS?"

"No. That's *CSI*. The one I'm talking about is kind of like the Canadian CIA. My dad works for them."

"I take it he's not a janitor." Jan chewed on her thumbnail. "Christ, you're just full of little secrets, aren't you?"

Josh swallowed, a sour taste in his mouth. "I would have told you if I could, Jan. It's kind of a hush-hush thing. Dad wasn't even supposed to tell Mom and me. He's not even a regular agent there. He belongs to this secret organization within the company. They go on special assignments and stuff, the type that creates a few enemies. Only reason we found out is we were attacked once."

"See?" Rebecca's voice was suddenly very shrill. "I told you this was his fault. Should have left him back there and we'd all be safe now."

"Enough of the psycho drama," Jan said. Her voice was little more than a whisper but the strange edge to it froze everyone. "Rebecca, take a pill and let him speak."

Josh felt his heart skip a beat. He'd been thinking exactly the same thing ever since he saw the blade in the tire. What if this was another attack like Lebanon? Were they after him to get to his father? He shook the guilt away and tried to think of what his dad would do.

"I wish it *was* all my fault, Rebecca, but I don't think it is. I think it's all about luck in this case. Bad luck."

"When were you attacked?" Brian finished his can of soda.

"When I was 16. Dad took us on a trip to Lebanon."

"I remember. You brought back that stupid urn."

"Hey! My mother loves that urn."

"Josh, it's ugly."

"Hardly the most important thing right now. Anyway, while we were there, this guy took a shot at my dad. Bullet went right through an open window in our hotel room. Sliced through my mother's arm. Long story short, my father felt he had to tell us what was going on so we'd be ready if it happened again. He taught me a few things after school and on weekends. I can handle myself really well. I'll do everything I can to make sure we get out of this alive."

Everyone looked to the back of the SUV without saying another word. Matt stared at his empty hands, tears falling freely down his face. His mouth moved but he made no sound.

"Last question." Brian looked out his window, studying the woods. "Any connection between your father's work and those things with wings?"

"I don't know," Josh said, his voice cracking. "Can't see how. Just more bad luck or something. Can you look at the map and find the next town? We've been driving forever and we've only got a half tank of gas. If those guys are following us I'd rather not meet up with them while we're still in the woods."

"Sure." Brian bent down to the pouch on the door where the maps were held. His hand stopped before reaching in. "What the hell?"

"What is it?" Rebecca leaned forward and put a hand on the back of Brian's seat.

Brian sat back up. In his hand was a single piece of white paper.

"Where's the map?" Josh took turns looking at Brian and the road.

"It's gone. All the maps are gone. This was the only thing in there."

Brian reached over and held the piece of paper out by the steering wheel. Josh looked down at it and hit the brakes.

It was a crude drawing, like something a grade school kid would do: a jet black peacock with glowing eyes. Beneath the drawing were two words written in red crayon.

"No escape." Josh read the words aloud, icy prickles jabbing into his skin.

"How the hell did that get in here?" Jan reached forward and grabbed the paper away from Brian. "Is this someone's idea of a joke? Brian, did you do this?"

Josh turned around slowly. "If you keep up like this we're all going to die. We need to stop the hysterics and focus."

Jan crumpled the paper and threw it on the ground.

"I didn't do this." Brian turned to look at Jan. "You know that. It was one of them. When was the last time anyone saw the map?"

"At the creepy gas station." Jan crossed her arms across her chest. Tears formed in her eyes. "I put it away because Josh was having trouble folding it."

"Right." Josh tried to think beyond the fear he felt. Despite his father's training, he realized he was out of his depth. "So we had the map then. That's when they took the maps and put this little note in there."

Brian wiped sweat off his forehead, turned around and looked out the back window. "If they've been tracking us that far, they're not going to stop now, are they?"

"Worse." Jan laughed and bit her lip. Tears flowed faster down her face. "We didn't see any cars pass us, right? They went ahead of us and set up a trap."

"Either that or there's more than one set of them." Brian wiped the sweat away again. "Josh, we need to get off this road. Fast."

Josh clenched the steering wheel. Up the road, a white van appeared. Impossibly fast, it shot up the road. It's engine roared, dirty and loud.

Rebecca screamed.

Before Josh could react, the van slammed into them. He felt a sharp crack as his head hit the steering wheel.

Then there was nothing but blackness and pain.

Chapter Four

July 31st

When Josh awoke, he was in a concrete cell. He blinked something – blood – out of his eyes. Blood-stained leather manacles bound his wrists spread-eagle above his head. His eyes traced chains from each manacle to thick metal hoops in the ceiling.

'You've got to be kidding.'

His shirt, shoes and socks were gone, his bare chest covered in bruises and abrasions. The floor was stained with red and brown smudges. Dried blood.

The cell reeked of spoiled hamburger. Two bare bulbs swung gently on short wires from the ceiling. They splashed cold light in puddles. He shook his head, trying to clear the fog in his brain. The only result was pain. Every part of his body ached. Although he knew it would be futile, he tried to pull his arms free of the manacles. He clenched his jaw as leather chewed into flesh. As expected, he could not get his hand through. The leather held tight.

He twisted to look over his shoulder. He was alone. The only entrance was directly in front of him. Like something from a horror-movie version of an insane asylum, there was a small window slot in the door. It was covered by a metal slab. On the other side would be a latch to uncover the window, allowing someone to look in on him without actually entering the room. He looked around for signs of a video camera. He saw no evidence of one.

'Stay calm,' he thought. 'Dad trained me for this. Keep pulling my hand through the manacle. If I'm lucky, I'll draw blood. Use it to lubricate the restraint and make it easier for me to escape.'

Through the walls, he heard a scream.

The sound was so shrill he could not tell if it was male or female. Either way, a scream like that was never a good thing. Someone was being hurt in ways he chose not to imagine. Moments later he heard another scream. He realized immediately it was Jan.

'At least I know she's not dead. If these people are after Dad, they'll keep me alive. At least for now. No guarantee for the others. I have to move quickly.'

He focused on his right hand, pulling it repeatedly down. Pain shot through his arm as leather bit into flesh. Maybe it was the pain or the streams of blood at his feet, but suddenly memories from the night of the bush party came back to him. He smelled charred flesh and feathers as the creatures' wings burned. He flinched as he recalled kicking in one of their skulls. In his memory, he moved impossibly fast: like Batman or Jet Li. His father had taught him things, but nothing like this, not when he was so young.

Then another image flashed before him.

***

He sat on his back porch with Tommy Delonki. It was a hot day in late August, the threat of going back to school imminent. They drank red Kool-Aid from plastic Jurassic Park cups. Inside the house, his mother sang along with the radio as she made the crust for an apple pie. Two skateboards lay nearby on the lawn. Nothing he saw or heard could explain the absolute terror the memory brought to him.

***

"Something happened."

As soon as he said the words he wished he'd only thought them. His voice echoed off the concrete walls, emphasizing how enclosed he was. It felt like a coffin. What if they did not come for him? What if they just left him hanging there until he starved to death? Claustrophobia set in.

"Stop it," he said. Sweat fell from his hair. The room was hot and humid, just like that day in August. "Think of something else."

'I can't stop them. One day they'll come to take me away and I know I can't stop them.'

Josh raised his head.

Goosebumps ran down his chest. The room suddenly seemed very cold.

***

"I can't stop them," Tommy said. "One day they'll come to take me away and I know I can't stop them."

"You don't know that." Josh picked up a chip of concrete that had crumbled off the back porch and threw it across the lawn. "Things don't work that way."

"You don't know them." Tommy grabbed his Kool-Aid and held the glass against his cheek. "You've never seen them."

"Yes I did." He put his hand on his friend's shoulder. "I saw what they did to you last night. It's wrong and it's weird but they're not coming back. Monsters always go away when someone else sees them. It's a rule."

"Maybe." Tommy set the cup down then looked away. "I still know I'm going to die."

***

'And he did,' Josh thought. 'In the hospital a few days after those things in the woods beat him up. Those things with wings. And I'd seen them before. How could I forget something like this?'

The two voices screamed again.

One of them cut off suddenly.

'Like a tape had been stopped. Or a throat had been cut. I could really use a miracle right about now. I know two in one day is pushing it, but please!'

The chain fell from where it was anchored to the ceiling and landed on the floor with a loud clang.

Josh panted, quick shallow breaths. He felt light-headed, his heart racing.

When the echoes ended, the only sound he heard was the pounding of his heart. He stared at the door, expecting it to open any second. They had to have heard that.

The door did not open. They weren't coming.

'Maybe they didn't hear. Even if they did, there's no way they would equate that sound with me pulling the chains out of the ceiling. It's impossible. A...'

***

"A miracle. That's what it is. It's a bloody miracle you weren't killed."

His mother, crying, held him against her chest, tightly, and kissed a cut on his forehead.

Josh was six years old. His body was covered in scrapes. His head felt funny and he could not feel his left arm.

"It's nothing," he said.

"Nothing? You were hit by a bus! Your body flew into that tree."

"Leave the boy alone, Therese." His father spoke from the doorway. He was dressed in a dark suit and sunglasses, like he was heading to a funeral. "Get him to the hospital. I'll take care of the police here. And that driver. I will definitely take care of him."

***

Josh pushed the memory away. 'Focus. That has nothing to do with this situation. I'm just lucky. Things just work out for me.' He looked around the room and laughed. 'Yeah. Things work out for me really well.'

A voice he recognized as intuition told him he couldn't risk the second chain falling. He'd been lucky once. He didn't want to push the luck he had left. As quickly as he dared, he lifted his right hand. The chain rose with it, a harsh metallic sound trickling through the room each time a link moved across concrete.

By the time his right hand was halfway up, he started to feel the strain. Each link was two inches of thick steel. It was heavy and, after two car crashes, his body was fatigued. Moving quickly would lessen the strain but increase the noise. If his captors caught him with one arm free, they would kill him immediately.

When his hand reached the manacle, he searched for clasps. Finding it locked, he searched the seams for a weak point.

'If I can pull the metal chain out of the ceiling, I should be able to snap this right off.' Only problem, he had no idea how he'd done that. All he did was pull and ask for...

***

"A miracle."

He looked down at Tommy Delonki. Once his best friend, he was now just a frail 16-year-old lying in the dirt. His body was battered almost beyond recognition. Tears smudged the blood and dirt on his cheeks.

"It's nothing." Josh, crying, held Tommy's hand.

"Nothing?" Tommy coughed. A trickle of blood dripped down his lips. "You took on those things. You beat them and you've barely got a scratch. You did that all for me? I guess we're still friends after all."

Josh looked over his shoulder.

Bodies burned behind him, scaly flesh now blackened and charred.

"They're called Edimmu," Josh said. He looked back at Tommy and squeezed his hand. Tommy blinked, the movement slow like a snowflake falling from the sky.

"How do you know that? I've never told you."

Josh swallowed and looked down at his hands.

"I don't...."

***

"...know."

Josh froze. 'What the hell is an Edimmu? It had to be those winged things but Tommy was right. There's no way I could know that. Just like I couldn't pull a chain out of the ceiling. Or survive getting hit by a bus at six. There's no way I could...'

The manacles on his both hands clicked open. The left swung away while the right fell with a thud at his feet.

"Impossible."

He looked around the room hoping to find his clothes. There was nothing in the room except him, the light bulbs and the chains.

And the door.

Then, Jan screamed again.

'Analyze later,' he thought. He walked to the door, assuming it would be locked. Still, when he turned the doorknob, he felt a stab of disappointment when it didn't move. 'Guess I've run out of miracles.'

'Damn.' He stepped back and studied the door. 'I've got to get them away from her. No idea how many there are or how they're armed. Dad taught me to run from this sort of thing. He said not to worry about him or Mom, just get myself out of the situation. I always told him I understood. On some level I guess I convinced myself I could be the stone-cold survivor. But I can't leave her. I couldn't live with myself. This door's only going to open from the other side. Guess I know what I have to do.'

He lifted a length of chain. He swung it above his head several times, gathering momentum. When it built up enough speed to create a humming sound, he threw the chain.

It slammed into the door.

The solid metal door didn't break but that wasn't his intention.

All he wanted was to get their attention.

He wiped sweat from his nose and walked back to the door. He put his ear against the cold metal and heard nothing.

The screams had stopped.

He picked up the chain and listened again. He heard a faint, repeating sound, like the tick of a clock.

Or footsteps.

'Wish I could remember how I killed those winged things. The Edimmu. Guess I'll have to rely on what Dad taught me.'

He covered his mouth, terrified for a moment. Then he stretched his arms and shoulders. He had to relax if he was going to do this. Mouth dry, he picked up the chain again. He threw it above him and it shattered into the nearest light bulb. He turned his head as glass showered down on him. When he looked back, the room was darker than he expected. With luck, it would make the fight more equal.

He shattered the other light and the room went pitch black. Josh closed his eyes to fight disorientation. He walked, arms outstretched, to the door. When he opened his eyes, he was surprised to see a crack of light under the door.

'Hinges open outward. Can't hide behind the door. I'll have to stand in their blind spot and hope for the best.'

He pressed his body up against the wall two feet to the right of the doorframe.

He waited.

With a loud slam the window opened. A square of light lit up the back wall. Josh held his breath.

"Lookee here, Simon. This bloke wants to have a go."

'Australian?' Josh thought. 'I'd expect a French accent this deep in Quebec. These boys aren't local.'

Josh heard two clicks. His father had trained him to recognize the sounds: guns being cocked. That was all he needed to know.

He heard keys jingle and, after a series of metallic clicks, the door unlocked. It opened slowly. The darkness dissipated into murky gray. Josh saw the silhouettes of two men against the back wall. The one in front was slightly shorter than the one behind. Their bodies cut off most of the light. Josh had only a few seconds before they saw him.

He sprung.

With his left hand he grabbed the wrist of the front man's gun hand. He held it out to the side and, in the same movement, punched with all his strength at his throat. His target's face went red even as his fingers twitched on the trigger. A bullet shot into the back wall. Josh grabbed the man's head, pushed it down and smashed his knee into the man's face. His body went limp. Josh threw him backwards into the second man. Instinctively, the bigger man's hands went around his friend, trying to break his fall. Josh tensed the index and middle fingers of his right hand and stabbed them straight through the second man's left eye. When he took his hand back it was covered in red and white goo. The second man screamed, hands rushing to cover his wound. Josh stepped on the wrist of the first man's gun hand. He put his weight on it until the man let the gun go.

Josh picked up the pistol and shot both men in the head.

The echoes hung in the air for a long time.

'That was too easy,' he whispered. 'Seriously. How did I do that? I've only fired guns at the firing range. Dad said if I was fighting for my life I had to be willing to kill. He said when the time came it was just about death, yours or the other person's. Still, shouldn't I be more freaked out? I killed these guys and I feel nothing.'

He stared at the gun in his hand. A moment later he bent down to retrieve the second man's gun. It was the first time he really looked at his captors.

The shorter man was a slightly balding redhead. The one in back bore an uncanny resemblance to a young Robert Redford. Both wore white surgical gowns over dark clothing.

'Not what I was expecting,' he thought. 'Maybe Rebecca was right. Maybe this isn't random at all. Maybe we are hostages. But if they're after my Dad, why weren't they questioning me? Dad said they would shoot a video with me to prove I was still alive. Who are these people?'

He stepped over the bodies into the hallway. The door to his cell was one of many that lined both sides of the corridor.

'So many doors,' he thought. 'I could shout out for Jan,

try to find out where she is. Stupid. That would give me away. I'll just have to check the doors one by one.'

Josh stopped in front of the next door and cautiously opened the window. Inside was a young woman in a torn blue dress. She hung from the ceiling just as like he had. Intravenous tubes pumped black and green fluids into her body. Strange symbols were drawn in blood down her arms.

'Who are these people?' He shook his head and closed the window. 'Questions for later. I have to find Jan and get out of here.'

The next door on the right was open. It led to a brightly lit room with three operating tables equally spaced around the room. One bed was empty. Jan was in the second. His eyes froze on the third.

"Brian."

Josh ignored Jan's pleas and stood over his friend's body. His legs had been removed. On a nearby metal tray sat a surgical saw with pieces of flesh embedded in the teeth of the blade. Brian's face was stiff, open mouth frozen in a scream that would last forever.

"Josh, you've got to snap out of it," Jan said. "Help me." It wasn't the words that got to him; it was the surprisingly calm tone. He forced himself to turn away from Brian and untied the straps that bound her to the table. She wore a blue dress identical to the one he'd seen on the other woman. The same strange symbols were drawn in blood down her arms.

"Are you okay?" He asked. "What were they doing to you?'

"I don't know." Jan slipped off the table. "They said I was a candidate. Kept muttering something about Eyeness and Activation. Who cares? They're crazy people. I've seen at least five of them. They come in shifts. Two left a little while ago."

"It's okay. I killed them."

Jan's eyes went wide and she took a step back from Josh.

Josh passed her one of the guns. "Take this. I know how much you hate guns. Don't worry about being accurate. If you see someone coming you don't recognize, point and shoot. Have you seen the others? Rebecca or Matt?

"No." Jan glanced briefly at Brian's body. She turned away and folded her arms over her chest. "They made me watch. Wanted to see if it triggered something."

"Damn." Josh swallowed down tears and stared at the ceiling. "We need to focus if we want to get out of this. Stay close and watch my back. Okay?"

Jan nodded. She grabbed the gun with both hands and followed Josh back into the hallway.

Chapter Five

"We need to find a phone," Jan whispered.

"No, we don't." Josh looked up and down the hallway, trying to think.

"Josh, we have to get help."

He turned and placed the palm of his hand against her cheek. "Jan. I love you. Trust me."

Now that Jan was safe, he realized he'd made a tactical error. He led them back to his cell and searched the bodies of the men he had killed. He found a set of keys and cursed under his breath.

"What's the matter?" Jan very deliberately kept her eyes off the dead bodies.

"There are a lot of keys on here. I've no idea which one opens what." He stood. "Here's the plan. We'll go up and down this hallway. There are doors on each side. I'll open the window on one side, you open the other. If you don't recognize the person, close the window."

"We've got to help them…"

"No, we don't. Look, by rights we should just get out of here and leave everyone behind."

"By rights?" Jan narrowed her eyebrows. "Is that what your secret agent father would do? Would he even save me? Or would he leave me to die?"

Josh looked at her and said nothing.

"I see. Well, whatever you think, you're not your father."

Josh walked away from her. She followed and grabbed his arm.

"You're not your father."

"I don't know *what* I am. Not anymore. But I know this scenario. My dad trained me for this. I can get us out of here as long as you trust me."

Reluctantly, Jan took her hand away.

They opened four windows before they found Rebecca.

Like Jan, she wore a blue dress and her arms were covered with strange symbols.

She wasn't alone.

An elderly blond man held a knife to her throat. His pants were around his ankles.

"Bugger off, Keith," the man said over his shoulder. "You said I could have this one. Leave me be."

Blood pounded in Josh's head. He looked at the gun in his hand. 'I can't risk shooting from this angle. I could miss and hit her.' He thought over his options. Then he kicked the door. Jan squealed – instinctive shock. Josh motioned for her to press against the wall. He knelt down, back on the opposite wall, and raised his gun.

"What the hell is your problem?" A face appeared in the window, eyes wide with realization.

Josh fired.

Rebecca screamed. With a thud, the body collapsed.

He tossed the keys to Jan. "Try them all if you have to. Get the door open. I'll keep you covered. He looked up and down the hallway. Sooner or later someone would investigate the shots. But that wasn't what ate at him. It was the look in the man's eyes. He'd seen it hundreds of times in horror movies. It was the look every victim had when he or she confronted the monster in the darkness. 'And I'm the monster,' he thought.

Jan didn't hesitate. It was one of the things he loved about her. Most people would collapse in hysterics. But not her.

"Hold on, Becka," she said through the window.

"Get me out of here," Rebecca moaned. "I'm not sure he's dead."

It took ten minutes before Jan found the right key. Once the door opened, she stepped over the man's body and tried keys on the manacles. Josh watched the hall. When she was free, Rebecca fell against Jan, crying.

"Move quietly," he said as he bent down to take the dead man's knife. It had smudges of blood on it, blood that had to be Rebecca's. He wiped the knife on his jeans and passed it to Rebecca. "We're going to find Matt and get out of here."

"What about Brian?"

'Crap', he thought. He turned to face her, opened his mouth and tried to think of the words to say it.

Her face went numb. "Oh," Rebecca said. She gave several quick, shallow nods, took a quivering breath and let the tears fall down her face. Then her eyes glazed over as Jan led her out of the room.

'She handled it better than me,' Josh thought. He searched the dead man's clothing and found a gun in a holster attached to his belt on the floor. 'But then, she didn't see the body.'

They found Matt in the next room. Thankfully, he was alone and unharmed. He still had his pants, but was also missing his shirt, socks and shoes. Jan unlocked the door with the same key that had unlocked Rebecca's cell.

Matt opened his mouth, his eyes asking where Brian was. Josh shook his head and passed him a gun. Matt took it, going pale as soon as his fingers touched the metal.

"I've never fired a gun."

"Like I told Jan, don't worry about being accurate. Point and squeeze. If nothing else, the noise might scare them. We have to find the way out of here. But not until we kill the last two."

Matt looked over at Jan, eyes wide. Then he stared down at the gun in his hands. "Josh, we can't do this."

Josh didn't turn around to look at him. He walked slowly to the open door at the end of the hallway. As he moved closer, he saw a set of stairs leading upwards.

"Josh," Matt hurried to get to Josh's side. "We can't kill these people. It's wrong. We've got to get out of here, get help."

Josh stopped but did not turn around to look at him. "That weapon in your hand is the only help we're going to get."

Matt put a hand on Josh's shoulder. This time Josh did turn around.

"Listen closely, Matt." Josh's voice was a harsh whisper. "Once we head up those stairs there won't be time for me to repeat myself. You're not an idiot. You know the situation we're in. These aren't the kind of people you just run from. You run, they follow. And they will catch you. It may take an hour, a day or a decade. But they will come after you. And when they do, they'll kill you. This isn't civilization. There's no help a phone call away. They've already killed two of us. I will not let there be a third. So, if you don't think you can pull the trigger when you need to, take the girls and go hide in one of the cells. I'll come back for you when it's over."

Matt dragged nails down his cheek and then bit them. He turned to look back at the others. Jan lifted her gun, resolve written clearly on her face. Matt took a deep breath and nodded. "Fine. Let's do this."

Josh raised his lips in the hint of a smile, then started up the stairs. Matt followed him with the two women close behind.

The air reeked of cigars and roast chicken. Josh held his hand up, motioning the others to stay put. Back against the left wall, Josh crept up the stairs. He kept his gun pointed at the top of the stairs. The unpainted metal door reminded him of the large walk-in freezers he had seen at the restaurant that Brian's family owned.

'Maybe that's why they didn't hear the gunshots,' he thought. 'Either that or they're just so used to hearing shots they no longer pay attention.'

He put a hand on the door. It was cool to the touch. When he took his fingers away, there was a thin layer of grime on them, like oil. He reached for the large handle, turning it slowly.

When the click came it was soft, like an inhalation.

Josh held the handle down for a moment, listening.

When there was no hint of movement or noise on the other side, he pushed the door open. It led to a room lined with unfinished wood shelves filled with metal cans of food. He looked behind him and motioned for Matt to lead the others up.

Josh moved into the pantry. There was another metal door with a large window near the top. Peering through it, Josh took in details of a bright, cheerful kitchen. An old woman stood at the stove stirring a pot. Her gray hair was up in a bun. She wore a sleeveless floral summer dress.

Josh cocked his gun and threw open the door.

The woman turned. Her smile turned to shock, then slid into disbelief and pain. She looked down at her chest, her fingers touching blood as it spilled out over her dress.

Josh realized he was holding his breath. He fought to breathe again. He couldn't remember pulling the trigger. He had not even heard the gunshot. He looked down at the gun in his hands. It was warm. He looked back up at the woman and watched her fall to the floor. The wooden spoon she held clattered against the floor.

"Jesus!" Matt rushed past him and knelt beside the woman on the floor. "Was the old woman such a threat? You're losing it."

Jan walked over to the woman, bent over and spat on her face.

"Have you all gone mad?" Matt stood up and led Jan away from the body.

"She has to be in on it." Jan stared down, unable to meet Matt's eyes. "There's no way she didn't know what was going on down there."

"Still, you don't know…"

With fast, large steps, Josh walked over and put a hand over Matt's mouth. He put a finger against his own lips, the sign for silence, and looked around the room.

It was a pleasant kitchen. There were two other doors, one leading outside and the other into the guts of the house. The walls, painted yellow with white trim, were lined with glass-covered cabinets. Inside, cups and dishes reflected the light that shone through the large window embedded in the western wall. Looking through the window, Josh saw the sun setting behind a distant row of trees. In between the house and the woods was a large red barn. Two brown horses ate hay in a pen. Josh saw movement. A man in overalls, with large arms and a pitchfork, ran toward the house.

Before Josh could react, something smashed into his head. Everything spun, the world blurring. It stopped when he hit the floor.

He saw a thin, black-haired man hitting Matt in the knees with a hammer. An olive-skinned man in a white ceremonial robe pointed a shotgun at Rebecca and Jan. Two redheaded men, who looked to be identical twins, stared down at Josh. Like the men below, they bore an uncanny resemblance to Robert Redford.

'Brothers,' Josh thought. 'What kind of family is this?'

"Damn maggot," one of the twins said. "You killed me mumsy."

The other twin kicked Josh in the ribs. Josh felt something crack. He coughed up blood. Then both twins began to kick him repeatedly.

He heard a door open. The beating stopped.

"What the hell happened?"

Josh looked up from the floor. It was the large man with the pitchfork.

"They killed Mumsy, Sasha," one of the Redford twins said. "Shot her like a bleeding animal. Let me skin him alive."

Sasha, the man with the pitchfork, stepped forward and looked down at Josh. "You know we can't. Otto will have our heads if he dies. Go check on the others."

"But…"

Sasha slammed the butt of the pitchfork against the hardwood floor. "Check on them now! Remember why we're doing this."

One of the Redford twins kicked Josh in the head before stomping off downstairs.

From the floor, Josh looked around the room. It hurt

to move his head, so his view was limited. Matt held up hands covered in blood as he screamed in pain. One leg twisted at an unnatural angle. Josh couldn't see much of the women from where he was, only their legs and the man who held the gun on them.

'If ever there was a time for a miracle, this is it.' he thought. Nothing happened. 'Oh well. Guess I'll have to make my own luck this time.' He closed his eyes and focused past the pain, numbing it.

Then, he opened his eyes and sprung.

With his right hand he grabbed the remaining Redford twin by the crotch. He pulled down and twisted as hard as he could. The man fell to his knees. Josh slammed his elbow into the man's nose. The man holding the shotgun pivoted, pointing the gun at him. Josh spun behind the Redford twin. He lifted him back up to his feet by the hair. Josh had another human shield.

The man with the shotgun cocked it, readying it for fire.

'Don't know if this will protect me or not,' he thought. 'Better not chance it.' He twisted the twin's head with a sharp jerk. There was a wet crunch and the neck broke.

"You mother...." The man with the shotgun fired, the sound drowning out his curse. Josh dropped, rolling away from the blast. He yelped as the movement brought sharp pain to his ribs.

"Josh!" Jan cried out for him. She curled her fist and punched the man with the shotgun in the back of the head. His head flew forward and Jan hammered her hands down on his skull. He fell.

The man with the hammer left Matt and slammed the hammer into Jan's side. At the same time Sasha raised his pitchfork and jabbed it like a spear at Josh.

"No!" Josh screamed.

The weapon stopped midair.

Sasha struggled, leaning forward into the pitchfork. No matter how hard he pushed, the pitchfork did not get any closer. Josh clenched his fists, his full attention on the pitchfork.

Then something clicked.

A grating hum filled his ears, like dozens of flies buzzing inside his head.

He reached out with his hands and grabbed the pitchfork.

His whole weight resting on the pitchfork, Sasha collapsed. Josh spun the pitchfork like a quarterstaff and brought the tines down into Sasha's chest. As the body twitched, dying, Josh pulled out the pitchfork. He jabbed it into the throat of the remaining Redford twin. Blood spewed everywhere. Then he yanked it loose again and walked toward the black-haired man.

"Stay right there, punk." The black-haired man stood behind Jan, one arm wrapped around her throat, the other held a hammer above her head. "None of your tricks or she's dead. You're off limits but she's not. Put the weapon down."

Footsteps came up from the basement. Josh focused his attention on the open door. Again, his head buzzed and the door slammed shut. The other Redford twin's face appeared in the window. The door rattled but, no matter what the Redford twin did, would not open.

"Listen, thin man." Josh walked toward him, pitchfork in front of him. He noticed that Rebecca had gone over to Matt and was trying to help him to his feet. "Here's what's going to happen. Run away or I'm going to run this pitchfork right through you."

"You'll have to stab through her first."

Josh took another step forward. "Yes, I will. I'll put the pitchfork through her. Then it's going through you. Afterwards, I'll bandage her up and watch while you bleed to death." Josh shrugged as if it didn't matter which choice he made. "Run or die. Those are your choices."

"You won't do that." The man took a step back, dragging Jan back with him. "You can't do that."

Josh put the pitchfork up against Jan's bared stomach.

"You have no idea what I'm capable of doing."

Suddenly, the room went dark. At first Josh thought it was just the sun going behind the clouds outside. Then, shadows turned pitch black, nearly opaque. Josh looked around. The shadows moved like liquid, rippling and swirling.

"Josh, what is this?" Jan asked.

"I... I don't know." Josh shook his head.

One corner was significantly darker than the rest of the room. Josh held the pitchfork toward it. He sensed movement, like an army of eels thrashing in a pool of ink.

'Am I being sent to hell for what I've done?' he thought.

An eight-foot-tall man dressed in a green business suit stepped out of the darkness. In his wake, the shadows rippled like eddies on a black lake. Josh tried to focus on his features but all he could see was the man's..."

"Wings..."

Josh dropped the pitchfork and backed away.

"Ah, there you are." The man's voice hissed like a serpent. "Come along. We've been looking for you."

"We? Are you an Edimmu?" Josh noticed other figures starting to come out of the shadows.

The buzz in his head went wild. He pushed his palms against his temples, trying to ease the pressure. He couldn't see straight. He stepped back, his body colliding with someone else. He felt a strong grip put an arm around him. The room became very hot.

"He's going nowhere with you."

Josh looked up. The man behind him was a black man dressed in a red three-piece suit. Something in the curve of his mouth, the set of his eyes, left a taint of very bad things.

"Why are you here, Wisdom?" The winged man's face flickered. For a moment, Josh swore he saw the face of a reptile instead of a man.

"Be gone, Edimmu." Wisdom tightened his grip on Josh. "Run back to your puppet master. You have one chance to sink back in your hole. Then I get angry."

The Edimmu glanced over his shoulder. The shadows flickered. Then, without turning his body, the Edimmu stepped back into the shadows. When he was gone, the shadows faded to gray and the sunlight reappeared.

Wisdom released Josh and straightened the lapels on his jacket. Josh ran to Jan's side and they embraced.

"Screw this." The black-haired man dropped the hammer and ran into the guts of the house. Jan collapsed to her knees, crying. Josh looked toward the basement door. There was no sign of the Redford twin in the window.

"What the hell was that?" Matt looked up from the floor. Both his knees were shattered. He wouldn't be standing for some time. "Was that like the other ones? The ones you killed?"

"You've killed Edimmu?" Wisdom cocked his head and focused on Josh. "That's very interesting."

Josh rubbed the back of his neck. "I don't remember killing them. Who are you?"

"A friend. You are capable of extraordinary things. I know why you can do the things you do. I can train you to use these abilities. Let's get your friends home. After that, we'll talk."

"My friends?" Josh felt his mouth go dry. "What about me? Don't I get to go home?"

Wisdom looked around the room. His eyes rested on the spot where the Edimmu had entered the room. "I'm sorry. I don't think that's an option anymore."

Chapter Six

August 1st

Thessaloniki had grown into the second largest city in Greece. Like most large cities it had great theatres, booming tourism, and wild dance clubs where people tried to forget how civilized humanity had become. Old women shopped at corner fruit markets and the police did their best to keep crime off the streets.

Unlike most modern cities, Thessaloniki's history reached back thousands of years. Many of its ancient buildings stood side by side with newer structures. Aside from the largest church in Greece, there was the famed White Tower: a this former fortification that later served as a prison. Not far from the White Tower was an apartment complex in a constant state of reconstruction. From the outside, it was nondescript, consisting of three eight-story buildings clumped together. Wood scaffolding covered most of the external concrete walls, obscuring the windows and balconies. Inside, cans of paint cluttered narrow hallways. Drywall dust hung thick in the air. Over the years, many tenants had left in a defiant protest to the incessant construction. With each departure, a member of the Council of Peacocks moved in.

By the time Wisdom rescued Josh Wilkinson, over 80% of the men and women in the complex were devoted to Propates. Beneath the complex was the real headquarters. Propates chose the complex solely for its proximity to an underground network of tunnels dug in the fourteenth century. Few outside the Council knew about their existence.

***

Propates sat behind a mahogany desk in a stone room. Across from him, Echo sat, legs crossed. Her gray suit was covered in dust and ash. Her hair lay loose around her face.

"I told you already, I was just doing him a favor." Echo pulled her hair back off her cheek. Using an elastic, she tied it in a ponytail. "I don't care about Council politics."

"I know you don't. That's why I'm so intrigued. Why were you sneaking around the ritual room?"

Echo rolled her eyes. "Spying, of course. Then you followed me back to Prague and destroyed my home. I think that made us equal. Then you dragged me to this ant-hill."

"You can't actually approve of the way Wisdom is collecting these little monsters. You know how he is. Wisdom and his toys. That's all they are to him. It's all we ever were."

Echo leaned forward. "They're not monsters. They're children. And I don't care what he's doing with them. Let it go. Whatever you're planning, Wisdom's onto it. Have you seen him lately?"

"Thankfully, no." The phone beside Propates buzzed. He picked up the receiver. "I'm busy. I don't care what Lucius said. Deal with it. Now hold the rest of my calls." He hung up and turned back to Echo. "I haven't crossed paths with Wisdom in years."

"I've never seen him so focused. He's going to stop you. You know that, right?"

"He can try." Propates leaned back. The smile disappeared from his eyes. The light in the room faded. Shadows slunk in the corner of the room like water breaching a sinking ship. "Times change, Echo. I've changed. We were together for a long time."

"Centuries, but that doesn't count."

"After everything he's done to you, to us, how can you choose him over me?"

Echo turned away. "Not this again. We had our moment. It's gone. And I'm not choosing Wisdom. I'm choosing me. Let me go and I'll disappear. Tell me, how exactly are you blocking my abilities?"

Propates put a finger to his lips. "It's a secret. I've learned so much from my time with the Council of

Peacocks. Things you couldn't even imagine. Why don't you stay? I can arrange rooms for you."

"Please," Echo waved her hand before her face. "Why would I stay in a dung pile like this? I told you. I want nothing to do with you or your Council. Just let me go."

Propates sighed. "Fine. I've released the barrier. Get out of here. But don't get involved in Council business again. I don't want to hurt you, Echo, but things are moving quickly. I can't let you jeopardize our plans."

Echo sighed as her powers rushed back to her. She stood and clenched her fists. A portal of light appeared beside her.

"We both know what Wisdom is," she said. "Whatever secrets you've learned, you can't hope to think you're as powerful as him."

"The plan is bigger than me. I couldn't stop it if I wanted to." Propates picked up a cigar. It turned to ice at his touch. He tossed it over his shoulder where it shattered into a dozen pieces.

Echo put one foot in the portal. "Then it's been nice knowing you." She stepped through the circle of light and was gone.

For several minutes Propates stared at the space she'd occupied. Then, a knock at the door interrupted his trance.

"Come in, Ferris."

Paeder Ferris walked in the room. He was dressed in white robes and carried a thick manila folder in his hands. He was in his mid-twenties with strawberry-blond hair and ice-blue eyes.

"Please tell me the tracker is working," Propates asked, even though he saw the answer in Paeder's eyes.

"He's difficult to track with all the teleporting, but we have the maggot." Paeder opened the folder and took out a satellite photo. "The signal's coming off the coast of Argentina. When can I kill him?"

Propates reached for a new cigar. "You can't. You know that. Josh's crucial to the plan. Wait until he's back on the mainland. Then bring him here."

"He killed me mumsy. Slaughtered my brothers. I watched him stab my twin. You can't expect me to just let that go."

Propates stood. "Yes, I can. We don't have time for vendettas. Not yet. When you retrieve him, bring him to me unharmed. Understand?"

Paeder nodded tersely but would not meet his eyes. Then he left the room.

Propates smoothed the front of his shirt and stretched his shoulders. He returned to his paperwork, humming happily. Everything was going according to schedule.

***

Echo stepped out of the portal and stood in the bedroom of her summer home. The island off the coast of Argentina was beautiful, a welcome retreat from the hectic city life in Prague. She had bought it from the French 150 years ago. She'd never been able to rightfully determine if the island had a name before she had arrived. At the time, it was uninhabited. She'd brought over a dozen locals from the mainland. They had built her home, cultivated the land, and tended her crops. Over the years, those dozen had become several hundred. A village had sprung up on the other side of the island. They called it Port Echo, which amused her to no end.

She sat on the edge of her bed and slipped out of her jacket. The heat was palpable, almost sentient. A cool breeze blew in through open windows, gently tousling the curtains. It sank into her bones, dissolving the tension from her shoulders. She closed her eyes and let her head fall back.

"Annisa? Roma?" She called out to the two servants who cared for the house in her absence. No response. She glanced at the alarm clock beside her bed. It was mid-afternoon. Perhaps they were in town getting supplies.

"Whatever. I need a shower anyway." She pulled her hair free of the elastic and slipped out of the rest of her clothes. In the bathroom adjacent to the bedroom was an extravagant shower: concrete and stone came together to create an artificial cliff. When she turned on the taps it became a waterfall. To each side of the shower, tropical plants in terracotta pots rose to the ceiling. They reinforced the illusion of bathing in the jungle. She kept the water cool as she washed the dirt and oil from her skin.

She toweled dry and walked back to her bedroom. As she dressed, she admired the room. In every direction, windows offered stunning views of the ocean. The water seemed to take over the rest of the world. From here, there was no sign of any other piece of land. It made it easy to believe she was on a completely different planet. Planes rarely flew overhead and, being so far from a major port, few ships dotted the horizon. Of all the homes she maintained, she chose this one now because of its isolation. For the moment, she wanted nothing more than to be alone.

"I'm sorry, miss. I must not have heard you come in."

"It's been too long," Echo turned to find Annisa in the doorway. She embraced her warmly. "It's good to see you. Unfortunately, I'm only here for the night. Can you get my blue suit ready? I'm heading to Toronto tomorrow to see Wisdom."

"Begging your pardon, ma'am, but Mr. Wisdom is not in Toronto. He's here."

"What?"

"Yes, ma'am. He arrived last night with a young man."

"That bastard. Where was he when the Edimmu torched my home? Tell him I'll be down in a minute."

"Yes, ma'am. Would you like me to prepare something for you?"

"No. Wait...yes. I'd love a mimosa. Several mimosas actually. And a quiche. What is he wearing?"

Annisa giggled, hiding her smile behind her fingers.

"Never mind. I'll be down in a minute."

Annisa curtseyed and left without another word.

***

Josh stared at his cell phone and chewed on an ice cube. He knew he should call his parents, but what could he say? Everything about yesterday seemed impossible. Still, every drop of sweat forced him to admit where he was.

'Barely slept last night,' he thought. 'That and this heat is making it very hard to stay awake. Every time I close my eyes all I see is blood and darkness. And wings.'

***

Back in the Laurentians, Josh wanted to chase down the remaining kidnappers. Wisdom stopped him.

"Bad idea," Wisdom said.

"We can't leave them," Josh countered. "You never leave guys like this alive. They always come back."

Wisdom narrowed his eyes, studying Josh. It was like he was truly seeing Josh for the first time. "Normally I'd agree with you. However, we have no idea what they are doing. They could be setting explosives or getting reinforcements."

"All the more reason to act quickly." Jan grabbed Josh by the chin and pulled him closer, making sure he only focused on her. "There are other people down there, people who need help. We cannot leave them."

"We can," Wisdom said. He looked Jan squarely in the eyes. "And we are. Call the police when you get home if you want. There are more important things at stake."

Jan grunted in frustration. "What kind of monster are you?"

Wisdom glared at her impassively. Finally, Josh looked away.

Wisdom created a disk of light.

"What is that thing?" Matt asked.

"Localized low-gravity wormhole," Wisdom said. "You can think of it as a teleportation disk. We can use this to get you home."

After a little coaxing, everyone stepped through the portal. Jan and Josh worked together to carry Matt since his shattered kneecaps made it impossible for him to walk.

Rebecca moved stoically, as if walking through a passive dream. On the other side of the portal was the Civic Campus of the Ottawa Hospital. As soon as Josh and Jan placed Matt on the ground, Wisdom closed the first portal and opened a second one.

Josh looked at Wisdom and nodded, understanding the ramification. He turned to Jan, kissing her on the lips.

"You can't go with him," she pleaded.

"If I stay, you won't be safe." With a look of apology, Josh turned away as Wisdom opened a second portal. "The Edimmu are after me. You saw that.

***

Josh glanced over at Wisdom. He stood on the veranda staring out at the ocean. Still dressed in the same red suit, Wisdom hadn't moved since breakfast. Then, Wisdom motioned to Annisa and whispered something in her ear. They both looked at the ceiling. The servant nodded and then headed toward the stairs that lead to the second floor.

When Annisa returned, she wasn't alone. Beside her was one of the most beautiful women Josh had ever seen. Long brown hair fell down over her shoulders in waves and curled around her face. It was hard to determine her nationality. She had high cheekbones and a delicate chin with large amber eyes. She wore a tight, white jacket buttoned over a cream-colored bustier. Along with loose white slacks, she wore matching white pumps.

"Found yourself another stray, I see," she said. She crossed her arms over her chest and fought the urge to scream at him.

"Something like that." Wisdom smiled but kept looking out at the ocean. "I'm sorry about your condo, Echo. You must be thrilled to see me."

"Well, somebody's having delusions of grandeur."

"I know you've been to see Propates." Wisdom stopped smiling.

"How?"

"You know me. I have my ways. We don't have much time. Events will move quickly now. I've tried to slow them down but nothing I do works. I could explain more to you but it would only make things harder."

"Christ, is it your father again? Did you have another dream?"

Wisdom frowned. "Didn't I just say 'no questions'? I'm fairly certain I just said that?"

"Zip it." Echo walked over to Wisdom and put a hand on his shoulder. "Cut the tough guy act. You're scared. I can see it in your eyes. What is going on?"

Wisdom turned and brushed a curl of hair out of Echo's face. "Just the thought of losing..." He stopped and pulled his hand away. "I can't stand losing, you know that. It is bigger than I expected. The Council made a deal with the Djinn. I know, I know. No need to hyperventilate. I have a few tricks up my sleeve yet. The boy over there is Joshua Wilkinson. He's an Anomaly, like the others but somehow different. I did not find out about him the first time. As far as I know, neither did Propates. He's a wild card, and I hope it's enough."

"What do you mean 'the first time'?"

"Just trust me, okay? It's for the best that you don't know any more. I need a favor."

Echo exhaled slowly and stepped away from him. "Of course you do. Not enough you get me to spy on Edimmu. Now you show up, tell me the end is nigh and not to ask questions. This isn't my thing, Wisdom. I gave up all this Illuminati nonsense nearly 200 years ago. I like my nice quiet life."

"I never stopped loving you. You know that."

She stopped, bit her lip and crossed her arms again.

Wisdom cleared his throat and looked back out at the sea. "I just wanted to tell you at least once before things get hectic."

Echo bit harder into her lips. "Bastard," she said as tears built up in her eyes. Then she walked back into the house.

***

Echo did not reappear until supper. Josh looked up occasionally from his seven-layer lasagna, unable to fully concentrate on eating with the tension in the room. Wisdom kept his eyes averted from everyone and barely touched his meal. Echo ate slowly, each forkful a statement louder than words.

Echo turned to Josh. "What are you staring at?"

"Umm..." Josh looked away.

"Echo," Wisdom said. "This is childish."

"Excuse me?" Echo's eyes flashed bright blue. Behind her a vase exploded. Her face went red and she placed her fork back on the plate.

"Thank you for proving my point." Wisdom stared at the space where the vase had been. "I need a favor and I can't wait any longer for you to calm down."

"I am perfectly calm. If I wasn't, it wouldn't have been a vase that exploded."

Wisdom shook his head. "Always the same. Such a drama queen. You know..."

Echo jumped up. "You did not just call me a drama queen!"

"Sit!"

Echo flinched as if struck. Tears fell down her cheek.

'Has he abused her?' Josh thought. 'The way she's looking at him, she looks terrified.'

"What do you want?" Echo glared at Wisdom. Each word she said was measured and overly precise.

Wisdom sighed and sat down. "You know what I want, Echo. I want to stop hurting you. It's why I left years ago and it's why I'm leaving right after dinner. But what I *need* is for you to take this boy to my London offices. The Council has seen him with me. They may be able to track my movements. Propates won't be expecting anything from you. Not so soon after he's caught you playing spy. Unless I'm mistaken, they plan to use Josh for something, some purpose I have yet to work out. Somehow his existence has been kept a secret from me. That's a story in itself. I'm heading to Toronto to meet a new arrival. I know you have questions. I would in your shoes. But believe me, I can't tell you. No good would come from telling you."

Echo seemed calmer now. Her eyes were dry.

"Is that it?"

Wisdom shook his head. "One more little thing. Another delivery I'll tell you about later." He looked around the room. "Just in case the shadows here have ears."

After a deep breath, Echo continued eating her lasagna. "Fine. But when this is over I don't want to see you for at least a hundred years."

Wisdom flinched and stared at his plate. "I pray you get the chance to stay angry at me."

Chapter Seven

August 2nd

David stared out the window of the Greyhound bus at the streets of Toronto. The view overwhelmed him. There were piles of garbage and throngs of prostitutes in one neighborhood followed by mansions hidden behind high walls and security cameras in another. Restaurants, their names written out in Chinese characters, cluttered entire neighborhoods.

'So many people,' he thought. 'It's like a zombie invasion. It was never like this back in Dartmouth.'

It was also much hotter than anything he had experienced before. He overheard other people on the bus saying it was the hottest summer on record in Ontario. The windows kept fogging over because the bus' air conditioning was on high. David cleared the window with the palm of his hand so he could watch the city slide by him. He tried to do the tourist thing, to keep his eyes on the busy and well-lit areas, but that was not who he was. At his core was something else. Again and again, he was drawn to the dark alleys, the vague hostility in the eyes of the homeless. In a city like this, it was easy for him to believe the world was filled with evil.

That made him feel a little less alone.

His reflection stared back at him from the foggy window, like a different person he was trying to ignore. He had not showered in days. It had been much longer still since he had slept through the night. His coppery red hair hung limp and greasy, an inch longer than he would have liked. His right ear was pierced with a small hooped earring constructed of surgical steel. The only other jewelry he wore was a simple medallion with the symbol for his birth sign – Aries – bound around his neck with a thin piece of raw leather. He had worn the same loose-fit jeans and light blue

T-shirt for three days now. His face was pale and bloodless with dark circles around his eyes. It made his bright green eyes seem all the more unnatural.

When he stepped off the bus, he saw a six-foot tall woman standing beside a black Hummer. She had broad, imposing shoulders and her skin was nearly as pale as David's. Her hair was a sharp blond crop cut, making her look militant and feminine at the same time. Despite the heat, she wore a dark blue turtleneck that matched the bruising on her face.

'That'll be Wisdom's assistant,' he thought as he struggled to pick up his canvas bag from under the bus. According to the letter David had received, her name was Elaine Radegund. As he walked toward her, she opened the door to the backseat.

"You're late," Elaine said. She grabbed his bag with one hand and threw the bulky weight effortlessly into the backseat. "Get in."

David tensed, thought of a thousand ways to respond to how rude she was, but in the end said nothing. He slid in and let her close the door. His eyes fell on the driver and he held his breath. The driver was well over seven feet tall, with shoulders like a human pit bull. There was nothing vague about his hostility. As soon as Elaine snapped her seatbelt, the driver took off.

They drove in silence for several blocks before David's skin started to itch.

'Someone is watching me.'

He turned slowly to look behind him. Two prepubescent girls stared back at him. They wore identical black skirt suits. One was Asian, the other Caucasian with blond hair and blue eyes. He saw in their eyes why they were there. 'Protection.'

"This one can read our minds," the Asian girl said. "He's stronger than he looks." She looked to be about ten years old. David noticed she was wearing lipstick and mascara. He hoped that his employer was not using them for more than one type of job.

"Don't be a pervert," the blond girl said. "We work for him the same way you do."

"She means the way you *might* work for him if you pass the test." The Asian girl jutted out her chest in a way that would have shown off her breasts if she had any. There was something monstrous about the two of them.

The Asian girl spat at him.

He wiped it from his cheek.

"We're no more monsters than you are. Now stop talking to us."

'They heard my thoughts,' David thought. 'How's that possible? Are they like me? Wisdom said he knew all about me, what I could do. He said he could train me but I never expected this. How many others like me are there?'

He turned back to the girls, questioning them with a look.

They stared at each other for a moment, as if holding a detailed conversation. Finally, the blond-haired girl turned back to him. "You'll find out soon enough. Now stop talking to us. Don't make me say it again."

"Play nice," Elaine said. "Back down and keep up the surveillance."

The blond-haired girl, Jessica, glared out the window. The Asian girl reached out and held Jessica's hand. After another silent conversation, Jessica nodded and closed her eyes.

"I'm not a monster," he whispered to himself. But he didn't believe it. He was a murderer. The first time was two years ago, an accident like a gun going off when you least expect it. Still, he knew there was a gun, knew it was loaded with no safety. He was just as responsible as if he had willfully pulled the trigger.

***

Prom. He stood by the punch bowl, uncomfortable in his tux. Around him, classmates danced, making fools out of themselves even though most were completely sober. His date, Ramona Straub, was a cheerleader with large lips, a small waist and long brown hair. He hadn't seen her in an hour.

When she first left, he assumed she was just in the restroom. Later, he assumed she must be just chatting with friends. Now, he knew something was wrong. Punch drink in hand, he made his way through the crowd of familiar faces. Quickly, he realized people were looking at him. Pointing. Snickering behind their hands.

He leaned up against a wall, took a sip of punch, and tried to stop his head from spinning. In the darkness behind his eyes, he saw everything so clearly. She was in the backseat of a car, topless with another man. Paedrag Lucki.

David dropped the cup of punch and walked out to the parking lot. He was furious. Ramona was cheating on him and everyone would find out tomorrow. Forget tomorrow; most of them knew now. Face flushed with anger, he wiped tears from his eyes.

He wanted them both dead.

Ramona and Paedrag didn't see him coming. They were too focused on each other. He stared at them through the foggy windows of Paedrag's car. David clenched his fists.

An explosion knocked people to the ground.

Car parts flew in all directions. People screamed, ran and cried. Everything around David dissolved into chaos and flames.

But inside, David was calm.

***

"You killed your girlfriend," Jessica said. "I knew you were a monster."

David's eyes flew open and he spun round to question them.

Jessica smiled and tapped her forehead.

"It was an accident." He turned around and stared at his feet. The first two times, he hadn't meant to use his abilities to commit murder. The last time, though, he knew exactly what he was doing.

The last time.

Maybe that did make him a monster.

In the back seat, the girls snickered behind their tiny hands.

The Hummer pulled into the parking garage of a tall glass skyscraper on Bay Street. David saw two armed men in the attendant booth. The show of strength was unnerving. It spoke of a back-story he knew nothing about. They pulled into a parking spot and Elaine opened David's door. He reached for his bag but Elaine shook her head.

"Leave that," she said. "I'll have it brought to your room. Wisdom will want to see you first. Girls, hurry back to class. No detours."

"Class?" David watched as the two girls walked away, hand in hand. He hoped he'd never see them again.

"You'll see in due time, Mr. Ross. Come."

Standing in the parking garage, David felt even more removed from reality than before. It was like an alien world, filled with concrete and too many shadows. There were no other cars on this level, nor were there any grease stains on the floor. With the exception of the soft rumble of the ventilation ducts, everything was quiet and still. Even in running shoes, his footsteps echoed loudly back through the empty garage.

Elaine placed her hand on a flat, red scanner to the left of the elevator. When the scanner turned blue, she punched in a series of numbers on a nearby keyboard. Only then did the elevator open to a dark-skinned giant of a man in a black suit, and a Doberman Pinscher on a short leash.

"Get in, Mr. Ross." Elaine motioned him forward but did not step into the elevator. "This will take you to Mr. Wisdom. I'll meet with you later this afternoon to go over some paperwork with you."

David hesitated. He looked at the dog and thought of what those teeth could to do to him. Could he stop the dog before it ripped out his throat?

Elaine shook her head. "We didn't bring you all this way to kill you, Mr. Ross." She pushed him into the elevator. "If you intend on lasting here, don't be so jumpy."

As the elevator doors closed, David struggled to keep his eyes off both man and dog. He was afraid either one of them could attack at any moment. There was no soft elevator music to fill the air, just the constant panting of the dog. David studied the mirrored walls of the confined space and fought a losing battle with fear.

'Too late for second thoughts,' he thought. Sweat ran in streams down his back. 'Besides, I can't go back home. The police are looking for me.'

The doors opened to a busy corridor. Men and women in dark suits walked in every direction. Over by the reception desk a man in a brown uniform delivered flowers. Another man in a rumpled grey suit shouted at the receptionist, something about rescheduling an appointment.

David got out of the elevator and looked back. He expected the giant man to get out and guide him to Wisdom's office. Instead the man let the doors close and disappeared.

He started toward the reception desk. A group of men in almost identical suits nearly crashed into him. They swerved mid-conversation without so much as an apology. Then, he felt a tickle in his skull and stopped. He turned in a circle until he saw a woman dressed in a tight, black business suit. She had long, straight brown hair but it was her eyes that captured him. They were emerald green like his, luminescent like a cat's at night.

"A word of advice, Mr. Ross," she said. "Most women do not take a gaping jaw and drool as a compliment. My name is Garnet. I'll take you to Wisdom. Follow me and try not to set anything on fire."

David swallowed. "Does everyone know about me?"

Garnet turned and walked away from David. He rushed to catch up to her. His eyes drank in her body, the way the fabric hugged her curves.

Garnet stopped and glared at him.

"Sorry," he said. "I'm not used to people reading my mind."

"Work on that," she said. "And, to answer your question, only a few of us know what you did back in Nova Scotia."

They passed several white doors that he assumed led to offices. All the doors were shut and there was not a window to be seen. It felt less like walking through an office building and more like being filed away in an archive. Occasionally, as he walked on, sounds came from behind the doors. He heard moans, laughter and muffled conversation. Once he had an impression of something large and not quite solid moving behind one of the doors. After that he kept his eyes forward.

"Is it much further?" he asked. His voice sounded pale and insubstantial in this place.

"Do you have another appointment, Mr. Ross? I do hope we're not keeping you from something."

The green-eyed woman slowed her gait.

David slowed his as well. He did not want to walk beside the woman. There was something about her that scared him as much as the unseen things behind the doors.

At the end of the hallway was a second reception desk. An old woman with grey hair typed at her computer. She was dressed in a bright dress of pastel flowers with matching gold necklace and hoop earrings. Garnet led him past the receptionist to a black door. She did not knock. She simply placed her hand on the face of the door for a moment and then pushed the door open.

David followed her in.

***

Wisdom stood from his desk as Garnet entered with David. "Right on time," he muttered under his breath. He walked over to the newest arrival and shook his hand.

"Pleasure to finally meet you, David," he said. "I'm sure you have a million questions. First, realize you are amongst friends here. No one will judge you on your past. Certainly not me. Garnet, can you pour us some drinks?"

Garnet bowed her head and went to a table covered with crystal tumblers and bottles of liquor.

"I don't even know where to start," David said. He glanced around the room, eyes wide in wonder. The room was luxurious, with thick carpet and mahogany furniture. Then he saw the wall of framed photographs to his right. He fixated on one of them – Wisdom sitting with a group of men on a beach – and his mouth dropped.

"Is that JFK?"

Wisdom smiled. "Yes. I met him a few times. Charming fellow. Always beat me at tennis."

David looked at Wisdom from the corner of his eye.

Wisdom smirked. "I'm older than I look."

"Who are these other people?"

"You wouldn't recognize their names, I'm afraid. The one to my left is Bill Bundy, one of Kennedy's advisors. The one with the big ears is David Rockefeller. He taught me how to play poker. But that's not important now. Let's talk about you. When did you first realize you were different?"

Garnet returned with drinks and handed one each to Wisdom and David. Then she returned to the bar to pour her own.

"When I was fourteen," David said as he sipped his scotch. "It started on my birthday. Mom had this cake all lit up with candles. When I went to blow the out, the cake exploded. Disaster. A few days later, I woke from a dream and my blankets were on fire. Mom thought I set it on purpose. She grounded me for a month and got rid of all the lighters and matches in the house. The next week, I heard her talking about how she was scared of me. Only she wasn't speaking. I realized I was hearing her thoughts. For years I thought I was crazy. Then there was prom and, well, it seems you know what happened there."

"Indeed." Wisdom motioned for David to sit on a red loveseat and then sat beside him. "No need to go over that right now. You're not alone. As I'm sure you've figured out, Garnet is like you. So were the other two you met in the car earlier, Jessica and Amy. Currently there are 48 young men and women just like you under my care."

"So many." David's hands shook. "What the hell am I? A mutant?"

"Not exactly. I prefer the term Anomaly. Each of you has advanced psionic abilities. No two Anomalies are exactly the same but there are some similarities. Over the years I've perfected a system of training people like you. I can make sure you never lose control again. I know the guilt is eating you, David. You can't live with yourself because of what you've done. I understand. I've done many things in my past I'm not proud of. That's why I do this."

"Have you killed people?"

Wisdom sighed.

"I'm sorry," David said. "I don't know what I was thinking. That was rude."

"No need to apologize." Wisdom finished his drink. Garnet came over with a crystal decanter and refilled it. "It's a valid question. You have a right to know about me, what kind of person I am. Yes. I have killed. Many times. Things were very different in my youth. As I said, I'm much older than I look. Back then, sometimes murder was a necessary tool. Then, years ago, I had a near-death experience in the south of France. I realized that, despite all my years on this planet, I hadn't achieved anything. No legacy. If I died, no one would remember my name. I needed a cause, so I chose you. The Anomalies."

"How did you find out about me? About us?"

Wisdom waved the question away. "Long story. For now, just know I have methods of finding people like you. In time, you'll get more details. You must be tired from your long trip. You must want to shower and get into some clean clothes. Garnet, can you show young David to his room?"

Garnet stood and offered a hand to David, helping him to his feet.

"Yeah," David said. "I'm pretty rank. One last question. Why is there so much security around here?"

Wisdom glanced over his shoulder. "I don't think it's enough security. I'm not the only one that knows about you, David. About the Anomalies. You have a power others would like to manipulate. They will stop at almost nothing to do so. Be glad that I found you first."

Chapter Eight

Garnet led him up a flight of stairs to a common room filled with plush beige couches and armchairs. Several strangers, all of them children or young adults, gathered around a large plasma television. They barely glanced at David as he walked by.

"This is your room." Garnet stopped in front of a white door. She handed him a keycard. "Someone will get you in the morning for breakfast."

The room was larger than he expected. It came with a private bathroom, a king-sized bed and a white leather sofa. His canvas bag lay on the floor beside the sofa on the rich crimson carpet. There was no TV or radio in the room but there were several shelves filled with books. A computer sat on a desk in the corner.

After a quick shower, he lay down and tried to sleep. Not long after, the two creepy girls from the Hummer paid him a visit. They walked in without knocking. Still, David knew they were coming before the door opened. He *felt* them coming.

"He's not surprised," the Asian girl said.

"Of course not, Amy," Jessica said. "Remember, I told you he was strong."

"Hmm, doesn't look strong to me."

"Are you little monsters here for a reason?"

Jessica put her hands on her hips. "Well, we're not here to make friends, if that's what you're thinking. We don't like you, remember?"

"We definitely don't like you," Amy said. She carried a Barbie doll in a red 'Gone-With-the-Wind' style dress and swung it gently in her right hand as she spoke. "But it's probably better for us if you don't die. You have to be careful now that you're here. Especially if you're outside. Of course, they don't let us go out much anymore."

"They say it's for our own protection," Jessica said. She

hopped up on David's bed not far from him and sat cross-legged, studying him while she tossed her blond bangs away from her eyes.

"It is, Jessica. You know what happened to Madeline."

"Who was Madeline?" David got off the bed and walked over to the sofa. It made him uncomfortable to be so close to them.

"We're not supposed to talk about her, Amy. Wisdom will do bad things to you."

"Will not. I'm his favorite."

Jessica rolled her eyes. "We both know that's not true. I'm the favorite. Anyway, since you've told first and I can blame this all on you, I'll tell him. Madeline was this old lady from somewhere in Spain."

"It was France." Amy walked over to the bed and sat on the corner.

"Whatever. She was pretty but not very smart. One night last month she decided to take off without telling anyone."

"She liked to go for walks at night." Amy brushed the hair on her Barbie with her left index finger. "And she wasn't that old, either."

"Was too. I heard she was in her late thirties. That's practically ancient. Anyway, later on that night, Amy and I woke up. There were all these people rushing around. Even Wisdom raised his voice and that never happens. Never. That's why I got out of bed and went looking. I knew it was bad."

"There was blood all over carpets. Even some on the walls."

"What?" David sat forward and pushed his damp hair off his forehead.

"She's exaggerating. Amy tends to do that because she's an only child. That's also why I adopted her as my sister. Not because she exaggerates but because she's an only child. No one should have to be an 'only' anything. The blood wasn't all over the carpet. It was just...I don't know...leaking behind Madeline. Now, *she* was covered in blood. I couldn't see very well but, from what I sensed in her mind, she was cut by very big knives. Knives that looked like peacock feathers."

"She was also set on fire. Don't forget that."

Jessica grabbed Amy's Barbie and threw it against the front door. "You're jumping ahead and ruining my story! Stop it!"

Amy walked slowly over to the doll, picked it up and adjusted its hair with her index finger. "Don't do that to my doll, Jessica. I won't warn you again."

Jessica opened her mouth, squinted her eyes, and then shook her head. "I won't. I promise. Don't be mad, okay? Anyway, David, we found out after she was dead…"

"Dead?"

"Well, yeah. We forgot to mention that, didn't we? Well, after she died, Amy overheard Elaine and Wisdom talking. It wasn't a random attack. This was deliberate."

David pulled a package of cigarettes from his canvas bag only to have them pulled out of his hands by an invisible force. The package fell onto the floor between him and the girls.

"No smoking in here, David," Amy said. "Wisdom has allergies."

Jessica rolled her eyes again and got off the bed. She walked over to the cigarettes, picked them off the floor, and threw them into a nearby metallic garbage can. "He does not have allergies, Amy. How many times do I have to tell you? Things, I mean people, like him don't have allergies. He just doesn't like cigarettes because they smell bad. They'll make you give them up in class, too, so you might as well stop now."

David stared at the garbage can. "So you're saying someone tracked her down and did this to her. That's the reason you guys are not allowed out of the building?"

"Sort of," Amy kept her eyes focused on her doll. "But we weren't allowed out much before that, either."

"Don't say anything else, Amy. You know you really do talk too much. We should get back to our rooms. We have studying to do. Just don't go out on your own. Bad things could happen and I haven't decided whether I want you dead or not yet."

After they left, David changed into jogging pants and sat on the sofa. He looked out over the city for a long time.

In the morning, he woke screaming and covered in sweat. This nightmare was even worse than usual. He tried to forget the crawling, scaly things from his dream. But he failed. He looked at the alarm clock on the nightstand. It was 5:30. He threw off the few corners of the sheets still clinging to his body and pushed himself to his feet.

He looked out the window and surveyed the streets of Toronto. From thirteen stories up, he could still make out the people below. A group of people his own age staggered and swerved down the sidewalk. It took him several minutes to remember what day it was. Saturday morning. They were probably students out all night dancing and drinking, coming home after an early breakfast. In another life that would have been him.

***

Elaine walked into Wisdom's office and sank to the floor, her back against the wall and her feet on the floor.

"Rough night?" Wisdom asked. He sat behind his desk pouring a glass of scotch.

"It always is, Wisdom." She cracked her knuckles and rubbed the soreness out of her trigger fingers.

"I don't need to ask, do I?"

She looked up then. "Of course you don't need to ask. They're dead. It was just…messy. There were a few civilians. A mother and child."

"It's not the first time you've shot a mother, Elaine. Your conscience confuses me. Those men killed Madeline. So when do you stop?"

"When you say we're done."

Wisdom smiled. "Not the killing, the self-flagellation."

"I think only your kind can do that. I'm still…"

"Still human? Well, yes. I guess you are. I could change that for you, you know? One of these days you will take me up on the offer."

Elaine shook her head. "Not yet. Maybe when I get old. For now it's too much to give up."

Wisdom laughed softly. "I do love you, Elaine. Just don't tell Echo I said so. Well, I won't keep you. You should get a few hours' sleep while you can. This may be the last moment of peace you know in this life. This will be our last night here."

"Hallelujah. I've never liked Toronto. Too many homeless people. It just depresses me."

"London has just as many homeless," Wisdom said. "Do you think your dislike of Toronto might have something to do with a certain blond-haired man who died here?"

"That was a long time ago." Elaine went silent for a moment and leaned her head back against the wall. Then she pushed herself to her feet. "It's starting soon, isn't it?"

"Yes. In a few hours."

"Are you sure you can still trust Echo?" Elaine's face was blank. There was something in the vacancy of her eyes that clearly showed disappointment. "She could turn the Anomalies over to Propates. You did say she was unpredictable."

"Unpredictable, not stupid." Wisdom drank the rest of his scotch. "She'll be here just in time."

Elaine dropped her shoulders and scratched her hair. "I don't know if I'm ready for this, Wisdom."

"Believe me," Wisdom said. "When the time comes, you'll be ready."

***

At 6:58 a.m. there was a knock at David's door. He looked away from the mirror where he had been attempting to straighten his hair. He was about to say "Come in" when Garnet entered. She was dressed in a tight black pantsuit with a red top underneath. He started to admire the way she looked but stopped the thought before it was fully formed. Around here it was hard to tell who was listening.

"You're up? Good. Ready for class?"

David looked back into the mirror and ran a palm over the stubble on his chin. "Do you think I need to shave?"

She tilted her head to the left and studied him. "No. You're good. You know, there's a whole closet full of clothes over there. Are you sure you want to wear that?"

"What's wrong with this?" David wore a clean pair of blue jeans and a bright orange Roots shirt. The shirt hung loosely over his trim body and made his shoulders look bigger than they truly were.

"Nothing. If you were going to bingo. People around here usually dress for class. There are suits in there. Expensive ones."

"I'm not here for my fashion sense. And speaking of fashion, isn't that jacket a bit tight?"

"No, it is exactly tight enough." David followed her out into the hallway. "Here, take this." She passed him a CIBC bank card and, after David locked his room, she walked down the hallway toward a set of elevators.

"You're not paid like most jobs on a weekly basis. In addition to your hiring bonus, Wisdom put $10,000 into this account. The PIN number is 1993, the year you were born, right? You won't have many expenses. You pay no rent and food is included, of course. I'm sure one of the others already told you we don't encourage you to go off on your own. There are scheduled outings, though. Spend away on those. Some of the employees send money home to their families."

"I won't be doing that." They stopped at the elevators and he felt her eyes on him. "So when do I find out what I do?"

"Do?"

"Yes, do. As a job?" The elevator doors opened and Garnet stepped inside.

Garnet looked at him sideways and frowned. "Wisdom will go into that later. For now, just go to class. They'll show you all sorts of fun things. Get you ready for your... job. Don't worry. As the letter said, Wisdom has a very specific need for people with your talents. He is willing to pay extremely well for your services."

"It doesn't involve killing people, does it?"

"Focus on your classes, Mr. Ross." She turned fully toward him, looked at him from crotch to face. No matter how cute you are with those bright green eyes and full lips, you're still a boy to me. A little boy with a head full of big ideas."

"You think I'm cute?"

Garnet pressed her lips together but said nothing.

The elevator doors opened. Once again, David saw a reception area filled with dozens of people. Wisdom stood there in a three-button suit. Like yesterday, it was blood red, however, the cut was completely different. Wisdom shook his head and looked at the ground.

"Leave the boy alone, Garnet." Wisdom handed a file folder to a woman behind the reception desk and signed several forms another man placed in front of him. "I need you in the Communication's room. Elaine has something for you. Come, David. I'll show you around and make some introductions."

"Do you own this building?" David walked side-by-side with Wisdom. "The whole building?"

Wisdom nodded and laughed. "Kind of hard to have a few secret floors in a building you don't own, Mr. Ross. Yes, I own the building and a few others in this city, as a matter of fact. I also have several more around the world. It helps to diversify a little in my line of work. But we'll get to that later. I've rented out the rest of the building: a few of the smaller banks, some lawyers and accountants, things of that nature. Helps fund certain projects and investments."

"What kind of projects?"

Wisdom looked over at him and raised an eyebrow.

"What? You mean like me? What am I, a project or an investment?"

"Definitely an investment. One I hope will pay off well in the end. I see you decided to wear your own clothes. Interesting. You were given several thousand dollars' worth of outfits, yet still you wear that. Why?"

"Is this a test?" Instinctively, David covered his chest.

"Test, test, test. Everything in this life is a test, my young Padawan. Do you like *Star Wars*? Of course you do. Everyone likes *Star Wars*. I'm not trying to lead you to the Dark Side, David, and I'm nearly positive I'm not your father. I'm just curious about your motives. Help me understand you. Why did you choose your own clothes over the ones you'd been given?"

David moved out of the way of two Chinese men in nearly identical suits. They were deeply involved in some conversation about an offshore project. They barely took the time to nod a hello to Wisdom.

"It wasn't a big conscious decision, you know. Not like I'm trying to rebel or something. I just know these clothes. Not that I'm not grateful and all, it's just...."

"Ah. You're wondering what the catch is. Smart boy. Always be careful of the catch. Luckily, in your case, I'm not going to try to pervert you or turn you into something that you're not."

David bit the inside of his lip. "With all due respect, sir, what am I doing here?"

"The answer is complicated. I could tell you that you'll be taking part in an epic battle that I've personally fought for the last sixty years. And while that's true, it really doesn't answer your question. There are bad men out there, Mr. Ross, very bad men doing very bad things. No one is standing up to stop them. Most people, the law of the world, wouldn't be able to stop them. I can."

"With my help?"

Wisdom nodded. "You and a few others. You've already met three of them. I found Jessica in California, Amy in Australia and Garnet in Vancouver."

"There are six in your class. You'll meet them in a few moments. You come from all over the world with seemingly nothing to tie you together. But your talents bind you in a very real and incomparable way. Unlike you, David, I know the hows and whys of who and what you are. When you're ready, I'll tell you."

"What if I said I was ready now?"

"Then you would be wrong. That knowledge will come when you're ready to accept what I have to tell you. There is nothing more dangerous than too much knowledge in untrained minds. You're not ready yet and telling you could make my investment in you completely useless."

David decided he did not like being referred to as an investment. It made him feel less than human. Still, he didn't have much choice. Wisdom was hiding him from the police. If he left, eventually they'd catch up with him. This was also his best chance to discover why he could do the things he could.

"You said you'd found 48 of us. Does that include Madeline?"

Wisdom jerked his head back. The lights flickered and dimmed. "Something new," he said. "No. It does not include her. It would be best if you don't speak about Madeline. It will upset the others. When you're ready – and I will tell you when you are ready – I'll let you know all about where you come from. If you wish, I'll even tell you about Madeline. But for now, you're late for class."

Wisdom walked toward a set of glass doors that opened as he got close to them. There were only a few people on this side of the doors. The first, a boy with light brown hair, sat on his feet. He looked to be about fourteen years old wearing a navy blue suit with a red tie and running shoes. He hit his head into the wall behind him repeatedly, not with a lot of strength but enough to make it look painful.

Wisdom leaned toward David and lowered his voice slightly. "That's Jared, one of your classmates. Since he's so busy, I think we'll leave the introductions for later. Don't worry, he's not troubled. A bit of a drama queen poseur if you ask me."

"What's wrong with him?"

Jared stopped banging his head against the wall and looked up at them as they walked by. He stuck his tongue out at David, an act that made him look younger than he really was. After they passed him, Wisdom said: "I believe he's upset with the mark he was given on his last assignment. I see from the look on your face that it shocks you. What shocks you more, that we have tests or that he acts like a normal kid?"

David looked back over his shoulder.

Jared was still sticking his tongue out at him.

"I hate tests. What happens if we fail?"

Wisdom put a hand on David's shoulder, his touch surprisingly warm. "No one fails these classes. If you don't perform as well as your instructors expect, you simply keep doing the assignment over and over until you've mastered it. It's more like karate class. There are levels. Jared is currently stuck at Level Three. He's been there for several months now, and I think it's bruising his pride. He came to us at the same time as Amy but she has progressed to Level Six. You, of course, will start at the bottom. Level One. From what I know of your experiences in Nova Scotia – and don't ask me how I know – you should progress to Level Two by month's end. Ah, and here are the last two members of your class. David, I would like you to meet Bethany and Todd.

The woman, Bethany, nodded and gave a little wave. From the wrinkles and weight on her face, David guessed she was in her early 50's. She had short, graying hair cut just above her ears, and calm brown eyes. She was actually knitting – like some sort of stereotypical grandmother figure. The younger man, Todd, read from a stack of papers gathered in a manila folder. He was a slightly overweight man not much older than David. He had short brown hair, smooth skin and a bright smile peeking out from his dark brown goatee.

"Hey, David." Todd closed the file and stuck out a hand to shake. David shook the offered hand and smiled back. There was something honest in Todd's eyes, like the comfort of a pastor or a young doctor. "I was just reading some of my dreams to Bethany. That's one of the first things they'll have you do in Level One, keep a dream journal. As much as I love the kids, it's nice to have another adult here."

"Don't lie." Bethany barely looked up from her knitting. "You don't love the kids and neither do I. Damn little demons, if you ask me. Oh, don't give me that look. You've had the same thoughts yourself and you know it. All that power and no emotion. I tell you, they're not quite human."

"Who amongst us is?" Wisdom smiled as he said this. "I'll leave David with you, Bethany. Do try and be nice."

David watched as Wisdom marched away. Before he left, Wisdom looked at his watch and mouthed something. David wasn't certain, but he could have sworn Wisdom said, "Almost time."

'Almost time for what?' he wondered.

Chapter Nine

Propates sat in his office holding an old photograph in his right hand. It was faded and yellowed with age, the edges worn from years of handling. It was Echo sitting on a beach in Thailand. She wore a one-piece bathing suit – blue with white polka dots – and an oversized, flopping sun hat. She was smiling at the photographer – himself – while children played in the waves behind her.

"Why did you go back to him?" He traced his finger down Echo's neck. "Things could have been so different."

He looked at the image emblazoned on the wall before him. It was a representation of Melek Taus: a large black peacock in a circle of gold. Christians and Jews regarded Melek Taus as Satan. The peacock represented pride, something the monotheists saw as an opening to all sin. Propates, however, knew it was simply a new version of an old power: Argus, a hundred-eyed, all-seeing god who never slept. By learning the lessons of the peacock, one could transcend humanity and become a God.

The phone rang.

"I'm busy," he said. "Be quick."

"Whatever you're doing will wait." The voice on the phone was familiar but not instantly recognizable. "We have an issue with the agent from away. Lucius and the others are meeting in the Vulture Antechamber."

"I'm heading there in a few minutes, anyway." Propates answered. "The shadows are not sitting well. The Orpheans are about to make an appearance. Is this Otto?"

"Tsk. No. I'll see you in a few, Propates."

The crass denial confirmed who the voice belonged to, but the caller hung up before Propates could name him. He pushed the button to open the elevator. The carriage was empty, for which he was extremely thankful. The Council of Peacocks was growing. Its membership was well into the tens of thousands now. Members of the upper echelon had taken up residence here in Thessaloniki; there were smaller outposts around the world. With growth, however, came an abundance of administrative duties: papers to sign, rewards and punishments to be meted out, initiations to oversee. The business of trying to save the world from itself was quickly becoming a real business.

"If I knew it was going to end up like this," he whispered to himself, "I wonder if I would have answered Wisdom's question differently."

He closed his eyes and thought back to the first time he'd met Echo and Wisdom.

***

In 51 AD, Propates was a sixteen-year-old man living on a farm in the countryside not far from Rome. He'd never been to the city, but he knew about it. Tax collectors and bloodthirsty soldiers came from the city. What more did he need to know? When he married his young wife, a fourteen-year-old beauty named Olivia, his family built an addition onto the main house. Olivia was pregnant with their first child. The oracle who lived nearby said the child would be a boy. In retrospect, Propates remembered the haunted expression on the oracle's face as she told their fortunes. She must have seen what was coming.

Early one summer evening, a nobleman and his entourage passed by the farm. Like most nobles, they treated the uneducated peasants as little more than worms. With the weight of muscle and steel behind it, they had the right to take whatever they wanted. In their philosophy, if you could not stop someone from taking your possessions, you did not deserve to keep them. The commander of the nobleman's soldiers wanted Olivia. Propates stood between his wife and the soldiers. He was beaten for his insolence. While the commander raped his wife, Propates, bloodied and sore, fed and watered the man's horses.

After fifteen minutes, the commander returned and forced Propates to smell his Roman fingers. Propates cringed at the smell of his wife on the brute's body. But he said nothing. He did nothing. The commander laughed and offered Olivia up to the rest of his men. Propates remembered the look on his father's face. 'Get used to it.'

Later, after helping Olivia wash the blood from her body, Propates snuck out of the house and into the darkness of the fields. The open air was the only place large enough for his fury. He knelt and pounded his fists into the damp earth. His eyes burned with tears but he dared not scream. On the way back to the house, he saw a woman. Her hair was long and tightly curled, done up in the style fashionable amongst Roman ladies of the time. In the moonlight the bared flesh of her arms and neck appeared as cold and pale as bone. When he realized he was staring at her, he forced his head down. If the lady complained to the soldiers, if she told them he dared look upon her, they could kill him. And then where would Olivia be?

"Come here, boy." The lady spoke, her voice soft like the wind through the grass.

Fear froze him in place.

"Don't make me repeat myself," she said. Now there was definite laughter in the voice. Propates felt the fury flush through his face. Who was she to call him boy? Even though she looked like royalty, her soft, wrinkleless face marked her as barely older than him.

"Yes, mistress." As Propates spoke, it felt like he had pebbles in his throat. Each word was painful. He walked closer to her, keeping his eyes to the ground.

"This anger you're feeling, boy, the rage that's welling up inside you…I've felt it. Oh, you can take that sneer off your face. Believe me or don't. Why should I care? I am not really sure why I'm bothering with you at all. I just…I guess I just had to talk to someone human, someone who still knows what it's like to feel pain, to watch everything you hold dear get demolished in front of you at the whim of some monster."

Propates looked up. His lips trembled. "You're rich and

powerful," he said. "A lady. You know nothing about being poor and powerless."

The woman stared over at him. For the first time, their eyes connected. There was just as much venom in her eyes as Propates felt inside himself. "I know more than you can possibly imagine about being powerless. Your woman was raped. So what? At least it wasn't your mother. Or your father. At least you didn't have to watch it being done to them. Imagine that captain forcing you to slit your brother's throat then stand still as he killed the rest of your family. Imagine…" Her shoulders slumped and she shook her head. "Oh, why bother? Right now you feel like the biggest victim in all of history. There, too, I've been. But you're not, boy. You're not the biggest anything. You will rage, you will die, and history will forget you." Then she looked up to the sky, a small smile on her lips. "But it won't forget me."

From behind Propates, a voice called out of the dark. It boomed like thunder in the distance.

"Andromeda? Where are you?"

The lady wiped under her eyes with her fingertips and was silent for a moment. "I'm over here, Wisdom." When she spoke, all the venom was gone, replaced by a mix of emotions Propates could not identify.

Behind him, Propates heard the jingle of moving armor and the plodding of heavy footsteps. The sounds moved toward him, but Propates did not turn around. He did not look up. He held his breath and waited for the sword stroke. Then the steps stopped. A firm, warm hand gripped his right shoulder, but he could not see the man who touched him. A mix of sweat and sulfur filled the air. Propates felt uncomfortably warm. The man behind him radiated heat like a living fire.

"What are you doing with the boy, Andromeda?" The man's voice no longer boomed like distant thunder. It crackled like lightning.

"Comforting him."

Wisdom laughed. "Comforting? Seducing is more likely.

If you want him, take him. There's no need to toy with…"

"Everything is a game to you, isn't it?" The venom was back in her voice.

"Andromeda, everything is a game. And not just for me. When you've lived as long as I have, you'll realize that. Nothing we do today affects the greater ripples of time. These people fade and die so quickly. Why be concerned with them at all? You have not been one of them for hundreds of…"

"Hush, Wisdom." She stepped away from the tree and approached Wisdom. Propates stood between them, wishing he could fade into the shadows. The tension between them stung like embers. "Never reveal a lady's age. You should know better."

"Humph. Do you want the boy or not?"

Andromeda grabbed Propates by the chin and forced his head up. She studied his eyes for a moment with a hard, icy intensity. Then her expression softened and she took her hand away. "No. He's too soft and angry."

The hand on Propates' shoulder gripped tighter. "Soft and angry, you say. I can use that."

Andromeda took at step back. "No, Wisdom. Please, don't…."

"If you don't want him for a toy, Andromeda, I will take him. I haven't converted anyone since I took you. This melancholy you're feeling, maybe it's just loneliness. Tell me, boy, what is your name?"

The hand on his shoulder spun him around and forced him to his knees in one movement. For a moment, the pebbles in Propates' throat seemed to clog up his entire voice. He looked up at the dark-skinned man before him and screamed. It was not the violence implied in the blood red flares of the cape or the highly polished metal of his Roman soldier's uniform. It was the orange-glow in the man's eyes, a glow that came from some internal flame.

"I said, tell me your name!"

As Propates watched, the orange glow faded and died.

The only light now came from the moon above. Propates fought past the pebbles in his throat and the fear clouding his head.

"I'm called Propates, lord."

Wisdom smiled and rested a heavily calloused hand on Propates' unwashed hair. "A fine name. An auspicious name. Tell me, Propates, would you like to live forever?"

Wisdom tore the thinly woven tunic from Propates. He placed a warm hand on the sixteen-year-old's trembling chest. In a flash, Propates sensed the pain and screamed. Wisdom's hand crackled and burst into flame. With inhuman speed and strength, he pushed Propates down onto his back and started chanting. Only later did Propates realize the words were Arabic; at the time, he only recognized them as magic.

Fire thrust from Wisdom's flesh, inserting its heat into every cell of Propates' body. As it pulsated through his quivering body, his marrow superheated, turning to plasma. His blood flash-boiled, turned to red vapor and hissed out from every orifice in his body. Only a force coming up from the earth, a shadowy darkness, cooled his body enough to keep bones and flesh intact. It was the worst pain he had ever felt in his life.

He spent nearly a month fading in and out of fever dreams. He was only dimly conscious of the outside world, but he remembered leaving the farm. He knew Wisdom left a sack of currency at the farm, payment to father for a son. He felt more than saw Andromeda come to sit with him. She came often. Propates knew she cried over him and held his hand. But mostly he was only aware of the dreams.

The place he dreamt of was nowhere on Earth. It was a red city with no sun. Pillars of orange and black shot up from the scorched, blackened earth to a crimson sky. He wandered through buildings as massive as mountains, filled with ephemeral creatures whose translucent bodies were constructed of living flame. In the distance, giant birds flew over a range of mountains composed entirely of glistening emeralds. Later he was in the presence of a man emerging from a pool of lava. Neither the flame nor the heat seemed to touch him. The man's face flickered, sometimes visible, other times not; but Propates knew the man was Wisdom. In the dream Wisdom grabbed him by the hand and led him into the pool of lava. As he sunk below the molten matter, Propates clearly heard Wisdom's voice say: "Welcome to Djinnistan."

Propates woke with a start, just managing to keep the scream in his throat. Andromeda was beside him, reading silently from a scroll. She was dressed in a fluid, graceful gown that was dyed deep purple. Her hair was down, flowing over her shoulders like water frozen in place.

"What did he do to me?" Propates forgot himself for a moment. He reached over and gripped Andromeda's hand, a presumption that previously would have scared him into paralysis. "What is he? What have I become?"

Andromeda put the scroll down and leaned over him. With a gentle hand, she pushed a lock of sweat-damp hair away from his forehead and out of his eyes.

"What has he done?" she repeated. "He's freed you and he's damned you. He's damned both of us. As to what he is, I don't really know. I've been alive a long time now, a very long time, and I've never met anyone like him. Sometimes he talks of his home, of the place he came from. He calls it the Kaz but I've never heard of such a place. Have you?"

Propates shook his head. His throat was dry and his whole body ached for moisture.

"As for what you've become, only time will tell. We are not like him. Not even close. The things I've seen him do, they are inhuman. Maybe he's one of the gods from Olympus and maybe now we are demigods. I don't really believe that, but it's a nice lie. A pretty lie. And it helps me get through the nights. I suggest you find yourself a lie, something that will help you, too."

For decades, Propates traveled with Wisdom and Andromeda. Most of that time was a blur of violence and excess. They traveled to England where Wisdom conferred with hidden remnants of the nearly extinguished Druidae. They met with barbarian shamans throughout Europe and mystics in China. Wisdom was looking for something, but he would not tell Propates what it was. A brief stop near Rome gave him the opportunity to revisit the family farm. It was mostly to confirm that Olivia was dead. She'd died in her early thirties, childless and unmarried. The family farm was now owned by the descendants of a distant cousin. Whatever hope he had held that his unborn child had survived the repeated rapes was destroyed.

Propates said goodbye to the last vestiges of his former life.

Then they traveled deep into the jungles of Africa, on the edges of the Kingdom of Aksum, and everything changed. On that day, Propates learned to touch the shadows. It was also the first time in centuries that Wisdom faced his father.

They arrived in the village just after midday. Fresh from two years amongst the Parthian tribes traveling the lands that would one day be Iran and Turkey, the three of them were dressed in rich embroidered beige robes with loose cowls to cover their heads. Wisdom still traveled with a small body of soldiers but the majority of them kept to the outskirts of the village, a gesture Wisdom hoped would avoid panic in the villagers. Wisdom spoke the language of the region – he seemed to know the language of every region – and quickly arranged for room and board. Then he left Andromeda and Propates, disappearing into a hut constructed of mud and straw with a man dressed only in bones and leather.

"What are we doing here?" Propates was uncomfortably aware of the smell of freshly spilt blood in the air. Something was being slaughtered nearby. He hoped it was for a feast. He hoped it was an animal. "What is Wisdom looking for?"

"Answers." Andromeda removed her cowl and ran her fingers through her hair to remove the tangles. "Wisdom is asking the medicine man here questions, the same questions he's asked the others. When he has answers, we will leave."

"Answers to what kind of questions?" Propates looked around for a place to sit and only found the floor. He decided to stand. "What does a man like him need answers for, anyway? The way he talks, you'd think he already knows everything."

Andromeda smiled and brushed Propates' bangs away from his forehead. "You've barely changed at all. After all these years you still look like you're sixteen. Sometimes I wish you were a little older."

Propates reached up and touched Andromeda's hand. "I am old enough. I had a wife once, remember? A wife who is long dead. Let me..."

"No. Wisdom will..." Andromeda pulled her hand away. "I cannot do this."

"Do you love him?"

Andromeda sighed and pulled even further away. "We have a long day ahead of us. While Wisdom is conducting his research, I suggest you find something to keep yourself occupied."

Then she was gone. It was the last time he would see her for several hundred years.

Propates stayed inside the hut, sitting on the dirt floor with his knees curled up to his chest. Whatever Wisdom had done to him all those years ago had not only retarded his aging process, it had also slowed his mental and emotional growth. Despite his age, he still felt all the roiling emotions of an adolescent.

"Andromeda doesn't love him," he whispered to himself. To his young mind, without love or the promise of children there was no other reason for marriage. Only royalty or heads of state married for political reasons. So to him, that meant there was still a chance he could steal her away from Wisdom.

He stood and began to exercise, using a series of fluid yet physically strenuous movements he had learned in Asia.

Within moments, he was lost in the rhythm of movement. Then he sensed something. A stirring in the shadows. He tensed, shifting his consciousness out of his body to become fully aware of his surroundings. At the back of the hut, behind a stack of clay jars and animal pelts, something was moving in the darkness.

"I see you," he said. "Come out." The shadows churned and Propates realized it was not someone or something moving in the shadows. Rather, the shadows seemed to be redistributing themselves around something.

"What are you?"

His heart beat forcefully in the silence. For a moment, there was nothing. Then a sound, sibilant like the clicking of pebbles underfoot and the drifting of sand in the wind, spoke from the shadows. "I come as a warning," it said. As it spoke, the shadows swirled in jerky motions. "One of the Invisible Ones is coming: one of the Smokeless Fire. All will be consumed by him. He comes for his son and nothing will stop him."

Propates took a step closer to the shadows. "That means nothing to me, demon. Stop talking in riddles. Tell me what you are!"

"We are friends, Propates. We have known you since Wisdom touched you the first time. He has shown you nothing and he never will. Come to us, touch us and you will be shown things beyond your current understanding. But we must hurry. The Invisible One is almost here."

Propates studied the figure submersed in the gloom, his whole being tensed and waiting for an attack. When it did not come from the shadows, he turned and exited the hut.

"Damnable shade," he whispered and spat on the ground. It was not his first experience with an incorporeal parasite. Several times in China, but more often amongst the Parthian tribes, he witnessed attempts at possession by creatures from Beyond. This was obviously some sort of fiend sent to tempt him, lure him to Hades so it could steal his body. He had to find Wisdom and let him know about the attempt. Wisdom would know what to do.

He was so focused on the need to find Wisdom that he did not see what was right in front of him. The village was quiet. Nothing moved, not even the leaves of the trees all around him. He looked above the trees and bit his lips. The sky was purple and red, like a bruise, and the clouds ran briskly through the heavens. A determined wind blew them but did not touch the earth.

"Wisdom?" The village absorbed his voice and offered nothing in return. He felt a chill that had nothing to do with wind rush through his body. As a child, he'd been taught this meant a larva, one of the restless dead, was reaching out to him in warning. He had never really believed it until that moment.

"Wisdom?"

A tree branch cracked in the distance.

"Andromeda?"

Silence.

Propates walked further into the village, past circular straw huts and the tree to which only recently the village had secured its cows. There was no one to be seen. Even the cows were gone, though the leather thongs that had held them in place remained. Fire still smoldered in the shallow fire pits and the smell of blood was thick in the air. But where were the people? Where were the bare-chested mothers grinding grain, the toothless old women making pottery, the naked children chasing each other through the dust? He'd seen them all as he had come into the village. He walked a little further and heard a soft sound. His eyes quickly spotted the source – a small red-clay bowl filled with grain spun with diminishing speed. Propates knelt beside it and stopped its spinning with his fingertips.

And one again, silence.

'Wherever they went,' he thought, 'they left recently. And very suddenly.'

Something moved behind him. Propates turned so quickly he tripped over his own feet and fell on the ground.

His eyes shot to the spot the movement had come from, but now he could see nothing. Then something charged out of the woods, an indescribable mess of torn flesh and exposed bones. Only as it grew closer did Propates recognize the dark skin, the threatening mounds of muscle in the shoulders and the look of rage on the shredded face.

Wisdom.

Something had done this to Wisdom.

"What...?"

Wisdom glanced at him. For a second, he was not sure he even recognized him.

A roar came from out of the jungle, a sound like screaming children and the smashing of boulders. Bolts of lightning danced a web of electricity in the now-cloudless sky above. Daylight bled out of the air. It grew darker and darker. Propates looked for the sun. It was still there, but with every passing moment it gave off less and less illumination. He jumped as Wisdom grabbed him by the arms and abruptly pulled him closer. Face to face, Propates determined the look he had mistaken for rage was actually fear.

Wisdom said: "Run."

The shredded man pushed him away and then turned back to the woods. Fire sprang up along Wisdom's body, shrouding him in bright red flame. The sound came again from the woods and it was enough to shatter the last of Propates' nerves. He screamed and ran wildly, barely aware of where he was going. It was as dark as night now, the only light coming from the web of lightning above. In his panic, Propates ran right into a hut and through the straw wall. There was movement to his left, something moving and twitching in the shadows, a swirl of barely visible colors with a sense of enormous mass behind it. Then from out of the darkness, there was a hand, human in shape but black and airy like a shadow. It was followed by a slender arm. It beckoned to him. Then something spoke.

"Last chance."

This time, there was no hesitation. Propates reached out to the shadow hand. He felt a rush of cold consume him. Then he was just gone.

***

Propates left his office, signed an invoice his secretary held out to him, and headed toward the elevator. One level down, he stepped off the elevator and nodded to the white-robed acolyte who sat behind the reception desk.

Even the ceremonial floor required administration now. Two stories below the apartment complex, the ceremonial floor was connected to centuries-old tunnels that ran from here to the White Tower in one direction, far beyond the city limits in the other direction. Most of the rooms currently used by the Council of Peacocks were newly constructed, like this foyer. The flooring here was pristine white tile. On the ceiling, fifteen feet above Propates' head, was a mosaic of a peacock landing in Paradise surrounded by Edimmu, while in the distance the spirit of Argus with his hundred eyes looked on with a smile. The ceremonial floor had been built mostly by the Edimmu and, being much taller than humans, they required more space. Enclosed spaces reminded them of their subterranean cities. It reminded them of their descent into slavery.

Propates left the foyer and walked briskly down a tunnel constructed from sand-colored bricks. There was no one else in sight, which annoyed him. Everyone else was probably already dressed and in the Vulture Antechamber. As Argus' representative on Earth, Propates should have been the first one contacted in case of emergencies, not the last. Lucius and Otto had apparently forgotten their place in the scheme of things. Maybe it was time to remind them.

The entrance to the cloakroom was guarded on either side by an Edimmu. Both were male, their scaly visages touched with flecks of black and yellow. Both wore ceremonial uniforms – leather kilts, knee-high sandals and heavy claymores strapped to their waists. Like most of the young Edimmu, neither guard wore a shirt nor had any body hair. Neither acknowledged him as he walked between them. They served him now out of need and fear, not loyalty.

He stripped off his business attire and slipped into a heavy robe lined on the inside with soft felt. The outside of the robe was constructed entirely of peacock feathers. Underneath it he wore a simple white tunic that hung to his knees. All members of the inner circle dressed the same, a remnant of times when to be a member of the Council of Peacocks was a death sentence. The cloak came with a thick cowl that hid the practitioner's face. What once was a pretext of privacy was now a reminder of humility and the heritage of the Council.

The Vulture Antechamber was dark. The only light came from small fires burning in copper braziers, one on each of the five raised funeral platforms that encircled the raised dais at the center of the room. The dais itself was thirteen feet in diameter, one foot for each lunar month in a year. If viewed from above, the platforms looked like black rays shooting out from a black sun. Around the edge of the dais stood life-sized statues of vultures carved from black marble. They looked outward over the funeral platforms, a carry-over from a magical rite that only Propates and the Edimmu remembered.

Frankincense and myrrh were heavy in the air, the incense so thick it hung like mist. In the shadowy recesses of the cavernous room, acolytes and Edimmu chanted quiet incantations in Greek. On the dais, just inside the vulture statues, five figures in robes identical to the ones Propates wore knelt nearly equidistantly around the circle. Their cowls covered their faces and they remained silent as Propates took his place at the Eastern Edge, completing the circle.

"Why has a full flock been called?" he asked.

"I called the flock because I have a concern about the agent from away." Propates believed this deep tenor voice belonged to Lucius. It was difficult to distinguish individuals in the Vulture Antechamber. The magics and the acoustics here turned each voice into a stronger, stranger version of itself.

"This is not news," Propates answered. "We all have concerns, but the coming war means we must accept strange allies. I'm much more concerned with the loyalty of the Orpheans than this Defksquar. The demons are called demons for a reason."

"But they are *our* demons," another voice said. "They come from our planet's evolutionary cycle, unlike the other one. Defksquar is moving behind our backs."

"Again, this is not news," Propates felt the heat of anger rise in him. "We've known for twenty years he wasn't going to give us the full story about why he was helping us. And we've known for five months now he was outright lying about some things. But he is not lying about what's coming. Our oracles have confirmed it. So have the demons. If we are to survive this war..."

"Of course we'll survive it," a third voice said. "It's just a question of who we kneel to. Some of us have concerns that the agent from away wants us to kneel to him."

"We kneel to no one but Argus." This came from a truly familiar voice. This one was definitely Otto.

"Exactly," Propates said with a smile. "And if we stay on this path that is where we will continue to kneel. As for Wisdom, I made it known long ago that he should have been informed about the coming war. I was outvoted. You all believed Wisdom's father that doing so would be disastrous. Like an idiot, I let you all keep him out of the loop. If we had his help, maybe we wouldn't need the agent from away."

"The agent from away has given us technologies and magics completely unlike anything on Earth." This voice, with its overriding tone of arrogance and assumption, was the one who had called him earlier. "Without his help we would never have perfected the process of Eyeness. Nor would we have the knowhow to design the weapons the demons are building for the coming war. What would Wisdom have given us?"

Propates fought the urge to rise and backhand the man. "He could have given us an army of immortals, demigods like me. Beings who could survive the yet imperfect process of Eyeness. We wouldn't need alien technologies. And we wouldn't have had to give over our children to the demons."

"Our children, not yours."

For a moment, the tension was nearly strangling. Some of those chanting in the corners stumbled over their incantations. Now Propates did rise. He moved to the center of the dais and raised a hand. The darkness dissipated and, in an instant, the underground chamber was filled with a bright, warm light. Sunlight. He pushed his cowl away from his face and turned toward the owner of the arrogant voice.

"Enough. Your petty power games have made you forget yourself. You are not my equal. So you sold your firstborns for a cause. So what? You all know what I went through. I lived in the Black Sea! I dwelt with demonic forces you can't even comprehend. I was found, saved by the spirit of Argus himself. When I returned to Earth hundreds of years ago, I was able to rebuild his church. The reborn Argusites. The Council of Peacocks. Perhaps you're thinking that I've led too long?"

None answered him.

"Your silence speaks for itself."

"Only some of us question," Otto said. "I am not one of them. My loyalty is to you."

"Some of us do have questions." This was Lucius. The magic that masked voices was gone now, but the bravado did not disappear with anonymity. "You're part of the old régime. Like Wisdom. The Djinnistani informed us the timeline has changed."

Propates moved quickly. He gathered the shadows around him, solidified them and constructed a spear. He slammed the butt of the weapon of darkness against Lucius' chest and knocked him to the ground. "You've spoken with Wisdom's father, have you? And you believed him? You doubt an alien but you believe a creature like that? By all my eyes, Lucius, you have just proven to me that you are too stupid to live. I banish you."

"No, Propates!" Otto stood and removed his cowl. "This is forbidden. The laws..."

"The laws?" Propates clenched his fists and the light of the room wavered. "I wrote the laws! And this insignificant termite is trying to eat away at everything I've built. Living in the shadows was good for my character. Maybe it will be good for his."

With a mental command, Propates called upon the darkness, a crepuscular world of death populated not by the demons or Edimmu, but by ghosts and fear. Long ago, this world had reached out to him, captured him and perverted what was left of his humanity. Ever since Argus had freed him from the land of the shades, Propates had become their master. The things in the shadows now obeyed him. The artificial sunlight quickly faded. In its place was a sooty gloom beyond night. This was more than the absence of light or the vacuum of space. It was the antithesis of life. Within the darkness, unseen by any but Propates, the denizens that haunted the netherworld moved. Little more than centers of gravity, they circled around Lucius, not placated by his screams of raging. Then rage gave way to pain as unseen hands tore at him and dragged him away. In a matter of seconds, the shadows retreated and all trace of Lucius was gone.

The Vulture Antechamber was silent. All chanters, Edimmu and human, stared at Propates in awe. Terror. 'Good,' he thought. 'That reminded them.'

From behind one of the vulture statues, someone, something, cleared its voice and said: "Sorry to interrupt, pets. We could come back later if you prefer."

Propates ran a hand through his hair, took a deep breath and relaxed his powers. He slipped the cowl back over his head and, on cue, the incantations began again. This, in turn, recalled the magic of the place.

The Vulture Antechamber had been used for over a

thousand years to contact other realms of reality. At first, the Edimmu had used it as a form of telecommunication, talking with encampments of their people in the underground cities of Kazakhstan and the subterranean country of tunnels and cities beneath South America. Then Propates, as head of the Council of Peacocks, used its energies to commune with the peacock-god Argus and the undead creatures of the gloom. Repeated dimensional warping here had weakened the boundaries of normal space. It allowed the agent from away to contact the Council. It also let these two beings, outcasts, stand and breathe in a world that should have been closed to them. These were the Orpheans, demons to most, partners to the Council of Peacocks.

"Why are you here, Sanchez?" Propates spoke to a hazy blur to the left of the statute. In this world, the Orpheans had no solid form. They were ghosts. Phantoms. The one he talked to was short and rotund. The figure beside the first one was taller and much more slender. Her name was Carla and, unlike Sanchez, she scared Propates just a little. There was a spark in her eyes that spoke of a long, burning rage.

"Are we unwelcomed?" Carla's voice was just as thin and strained as Sanchez's, as if they were shouting from somewhere far away.

"Of course not," Propates said with conviction. "Our allies are always welcome here. Did you need bodies to possess?"

"No," Carla spoke quickly and looked down at Sanchez with an expression that told him the subject was not up for debate. "We cannot stay long. We will find bodies elsewhere soon enough. We bring word from our Lord Ahriman. He confirms what the Djinnistani told us. Wisdom has been traveling in time. The ripples are faint, well-hidden, but, once Ahriman knew what to look for, they were easy to see."

"Has he changed anything?" Propates was glad his face was covered. It allowed him to conceal the loss of blood to his face.

Carla and Sanchez exchanged a slow, meaningful look.

Then Sanchez spoke. "He has changed much, but nothing of consequence to our plans. He still does not know what is coming and, in the end, his father will take him away. We must focus instead on our own concerns. Our children must be gathered. Initiated. The time of the Activation approaches."

Then the Orpheans were gone. In a wink, the hazy figures faded from view, leaving only natural darkness. For a moment Propates kept his silence as everyone in the room reflected on the warning.

"I suggest you all remember their words," he said. "Our world is in jeopardy. Everything we hold dear is in danger of being ripped away from us. We do not have time for in-fighting. I will waste no more time on it. I strongly suggest you do the same. And as for the agent from away, we've been in bed with him for too long to start wondering now if he's diseased. Our path is set, for good or bad. The Activation is coming."

Chapter Ten

The classroom was larger than David expected. It was the size of a small banquet hall and, for the most part, empty. When he stepped through the door, the first thing he noticed was a long oak desk at the head of the room. Three stacks of files were piled neatly upon one corner while the rest of the desk remained empty.

The second thing he noticed was the big-boned woman by the windows. She looked out over the city as she ruminated on her lower lip. Her left arm was in a cast and sling. Taking in the rest of the room, David saw three rows of reclining chairs, all black leather and surgical steel. Each chair was five feet away from the others, spacing them out over the width of the classroom. They faced a chalkboard that took up the majority of the wall opposite the windows. There was nothing else in the room.

Amy, Barbie in hand, sauntered in with Jessica. Jared gave up pounding his head against the wall long enough to take a seat. Garnet did not show up. David assumed she must be in another group. He waited until everyone else was seated before selecting a chair. He chose the one furthest away from the other students.

"How is your arm, Ms. Ryerson?" Jared asked. When he spoke, there was a dangerous glint in his eye. To David, he looked more like a boy with a magnifying glass over an anthill than a student asking a teacher about her injury.

"It's still broken," she answered. She moved away from the window and David inhaled sharply. The right side of her head was covered with a large white bandage. Her neck and cheeks were red and raw with visible burn marks. Her eyes ran over Jared then settled on David.

"I am Ms. Amelia Ryerson," she said. "As you've probably been told, I teach a few things here you don't learn in a normal classroom. So let's set some ground rules right now."

She took a deep breath and suddenly looked back out the windows. Her expression, like looking back on a lover she was forced to walk away from, made it very clear she wanted to be somewhere else. Lips pursed, she looked at the ground and then began to speak again.

"This is not high school, so there is no acting like children. I have no time for it, and after yesterday it seems like none of us do. I need to also point out that I am nothing like you." Her good arm fell free and she paced back and forth in front of the chalkboard. "Jessica, will you please explain to the verbose Mr. Ross what exactly you are?"

The young girl opened her mouth to respond, stopped for a moment and then looked to Ms. Ryerson. They stared at each other for a heartbeat before Ms. Ryerson responded.

"Oh, for God's sake, child, give him the simple version for now. I can't believe you had to ask that. Now go on."

Jessica's face went slightly red at the word 'child', but she turned in her seat to face David anyway. "All of us were born with certain abilities that are anomalous in humans. We call these abilities EFHB, which stands for Extraordinary Functions of the Human Body. EFHB, a term first used by Chinese scientists, is used here to distinguish what we can do from the stigma attached to words like 'paranormal' and 'psychic.' Almost everyone has some degree of psychic powers. They experience moments of déjà vu or brief telepathic contact with their loved ones. That's normal. It differs from person to person, kind of like the propensity toward sports and puzzle solving. Some people are stronger than others. What we do is very different. That's why we are called Anomalies. We are outside the realm of normalcy."

Jared squirmed in his seat. "Can we talk about my re-test?" He focused on cleaning his fingernails as he spoke. David realized that Jared barely looked at Ms. Ryerson and, when he did, the look was one of contempt. He wondered just how Ms. Ryerson had gotten that broken arm.

"No, Jared," Ms. Ryerson answered. "At this point in time I'm not sure there will be any re-tests. Wisdom wants me to ensure you're ready for more concrete scenarios, so I'm going to have to skip fairly quickly through a few lessons. Now, each of you lean back in your chairs. Go on, get comfortable. David, I would appreciate it if you would stop clawing at the furniture. You may be a freak of nature but, nerves aside, you are not a cat. The first thing we learn is how you can access your abilities at will. I am going to teach you some concentration exercises before we move on to the big stuff. What is the first step in relaxation? Anyone?"

Bethany opened her mouth to answer. Then her face went lax.

She looked around her, as if searching the corners of the room for something.

"Bethany, what …?"

"Hush, Toddie. Do you hear that?"

The room was silent.

Bethany got up from her chair and walked to the windows. "It's coming from outside."

Ms. Ryerson stared at Bethany's back, her lips tense and white.

"Do you hear anything?" she asked Todd.

"No, Ms. Ryerson, but then I'm not as strong as Beth. What about you, David? Anything?"

David's eyes went wide and he shook his head. "What am I supposed to be hearing?" He stopped and looked around his mind to see if anything seemed out of place. "I do feel…something. Almost…I guess it does kind of feel like I'm being watched."

"This can't be good." Amy got up from her chair and went to stand beside the older woman.

"What the hell is this?" David asked. He stayed in his seat. "Bethany?"

Bethany shook her head, her eyes focusing between the city streets below and the windows of the nearby glass buildings. "I don't think they know I've spotted them. They are cloaking their thoughts. I only caught it because I was thinking of how that creep Jessica is so hard to read."

"I'm not hard to read," Jessica said. "You're just a bad reader. And I am not a creep. I'm just stronger than you and you're jealous. There are three of them, Ms. Ryerson. They are about to enter the front lobby. Do you want me to send for Elaine?"

Ms. Ryerson nodded, slowly clenching her good fist over and over. Then she shook her head. "No, I'll take care of it. Jessica, I am putting you in charge until I get back. David, you're new, but trust me on this. Follow her lead. I want the five of you to meet up with the others on the roof. A helicopter will be waiting by the time you get there. You've all got to get out of the country ASAP."

Amy looked at the ground for a moment, glanced at Jessica, who only shook her head, and then bit her lip. Then she said: "It is them, isn't it, Ms. Ryerson?"

Ms. Ryerson blinked and looked away. "Do as I say. If you're lucky, you will never find out. Now go." With that, Ms. Ryerson ran off faster than humanly possible, little more than color in motion.

"How...? What...?" David was out of his chair now.

"You're such a newbie." Jessica rolled her eyes and walked toward from the main bank of elevators. "Do you think Wisdom would hire someone normal to teach us? Come on, we'll take the private elevator."

David started after her. "Shouldn't we wait for one of the guards? You know, the guys with guns and training? It could be dangerous."

"Don't be stupid," Jessica answered. "Of course it will be dangerous. But so are we."

David looked over at Bethany, who was still looking out the windows.

"See," Bethany said. "I told you she's creepy. Come on, we should follow them. This could be bad. Poor guy, you have no idea what you've got yourself into, do you? I wish I could tell you, but somehow I don't think you're ready for the truth."

"So I hear. Can you tell me why the hell everyone's

acting like the Russians are coming?"

Bethany laughed and put her arm around David's waist as they followed the others out of the classroom and through the halls. "You are far too young for that reference. Hell, I'm too young for it. Well, not really, but I feel too young for it. The reason we are leaving is that a group of...well let's just call them a group for now. They are coming and they want to kill us. No, I can't tell you why. Of course I know why. I'm just not allowed to tell you. Not yet. Mr. Wisdom has some enemies, very bad men who do very bad things."

"You know, the whole answering questions before I ask them is also very disturbing. Can you stop that? Are these the same ones that got to Madeline?"

The color drained from Bethany's face. She shook her head, clearly upset. "What do you know about that? Never mind, I'm still not telling you anything. But yes, I do think so. Maybe not the same ones, exactly, but the same group. Listen, we don't have much time and I don't even know what you are capable of. Do you know?"

Ahead, he saw Jessica point her finger at the two Chinese men that had almost run into him earlier. While he watched, both men nodded their heads and took guns out from inside their jackets.

"Yes. I know what I can do."

"Good. Because if we don't get to that helicopter on the roof you may have to do some of whatever it is you do. Look, don't give me that face. See guns? People running? This is not a 'let's talk about it' situation. This is not an 'Orange Alert.' This is a 'kill or be killed' type of situation."

They caught up with Jessica and the others just as the door to the elevator opened. Once inside, Todd pressed his hands against the metal doors and they started to rise very quickly.

"Todd, can you make this go any faster? They're in the building now." Jessica pulled on her lower lip with her fingers. She looked like an old woman worried about her taxes.

"If I make it go any faster the cables could snap and we'd fall right into their laps. Now let me concentrate."

Although he did not seem to be pushing very hard, there was a lot of sweat pouring off his forehead. David could not begin to fathom exactly what Todd was doing.

"What happens if they find us?" David asked. "They just kill us and leave? Won't they try to kill Wisdom and the others first?"

Jessica shook her head. "You don't go after Wisdom. Even these morons know that. I can smell it in their brains. They will come right for us and the other Anomalies, but they will eliminate anyone that gets in their way."

"Except Wisdom." Todd was starting to show signs of weariness. His eyes twitched and sweat poured freely from his damp hair.

"Oh." Jessica let the sound drop from her mouth. It was soft, barely audible but the word filled the elevator like a large, heavy object.

"I can feel it too," Amy said. "They have started to kill people."

"Most of them don't even know anything about us. Todd, please try to make this go a little faster. It's not that I'm scared or anything but I...I just don't want..."

The elevator stopped abruptly and everyone let out a short yelp.

David wiped his own forehead. Until that moment he had not realized he was sweating. Part of him wondered if this was some sort of bizarre test. The only thing that convinced him it was all completely real was the messages his brain kept sending him. While he could not decode them all, the general meaning was clear. Somewhere nearby, people were dying and people were screaming.

The elevator door opened.

***

Ezekiel Scratch was a security guard. He had no particular love for the work and he certainly felt little or no honor in the profession. Still, he did not think about quitting daily as so many people do at their jobs. People checked in with him when they entered the building at 333 Bay St. It was a big building, lots of visitors, and most of them really had no clue how to make their way around. It was his job to point them in the right direction. As security jobs go it was one of the best. He did not have to wander around some warehouse with a flashlight pretending to watch for thieves and vandals as he tried to stay awake. He did not work with money or anything valuable, so the risk of robbery was barely calculable. Here he was able to interact with people, see the light of day and be home each night to Dianna and the kids.

Downtown Toronto is also one of the most peaceful cities of its size in the world. It does not attract the same type of crazies as New York or Los Angeles, and its murder rate is next to non-existent compared to places like Chicago and Detroit. In the five years Ezekiel had worked on Bay Street the most violence he had seen was a freshly-fired accountant point his finger at his former boss and threaten to break his skull for letting him go. The guy never followed up on the threat. Violence outside the hockey rink just did not come natural to Canadians.

Which is why it took him a long time to realize the gunshots and the screams around him were real.

Then the elevator gave a sharp 'Ding!' A group of muscular men and women in dark suits rushed off the elevator touting large rifles and handguns. For a moment, Ezekiel wondered if they were just filming some movie here again. The absence of cameras and the very real smell of blood made it hard to believe the comfortable lie.

Ezekiel rose from his hiding spot and started to follow after the people with guns. That is what security guards do, he thought. Then a woman with a blond crop-cut and a lot of firepower told him to stay back. She pointed out a coffee stand where a few people who worked in the building were hiding.

"Protect them," the blond woman said.

He crouched down and did just that. For five minutes there was nothing but screaming and gunshots. Then a relative silence.

"What are they doing now?"

Ezekiel checked his gun again, to make sure the safety was off. It was the third time he had checked since the shooting started. As before, it was ready to fire. He had never shot a gun at another person, although he was not sure the things he saw qualified as people.

"Zeek, I said what the hell are they doing? Can you see?"

Ezekiel looked at the people huddled in the corner with him. Then he looked back down the hallway that led to the lobby. He saw the three 'things' causing all the damage. Bodies and bullet shells littered the floor. He watched as one of the three 'things' (he could not bring himself to use the word monster) lifted the body of a young man up by the legs and tossed it two hundred feet down the hall. Another picked up a white-haired Chinese woman, bit into her neck and started to chew.

"Don't ask." Ezekiel swallowed hard. He was proud of himself for not fainting. "Besides, I can't see much. It's starting to get smoky." He said this to the woman who owned the coffee stand. He had bought coffee from her every morning since he had started the job. He had no idea what her name was, and no clue as to how she knew his. In the moment, he forgot he wore a nametag. "I think they've started a fire."

"A fire!" She stood up and Ezekiel grabbed her arm to pull her back down.

"It doesn't look big. For Christ sakes you can't go out there. You didn't see what they are.

The woman took a strong grip on his hand, tore it from her arm and got back up. "Don't you be grabbing me! I am not your property and you are definitely not my knight in shining armor. Shouldn't you be out there stopping this?

You're a security guard, aren't you? Or are the uniform and flimsy badge just for show? And of course I've seen what they are. Just a bunch of guys in suits. They came off the elevator. You were there when they did."

Ezekiel shook his head. "That wasn't them. There are only three of them. They came in the front door and they…"

"There's only three?" She grabbed her purse and started to walk away. "We outnumber them even here. You can do what you like but I'm not staying here."

An African-Canadian man behind her, still gripping his cappuccino, spoke up.

"Melinda, for Christ's sake, get down!"

"I am not getting down," the woman said. "I'm getting out. There's got to be a fire door around here. We can…."

She was cut off by another round of gunshots. The woman flattened herself against the floor several feet away from any sign of protection. Ezekiel, the black man and the two women still behind the coffee stand shrieked. Ezekiel nearly dropped his gun. He was sweating through his uniform now and he could barely keep his stands steady. But the coffee-stand lady was right. He did have a job to do. He took several sharp breaths and then got out from behind the coffee stand to protect the stranger.

He pointed his gun at the spot where the hallway met the foyer. He could not see much except shadows and smoke, but he could hear the chaos. His teeth felt fragile as he clenched his jaw. Sweat dripped into his eye. He did not dare take the time to wipe it away. Something could show up in that moment. If it did, he wanted both of his hands on the trigger.

The gunshots were coming pretty steadily now. In fact, they seemed to be getting louder. That could only mean the fight was coming into the elevator area.

The coffee-stand lady lay face down on the ground, holding her purse up to guard her forehead.

"Miss, get up." Ezekiel knelt down beside her, still pointing the gun as stiffly as he could. "We've got to…."

He stopped.

Shapes came out of the smoke, walking backwards. They moved very slowly, gracefully, the shooting and the screaming little more than an annoyance. When they were free of the smoke, one of them turned around and looked directly at Ezekiel.

Ezekiel stared back.

He felt as if the gun was going to drop out of his hand at any moment. The only thing that kept it there was the knowledge that the safety was not on and he had no way of knowing if or where the bullet would go.

"Mother of god." He wanted to look away but found that he could not move. A deer in headlights. He was frozen, watching the shadows move through the smoke into solid objects. Then the evil thing turned away from him, faced the nearest elevator and ripped the metal doors open with its hands. Steel tore like paper. Ezekiel looked down at his gun. Sweat ran onto his lips now. What kind of person could turn their back on a gun? But then again, what kind of person....

"...has wings?"

The other two winged creatures turned to look at him now, their eyes empty holes of red-trimmed white light. All three appeared to be male but their facial features slipped when he focused on them. One moment they were blond Caucasians, the next their skin was covered in green scales. One snapped his fingers and the area connecting the foyer with the elevator area suddenly disappeared. A wall of darkness appeared where once there was only smoke. It seemed especially dark against the luminescent white of their wings. The second the darkness settled in place, Ezekiel could no longer hear the gunshots and screaming from the other room.

The first winged man now had all the metal torn away from the elevator door. There was no sign of the actual carriage but that did not stop them from stepping inside. One by one they jumped into the elevator shaft. And flew up.

Ezekiel flipped the safety on his gun, placed it quietly beside the coffee-stand woman and ran toward the back doors.

***

"Damn!" Elaine pounded the butt of her shotgun against the wall of swirling blackness for a third time. It was getting hard to breathe with all the smoke in the air. Most of the civilians ran out into the streets as soon as they caught a good look at the Edimmu. The rest were currently being escorted out by her security team. She turned on the two-way radio installed in the collar of her trench coat and called Wisdom.

"Yes?" His voice sounded tinny and even more inhuman than normal.

"They're inside. They've put up some sort of wall. We can't follow. Are the others away?"

"Should be," Wisdom's voice came back. "Don't worry about the Edimmu. I will take care of them. Get the others and leave the building. I can't guarantee it will still be standing when this fight is over."

"Affirmative."

She turned off the radio and motioned for the rest of her security team to get out of the building. Elaine had served Wisdom for over ten years. In all that time, she had never actually seen him in action. Each time they had encountered an Edimmu or Council member, the bad guys had always made a hasty retreat. There was something in Wisdom even the inhuman feared.

She prayed, for all their sakes, Wisdom lived up to his reputation.

***

David was the first to walk out onto the roof. Three helicopters were there, but each of their blades had been shattered like glass. Black smoke poured out of their interiors like liquid sewage overflowing from a toilet. Near the edge of the building, a pocket of strangers stared at the metallic corpses. He recognized some of them from the common room yesterday. Perhaps these were the rest. He did not, however, see Garnet.

"What should we do now, Jessica?" Amy asked.

"How the hell should I know?"

"Ms. Ryerson did put you in charge. Any clue?" Todd took a step toward the helicopter.

Jessica stomped her foot and her face became a mixture of wrinkles and tense expressions.

"They're coming up the elevator shaft." Bethany stared into the heart of the building. "They know we're here. We can't stay. We have to get down."

Jessica stared at the helicopters and the other Anomalies. "Todd, can you stop the elevators from working?"

"They're not taking the elevators," Bethany said. "They're flying up the elevator shafts."

"What do you mean, flying?" David asked.

"She means they're flying," Todd said. "Keep up. They're in the main elevator shafts, right? Good. They don't connect with the roof. We're safe for now."

"Safe isn't exactly the word I would use."

The five of them spun around as soon as they heard the new voice. A short woman in a white jacket with matching pants walked out of from the black smoke. The smoke did not seem to touch her. If anything, it moved out of her way.

David felt fire spring to his fingertips. His head buzzed so loudly he could almost see the noise. Beside him, Jessica suddenly seemed a few inches taller and her hair blew backwards in a wind that had not been there a moment ago.

"Relax, children." The woman kept walking toward them. "It's not me you need to fear. I'm a friend. Promise."

"If you're a friend, why did you blow up our helicopters?" Amy hid behind Jessica but spoke with confidence.

"Not what you would call a bright girl, are you?" The

woman was only a few feet before them now. "I didn't. That was our dear friends below. The thing you have to ask yourselves is why creatures who can fly, who flew up here to destroy the helicopters before going all Matrix-like on the lobby, didn't just fly up to the 13th floor in the first place."

"Good question. Why?" Bethany chewed on her nails and studied the woman with surprising calm.

"Because they want to make a statement." David walked past Jessica to stand in front of the woman in white. "Is that it? They want to destroy the building one floor at a time as a show of strength or something?"

"Close," the woman in white said. "But not as close as I expected. Maybe Wisdom is expecting too much of you lot. Actually, shouldn't there be two more of you? Where are Jared and Garnet?"

It was in that moment they realized Jared was no longer amongst them.

"Damn it!" Jessica pushed her way past David and stood immediately in front of the woman. "Where did he go? Did anyone see him in the elevator? And who are you? Did Mr. Wisdom send you here?"

The woman laughed. "Of course Wisdom sent me. Call me Echo. Most people do. Wisdom and I go way back. But we really do not have time for this right now. You're not safe here and Wisdom is not going to be able to protect you."

"And you can?" David asked.

The woman looked down into the building. "Doubtful. Not if we stay here. Hence the need for speedy retreat."

"What about Wisdom? Is he going to be okay?"

The woman looked at David closely. "Wisdom can take care of himself, but not if he has to watch out for you guys as well. I am supposed to take the 48 of you somewhere the Edimmu won't be looking. We can all hide out for a few days, throw these losers off our trail and then my babysitting chores are over. It's just a shame the other two aren't here."

David looked behind Echo. "And how are you going to get out us out of here? Do you have a spare helicopter handy?"

Echo shook her head. "That's a little too primitive for me. Wisdom may like all this blending-in crap but I prefer a much more direct approach." She pressed her left arm out and flexed her wrist. Ten feet away the air sliced open and a multi-colored oval appeared out of the air. It was at least nine feet tall and three feet wide. "Do close your mouths, children. Although I'm sure Wisdom has not been completely forthcoming about the true nature of things, you all realize there are people out there able to do things other people can't. This is one of the things I can do. Now go on, step through there. It will take you to the safe house before you can say 'Beam me up, Scotty.'"

***

Wisdom felt a hole open in the space-time fabric nearby. He took a deep breath and smiled.

"Echo. Right on time."

He stood in front of the elevator shafts on the top floor and took off his jacket and tie. He was nervous the first time he lived these events. Just a little. You never really know when you step into a fight if you will win or not. Even when you are stronger and faster than your opponent, there is always the element of chance. This time there was no trepidation. He knew he would win because he had already done it.

The elevator door opened, slowly at first as fingers fought steel, then, with a sudden final violence, the shaft was completely visible. Wisdom smirked and spread his arms, palms out and parallel at waist level. Then he called forth the power of Hellfire and Brimstone.

***

"Can you believe this crap?" Sammy Laymon took a bite of his Polish sausage and spoke to his sister who was putting sauerkraut on her own. "First she's all about 'You don't show me enough affection' and 'I want more of a commitment,' then she starts with this whole handcuff-bondage and 'wanting to be with a woman' type stuff. She's just so confusing. I'm not sure if I want to institutionalize her or marry her."

"I told you she was a psycho." Catherine gave the hot dog vendor a $20 and waited for the change. "Can you see what's happening over there?"

Sammy shook his head. "They've got the whole thing blocked off. I haven't seen this many police since the Pope came for that Catholic youth thing a few years back."

"You're comparing explosions and tragedy to the Catholics? When was the last time you were in church? Do you want to head over to see if we can see anything?"

"If we can get through the crowds. Do you even know where the whatever-it-is is at?"

She shook her head. Traffic was stopped all around them. The roads had been closed off and pockets of people, like stones in a stream, pointed fingers all the way up to Yonge St. Sammy saw smoke fill the air, heard the roar of fire and police sirens, but he could not see what everyone was pointing at.

At first.

Then they saw black smoke pouring out of a window at the top of a nearby building.

"Must be quite the fire," Catherine said as she saw it, too. "Take my advice, dump her. Do you really want someone like that raising your children?"

"Well…"

He never finished the sentence.

At that moment the top of the building exploded. Red and orange light mixed with bright yellow flames, shattering the windows. It started to rain glass and burning shrapnel down on the crowds.

Then the screaming started.

And the running.

***

Wisdom walked through the flames as the ceiling fell around him. He stepped on the skull of the first Edimmu he had killed. It crumpled beneath his foot.

As soon as the Hellfire started burning their flesh, the three monsters dropped their human disguises and took on their natural reptilian form. They stood over eight feet tall, grey-green lizards in man-made suits. Their wings, oily black like wet vultures, twitched and spasmed as the fire spread. Wisdom reached into the flames and turned flicking fire into a solid steel spear. He used it to pin the second Edimmu to the wall. It still screamed that inhuman wail unique to these creatures long after the others fell silent.

The last of the three crawled away from him, five-fingered talons pulling it desperately over rubble and ash. In one hand it held a portion of a wing Wisdom had torn off its back. The rest of it lay somewhere in the flames.

"Tsk, tsk, not too far, lizard." Wisdom bent down, grabbed the thing that had once looked very much like a man by the head and lifted it off the ground. "First I'm going to give you a message to deliver to Propates and his arrogant cult. Then I am going to throw you out the window. It should be a new experience for you, flying without your bloody wings. Then you will hit the ground and be in a great deal of pain. Fortunately for me, it won't kill you. It is only twenty stories and you're a whole lot less human than I am. Then you will run back to your master as fast as you can. Understand?"

The creature tried to nod its head but it could barely move. Most of its scales had melted off the flesh.

"Good. The message is this. Tell him I know what he has planned. Tell him I know he's in bed with my father. Then tell them I will accept the loss of this building because I am a patient man. But if he comes at me again I will forget how patient I am. Do you think you can remember that?"

The Edimmu tried to nod again.

"Good." Wisdom kept his grip on the creature's head and dragged it through gaps in the flame to the space where a wall of glass had once stood. The Edimmu tried to struggle, kicking its legs and flapping the joints where wings had once attached to body. It refused to let go of the portion of its wing it held in hand. Wisdom did not wait until he was at the edge. When he was five feet away, he bent down and, with his other hand, grabbed the creature by the groin, raised it over his head and threw the Edimmu. Then he walked to the lip of the building to watch it fall. After the Edimmu bounced off a fire truck and hit the ground, Wisdom crossed his arms and waited. A group of firefighters and police officers rushed to form a semi-circle around the twisted body. Only when it got up and ran – causing police and firefighters to run away as well – did Wisdom back away from the window.

As he teleported away, he said, "Let's see how it goes this time."

***

"I have to go to the bathroom."

Sammy looked over at his sister and shook his head. "You've got to be kidding. Can't it wait?"

Catherine glared at him. "If it could wait, I wouldn't have brought it up. Let's head to that falafel joint over there." Without waiting for a response, she started the slow process of pushing through the crowds.

Downtown Toronto was thick with crowds of onlookers, all gaggling at the destruction of the building on Bay Street. The air filled with a strange oily smoke that made it hard to breathe, but people flooded the streets. Reporters and police were everywhere. After two minutes of it, his sister Catherine was ready to go home. Ten minutes later they were still pushing their way through the crowds trying to get back to the subway.

They stepped through the door and found the restaurant empty. The guy behind the counter smiled, a perfunctory action, and then started the questioning. "What happened out there? Did you see it?"

Catherine pushed Sammy forward, forcing him to answer the question while she headed to the back of the restaurant to use the bathroom. "Yeah, we saw it," Sammy answered. "Whole building blew up. Fire everywhere. From what I heard, they're wondering if the whole building is going to come down."

"Like our own 9/11," the counter attendant said, slowly nodding his head.

Sammy shook his head and winced. "Not even close. It's probably just a gas leak." He looked toward the back of the restaurant and willed his sister to pee faster.

"So what will you guys have?" The guy behind the counter washed his hands as he spoke.

Sammy looked over the menu. "How about two beef shawarma plates? I might as well sit in here while the crowd disperses." The counter guy nodded and started to slice the meat for the orders as Sammy went to sit at the nearest booth. He focused on the crowds outside, most of them still pointing up at the darkened sky. He was so caught up in crowd watching that he forgot about his sister until the counter guy brought the food over to the table. Sammy smiled up at him, said thanks and then turned to the back of the restaurant again.

"Where the hell is she?"

He stood up and walked toward the bathrooms. A chill went down his spine. In that instant he knew without a doubt that something had gone inexplicably and horribly wrong. Each step he took made his body feel heavier, as if time was slowing down and gravity increasing. Invisible hands seemed to push him back, telling him to turn around and run. But he could not leave his sister.

"Catherine?"

He knocked on the door to the women's washroom.

No response.

"Cathy?"

He put his ear to the door and listened. At first he heard nothing. Then, softly, he heard a whimper. And heavy breathing. Images of rapists and mass murders flew quickly through his head. He slammed his shoulder into the door. It caved so easily that it took him a second to recover. When his eyes caught up with his brain, he started to scream.

It happened so fast the scream never left his throat.

He saw his sister, hair tousled, talking to a black hole that swirled in the mirror over the sink. She turned toward him. From the look in her eyes, he knew she was no longer herself. When he tried to scream, something shot out of the black hole in the mirror and lodged itself in his body. It all happened so fast, he never knew what happened.

From inside the body of Catherine Laymon, a voice like static and the hum of electricity spoke.

"Well, that was convenient."

In response, a voice came from inside Sammy's body. It was similar in cadence but with a quirky yet masculine quality to it. "Dear poppet, nothing is convenient for us nowadays. I tell you, it is destiny."

"Humph. Well 'destiny' could have given me a prettier host. How can I possibly have any fun with this thing?"

"We're not here for 'fun,' Carla," the thing inside Sammy said. "No fun until after this whole thing is over, if you ask me. At least now we can move around in the world."

"Fine," Carla answered. "But, nothing's worth doing unless it's fun, if you ask me. I suppose we should just move quickly and track down that Edimmu before it reaches Propates. We have to make sure it delivers the right message and not the one Wisdom told him to deliver."

"Absolutely. Do you think we have time to get a bite to eat?" Sanchez looked down the hallway, his eyes searching for the guy who had been working the counter. He saw nothing.

"Eat later. If I can't have fun, you definitely can't eat. Come on. Call him."

Sanchez manipulated Sammy's body and completed a complicated series of motions while chanting in an ancient language. More shadows flew out of the black hole in the mirror and coalesced into a pool of night between the two possessed beings. The pool shimmered and twirled and the restaurant filled with the sounds of thunder. Then the pool of darkness disappeared in a flash and, in its place, stood a wingless Edimmu. It was the same one Wisdom had thrown to the ground.

"Masters," the Edimmu said. It knelt on one knee, the action obviously putting it off balance without the extra weight of its wings. It did not look them in the eyes. Instead, it trembled in place.

"Tell me what happened," Carla said. "Don't forget anything, either. Tell it all."

The Edimmu bowed its head. A quiver ran through its body.

"Yes, master. I will tell you."

Chapter Eleven

August 3rd

David stepped through the portal and found himself in a very different place. If Toronto had felt like a different country to him, this was another planet. As people streamed out behind him, he looked around at what he first assumed to be an enormous, natural cavern. Then his eyes adjusted to the dim light.

"Whoa," he said. The 46 Anomalies gathered in a circular foyer the size of a basketball stadium. Fist-sized crystal spheres placed on pillars emitted a soft, steady light. What he first assumed were stalagmites and stalactites were actually thick granite columns. They rose from a tiled floor to a smooth ceiling fifty feet above his head. Numerous passages branched out on either side, many blocked by twelve-foot-diameter stone wheels, their edges cracked with age. A spiral staircase carved from stone rose to a second floor.

"Look at that," Todd said. He pointed at one of the walls covered in an immense mosaic of a peacock crafted from blue, green and black tiles.

"That's bloody creepy," Bethany said as she wrapped her arms around herself. "Gives me the chills."

"What is this place?" David felt a dry breeze blow along the back of his neck. "How far underground are we? The air actually smells fresh."

"This is Turkey," Echo said as she brushed dirt off her suit. "This is what I get for wearing white. Well, actually Kurdistan, but Turkish officials don't like to acknowledge that. We're currently about 500 feet below the surface."

"Did you build this place?" Todd asked.

"Hardly," Echo turned to the portal and closed it with the flick of her wrist. "These caves were built around 9500 B.C. There are hundreds of these underground cities in this part of the world. Best thing about this one is that you can't get to it from the surface. The old entrances are still caved in. Odds are this place won't be discovered for at least another hundred years. Only way in or out is the way we took."

"How many others can make those things?" Jessica asked. "Those circles of light."

Echo raised her hands and shrugged. "A few. You should be less interested in the portals and more in Wisdom's little vendetta."

"What vendetta?" Jessica cocked her head to one side and grabbed Amy's hand. "Wisdom never said anything about a vendetta."

"Right. Because Wisdom is always so good about explaining himself. We'll be here for a few days until Wisdom comes." Echo walked away from them and headed up the spiral staircase.

Jessica stormed after her. "How are we supposed to stay here for a few hours, let alone a few days? It is just a dirty cave. There's nowhere to sit and there's…. whoa."

Jessica stopped talking when she reached the top of the stairs. David pushed his way through the crowd to where she stood. Before he reached the top, he saw what made her speechless.

The second level was furnished like the loft apartment of a Hollywood celebrity. Silk curtains hung from the wall, giving the illusion of windows. Fifteen red plush sofas and chairs stood atop several hundred square feet of thick gold-colored carpet. Ornate marble statues and gold-trimmed light fixtures were everywhere he looked. Crystal vases filled with scented, artificial flowers helped hide the sensation of being submerged in earth. The whole thing was far too gaudy for David's liking but, in this setting, it was nothing short of magical.

Echo smiled. "It's amazing the things you can afford when you don't have to pay for them."

"You stole these things?" Bethany asked.

Echo shrugged. "Listen up, everyone. Watch where I'm pointing. Down that hallway you'll find the library on the right and the media center on the left. I have a few large televisions so you should not have to fight about what you watch. There's obviously no cable or satellite but there is an extensive library of movies and video games. If you follow the other hallway over here you'll find the apartments. There are fifty-three living quarters on this level. On the lower level is the gym, the pool and the greenhouses. Feel free to visit them. Your rooms have already been assigned. Look for your name on the door and make yourself at home. I did not have time to arrange for much clothing but make do for now. The room at the very end of the hallway is mine. Steer clear of that one, please. Now, if you'll excuse me, I have to send a message to Wisdom. He'll want to know we made it here safely, and that Garnet and Jared didn't make the jump."

With that, Echo smiled and walked away, heading toward a second set of stairs leading to a level above them.

"Wait. Aren't you going to tell us what's going on?" David suddenly realized that everyone was looking at him. He wished he had the ability to turn invisible. "I mean, uh, what were those things? Why were they after us and why are you helping us?"

Echo turned around and walked away. Over her shoulder she said: "Maybe we'll talk after supper. Let's meet back here in four hours. I'll have the chef prepare a meal for us."

Todd and Bethany exchanged a look. "Chef? She has servants down here?"

Most of the Anomalies went to look for their rooms immediately. For several minutes, David and his four classmates kept to the living room area. Todd rummaged through a stack of newspapers from various parts of the world that had been left on a large oak desk. Jessica and Amy sat on one of the couches, engaged in a quiet conversation. Bethany leaned back in one of the chairs, eyes closed. The expression on her face was far from peaceful.

"Am I the only one with a serious case of not liking this?" David asked as he sat down on a loveseat near Jessica and Amy.

No one responded.

"What exactly do you guys know about Wisdom? To start with, how did you all meet him?"

"Why should we tell you?" Jessica asked. She pulled her legs up on the couch, crossed them and leaned back against the cushions.

"Try not to be such a worthless prat, Jessica," Bethany said. "It's unbecoming. And you can stop looking at me like that. Amelia Ryerson may have put you in charge of our little escape, but that was only because you've got a lot of power in that frail little body of yours. Don't go letting yourself believe you're some sort of leader. I can still take you down a peg or two."

Jessica raised her lips in a smirk. "Any time you think you're ready, old woman."

A ball of crunched up newspaper sailed through the air and hit Jessica in the side of the head.

"Knock it off, you two," Todd said. He walked over to sit on the coffee table in front of David. "Wisdom found me in Alaska. My parents work for an oil company up there. At least they did until I accidentally blew up an oil container at the plant. I was dropping by so I could walk home with Dad after school. The school was pretty close to the plant and all. My dad and me, we were pretty close. Kind of like best friends."

"Why don't you be a little more melodramatic, Todd," Jessica said.

Amy put a hand on Jessica's knee. "Don't be mean. Say you're sorry."

"Sorry." Jessica turned red in the face and clenched her lips.

David looked over at the two girls and shook his head. There were some strange power dynamics in that relationship.

"Go on, Todd." Bethany came over and sat beside David on the loveseat.

Todd nodded and looked down at his fingers. "Well one day – it was a Tuesday, I think – I was walking by this truck they were filling with petrol and I noticed the driver. His name was Emilio Lee. He was this neighborhood bully a few years older than me. Got a job at the plant right after school. He used to beat me after school. Nothing sinister, really, just the typical 'give me your lunch money' crap. My dad told me to take it if I couldn't stand up to him. You see, I was never much of a fighter. Didn't have the guts for it. But what I did have was a good imagination. That day as I walked by the truck, I saw his face and I thought – no I wished – dozens of little demons would crawl out of the ground and set him on fire. I imagined him burning in hell."

David started to nod. It all seemed disturbingly familiar.

Todd continued. "Well, the next thing I know, the truck just explodes. Fifteen people, including yours truly, were sent to the hospital for burns. Two, including Emilio, died. I was far enough away that I didn't get burned too badly. I was out in a few days. By that time, Mom and Dad had been laid off. The company had to repair the damage. It ..." Todd let out a deep breath and stood up. He stretched his arms behind his back and started pacing in a circle. "It wasn't just the truck. A few pipelines were compromised, too. Millions in damage, from what the TV said.

"When I got out of the hospital, there was a letter from Mr. Wisdom. He offered me a job in Toronto. He did not go into much detail at that time, but I was looking for an escape."

"How did Wisdom find you?" David asked. "Did you, like, send a resume or something?"

Todd stared at David. The way he blinked his eyes showed contempt very clearly. "No, I didn't send a resume. He found me the same way he found you, the same way he found everyone. He felt me using my EFHB."

"EFHB?"

"Extraordinary Functions of the Human Body," Bethany said. "We've already covered this, so try to keep up, dear. If we ever get back to taking classes, you'll learn more about them."

"What do you mean 'if'?" Jessica uncrossed her legs and leaned forward.

"Well," Bethany said, her eyes narrowing and her lips twitching. She looked uncertain. "I just thought, I don't know, maybe things are going to change after this. Nothing like this has ever happened. People died. Maybe Wisdom won't want to continue."

"Wisdom will need us more than ever now," Jessica said. "Things progressed faster than expected, that's all."

David felt his head buzzing. "Do you mean you guys know what's going on here?"

Bethany opened her mouth to speak but Jessica held up her hand. "Don't say anything. He's not ready."

"Damn it!" David said. "Teleporting around the world to escape an exploding building and flying guys that want to kill me makes me ready. Now tell me what the hell is going on!"

Silence.

"We don't know everything," Amy said.

"Don't you dare say another word, Amy!" Jessica whirled to face Amy so quickly David thought she was going to hit the other girl.

"Jessica, he's right," Todd said. "We should tell him what little we know."

The four of them looked at each other for some time. Their eyes darted to each other, holding a silent vote. When the tension reached a point where David felt it painful to breathe, Jessica lowered her head and said: "Whatever. Tell him."

Amy put a comforting hand on Jessica's shoulder. The other girl pushed it away.

"I'll tell you a little story," Bethany said. "I'll start with how Wisdom found me. I was living in England – Liverpool, actually. Life was brilliant. Then, I made the dim-witted blunder of going with my friend Tanya to this psychic fair.

"Any who, I got this reading from this funny-looking woman all dressed in black. Her hair was all wild-like. She looked like a bad actress trying to pretend she was a psychic. There was even a crystal ball standing on the middle of the table.

"So I sat down in this metal chair, ungodly uncomfortable. She told me her name – can't remember it now for the life of me – and pulled out a deck of tarot cards. She told me to shuffle them while focusing on a question. So I did. I felt this strange sort of buzzing in my head like I was getting a headache. My body went numb and my head started to sway. The woman reached over and took hold of my hands. 'That's good enough,' she says. Turns out I'd been shuffling them for a couple of minutes.

"She laid out the cards and said "I see a tall, dark man in your future'. I burst out laughing. I mean, it was such a campy thing to say. Like something out of an old Roger Corman movie or something. The psychic lady – I think her name was Sue or Mary-Sue, something like that – she just smiled like she was used to that sort of reaction. Then, quick as I can snap, she wasn't smiling anymore. Her head flew back and I could feel this wind. It blew back her hair but didn't touch the cards at all. Other people felt it, though. I could tell because all around me the noise just dropped off. It was actually quiet, except for the beating of my heart in my head and the words of Suzette. That was her name. Suzette.

"'The Dark Man will lead you into a battle against powerful demons,' she said. 'Many people will die. You may be one of them.' So by this point I'm kind of getting freaked out. I'm not sure I want to stay and hear the rest of it. But I can't seem to move my muscles to get up. The wind grew stronger and so did the buzzing in my head but I could still hear her perfectly. 'But you are not like other people,' she says. 'You have more in common with the demons.'

"Then the crystal ball shattered. Well, as soon as she stopped screaming, she pushed the money back in my hand and told me to get out. A few days later I got a letter from Wisdom.

"You see, Wisdom can sense things. Amy was right. We don't know everything. One thing we don't know is exactly what he is. I mean, it is possible he's just somebody like us, someone who has EFHBs. But sometimes I feel he is something else. I can't put my finger on it but I don't think he's really human."

"He's partly human," Amy said. "But he's partly something else, too."

David whistled. "Do you think he's related to those winged things?"

Bethany bit her fingernails for a moment then shook her head. "No. I don't think so. I can still remember how those things felt in my head, kind of wet and slippery, like snakes in black water. Wisdom is something else. There is something very hard and very fiery about him. What I do know is what we've been taught in class.

"Ms. Ryerson taught us that humans aren't the only people on earth. Now I am not talking about UFOs or people from Mars. There are civilizations on Earth that have been here for thousands of years that do their best to keep away from mankind. They've gotten very good at it over the years. Partly they hide out of fear. There are not as many of them as there are of us. The bigger the world gets, the harder it is for them to hide in one sense, but in another it gets a lot easier. They can't hide out in the woods and country graveyards anymore, so instead they hide in high-rises and sewer systems."

"What are you talking about?" David asked. "Vampires?"

Jessica scoffed. "Newbie."

Bethany shook her head. "Not vampires. I don't think those are real. But then again, maybe that is something else that's being hidden from us until we're ready. We were never told their names, only that they had an ancient civilization that thrived all over the planet 1200 years ago until their culture destroyed itself in an idea-war. Truth is, if Echo was telling the truth about how old these caves are, they were probably the ones that built them."

"What does that have to do with Wisdom?"

Bethany looked into David's eyes. "Ms. Ryerson said these people are getting tired of hiding in the shadows. They are making deals with a group of humans, some sort of cult that's doing experiments on humans. They are planning a war. We're being trained to stop them."

David put his hands on his head, scratching idly. "So is that what we are? The result of some cult doing experiments on humans?"

Bethany looked over to Jessica.

"Don't look at me," the little girl said. "You started it. You might as well finish it."

Bethany bit her fingernails again, speaking through her fingers. "No, we're not that. We're something else. Something evil."

David lowered his head. "Evil? As in not the good guys?"

She nodded. "As in pretty far from the good guys. I don't know anything more specific. Wisdom always said he would tell us before the big day, before the battles began. Seems he was a little late there."

David jumped off the sofa. "I'm not a monster!" He walked in the direction of the living quarters. "No matter what you say, I'm not evil!"

When he left the room, Jessica crossed her legs and smiled.

"I told you he wasn't ready for it. Newbies never are."

Todd got up from the coffee table. "Jessica, I'm not sure I'm ready for the truth. Even after everything we've seen and done in the classes, it's never easy to learn you have a little demon inside you."

Chapter Twelve

David brushed past a group of teenage girls. He was barely aware of the tears streaming down his face. Teeth clenched and red-faced, he headed down a hallway lined with living quarters and looked for his room. While the mottled walls were unevenly carved out of stone, the doors and frames were constructed of polished wood. Many of the doors were open to luxurious apartments. Thick slate-grey carpet covered the dirt floor. Electric sconces shaped like nymphs supported the illusion that they were in a hotel rather than an old cave dwelling. Anomalies, young and old, gathered in small groups along the hallway. It seemed no one wanted to be alone.

He found his assigned room halfway down the hall. He stepped inside, quickly closing the door behind him. He leaned his forehead against the cool wood until the pounding in his head stopped. Then he turned around and looked for a place to collapse.

His quarters were luxurious. There were two dark green couches in the front room. Deep umber and rust-colored pillows were thrown in a carefully constructed chaos on the furniture. Pillows filled the corners as well. Past that was a round room with a bed twice the size of a normal king-sized mattress.

"I'm not a monster." The words fell out of his lips before he realized he was still thinking about that. "Bethany has to be wrong. It's probably just genetic mutation or something." The only problem was the evidence piling up around him. He wasn't the only one who had hurt people. Todd had killed two people because he could not control what he was. Did that make him a monster?

'No,' he thought. 'But I can't pretend I'm like Todd. He killed by accident. I went out of my way to kill. Maybe not the first time, but I knew what I was doing the last two times.'

He shook his head. That was not quite right. The second time he killed someone he didn't really know what he was doing.

'But I hoped.' He lay down on the bed and closed his eyes.

***

The second time he killed with his power was not long after the prom. People were still reeling from the strange explosion that had killed Ramona and Paedrag. At first, the police suspected a car bomb. They questioned David and a few others several times but soon admitted they couldn't find any evidence of foul play.

Many people came to him in the weeks after, offering condolences. He nodded, even cried a few occasionally. Most of the time, the tears were even real. Most of the time.

Then he started to play with the buzzing in his head. He knew it was somehow connected to the explosion. He realized he had to control it or someone else was going to get hurt.

That next someone was Dunstan Joyce.

It was lunchtime.

David sat with a few friends playing cards. He heard laughter and raised voices. The whole cafeteria turned to look over at Dunstan. He stood on top of a lunch table while two Goths in black makeup with purple hair shouted at him. Dunstan and his friends were laughing.

"Must be going into all that gay stuff again," David's friend Mark said.

David rolled his eyes. Dunstan was always going around telling anyone who would stop long enough to hear that homosexuals were going to burn in hell.

"God," David said. "I just wish he would shut up. Or die or something."

Then the laughter stopped. It was replaced by a scream. Dunstan clawed at his own throat, as if trying to scratch out whatever was in there preventing him from breathing. A flurry of people rushed to him but nothing worked. The thing was, David felt a part of his mind drift across the room, tightening around Dunstan's throat. He couldn't draw that part of him back. And the scary part was he didn't really want to.

***

He slept through the night and woke the next morning with a headache. He opened his eyes and shut them quickly. Even the dim, recessed lighting around the room was too much. He rolled onto his side as the nausea took hold.

'Damn migraine.' Slowly he threw off the covers and sat up. 'No wonder, really. After all that crap yesterday, I guess my mind is going through a required meltdown.' Keeping his eyes closed to fight dizziness, he reached out for something to steady himself. His fingers touched stone and a jolt of electricity shot up his arm. He screamed and opened his eyes.

He was no longer in the bedroom. Instead, he was on a rooftop looking down on a city. It wasn't a city he recognized. Figures moved below him in a rush. Unfamiliar scents streamed around him: spiced meats and flowers, perfumes and sweat. He looked above and saw nothing but darkness and dry earth.

'I'm still underground,' he thought. 'An underground city.'

He looked back at the people milling about the streets below and realized they were not really people at all. Tall and slender, their faces and bared arms were covered with sleek, moist scales. He'd never actually seen one before, but he knew these things, these winged beings, were Edimmu. They were far different than the savages who attacked the building in Toronto.

These Edimmu were as civilized and refined as any city dweller of the modern age. Women carried babies in their arms. Children played in front of stores where merchants bartered in a sibilant chatter, a series of clicks and growls that was at once magical and threatening. Something flew above his head. He looked up and saw a trio of bare-chested Edimmu playing a game consisting of throwing a gold discus while flying backwards. They flew over the city, dodging taller buildings.

Another Edimmu wearing a plain, white tunic flew from house to house with a large cloth sack draped over his back. It appeared he was the equivalent of a paperboy or mailman. He dropped parcels off at each stop. That implied that the Edimmu were not only civilized, but literate as well. Closer to him, he saw an open window leading to an apartment. He blinked slowly as his eyes fell upon two Edimmu in the middle of lovemaking. The slow kisses and gentle thrusting motions made him blush.

Then he heard something. He realized it was the first sound he'd heard in awhile. It started as a soft 'ting,' like a small bell being rung or the chinking of crystals. Then, not only could he hear the sound, he could see it. He saw it ripple throughout the city. Translucent rings of light and shadow touched every subterranean corner. He looked back to the open window and the couple making love. Suddenly, he was gone from the rooftop. Now he was inside their apartment. He watched as they stopped what they were doing. They cocked their heads to the side, trying to find the source of the sound. The male Edimmu stood, wrapped a blanket around his waist and went to the window. His female partner said something to him, an incomprehensible series of clicks and hisses. The male shook his head and then turned sharply toward David and started moving. For a moment, David thought he was discovered. Then the male rushed past him, heading to a smaller room off the bedroom.

'A bathroom,' he whispered. It looked distressingly similar to bathrooms of the modern world, complete with shower, sink and toilet. All three devices were running now. Water flowed from everywhere. Hot water caused the air to mist and steamed over the wall-length mirrors that lined one of the walls. The male yelled now as he struggled to turn off the taps. The ringing sound grew louder. It filled David with a tingling sensation that started at the base of his spine and spread throughout his body.

"Something's coming," he said. Even as the words left his mouth, the darkness appeared. The steam on the mirror was wiped away by an unseen hand. It created a murky hole that reflected nothing of the real world. As the hole spread further, the sound grew louder. Then, things started to flow out of the darkness, impossible shapes with horns and tentacles wielding swords. The male Edimmu screamed as one of the dark shapes slashed at it. Blood shot from the Edimmu's throat, splattering the walls and floors. David squealed but the blood did not touch him. It flew through him, covering the rest of the room. He watched as more and more shapes streamed out of the mirror. Something killed the female and then flew out the window into the city.

Then David was back on the rooftop. All around him, dark figures poured out of every mirror and reflective surface in sight. They slaughtered every Edimmu they found. Flying shadows, crow-like monsters the size of large dogs filled the sky. He watched as they tore the flesh from the three Edimmu playing the discus game. Silent explosions rocked the city. Flames erupted from every quarter and the scent of blood grew thick in the air. A female Edimmu ran toward David, a small baby in her arms. She screamed for help, desperation in her eyes. He reached out for her and....

He was back in the bedroom. When he reached for the female, he had removed his hand from the wall. When he lost contact, the images disappeared instantly.

"What the hell was that?" He lay back down in bed.

As frightened as he was, he still was self-aware enough to realize the headache was gone.

***

He left his room and followed the sound of voices to a dining area. Echo and the other Anomalies sat around large glass tables eating breakfast. He was the last to arrive. Two servants, women with dark brown skin, moved around the room. One poured coffee while the other dished out scrambled eggs. Bethany had saved him a seat near the head of the table where Echo sipped wine from a crystal glass.

Jessica took a sip of the coffee before her. Her face twisted around her lips like she had just sucked on a lemon. "That's gross. Do you lose your taste buds when you get older?"

Echo smirked. "No. We just learn to appreciate different tastes. How old are you, Jessica? If memory serves me right, you would be 13, correct?"

"I'm 12." Jessica reached for the cup of coffee again, her face firmly set. "And a half."

"Of course," Echo laughed again. "That half is very important."

Amy stirred her eggs with a fork. "How old are you, Echo?"

"Amy!" Todd nearly spat out the eggs in his mouth. "You know it's not polite to ask that kind of question."

"Oh please, children," Echo said, the laugh still thick in her voice. "I'm well past worrying about my age. In fact, I've stopped counting. You do after awhile."

"You can't be older than Bethany." Jessica took another sip of coffee. Once again, her face contorted but she forced herself to keep drinking. "She's ancient."

"Hey!" Bethany said. She threw a napkin across the table at Jessica.

Echo turned to Bethany. "Behave, now. To a child's eyes you would be ancient. To me, you are just a babe. Let's just say when I was 12 there was no such thing as Christianity and the Jews still worshipped a god and a goddess. Well, I can see from the looks on all your faces you don't really believe me. Why should you?"

"What are you?" Todd leaned forward, elbows on the table.

Echo leaned back in her chair and studied Todd. "I was

human, once. That changed when I was sixteen. I paid a price. You could say I sold my soul but I don't regret the price. Not often, anyway."

David cleared his throat. "Is Wisdom like you? Did he sell his soul, too?"

"If you have questions about Wisdom, ask him yourself." Echo put down her wine. "But enough questions about me. I'm sure you have all sorts of questions about what you are."

"We know what we are," Jessica said.

"Do you?" Echo motioned for one of the servants to clear way her plate of eggs even though she'd barely touched them. "So what has Wisdom told you?"

Amy glanced at Jessica before speaking. "Ms. Ryerson and Wisdom tell us we're a little...evil."

"Evil?" Echo laughed. "Hmm. I didn't expect that. Not from Wisdom. Listen, there's one thing I've learned over the years. One person's devil is another person's god. Literally. Have you ever heard the name Azazel? If you buy one of those pretentious books on angels, he's listed as a demon. Yet the people in this area worshipped him as a god, represented by a black peacock. The only reason he's seen as evil is because of a cultural battle between the Hebrews and the Yezidi. In every war I've seen, it's important for morale to demonize your enemies. Make their gods into things of darkness and evil. It's almost as if two people on different sides of the same conflict can't possibly worship the same god.

"There is no evil. Not any absolute evil, anyway. Killing babies could be seen as evil, the slaughter of innocents. Or it could be seen as ridding the world of a threat in the making. It all depends on the spin you place on it. Depends on who writes the story and who reads it."

Echo took several slow breaths. "But I digress. What has Wisdom told you about the Council of Peacocks?"

David looked around the table. Everyone looked as confused as he felt.

"It's a pretty amazing bird, the peacock." Echo leaned back in her chair. "Have you ever heard its cry? It sounds like a person screaming in pain. It was the sacred bird of Hera. Let me tell you a little story, the myth of the peacock."

"Oh, dear god, she's going to give us a history lesson." Jessica pushed her coffee away and turned to Amy. "Can we please leave?"

"No," Amy said. "I want to hear this."

"If I may," Echo said. "Hera learned her husband, Zeus, was having an affair with a young nymph. So she hid the nymph in a cave and stationed a hundred-eyed giant as her jailer. The giant, Argus, was a hero. The stories say he slew Echidna, mother of monsters. They also say he was killed, in turn, by Hermes when Zeus decided he wanted his mistress back. But it's just a myth. See, the myths about Argus actually refer to a religious cult, a group of worshippers. They worshipped Hera and a giant, all-seeing god. The Argusites were at war with the worshippers of a water goddess – Echidna. When the war was over, the followers of Echidna were either killed or banished. Another cult rose in their place, a group of magicians who worshipped Hermes. Unfortunately for the Argusites, they weren't as lucky against the Hermetics. One religion fell to another. Symbolically, the god Hermes 'killed' Argus, just as Argus 'killed' Echidna.

"When their temples were destroyed, the Argusites were forced to flee north to underground cities like the one we're in now. The locals also worshipped a peacock god, Melek Taus. The two gods were very different but the Argusites adapted. They became the Council of Peacocks.

"During the middle ages, the Council spread all over Europe. It wasn't a popular time to be a pagan, so they kept very quiet. Then they gained a powerful ally, a very annoying man named Propates. He has access to dark powers. He's capable of things even I can't explain. Propates has led the Council for several hundred years now."

"Is everyone immortal?" David asked as he rubbed his

temples. His migraine was returning. "I mean, seriously, how many of you people are there?"

"I'm not immortal. Neither is he. We've just been alive for a very long time. All you need to know is that the Council of Peacocks sent the Edimmu after you. They're the ones Wisdom has been training you to fight."

Amy looked up from her plate. "What exactly is an Edimmu?"

"That's a long story," Echo covered her mouth as she yawned. "And I'm through with history lessons for today. Please excuse me." She stood up from the table and walked briskly out of the dining room.

Amy looked around the table. "Do any of you know what an Edimmu is?"

Everyone shook their head.

David thought back to his vision of the Edimmu city. "I think that's one of the many questions Wisdom is going to have to answer when we see him again."

Chapter Thirteen

August 4th

Josh stared out the window at London. He couldn't see any landmarks he recognized. Having never been here before, he wondered how far he was from Big Ben and London Bridge. Lights shone from vacant offices in concrete buildings all around him. They gave the city a sense of life, but it could just as easily have been New York, Toronto, Tokyo or Chicago. He'd seen so little of the world that it all looked the same.

His living quarters were comfortably ordinary. Dark-stained wood and plush green furniture filled the carpeted room. The closets were filled with presents: dozens of Armani suits, well-tailored pants, high-quality shirts, belts and ties, all pre-packaged, creating an artificial sense of home. The building was quiet now that the workday was over. It would have been peaceful if not for his constant fear that the world was going to explode.

He had arrived in London two days ago. The first day was filled with doctors. They drew blood and placed him in large magnetic chambers to take pictures of the blueprints of his body. He ran on treadmills and did three-hour-long I.Q. tests.

Yesterday, he spent two hours with a staff psychologist who made him talk about his parents, his love life, and the blood-soaked trip to the Laurentians. Then alarms went off throughout the building. People ran in all directions, faces drawn and pale. While no one gave him any significant details, Josh determined something catastrophic had happened in a building Wisdom owned in Toronto.

During the chaos, he caught his first sight of others like himself. Dozens of staff members – mostly research assistants and scientists – from Toronto were assigned rooms on the same floor as his. Amongst them was a beautiful woman with the most stunning eyes he'd ever seen. Her name was Garnet. They spoke briefly in the hallway before she disappeared.

He pulled back the covers of the bed and slipped under the sheets. Hands folded behind his head, he stared at the white ceiling. Every time he closed his eyes, he saw creatures coming out of the shadows. Edimmu. He saw flashes of himself fighting them in the woods, setting their wings on fire for what they did to Tommy. What were they? Aliens? Demons? And why were they after Tommy?

Why wasn't Wisdom giving him any answers?

There was a knock at the door.

Josh threw the covers off, walked to the door, and glanced through the peephole. Garnet stood outside wearing a green summer dress. She held hands with a young boy wearing a blue t-shirt and white shorts.

"Hi," he said as he opened the door. "It's a little late for visiting, isn't it?"

"It's 9:30."

"Oh." Josh saw in her eyes she wasn't going anywhere. He stepped aside and let her in. "Who's this?"

"His name is Jared."

Jared walked straight to the couch and sat down hard. He folded his arms, grumbled something inaudible, and stared at the floor. He reminded Josh of his cousin Adrian. There was even a vague family resemblance he wished he could ignore.

Jared looked up at Garnet. "I told you I won't like him."

"Be nice, kiddo," Garnet said to Jared. "He's had a bad few days."

"Who hasn't?" Jared's face blanched. "I can still feel those people dying in my head."

Garnet knelt down by the couch and stroked the boy's brown hair. "Me too. Lucky for me you got separated from the others and never made it to the roof. I need you to give Josh a break. Don't pull any of the crap you did with

Madeline when she first came to us, okay?"

"I miss Madeline," Jared said. "She used to play Super Mario with me. She didn't deserve what they did to her."

"No, she didn't." Garnet frowned, tears forming in her eyes. "Well, enough of this maudlin crap. We came to ask you to join us in the common room. It's far too early to sleep, and I'm sure we'll all feel a little safer if we stick together. Maybe we can even scrounge up a Playstation from somewhere. Just don't expect me to be much good, Jared."

Jared smiled and ran for the door. "More fun for me if you suck. Means I'll win."

"Deal." Garnet turned back to Josh and winked.

Josh smiled and followed them out.

***

Below the surface of Thessaloniki, in the caverns carved out by Edimmu, Paeder Ferris was being prepared for the third ceremony in the process of Eyeness. Two lower Council members in unadorned white robes anointed his naked body with fragrant ritual oil. He stood, legs spread, arms stretched out to the sides, allowing access to every surface of his flesh. The markings of previous initiations glimmered under the oil. Five intricate eyes were tattooed down the side of each leg, outlines of blue with green irises. Ten similar eyes were tattooed on his back, placed to form the kabalistic Tree of Life.

"There will be considerably more pain this time," Propates said. He watched the process from the edge of the room while Otto prepared the required chemical injections.

"I can deal with the pain." Paeder grimaced as one of the acolytes anointed his inner thighs. "That maggot destroyed my family."

The acolytes finished and withdrew to an adjoining room. Otto injected a syringe filled with a luminous green liquid into Paeder's jugular vein. He injected a second needle filled with a clear solution into his left arm.

Grabbing him by the arm, Propates led Paeder to the octagonal crystal chamber at the center of the room. It was exactly five feet in diameter and stood fifteen feet tall. Entrance was through a crystalline hatch that was raised or lowered from the outside. When closed, the hatch vacuum sealed the chamber.

"This is not physical pain we're talking about," he said. "It's a spiritual pain. All rebirths start with a death. Once you enter this chamber and the process begins, parts of your soul will be ripped apart and replaced with something else. I need you to comprehend what that means. We're not talking about alterations at the genetic level. That happens, but it's just an offshoot of the real magic. You are about to lose your mortality and ascend to a level of divinity."

Paeder took a last look at the chamber before stepping inside. "I don't need to know how it works. Just as long as it gets the job done. I can't stand by and let him get away with it."

Propates exerted his will and activated the nerve centers in Paeder's body. Paeder dropped quickly to his knees. The pain came so quickly he was unable to stop the screams.

"You are to take him alive, Paeder. If I even suspect that you're trying to kill him, I will send you to the shadows the same why I did Lucius. The boy is too important. I won't let an insignificant twit like you get in the way of our plans. Now, convince me I'm not making a mistake sending you."

Propates relaxed and Paeder, regaining control of his body, rose to his feet. Calmly, he wiped the sweat from his forehead. Every ounce of his demeanor spoke of potency and resolve.

"I will do as you command. Doesn't mean I can't make him hurt a little."

"No, you can hurt him. Just nothing permanent. Now, you said you don't need to know how this process works. Unfortunately, ignorance is a luxury you can't afford. We've learned from our mistakes. If you enter this blindly, it will kill you. Not might, will." He handed two fist-sized emerald-colored crystals to Paeder. "The first thing you'll notice is the gas. It's a mixture of Earth chemicals and gases from the

Axeinus, the Black Sea. Breathe it in deeply. Saturate your lungs. You'll also have to chant the second invocation of the Black Peacock while channeling your pain into these crystals. No matter what happens, maintain focus on the crystals. They will keep your mind intact. As the gas fills the chamber, Otto and I will start what we need to do on our end. That's when the pain will really kick in. Your mind will expand as your body disintegrates. Then it will reconstitute. It's not pleasant but you need to work through it. The last thing that will happen is a gift from our friend from away."

Propates lowered a gold necklace over Paeder's head. It was a simple design with a small lapis lazuli amulet engraved with magical sigils. "In the final stage, the necklace will be broken down and fused to your spirit. You'll feel a different pain then, unlike anything you've ever felt. In that moment you will cease to be human. You'll become, for lack of a better word, an angel of Argus."

"How long will this take?"

Propates glanced over at Otto.

"That depends on you," Otto responded. "No matter how willing you are, your body is going to fight this. If it doesn't fight very much, you'll probably be done in an hour. If it fights a lot, we could be here for up to eight hours. Based on what I know about you, you're an animal. Which means your animal nature is going to fight back. I hope you didn't have plans for dinner."

"I'm ready." Paeder sneered at Otto and tightened his grip on the emeralds.

Propates closed the door to the chamber and motioned for Otto to start the flow of gases. Filmy green vapors twirled through the air, slowly sinking around Paeder.

To his credit, he lasted an entire five minutes before the screams started.

***

Six hours later, Propates stepped into his apartments and closed the door to the world. Personal time was something of a commodity in his life. With each passing day, as the Activation approached more and more quickly, preparations and politics stole more of his time.

Even now, away from work, he was not alone. Three acolytes were assigned to his quarters: a cook, a masseuse, and a general assistant. It was humbling to admit he couldn't do everything himself but he was simply too busy trying to save the world to eat properly.

"I can't wait for this nonsense to be over," he mumbled to himself. He waved the acolytes away and bypassed the food laid on the dining room table. Brushing off their protests, he walked straight to the bathroom and locked the door. He leaned over the bathroom counter and studied his reflection in the mirror. He looked for signs of the young farmer he used to be. There was nothing left of that boy. The parts Wisdom left undamaged were destroyed by years living amongst the shadows of the Black Sea.

Something tingled at the back of his consciousness. The faucets spun open, hot water flowing freely. Steam flew up, fogging over the mirror.

"What do you want?"

From behind the shroud of steam, a voice came. "We have much to discuss, Propates." It was noticeably inhuman with a grating, chalk-like undertone.

"If you have something to discuss, there are proper channels. I don't care what you do with the rest of humanity but you will show me a proper respect if you wish to maintain our allegiance. Now, say what you will and get out of my sight."

The voice murmured something inaudible, as if it was conferring with someone else. Then, it spoke again. "We show you respect. We let you believe the lie that we never see you naked, that we don't watch you as you sleep. We allow you your comfort because it benefits us. Perhaps it is you who need to show us some proper respect. Why are you sending an agent after my child?"

"You're being ridiculous." Propates exerted his will and

the mist covering the mirror dissipated. In its absence was not a reflection of the room, but a blackness that continued on with no apparent end, broken only by faintly luminous bodies. Though he'd only heard one voice, dozens of glowing red eyes stared back at him. "He is not your child, any more than he's Richard Wilkinson's. Josh isn't a person. He's a tool. An important cog in a complicated machine that has fallen out of place. We need to put it back in place before the machine falls apart. My agent is not going to kill him. He's going to retrieve him. Now, if there's nothing else…"

The voice murmured something else. The luminous bodies shifted, huddled together, but most of the eyes remained on him. After a moment, the voice spoke again. "We are glad our need for each other is coming to an end. We have never forgiven you for stealing the Edimmu. There will come a time when you must make restitution for your betrayal."

"Your threats don't frighten me, demon, no more than they ever have. As long as you're imprisoned in the Axeinus, I have nothing to worry about. Now, our conversation is done. Do not contact me this way again."

With another exertion of will, Propates broke the connection to the Axeinus. Once again the mirror reflected on the bathroom. He closed his eyes, more exhausted than ever.

Chapter Fourteen

August 5th

Two days after the attack in Toronto, Wisdom appeared in London. No one was exactly sure of the time of his arrival. One of his London secretaries, a middle-aged woman named Shirley, found him in the morning working in his office.

"Dear God, sir," she said. "You know everyone's been looking for you."

Wisdom looked up from a folder filled with black and white photos. "The search for Wisdom continues, eh? The subtext is amusing. Be a doll and get Elaine on the phone for me, would you? She should be in Hong Kong."

Shirley nodded and left the room.

Wisdom turned back to the photos. They'd been taken by Ms. Ryerson. She was tracking men with ties to the Council. One was Otto Siegmar, a bioengineer from Germany. The other was Lucius Vitalli. He was an Italian businessman now living in New York. Lately, Lucius had fallen off Ms. Ryerson's radar, which made Wisdom nervous.

He'd been busy himself spying on a third member of the Council. Paavo Rothschild was the liaison between the Council and the Bilderberg Group. Despite what the swarms of the paranoid believed, the Bilderberg group was not involved in a diabolic plot to overthrow the world. Having been a member of the group since its inception, he knew all too well what their real purpose was.

Yesterday, Paavo and Otto had met in Munich. The first time through these events, Wisdom had learned about the meeting afterwards. This time he wanted to be there when it happened. Somehow, events had changed again. Security around the meeting was increased with extra surveillance-blocking technology installed. It appeared they knew their location was compromised.

Several minutes later, the intercom beeped.

"Yes?" Wisdom slipped the photos into his desk.

"Elaine is on line four. I thought you should know, sir. There is a Mr. Icke in reception. He says he has an appointment with you."

Wisdom groaned.

"Didn't I put a contract out on that wackjob? Oh, never mind. Just tell him I'm in the middle of something and I'll have to get back to him. Hmm, better yet, escort him to Meeting Room Six and have Sylvester and Kyle pay him a visit. Let's end that whole business once and for all."

"Yes, sir."

"Wisdom," Elaine said once Wisdom put the phone on intercom, "thank God you're alive."

"Don't tell me you've lost faith in me."

Elaine sighed. "After everything you've told me about traveling through time, I'm not sure what I believe anymore. If even the past is subject to change, absolutely nothing is absolute."

"You should be able to relax for a few days. Are the children secure? Be careful what you say on these lines. I can't guarantee they're secure."

"Of course," Elaine said. She was in Hong Kong with a group of look-a-likes. They'd been hired to make the Council believe all the Anomalies were there. Energy emitters designed to mimic the use of EFHB were activated at irregular intervals. "Everyone is secure here."

"History tells me it's vitally important no one find the Anomalies at least until next week. You'll know everything you need to by then."

"Is that when it happens?"

"Yes," he said. "That's when the Djinn shows up."

***

Josh pressed the bandage firmly against the inside of his elbow and stepped onto the elevator. After a fourth day of tests and bloodletting he'd developed a new-found loathing for doctors and needles. In the elevator with him were two Chinese men speaking Mandarin in hushed tones. Both were dressed in nearly identical dark suits. Only their ties were different.

There was no one in the lounge but the television was on. On the screen, was a thin, black woman with a thick accent. She walked down the aisle of a talk show studio audience asking the crowd if it was possible to ever really know someone. This led to a story about a woman who, after five years of marriage, found out that her husband was actually her biological father.

"Good to know trash TV isn't confined to North America." Josh turned the TV off and headed toward the cafeteria.

The lights flickered up and down the entire length of the hallway. A feeling settled over him. He looked up and down the corridor. It was empty. He clenched and unclenched his fists repeatedly, searching the fitful shadows in each doorway. Then, near the end of the corridor, something caught his eye. Movement. He took a step forward and peered closer at a half-open door. In the last few days he'd passed by it many times. A closet. He'd seen the middle-aged janitor pull cleaning supplies and a mop from there.

'Something's wrong.' The door was open, just a crack. Previously, it had always been locked. Worse, the light that pulsated above from the rows of fluorescent bulbs did not touch the darkness on the other side.

The door swung slightly more open.

In that second, rational or not, he decided it was not his imagination. Someone was watching him. He charged toward the unseen watcher, fists at the ready and jaw clenched. Then he saw movement again. A flash of gold light, like sunlight off a ring, hit him in the eyes. He slowed. He stopped, head throbbing.

The door swung open even further and a voice, at once familiar and alien, hit his ears.

"Remember," it said.

And he did.

***

Four summers ago, life in the Wilkinson house changed completely. After the death of Tommy Delonki and the shooting in Lebanon, Josh found himself jumping at shadows. He barricaded his closet door at night and consistently slept with his weapons – a knife under the pillow and a baseball bat beside the bed.

One day after school, he walked in on his mother. She sat on his bed holding the baseball bat across her lap.

"What exactly do you think is going to attack you?" She asked the question with barely concealed worry in her voice.

Josh could only shrug in response.

"The world is not a scary place, Joshua," she said. "I don't want you living in fear for the rest of your life. What happened in Lebanon was terrifying. And the way those savages killed poor Tommy, well, I can see why you're frightened. But you're home now. You're safe."

Josh blushed, his face heated and eyes watery. He couldn't tell his mother what had really happened to Tommy. He couldn't tell her about the monsters with wings or the horrible things he'd done to protect Tommy. He just shook his head and learned how to better hide his weapons.

A week later, his father was shipped off to a seminar in Greece.

Therese decided it would do Josh some good to get away from Ottawa for a while, so they flew down to Windsor to visit her brother. Eugene Froese was older than her by two years. Although brother and sister remained close, they rarely saw each other. Josh barely knew his cousin Travis. What happened in the woods that week put a wedge between them. They never spoke again.

Josh and his mother landed at Windsor airport where they were met by Gene and Travis. While brother and sister hugged, cousins stood by, bonded by feelings of discomfort.

During the car ride from the airport, Josh's mom talked and laughed with her brother while Travis hid by playing his Nintendo DS. Josh looked out the window and watched the rain fall on the gray city.

The Froeses lived on the east end of Windsor in a neighborhood of wartime homes and bungalows. They ate well that night. Gene's wife had cooked a feast. The food put Josh in a better mood. By the time they were on dessert, he found he was actually smiling for the first time in weeks.

"I have to say, Travis," Therese Wilkinson said. "It actually looks like you're turning out okay. You gave your mother more than her share of headaches when you were younger."

Travis grinned. "I have no idea what you're talking about."

Gene and his wife, Margaret, shared a quiet but genuine laugh. "Yeah, he's a perfect angel. In fact, the last time you guys were down, didn't Travis get Josh arrested?"

Josh looked up from his pie, startled for a moment. With everything else in his life, he'd completely forgotten. "That's right! I was thirteen. You and those damned friends of yours convinced me there was a Windsor by-law prohibiting bathing suits."

"Hey, I was the injured one," Travis said. 'I had to see you naked. It took three months of therapy to stop the nightmares."

"He's still no angel," Margaret said. "But he's doing better in school."

"Volleyball team still kickin' butt, too." Gene beamed with pride. "You should see him on the court. Moves like a tiger."

Travis grinned and hung his head in modesty.

"Josh is quite the athlete, too," his mother said. "Oh I know what you're thinking. He used to be so skinny and gangly but in the last six months or so he finally hit his stride."

Josh groaned. "Dear God, mother. You know that never gets any funnier, right? I'm a runner. Cross-country. She throws in that 'hitting my stride' crap all the time. It's so weak."

After learning he was a runner, Travis invited Josh to join him in the morning for his daily run. Josh agreed, happy for the chance to work his muscles. They ran down to the banks of the Detroit River, then along parkland paths all the way downtown. Josh was surprised at his cousin's endurance. Halfway through the 10k run, most people would have been winded. Travis barely broke a sweat. Josh, as usual, barely felt the exertion. His body was fueled by willpower. He never tired. It seemed in his cousin he'd found an equal.

For the next three days, they repeated the pattern. Then, on Friday night, Travis invited Josh to a party his friend was throwing.

Ignatio – Iggy to his friends – came from a rich Italian family. They lived in a sprawling mansion in South Windsor, in a neighborhood filled with luxurious houses. It was a pool party filled with thin girls in small bikinis and fit guys, mostly volleyball players or other athletes from Travis' high school. For several tense minutes, Josh was reminded of the bush party, the one where he had watched Tommy Delonki die. Then he caught the attention of two girls and his mind was otherwise occupied.

Hours later, Travis appeared, his knuckles bloodied and chest covered in scratches.

"What the hell happened?"

Travis shook his head and looked over his shoulder. "Nothing. Nothing much. Some perv watching us."

"Travis nailed him!"

Josh looked over at the thin olive-skinned Italian slurring his words by the pool. Iggy hadn't changed much since the first time Josh had met him two years ago.

Josh felt tense. "Is he still here?"

Travis shook his head again. "I don't think so. It's dark

back there. I was just getting a drink when I saw something moving behind the pool shed. First I thought it was just an animal. Then I saw something shiny. Like gold in sunlight. Wasn't sure if it was a watch or something else. I started walking toward it. That's when I saw him. Some jerk was back there watching us. Anyway, I shouted out to him. He started to run away and I just booked it. I ran at him and started punching."

"What did he look like?" Josh found the whole thing unsettling and very familiar.

"I'm not sure. It's kind of a blur. I remember seeing him, remember running and hitting him, but it's strange. When I stopped hitting him he was already gone. Guy must move pretty fast, whoever it was."

The next day they were both too hung over to go for the morning jog. Then, that afternoon, they were both kidnapped. The Froeses decided to take their guests on a picnic in Ojibway Park.

***

Josh felt his knees buckle and threw himself against the corridor wall for support. This flash of memory was different from the other ones he'd had recently. Rather than bubbling up from behind a wall of sludge, this one felt like it was being sucked out of his marrow. His head throbbed and all the strength in his muscles dissipated.

"What the hell are you doing to me?" He forced himself to stare into the darkness, to see what was in the closet down the hall. Once again, he caught a flash of gold and memory overwhelmed him.

***

Ten minutes into the picnic, Josh began to feel something. Fear. He kept looking over his shoulder, scanning the woods, not sure of what he might see, hoping he wouldn't see anything. 'Come on, Josh,' he told himself. 'This isn't back home. There are no Edimmu here. Nothing is going to come running out to get me.'

That's when he saw it. The glint of gold.

He froze, staring at the reflection. He dropped the piece of chicken he'd been holding and slowly slid off the picnic bench.

His mother looked annoyed. "What is it, dear?"

"Nothing," Josh lied. "Just thought I saw a friend from the party last night."

"Really?" Travis followed Josh's eye into the woods. The gold light flashed again and silent rage washed over Travis' face. "Oh. A friend. Dad, we'll be right back. I have to go say hello."

"For God's sake, Travis, no fighting, okay?" Gene looked into the woods blankly. "Where is your friend? I can't see anyone back there."

Josh looked over at his cousin. Without saying a word they silently agreed to do whatever it took to show this guy the downside of spying.

Past the mowed and paved façade of the picnic area, the woods took on another life. All sounds of civilization faded away, leaving only the call of birds, the whispers of the wind through the trees, and the hushed steps of their feet in the underbrush.

"Where did he go?" Travis whispered. The trees were far enough apart that they could see for quite a ways.

Nothing moved.

Josh put a finger to his lips, motioning for silence. Even at 16, when he decided to take control of a situation, his entire demeanor changed. His shoulders stiffened and he seemed to grow several inches taller. There was a gleam in his eyes like a wild panther. Now when he moved, his feet made no sound against the ground. Josh was barely conscious of the change. It was only when he saw Travis staring at him that he realized anything had changed at all.

"How did you do that?"

Josh looked confused. "Do what?"

Travis stared for a second longer, then shook his head.

"Never mind. Just for a second there, I thought....Must be the nerves.

"Must be." Josh turned away from his cousin, afraid his face would betray him.

"Wait." Travis mouthed the word. He put a hand on Josh's shoulder and pointed at a spot several yards away. "Over there."

Josh looked where Travis pointed. He caught the blur of shadows and the glint of gold disappearing behind the trunk of a massive oak. He sprang. Behind him he heard the heavy thud of footsteps as Travis followed. His body seemed to take over his mind. Gone was the anxious depression that had weighed on him since Tommy had died. He wasn't jumping at shadows; he was chasing one.

"Wait!" Travis whispered behind him. Josh stopped sharply. He nearly caused a collision with Travis, who could not stop as quickly. Even stationary, he kept his eye on the shadow.

"You're moving too fast!" Travis said. "I can't keep up."

"I'm not the one moving fast." Josh watched the shadow spin quickly and disappear. "The thing we're following? That's moving fast. Too fast for..."

"Thing? Too fast for what?"

"Too fast to be human."

Travis stared at him.

He stared right back.

"I'm guessing you don't mean it's a deer."

Josh shook his head and looked back into the woods. "I think I know what this is. You should go back. It's not safe."

"Not safe? And what are you? Wolverine? No offense, short stuff, but, well for one thing, you're insane. We're not chasing a Sasquatch here."

"I know. They don't migrate this far south."

"For another thing..." Travis stopped and did a double take. "Wait. Did you just...? Come on. There's no such things as Sasquatch, wastoid. And that thing we're following is totally human. I saw it last night, remember?"

Josh turned slowly back to Travis. "Did you? Really? And what did 'he' look like?"

"Well he..." Travis chewed his lip. He looked around the woods as if searching for a way out of this ridiculous situation. "It was dark. I didn't get a good look."

"You didn't get a good look at it because it wouldn't let you get a good look. Think I'm crazy all you like, but I've already lost one friend to these things. I'm not going to lose another."

Travis took a step back, then lowered his head. "Is this about that friend of yours? The one killed in the gang fight?"

"The what?"

"Look, I didn't mean to eavesdrop or anything, but I overheard your mom a few nights ago. She was talking to my parents about how a friend of yours got stabbed during a gang fight a while back."

Josh rubbed the back of his neck. "Tommy didn't die in a gang fight. And that thing we're chasing is moving about 100 miles per hour without so much as snapping a twig. If we keep chasing it, you're going to find out I'm right. So it would probably be best if you headed back."

Travis looked at his hands for a moment, then looked down into Josh's eyes. "There's no way in hell I am heading back without you. When we catch this guy and you see he's nothing but a perverted Peeping Tom, will you please do me a favor and start taking your meds?"

Josh smiled. "Deal."

In the distance Josh saw the glint of gold again. For the first time he got the impression they weren't really chasing the thing. Maybe it was luring them somewhere. Normally that would have been enough to make him change his tactics. But something about the light drove him onward. It compelled him.

"I've never been this deep in the woods before." Travis jogged easily behind him. Though both had been running for more than twenty minutes, neither was out of breath. "I had no idea it even went this far. We must be over the Salt Mine by now."

A few seconds later, Josh began to notice changes around him – subtle at first but increasingly hard to ignore. First he noticed a light mist hanging between trees and covering the underbrush. Then he heard strange bird calls, completely unlike anything he'd heard before. They sounded more like vulture-sized parrots than anything native to North America. Then he saw the trees and stopped in his tracks.

"What is it?" Travis stopped beside him. "Did you lose him?"

Josh shook his head and studied the trunks of trees ten feet in diameter. They rose 100 feet above him before the foliage began. The bark was ruddy, like redwood, but the leaves were long and flat stars like elongated maple leaves. Looking past the leaves he saw the sun. It took a moment for his brain to process what he was seeing. The sun had a light blue tinge to it. It was also twice as big in the sky as it had been when they'd entered the woods.

"Where the hell are we?"

Travis looked up at the sun. "This isn't right." Mouth gaping open, he spun around quickly. "This can't be Windsor. We don't have Redwoods or any type of tree this massive. What the hell is going on?"

"I don't know." Josh suppressed a shiver. "But I'm guessing our friend does. Still want to put money on him being human?"

Travis punched Josh in the chest.

"I take that as a 'no.' Are you sure you don't want to head back?"

Travis his put hands in the back pockets of his shorts and looked around. "Sure. I'll head back. When you can point out exactly where the way back is. I'm completely lost. Hell, I can't even use the sun to find east or west." He pointed to the sky and then looked into the woods. "Where the sun is now, if that way is east it would be about 9:00 in the morning. If that way is west it's closer to 7:00 p.m. So unless we've pulled a Superman and ran back in time...."

"Or we've been running for six hours. I get you. Neither one makes much sense. What time do you have? What does your watch say?"

Travis looked at his watch, then brought his wrist up to his ear. "Broken. Yours, too, eh?"

Josh nodded. "You wouldn't happen to have a cell phone, would you?"

"It's back on the picnic table. But even if I did, I'm guessing it wouldn't work, either. Maybe we should just find this guy and find out what's happening."

They started walking after that. Josh saw no sense running when their quarry was obviously not trying to escape. The underbrush grew thicker the further they went, as did the mist. He only caught occasional glimpses of the thing they were following, but it was going in a straight line now. It seemed to be moving slower as well, although Josh could still not make out any features except for the fact it was in the shape of a man.

"Do you hear that?"

Josh stopped and held his breath so he could hear more clearly. He heard a hushed rumble that sounded somehow familiar and yet inexplicable. "What is that?"

Travis went visibly pale. "It sounds like flippin' Niagara Falls."

Josh listened again and nodded. "Yep. That's definitely a waterfall. So I think we can safely say we're no longer in Windsor. Come on. Let's get this over with."

They walked through the strange woods for another ten minutes before they reached the banks of a river. It was easily as large as the Detroit River, several kilometers wide. Unlike the river that ran between Windsor and Detroit, this one glistened a translucent blue. It reminded him of the waters along the beachfront in Bermuda. It smelled salty, too.

"Over there," Travis said.

Josh glanced at him and then turned toward the

waterfall.

"Whoa."

For a moment, he found it hard to breathe. It was one thing to come to grips with his situation mentally. Actually seeing the waterfall and everything around it was an altogether different matter. It was easily one of the most imposing physical landmarks he'd ever seen. Before him, an escarpment covered with foliage shot up over five hundred feet. A section of the greenery gave way to rocks and grassland, as if the forest there had burned to the ground years ago and was only slowly coming back to life. Above the escarpment, birds with large, green beaks and leathery wings circled above the trees. The fact he could make out their wings and beaks from such a distance suggested they were as big as elephants.

The waterfall ran like a slash of blue and white down the face of the cliff. It slammed into the river below, hiding the base of the escarpment behind a roar of mist and noise. The only thing he could compare it to was Niagara Falls, but he'd never stood in the shadow of anything like this.

"Dude, where the hell are we? Is this Africa?"

Josh blinked. "Africa? Are you on drugs? Does this look like Africa?"

"Well, kinda."

"No! This is not Africa. This isn't anywhere on Earth."

Travis punched Josh in the chest again. "Now who's the one on drugs? If we're not on Earth, where are we?"

"Maghe Sihre."

The cousins turned as one at the voice, their hands clenched into identical fists. At the edge of the woods stood a strange-looking figure. He was a tall man with braided gray hair that hung down to the middle of his back. He was pale, with a complexion that could pass for Caucasian until you noticed the green tinge to his flesh. Ridges along his neck reminded Josh of vestigial gills, like he'd seen on aliens in Star Wars. His fingers also seemed unnaturally long and slender, but these things were only noticeable if you were watching closely. At first glance, he was just a man standing at the edge of the woods, dressed in green leather and a thick black traveler's robe.

"Is that the guy you saw?" He asked Travis the question over his shoulder; he kept his eyes on the stranger.

"How should I know? It was dark, remember?"

The stranger took a step forward. Travis flinched. Josh did not. "I'm afraid there won't be time for introductions. Not today. You are here because I made a promise, Joshua. Your father is a very powerful creature and he's worried about you. He's concerned about the way you slaughtered his employees."

"What the hell are you talking about?" Now it was Josh's turn to step forward. "My father isn't a powerful man and he definitely doesn't have Edimmu as bodyguards."

"Who exactly do you think your father is?"

The stranger was smiling now. He crossed his arms over his chest, giving Josh the first clear sight of the source of light they'd been following. A simple gold ring on the man's left hand shone brightly even in plain daylight.

"I know exactly who my father is. You have one minute to explain who you are and why you've brought us here."

"And how," Travis added abruptly. "Tell us how you've brought us here."

"Or what?" The man laughed with what sounded like genuine humor. "Oh my, Joshua. You are so much like your father. Always throwing around meaningless threats. Tell me, do you actually believe I'd let you get close enough to lay a finger on me?"

Thorny vines shot out from the darkness of the woods and wrapped around Josh's and Travis' wrists. Before either of them could react, the vines lifted them off the ground. Pain seared through Josh's confidence. He couldn't see Travis but he could hear him screaming. Blood dripped down his forearms. He felt completely helpless.

"Ah, silence." The stranger walked away from the edge of the woods and stood below them. Only then did he realize how far up in the air he was. His knees were level with the stranger's head. "Not even a whimper from the demon son. So tell me, Josh, what do you know about your father? What do you remember?"

Josh tried to answer but the pain from his wrists made it hard to concentrate. He saw a flash of light from the gold ring and his mind went blank.

The stranger smiled. "Just as I thought. You know nothing. We have big plans for you but you're a little too, shall we say, unpredictable. That nonsense you pulled killing all those Edimmu, well, we just can't have that. The alliance is far too new for in-killing. Unfortunately, we need you. Killing you isn't an option. For either side. Fortunately, I have an alternative. With this ring I slip into that pretty little brain of yours. I can repress all memories related to the Edimmu, your powers, and who your real father is. As an extra bonus, I'm going to make you forget about me, too. When the time is right, and only when the time is right, I'll make you remember. By then, it will be too late for you to stop what's coming."

There was a flash of light and a sensation of falling backwards. Then Josh woke up in darkness. It took his eyes some time to adjust. He realized he was in a forest lit by moonlight. His shoulders ached as if they'd nearly been pulled out their sockets. His wrists were mangled and bruised, covered in still-wet blood. He stood and looked around. His cousin Travis lay crumpled in a fetal position nearby. Nothing else looked familiar.

"What the hell happened?"

***

Josh woke up in his room. Garnet stood beside his bed.

"What the hell happened?" She asked as she chewed the fingernail on her right baby finger. "Did all the stress finally catch up with you?"

Josh sat up quickly and grunted as hot searing pain shot through his head. He fell back to the bed and looked at his wrists to confirm that they were still in perfect shape. Then he sat up again, slowly this time. "There was a man. I have to speak to Wisdom. There was a man in the building. He has to know."

Garnet stared down at him, her face slowly fading from condescension to fear. "You're telling the truth. I can feel it. How did he get past security?"

"Forget that." Josh gripped her by the wrists. "What I want to know is how he got past Wisdom."

Chapter Fifteen

Wisdom stared out the window and watched the light from the sunset bounce and beam off the pillars of glass and steel. He couldn't shake the feeling that he should be doing something. Since heading back in time, these were the hardest times. Nothing he did now mattered. Going through these days the first time, he'd believed, like most, that our every action is vital, that every choice could fundamentally alter our reality.

Now he knew better.

Nothing he did in the next two days would have any bearing on whether or not Propates won. Nothing he could do would help keep Echo alive or reduce the chance that the Council of Peacocks would subvert his students. He knew this based on the evidence he'd collected. Hard facts. But he still didn't like it.

The intercom buzzed.

"Yes, Shirley. What is it?"

"Sorry, sir, but you have some messages. Is it safe to come in?"

Wisdom groaned. "Yes, yes. I'm not going to hit you. That was one time, like five years ago. Let it go."

The intercom clicked off and Shirley opened the door to his office. "One time, you say. But you hit bloody hard. I lost two teeth!"

"Which I grew back for you. This may surprise you, Shirley, but I'm not always in control of my temper."

"You don't say. You received twenty messages this morning. Shall I go through them alphabetically or by phone number?"

"Neither. Just tell me the important ones."

"Very well." Shirley sat down in one of the chairs facing Wisdom's desk. "That reporter, the one from People, called again for the tenth time. Her deadline has been moved up and she wants to reschedule. What should I tell her?"

"Tell her too bad. I'm a busy man and she either makes the appointment or not. Next."

"Your broker called. He's got those stocks you were asking about. Are you sure about Livedore, sir? Last night I saw this documentary on them and…"

"I'm sure. I'm going to make a mint. Trust me. Any word on that other matter? The three men I asked you about?"

Shirley shook her head. "Not yet, but you did get a fruit basket from David Cameron. Shall I send it in?"

Wisdom rolled his eyes. "No. I don't want a bloody fruit basket from the bloody Prime Minister. And who sends fruit baskets anyway? Why not send me a car or a watch? No, I get a fruit basket. Maybe I should kill him. That *could* possibly alter the fabric of time enough."

"I'm sorry, sir," Shirley said. "But you're raving again. Should I get you some Turtles?"

"No. Wait! Yes. Get me a platter of several types of chocolates, but mostly Turtles. And you may as well send in the chocolate oranges from the bloody fruit basket."

"How did you know?"

Wisdom smirked. "Come on, Shirley. How long have you worked for me? I *know* things. It's the reason David bloody Cameron tries to be nice to me. He should try a little harder, if you ask me. And get me that detective from New York on the phone. I need to track down those men."

Shirley nodded and left. When the door opened seconds later, he expected to see his chocolate. Instead, he was surprised to see Garnet and a rather pale-looking Josh.

"What are you doing here?" Wisdom had always been sensitive to the vibrations of time. He could instinctively sense important fluctuations in history – times when something significant and rare was about to happen. It had helped him stay alive and remain a person of power for thousands of years. He sensed it now, in a moment experience had taught him should be completely free of importance.

"We have a security issue." Garnet turned back to shut the door. Shirley tried to walk in with a tray filled with Turtles and chocolate oranges. Garnet took the tray and shooed her away. She handed the tray to Josh, then closed and locked the door. "Josh has a story to tell you."

They sat around Wisdom's desk while Josh told the story of the mysterious stranger with the gold ring and the trip to another world. In the course of the telling, Wisdom ate the majority of the Turtles with alarming speed. Only when Josh finished did Wisdom stop reaching for the treats.

"Did you sense anyone in the building?"

Wisdom focused on Garnet as he answered her question. "No. I didn't. Up until right now, this moment, I believed I'd encountered just about everything you could experience on this world. Once again I have proof that I've just been stupid. I don't know how, but something has changed. This was not supposed to happen. Garnet, I need you to contact the head of security and bring him here. I have some arrangements to make."

"So you believe me?" Josh reached for the tray of Turtles. Wisdom raised an eyebrow and Josh withdrew his hand.

"Yes, I believe you. This flash of light you saw, the glow of the ring, I've seen it before. Not here, but in Niagara Falls. Long story and I have no intentions of telling it. But yes, I believe you... Now I just have to find out what it means."

***

There is an old saying that a wise man knows much but says little. So it took more than a little arrogance to portray oneself as the embodiment of Wisdom. It was not the name he'd been given at birth, but he had been known as Wyndam Wisdom for at least the last three thousand years.

Of course, there is a second part to that old saying: a fool knows little but says much. Wisdom had to admit now how foolish he'd been. Since gaining his freedom he had been reckless and brash, conceited and short sighted. If he'd thought things through with the foresight his name implied, Echo would still be alive.

Wait.

"Echo still *is* alive." Wisdom shook his head and opened his eyes. He'd fallen asleep on the leather sofa in his office, something he never did. It seemed like a very long time since he'd slept anywhere at all. "Still alive," he repeated: a mantra. If he wanted her to stay that way he couldn't afford to sleep. Maybe if he tracked down this off-worlder he could alter events enough to prevent the murder of the only woman he truly cared for.

He spent the next hour and a half making phone calls and signing papers experience told him could not wait. He returned to his living quarters and changed into a well-cut Sean John suit in shades of crimson and scarlet. Then he called Elaine in Hong Kong and told her what he planned to do.

"You know this is insane, right?" Her voice came in clearly over the speakerphone.

"No more insane than time travel." Wisdom smiled and ate a Turtle from a second tray of chocolates Shirley had just brought in.

"But isn't this different? When you traveled back in time, you knew what was going to happen. You knew all the players. Wisdom, you know nothing about this guy or the planet he comes from."

"That's precisely why I'm going."

"What if he hurts you? Or kills you? What happens to Echo and us if you're not here to stop Propates?"

The smiled dropped from Wisdom's face. "Trust me when I say this, Elaine. I've tried everything else. Everything. Obviously the Council of Peacocks has been working on levels I never even conceived of. Turns out I only thought I knew my enemy. I don't even know what battle I'm in. How the hell can I win the war?"

"You're not taking anyone with you, are you? Not even

me?"

Wisdom shook his head. "No. You're going to be needed here. Echo will come for you soon. She won't want your help but she'll need it. When you see them you'll know why. Just know I tried to save them. I made a choice. They lost."

"See whom, Wisdom?"

With a sigh, Wisdom turned to the window. "Just know I'm sorry. If everything goes well, I should see you in a few days."

"And if things don't go well?" Elaine did a masterful job of hiding the tremor in her voice, but Wisdom had known her too long to be fooled.

"I can't believe you need to ask," he said. "You have seen me, haven't you? Big man, big muscles, major voodoo? I can take care of myself. Just don't sleep with him this time, okay?"

The other side of the phone connection went silent for a moment. "Sleep with whom? Wisdom, I..."

Wisdom cleared his throat. "Forget I mentioned it. Maybe it'll be better if you do bed him, anyway."

Wisdom hung up the phone, stood and walked to the center of his living room. With a gliding wrist motion, he distorted space-time. A glowing oval of light appeared beside him and he stepped through the portal.

***

He emerged in a vacant hotel room in Niagara Falls. It was the same one he had confronted Propates in, back in a future he hoped no longer existed. It seemed the only logical place for him to start his search for the off-worlder. At least here, he could catch the scent.

After he left the hotel, it didn't take him long to find the alley where he'd seen the glint of gold and the moving shadow. He stretched out his consciousness, seeing layer upon layer of reality with his mind. There was no physical trace of the off-worlder. Fortunately, being here was enough for Wisdom to reawaken the sensation of being watched. He held the sensation, and breathed in. He had the scent. Now all he had to do was follow it back to the source.

Wisdom warped space-time again and stepped through a disc of light. He traveled from Niagara Falls to Ojibway Park in Windsor. It was late summer, the trees still at the height of strength and beauty. He breathed in the rich oxygen of the woods and tried to remember how long it had been since his last visit to a natural area. Unable to do so, he closed the teleportation field and stretched out his senses.

"Where are you?" He spun in a slow circle trying to pinpoint where the scent of the outlander was strongest. Presumably, it had been many years since the stranger had made an appearance here. To Wisdom's sense, time was only a thin barrier. Beneath the tranquility he originally felt, there was deep anger in the woods. He stopped spinning and unbuttoned his suit jacket. Something was very wrong with these woods. The trees screamed out with rage. The underbrush murmured secret plots to the ground. The air tasted of sulfur and burning coal.

He cursed under his breath and withdrew his senses. He clenched his fists and slowly walked to a clearing 100 yards away. In the sunlight, it was difficult to see the figure at first. Thankfully, Wisdom knew how to see the invisible. Before him, standing fourteen feet tall, was a bipedal incarnation of fire. Thick legs like tree trunks and bulging muscular arms gave the figure an undeniable impression of menace. His flesh curled and flickered in slow flame, like superheated gases or the shimmering of an oasis in the distance. Despite being translucent, the figure implied solidness. His presence was over-towering, like a mountain. The look of pity on his face was enough to shake Wisdom's resolve.

"What are you here for, father?"

"Oh, it's not what I want that matters." His father spoke in a voice like static and the burning of tree sap. "You came here looking for something. What was it?"

"Not you. Go back to your Hell. I'm more powerful than you remember, and I don't have time for this."

The figure laughed lightly. "The way you've been jumping back and forth through time tells me you have all the time in the world. Tell me, do you honestly think you can change what has already been written? Creation is like a painting. If you try to erase what's on the canvas, you improve nothing and ruin everything. Just let her die and be done with this nonsense."

What little resolve he'd mustered dissipated. Were any of his actions a secret? "If you know about the time traveling, you must also know I've killed you before. Just stay out of my way, you old bastard, and I won't do it again."

The towering figure of smokeless fire took a step back and shook his head. "You killed me? Really. How interesting. Well, that would explain why the future is unclear to me. Partly. You should know, as a Djinn I don't fear death. I exist outside of time as the humans see it. If you destroy this body, this incarnation, I simply return to the Mother Flame from which all our kind are made. If you had been born in Kaz you would understand that. But look at you. You're useless and lazy. You were given amazing talents and what do you do with them? Petty intrigues and capitalism. You've always been a disappointment to me, Akushula."

"My name is Wisdom." He clenched his fists and felt old angers stir up the fire in him. "You're no one to talk about wasting gifts. Especially to me. I've made a difference with my life. Each day, because of me, people's lives are better. Over a thousand people work for me directly. I teach the Anomalies to live with their demonic nature. If not for me, every one of them would have succumbed to their darkest nature by now. So, don't you dare say I'm wasting my life!"

"But you could have been so much more if…"

"If what? If I'd been more like you? What do you do with your life? You watch. That's it. You bathe yourself in the narcotics of voyeurism while I'm actually in the world making a difference. Just because you've wasted your life doesn't mean I'm wasting mine."

The Djinn took a step forward, the heat of his body pushing Wisdom back. "If you had spent more time watching and less time doing, you would understand why I withdrew from the world. Something is coming, Wisdom. Something far beyond anything you can handle. The only reason I'm here is to take you back where you belong. For once, live up to the name you've chosen and come with me. You can't be here when the end game starts."

"I am where I belong. And I'm not going anywhere. I remember what you did to my mother. You raped her. Tried to murder her."

The Djinn sighed. "I apologized for that. What more can I say?"

"What more can you say? It's not something you can apologize for! It pretty much puts you under the bad guy column for all time. Growing up, you beat me, treated me like a slave. So now you're old and you want me to forgive all your sins? Well, sorry. I do not forgive!"

For a moment, the clearing crackled with unseen energy, a tension on the verge of breaking. The Djinn shook his head and sighed again. "Fine. Have it your way. I've tried to be reasonable but you're still weak, short-sighted. A complete waste of life. If you won't come home willingly, I will beat you into submission."

Wisdom called forth the hellfire. "Old man, that's not going to work anymore."

And the battle began.

Chapter Sixteen

August 6th

"I won again," Jared said.

By 11:00 p.m., the common room in London was deserted. Most of the refugees from Toronto chose the isolation of their private quarters over the threat of conversation with others. Small talk inevitably led back to the attack, which made everyone uncomfortable.

"Give her a break." Josh took the controller from Garnet as Jared did his happy dance. For the third night in a row, the three of them had played *Mortal Kombat* after supper. "She's getting better. At least this time she landed a punch."

"Bite me," Garnet said as she ran her fingers through her hair. "Some of us haven't wasted our lives mastering video games."

"Your loss," Jared said. Then he put his controller down, no longer smiling. "Something's very wrong, isn't it?"

"D'ya think?" Garnet rubbed the back of her neck and sighed. She looked several years older than she had when Josh had first met her. "Wisdom disappeared again and no one seems to know where the rest of the Anomalies are. I'm glad to see those psychic powers of yours aren't going to waste, bud."

Jared rolled his eyes. "You know what I mean. It's worse than anyone is letting on. There's way more security than normal. Since when does Wisdom need security, anyway?"

Josh raised his hand. "If we're taking votes I'm all in favor of enhanced security. Maybe Wisdom just realizes that, whatever he is, he's not immortal."

"He's close enough." Garnet frowned and went to the window. Late at night, the city was lit with street lamps and illuminated rectangles from office buildings.

"You can't be serious," Josh snorted.

"Of course I'm serious. I'm telling you, I've seen the things he's capable of. Unbelievable things. You've seen the way he travels. How is that even possible? The physics are mind-numbing. Nothing our scientists know about reality today can explain it, and I've done the research. Aside from that, do you have any idea old he is?"

"No," Jared said, returning to his game. "And neither do you."

"Well, not exactly. But I have a pretty good idea. I know for a fact he was alive during the Inquisition."

"Bull," Josh said. He returned to the game but it was difficult to concentrate. Pressure kept building up at the base of his neck. His head started to spin.

"Scout's honor." Garnet put her hand on the window. She squinted her eyes as if trying to focus on something down on the street. "In fact, I'd put money on him being over a thousand years old."

"You're on drugs." Josh threw the controller down on the couch and pressed the heels of his hands against his forehead. The pressure was unbearable.

"Every chance I get, but that doesn't change the facts." Garnet leaned back. "He's definitely not human."

"So, if he's not human, what is he, then?"

Jared slowly lowered his controller and turned toward the window.

"A demon."

"What?" Josh almost choked on his own tongue.

Jared stood and shook his head. "Not Wisdom. Out there. I can feel it. A demon is heading up the street. I think it's coming here."

Garnet backed away from the window. She walked over to the phone and dialed an extension.

"We have incoming," she said into the receiver. "I don't know how many. Just get the entire staff on alert. Have someone check with Hong Kong, too. I need to know if this is a coordinated attack."

She hung up the phone and turned to face Josh.

"I hope the reports on you are correct, Wonder Boy, because this could get really interesting."

***

Garnet looked down her nose at the building's chief security officer. He was a white-haired old Irishman with a bulbous nose on a bulbous face. He was currently tracing out escape routes on a blueprint of the building. Garnet had already explained, at length, that she knew the layout of the building better than he did. He didn't seem to hear her. In fact, all he seemed to notice was the curve of her cleavage.

"Enough," she said, biting the word. "Just go watch a door or something." She waved him away and turned her back on him. The old man grumbled something and walked briskly away. This left the security room deserted, except for the three Anomalies. A bank of video monitors showed several sections of the building, the visitor's parking area, and all entrances. There were even cameras in the surrounding sewer system. The security room was overtly luminous and spartan in its décor. Being here helped Garnet feel safe. No matter which direction the demon took to get here, they would see it coming.

Jared sat nearby in a wooden chair that faced north. He did not turn around at the sound of Garnet's heels against the tiled floor as she approached. She placed her hands on the back of the chair and lowered her lips to his ears.

"Anything?"

Jared shook his head and kept staring forward.

"Does he know you've spotted him, Jared?"

"I can't tell."

"Is it an Edimmu?"

"Don't think so. He's powerful, though. Worse than them, I think." Jared looked up. His lower lip trembled slightly. He opened his mouth, on the verge of saying something else. Garnet, sensing what it was, bent down even further and gave him a kiss on the forehead.

"Don't worry, little man," she said. "We're not exactly powerless ourselves."

"How do you know it's a demon?" Josh paced back and forth in front of the wall of monitors. He had an open bottle of water in his hands. He had been holding it for some time and had not yet taken a drink.

Garnet straightened and turned to him. "What's your deal, anyway?"

Josh stopped pacing. "What do you mean?"

"I mean, what do you do?" She crossed her arms and shrugged.

"How the hell should I know? I haven't been to X-men school like you guys." Looking at the drink in his hand, Josh moved it to his mouth. Then, letting out a sigh, he placed it back on the bar. "I don't know. I guess I'm just lucky. Things just happen around me. Things that shouldn't happen."

"Well, that sounds particularly useless." Garnet rested her hands on her waist as she scanned the monitors. "Jared, how much longer before...?"

The lights went out.

Josh stood frozen. He listened to his heartbeat until his eyes adjusted. With a clunk, the air conditioning stopped. The absence of background noise was almost as unnerving as the power failure.

"He's in the building."

The voice was Jared's. Josh squinted his eyes until he could distinguish which shadow was the boy's. In the dark, he seemed very far away.

"Shouldn't a building like this have a backup generator?"

A shadow moved close to him. Garnet. "It does. It should have cut in by now. It must have been taken out, too. Look, Josh, I don't know you very well, but – no offense – what I've seen so far hasn't really impressed me. I'm sure you're a nice guy and all, but...."

"Don't worry. I'm not always so nice."

"Well, thanks for that uninspired bit of machismo, but I'm still not impressed. I'm just saying the security team here is good but I don't think they can stop the demon."

"Don't talk like that," Jared said. "You're talking like they're going to fail. Like we're all going to die. We can't think that way."

Josh lifted the bottle of water to his lips and gulped half of it. Then he shook his head clear off the last of his uncertainty.

"You're right about one thing, Garnet," he said. "You don't know me very well. Let's move."

"Where are we going?" Garnet started after him, then paused. "I mean, where do you think you're going?"

Josh smiled and started walking toward the door. "We are not going to just sit here and wait for that thing to take us down. Whatever it is, we outnumber it. We may have to be sneaky about it but we are going to take this demon down."

Chapter Seventeen

David rolled over in bed, on the verge of waking. He needed to go to the washroom, but it was so warm and numb under the blankets, he balked at leaving. The last few days had been lazy. He'd spent hours talking with Todd and Bethany but most of his time was spent alone in his room. He read Robert Jordan novels on an ereader, making sure he didn't touch the walls.

He pushed himself up slowly. A strange feeling was building in his stomach. It was like the fear that settled over him when he was immersed in a scary movie. Dread. The room was still fully lit; he still hadn't found the light switches. He could see everything around him. There was not even the hint of a shadow anywhere. Still...

He quickly searched the edges of the room again, listening for any sound, any movement.

Nothing.

He pushed the sheets away. Beads of sweat accumulated along his forehead. The veins in his temples throbbed violently, like the onset of a migraine. He massaged the back of his neck, trying to coerce the pain away. It was no help.

He heard a loud bang followed by a scream.

Trickles of dust fell from the ceiling.

He rubbed the sweat from his palms against the lower edge of his t-shirt and crept tentatively toward the front door. Each breath he took seemed very long: exaggerated. He was very aware of the sound of his exhalations, the beating of his heart and the pounding in his head. He could not stop blinking and his mouth was dry.

"I keep this up and I'm going to hyperventilate," he whispered to himself.

'They've found us', he thought. It was the only explanation for the way he felt and the things he had heard.

He ran a hand through his hair. When he brought it

down, it was soaking wet. A slow survey of the room confirmed what he believed: no weapons. One step at a time, he approached the door, opening and clenching his fists, not sure what to do. He couldn't just walk out into the hallway, not without knowing what was going on. But he also could not ignore the scream and just hide under the bed.

He heard a young girl call out for help.

David inched toward the door, his breaths short and shallow now. He turned the knob and let the door swing open.

Jessica fell onto the carpet just inside the room. She must have been lying on the ground, her back pressed up against the door. David grabbed her by the shoulders, dragging her completely into his apartment. She cradled her left arm. Jagged bone jutted out from the top of her left shoulder. Her clothes were charred as if she had run through a fire. A large bruise was forming around her eyes. It looked like her nose was broken.

"Amy," she said. Tears streamed down her face. Her lips were coated with blood.

"Where is she?" David asked.

He looked up in time to see something fly through the air. He howled, a primal scream, when he realized it was Amy. She flew like she'd been thrown, like a ball. He peered out the doorway to see where she landed. She hit the floor thirty feet away. She did not get up.

Then shadow sprayed up from underneath her, a fountain of black ink that spread out over the hallway and covered her body. As quickly as they appeared, the shadows retreated. In their absence there was no sign of Amy.

"She's gone," Jessica said. "I can't feel her anymore. I think they killed her. We've got to..." She pushed against the ground with her right hand. "We've got to get away."

"What about the others?" David knelt beside her and searched for a part of her body that wasn't wounded. With his help, she got to her feet. He led her to one of the sofas, then rushed back to look back into the hallway. "Are they safe?"

"Close the door. Quickly." Jessica rubbed at her eyes with her fingers. Then she took a look at how filthy her hand was and stopped. "They took most of them. Killed the rest. I can still feel Bethany, though. I think she's hiding in her room. Todd … I think they're doing things to him right now."

"Who is it?" He bolted the lock on the door. Then he ran to one of the larger sofas, dragged it over to the door, and pushed it until the entrance was blocked off. He was thankful the living quarters did not have the rollaway round doors he'd seen in different parts of the underground city.

Jessica glanced at the bone poking out of her shoulder. She bit her lip. "Those guys with wings. They followed us. Somehow. I was…" Tears fell down her face and she sobbed. In that moment, she looked just like the little girl she really was. She shook her head, becoming cold and impersonal again.

"I was in the sitting room with Amy. We both got up early. We always do. A bunch from the other classes were out there talking to Echo, trying to get more information out of her, I think. Todd was there, too. Next thing I knew, something picked me up. I slammed into the ceiling and I felt something crack. Then I fell. When I hit the ground, I think that's when I dislocated my shoulder. Her face went slightly green. Before David could reach her, she coughed up blood.

"Perfect," she said. She wiped her chin with her right hand and then scraped it clean against the fabric of the couch. "I don't know what to do. I don't know how they snuck up on us. I didn't even feel them coming, and I always feel them coming."

"They've come for you guys before?" Breathing heavily, he lifted and twisted the couch until it was flush against the entrance. From the other side of the door, he heard a man scream out in pain. It sounded like Todd.

"They've poked around before. Or something has.

Many times. Never as bad as this. Usually they just watch us. When they attacked in Toronto, that was the first time they ever came into a building. Wisdom has been moving us around. At least he has since I got here. We never spent more than a few months in one building. It must have been Madeline. Maybe they made her talk before they killed her."

Something pounded on the door.

"We are so dead." David slowly backed away from the door. He pounded his fists against his head in frustration.

The pounding came again. This time, the sofa moved back an inch.

***

"No!"

Bethany screamed as an Edimmu grabbed her by her ankles and dragged her face down toward the sitting room. Reptilian hands dragged her over the carpet. Her chin slammed repeatedly into the hard floor as she bounced along. She was certain her back was going to break at any moment.

Then, out of the corner of her eye, she saw a dead body and she stopped screaming. It was a teenage girl from one of the other classes. Bethany didn't know her name. The girl's face was frozen in a scream; eyes wide and face ridged with burn marks. The side of her neck had been chewed open, but there was little blood. As if something had sucked the blood away. She saw dozens of other children dragged into the shadow, disappearing.

Bethany felt numbness shoot through her.

Then her chin bounced against the floor again and everything went black.

***

It only took Echo an instant to realize she couldn't stop the Edimmu from taking the children. So she ran. Before most of the Anomalies registered what was happening, before the first of them fell to the ground with broken bones only to be swallowed by darkness, she warped the spatial field and jumped into the light. She closed the circle as quickly as she had summoned it.

Silence.

She looked around, not sure at first where her panic had taken her. The air was clear, clean and brisk. Below were thick, green forests of healthy trees; above, snow and ice hung to the ridges of untamable mountains. It took her brain several seconds to confirm what her body knew instinctively.

"Home," she said. She did not know if this particular mountain had a name but she was somewhere in the Jeseníky mountains in northern Moravia. "I was born not far from here." The village no longer existed, of course. Everyone she had known in that old life was dead and buried. Even their graves were long forgotten now.

"Mother would have loved the view from here." She sat down on a nearby rock, took deep breaths and stared out over the wilderness below. It was strange for her to think how old she was, far older than the trees. Most of the years slid through her memory, mercurial and jumbled, but her childhood stayed with her. Playing games by the river. Days watching clouds and birds. And the day Wisdom took her. He had been a different person then. Violent and cruel. Now he genuinely seemed to care about her. It was easy, sometimes, to forget what he had done to her. To her family. Now, it was all she could think about.

Echo covered her face with trembling hands and tried to push the memory of screams away. Somewhere in the world, people were dying because she had run out on them. In and of itself, that was no concern to her. Humans died every day, after all. But she had made a promise. A promise to Wisdom to keep the children safe. If they died on her watch, he would be angry. Or worse, disappointed.

She shut down the voice of instinct and rose to her feet. She opened another circle of light. Echo looked back once more on the mountains and forests of Moravia. Then she was gone.

***

Something pounded against the door again.

The sofa moved back another inch.

"We have to do something." Jessica said. She brought her right arm up to her head and squinted her eyes.

"What?" David licked his lips. He slapped himself across the face several times. "I can't die like this." He ran forward and slammed his body against the sofa until it slid firmly back up against the door.

"Not that way," Jessica said. "Use your EFHBs. They're stronger than your body."

"I don't know how!" His voice came out in a shrill and broken fashion. The realization that this little girl was handling the situation far better than him embarrassed him. The only thing that infuriated him more than his own weakness was having someone else recognize it. He howled and slammed his fists against the floor. "I'm flippin' useless! Damn!"

"Stop it!" Jessica shouted. She tried to push herself off the couch with her good arm but the effort made her woozy again. "Stop your whining or they're going to kill us! Quit being a baby and fight back!"

Radiant rage and a kind of hush crept through David. He turned to Jessica. He wanted to slap her. Then he set his jaw in determination.

"Good. I'm angry," he said. "Now I can fight back."

He stood up, moved away from the couch and focused his mind on the other side of the door. Beads of perspiration built up along his arms as the temperature in the room rose sharply. The air around the door rippled. Sweat dripped off his face and fingertips.

The pounding stopped.

On the other side of the door, something hissed.

Then it began to scream.

***

Echo stepped out of the portal just as an Edimmu

grabbed Todd by the throat. The lizard with wings stood over eight feet tall. It slammed Todd's head against the ceiling several times in quick succession until the stone was dark with blood. The creature turned at the flash of light as the portal opened. Before he could focus on Echo, though, Elaine stepped from the portal and started shooting.

Three more Edimmu appeared, one of them dragging a mess of clothing and flesh that looked like Bethany. They stopped, eyes flashing yellow as Elaine fired her modified Mossberg Mariner shotgun in quick succession. Echo stretched out her hands, took a strong grip on the magnetic strings of reality, and twisted them. Bolts of lightning shot through the air and singed the Edimmu's chests. They dropped the body and rushed toward a pool of shadow that hung suspended in the air a few inches from the wall.

"Not today," Echo said. She brushed her hands through the air toward the Edimmu's escape route. She clenched her fingers into a fist. The dark portal warped like a piece of paper, crinkled and shredded. Then, with a soft pop, the shadows disappeared.

The Edimmu stopped mid-stride, wings flapping. They turned as one, joined by a common intelligence.

Elaine emptied her shotgun into one of them. When the creature fell, she threw the shotgun aside, pulled out her MP-5 sub-machine gun and turned it on the other three. Echo rushed to Todd, who now lay slumped atop a table under the body of the Edimmu. Fingers to his throat, she felt for a pulse and let out a sigh of relief. At least the boy was still alive.

The remaining Edimmu each held their right arm outstretched, palms open and outward. The bullets from the sub-machine gun sprayed against an invisible barrier several feet in front of them. They started walking toward Elaine.

"Enough, Elaine." Echo said. "I'll take care of these three. Go check on the others."

With a nod, Elaine stopped firing and rushed toward the living quarters. A few steps later, an unseen force lifted her off the ground and tossed her backwards. She landed on her back with a thud. One of the Edimmu laughed, a mixture of hissing and guttural sounds.

'I hope I made the right choice,' Echo thought. 'Even with Elaine's help, this isn't the sort of thing I'm good at.'

From somewhere deep in the living quarters, a scream that was not human filled the air.

Chapter Eighteen

David waited until the scream stopped and then moved toward the door.

"Don't," Jessica said. She pulled her tattered shirt closer to her skin, closing the holes in the fabric. "It's not dead."

'I wish I could feel that,' he thought. He gave his head a single shake but kept moving. 'It has to be at least incapacitated. I felt the flames hit his flesh. Whatever these creatures are, I know now they can be hurt.'

He bent down, braced his feet, and pushed the couch away from the entrance. When there was enough space for him to open the door just a crack, he stopped pushing. Just in case.

He put his hand on the doorknob and started to turn.

"You're being stupid." Jessica was standing now. She brushed sweaty hair away from her face. Whatever signs of weakness there had been when she had broken down in tears was gone. She still looked like a broken doll with her damp, red eyes and the ugly break of her arm. Her stance and the steadiness of her eyes radiated nothing but strength. "It's stronger than that. It's stronger than us."

David turned the knob all the way and heard it click open. "You don't know how strong I am," he said. Slowly, he let the door open.

He peeked through.

On the ground, black as coal, was a pile of scaly legs and arms and wings. It twitched, the movement amorphous and subtle like snakes squirming under a black blanket. Then he saw the eyes, white ovals with thin green slits down the middle.

Looking at him.

"Damn."

As quickly as he could, he pushed against the door to slam it shut. His arms felt heavy and thick like he was moving through water. Before he could blink, the Edimmu was on its feet. It hissed – a forked tongue shooting out through human teeth – and slammed its shoulder against the slightly open door. Pain shot through his forehead where the door hit him. He flew back, falling on his shoulder as the creature charged into the room. Its black, oily wings fluttered back and forth. It grabbed the sofa in one enormous hand and tossed it away like so much cardboard.

David's anger was gone, replaced again by the fear that made him powerless. He closed his eyes, instinct screaming at him to flee. He pushed and pushed with weak arms that kept buckling at the elbow as he tried to get up. Something smacked him in the back of the head. His face slammed forward, breaking his nose. Somewhere behind him, Jessica screamed.

***

The Edimmu, caught off guard by their colleague's howl of pain, turned slightly toward the living quarters. For just a moment their concentration was divided between curiosity and keeping the shield in place.

"Go!" Echo shouted at Elaine.

Elaine jumped to her feet and ran toward the scream. Echo reached out, twining her fingers within the weave of energy and force that held the atoms of the room together. Then, once again, she clenched her fists. Nosebleeds accompanied tiny hemorrhages she set off in the Edimmu's brains. Elaine rushed past them as each Edimmu fell to its knees, reptilian hands over the all-too-human faces.

Echo tore at the magnetic strings again. Forks of lightning shot from her fingertips across the dry air. Scaled flesh sizzled. The Edimmu shrieked.

Then, corner by corner, the shadows began to grow.

***

Elaine fought the urge to run down the hallway. The submachine gun hung around her neck on a tight strap. She held it firmly with sweaty palms. Recklessness could be fatal.

She inhaled through her mouth to avoid the stench of the scorched bodies and smoldering fabric that littered the hallway. All the doors she passed were open, revealing room after room of carnage.

'Only a few bodies,' she thought. 'They must have taken the others.' Several of the dead wore white uniforms. Garnet's employees. 'Wisdom knew this was going to happen. He chose to let this happen. I can only imagine the alternative.'

Down the hallway, she heard a scream. Jessica.

'At least she's alive,' Elaine thought. Wisdom would have been most upset if he lost her. From what Wisdom had told had her, Jessica was vital to their success. She let the submachine gun fall back against her body and took an M-9 handgun in each hand. These weapons would minimize the risk of Jessica getting caught in the crossfire.

Jessica screamed again.

Elaine moved quickly now, a brisk walk with outstretched arms. She fired as soon as she stepped into the room. The Edimmu had its back to the door, both hands round Jessica's neck. It held her above its head while she kicked at its body and beat at its hands. Neither made its grip on her any less firm. Elaine aimed both guns at the Edimmu' knee caps. The creature howled and tossed Jessica like a sack of potatoes aimed right at Elaine. She rolled out of the way, letting the tiny body crash behind her. Whatever damage Jessica took in the fall, Elaine had still accomplished her goal. There was nothing now between her and the Edimmu.

The Edimmu hissed again. The air filled with the stench of ozone, like damp air after a lightning strike and, hands clenched in fists, it vomited bright red flame from his mouth. Elaine twisted to the left, barely escaping the attack. She dropped to the ground and tossed the gun in her right hand away. Then she grabbed the handle of her hunting knife, throwing it as hard as she could. It spun a full rotation in the air before the blade stabbed into the Edimmu, firmly in the middle of its forehead. It looked up, struggling to see the thing imbedded in its skull. It screamed again, a war cry. Then it fell and was silent.

Elaine ran to Jessica. The girl coughed but wasn't moving. Elaine recognized five serious injuries that were potentially life threatening.

"No time for caution," she whispered to herself. She squatted down and carefully helped Jessica to her feet while she talked. "Listen, Jessica. We have to get you away from here. I know you are hurt, but we're going to have to move quickly. Can you do that?"

Jessica nodded. Elaine put an arm around her waist and let the child put most of her weight on her. Then Jessica pointed at a nearby body.

"David is still alive," she said.

Elaine looked over at the crumpled man. The back of his head was a mash of blood and matted red hair. As if prodded by her eyes, David twitched and pushed himself up on tenuous arms until he was on all fours. He blinked several times, every movement maddeningly slow. Then his eyes landed on Jessica and Elaine.

"You look like hell, Ross." His face was a mass of broken and bruised flesh. "Injuries like that require a hospital. You're lucky to be alive. You wouldn't be standing if you were a normal person. Anomalies are fast healers. Just don't pass out. You're still vulnerable to concussions." Elaine looked at Jessica. "How many others are still here?"

Jessica shook her head, a tear falling down her cheek.

Elaine bit her lips, took hold of her sub-machine gun again and used it to motion them out into the hallway.

Then there was a series of screams. A whoosh of hot air rushed past them.

Silence.

Elaine raised a hand, motioning for them to be silent. Guns drawn, she stepped away from Jessica and crept forward into the sitting room.

"It's clear," she said.

Jessica walked forward, stumbled and nearly fell. David

tightened his grip on her.

"Holy. Crap." David stopped in his tracks, mouth open. Echo was burning. Blue and pale green flames streaked up and down her arms, tracing her breasts and legs without consuming her flesh or clothes. She stood in the middle of three piles of black ash. Echo looked up from the piles. David caught Echo's eye. She flinched. Her pupils shone bright orange for a moment. Then her eyes cooled to a deep black and the flames on her arms disappeared.

Everything else in the room was destroyed. Todd lay on top of a table, legs bent at the knee and raised so that his feet were flat on the table close to the base of his spine. Elaine exhaled with relief when Todd coughed, a harsh wet sound that confirmed he was still alive. Barely. The table was one of the few pieces of furniture still intact. The paintings that had given the subterranean apartment a sense of sophistication were now squares of half-burnt paper, their surfaces marred by black smears and holes where the canvas had been burned completely away. Under a long red sofa, upended and blackened, Elaine glimpsed grey hair. Bethany. Her legs hung out twisted at an odd angle and she was not moving.

"Is it safe?" Jessica asked. The strength was gone from her eyes now. Only the tears remained.

Echo shook her head. "No. There's something else here." She walked past them and stood at the mouth of the hallway. "It's down in my room."

Jessica shook her head. "It doesn't feel the same way these monsters do. It's very powerful. And it's not alone."

Echo wiped the palms of her hands against the sides of her pants. "You're right. It feels slimy. This one I know. Elaine, take the others and get out of here."

"That's not happening." Elaine took one step forward then stopped. Once again, Echo was covered in blue flames.

"Get them out of here," she said.

For a moment no one moved. Then Elaine let the gun fall against her body and nodded.

Echo turned and walked out of their sight.

A dark wind began to blow.

***

David watched Todd squirm in pain. He knew they had to move him, knew they couldn't.

"She's dead, isn't she?" Todd said. His face was contorted, eyes squeezed shut, and lips open to reveal teeth covered in blood. "Bethany's dead. I heard her scream for a while, then nothing."

"Yes," David said. "They broke her back." He left Jessica and walked over to Todd. He light squeezed Todd's shoulder in support. "It looks like she managed to crawl…" David stopped, realizing what he was saying.

Todd yelped, like a dog hit by a car. He sobbed, bringing a hand covered in blood to cover his face.

"Damn it," Todd howled. He let his hand fall away from his face and opened his eyes. "She was my best friend in the whole world." He stopped talking, let his head fall to the side and stared off into the rubble. "Help me up. I have to see her."

"I don't think…." David started.

BOOM!

An explosion shook the walls. A white blur flew down the hallway and crashed into a wall. It hit with a solid thud and dropped to the floor. Only then did David realize what the blur was.

"Echo!" Elaine ran to where the other woman lay in the dirt.

Before Elaine reached her, Echo pushed herself to her feet and brushed the dirt from the lapels of her white jacket. "Damned suit is ruined," she said.

"Echo." Elaine's mouth fell open and she quickly forced it shut, tightening her grip on the submachine gun. "You're bleeding."

"What?" Echo looked up and saw blood dripping down over her eyebrows. "Yes, it appears so. Put the gun away, Elaine. It won't do any good here."

"Is it one of them? One of the bastards on the Council?"

"No, Elaine. Just an old friend." Echo's eyes flashed orange. "I thought I told you to get them out of here. I'll meet you in the city below."

"Echo," Elaine started. "You can't."

"Don't presume to tell me what I can or cannot do, Sweetie. You have a very special place in Wisdom's heart, but you are only human to me. Remember that. Now, get them down to the city. Fast. He's coming."

Pale and shaken, Elaine nodded. "Grab Todd," she said to David. Despite the crazed look in her eyes, her voice was calm. "Help him off the table and move quickly."

He nearly toppled over. David offered him a shoulder for support. Elaine went to help Jessica. The four of them ran down the spiral stairs.

"This is bad," Todd said. He grimaced every time his right leg hit the ground.

David focused on the worn stone stairs as they descended. Something kept coercing him to look back. Echo stood there alone, arms outstretched, enveloped in flames again. Her hair churned and swirled slowly around her face, caught in turbulent, heavy wind. Dust devils sucked up sheets of paper and small clumps of fabric from the rubble, making strange sounds as they slid through the caves.

Todd tried to look back but the movement upset his equilibrium. He stumbled and, if not for David's support, would have tumbled down the rest of the steps.

After that, he kept his eyes forward as they entered the foyer where they had first entered the underground world. Then they turned and watched Elaine help Jessica down the steps. The wind gathered strength. It howled now, an animal sound.

"Go!" Elaine shouted. She waved with her free hand, motioning them toward one of the unblocked corridors. The floor was smooth and the lights down here were all intact; otherwise, David was sure they would have tripped.

The hollowed-out passage was ten feet tall and thirty feet wide. They rushed down the corridor until they hit a doorway half-blocked by a giant stone wheel. One by one they crept through the small opening next to the wheel, not risking the time it would take to move the massive stone. Behind the slab of stone another rough-cut staircase crafted a spiral path down to a still-deeper level of the caves. When David and Todd reached the bottom, they barely stopped to look around before they each dropped to the ground. The others arrived seconds later.

Jessica sank down next to them. "What do we do now?"

"We wait for Echo," Elaine said. She reloaded her handguns. "She can get us out of here."

There was another explosion, this one much louder than the last. The air flashed red and yellow. Jagged pieces of rock flew through the air. One shard hit David on his broken nose and he screamed. He fell, closed his eyes and waited for the sound of falling shrapnel to stop. When he opened his eyes again, he couldn't see anything past the top of the staircase. The small opening was filled with dirt, small rocks and large fragments of the stone wheel.

"Cave-in." Todd's voice was cold.

Elaine crossed her arms and rubbed her biceps. As she brushed the dirt from her face, David heard her thoughts. 'This isn't supposed to be happening. Wisdom said it would be over by the time Echo brought me to the caves.'

"What do you mean 'this isn't supposed to be happening?'" David asked. When he saw the look of outrage and shame play on Elaine's face, he realized he'd read her thoughts. "What do you know?"

Elaine grabbed him by the collar of his shirt. "Stay out of my head!" Her voice was low and steeled.

"Whoa."

Everyone turned to face Todd. He stood at the edge of a cliff a few feet away, his back to them. Jessica limped over to him. Within seconds, David followed her to see what

Todd was talking about.

"What the hell is this place?" Jessica asked.

Todd shook his head.

They stood on a ten-foot wide ledge that ran around the edge of a colossal cavern. Far below them, several hundred stone buildings formed a city. Despite no visible form of illumination, the entire city was well-lit and visible. It was hard to discern any real description of the buildings from this far up. They were several stories tall and strictly functional, void of unnecessary ornamentation. In between the buildings were roadways defined by light grey bricks. Above them, the ceiling rose until it disappeared into darkness, the top invisible to their eyes.

"I know this place," David said. "I had a sort of dream about it."

"This can't be real," Todd said. "Did Echo build this place?"

Elaine shook her head. "I don't think so. We have to look for a way down. We're too open up here. Fish in a barrel. We have to hide until Echo or Wisdom can get to us."

"What if...?" David stopped when Elaine turned to stare him down. She lifted her chin, daring him to finish the thought. David opened his mouth but could not speak.

"She's not dead." Jessica said.

"Can you feel her?" Todd asked.

Jessica looked back toward the cave-in at the top of the stairs. After a moment, she shook her head. "But I don't always feel her."

"She's hiding." David looked at the top of the stairs now. His head buzzed as he tried to look past the stone. "I see what you're saying, Jessica. You don't think she is dead because you can't see her in any way. If she was dead you would see some of her. The ghost of her."

Elaine sighed with relief. "You may come in useful after all, Mr. Ross. Come on. Let's find a way down."

Chapter Nineteen

Josh Wilkinson was blind. With the lights out and no windows nearby, the hallway was utterly dark, like an underground cavern. He kept his right hand on the wall as they walked. His fingertips brushed over the smooth, cool surface to keep walking in a straight line. Twice already he'd tripped over dead bodies. The stench of blood and gunfire was putrid.

Occasional bursts of gunfire broke the otherwise oppressive silence. Behind him, he heard two distinct sets of soft breathing: one slow and steady, the other quick and short. They comforted him, reminding him he wasn't alone.

"Does the security staff have nightvision?" Although he whispered, the words cut through the air like shards of glass.

"No," Garnet whispered. "They're human."

Josh rolled his eyes. "I mean do they have nightvision goggles? Haven't you ever seen a movie with the army in it?"

"Oh." Garnet's voice seemed very close to his ear now. "Maybe. Believe it or not, this sort of thing doesn't happen very often."

"What about you?" He swallowed; his throat seemed very thick and heavy. "Can you see in the dark?"

"Sorry. I'm human, too. Same with Jared. However, I am starting to think *you* can see in the dark. Where are we going?"

"I memorized the layout days ago. It's a little trick my dad taught me."

His hand hit emptiness. He stopped and stretched his arm back until he found the wall again. It was slightly cooler than air temperature. Slowly, he dragged his fingertips forward until he found the edge of the wall. He caressed the sharp angle and folded his hand around the corner. No trim. That meant it was likely not just a door. With his left hand, he reached back until he touched warm fabric. He caught a whiff of sweet perfume.

Garnet's voice was barely a whisper. "Watch the hand."

"Sorry." Blood rushed to Josh's face as he blushed with embarrassment. "Stay close. Jared, you still there?"

"Yes." The voice was barely audible; the word said quickly, the final "s" clipped almost to nothing. "Hurry. It just killed another guard."

"Where are you going?" Garnet pressed close to his ear again. "This isn't what Wisdom would have done."

"Wisdom isn't here, though, is he?" Josh turned the corner and headed further into the heart of the building. He nearly stumbled when his fingers came upon something hard, cold and cylindrical. A fire extinguisher. He came to a sudden stop and lifted the extinguisher off the wall. Behind him he heard a grunt and a soft thud. It sounded like Jared had run into Garnet's back.

"What is it?" Garnet asked.

"A weapon. Not much, but something. Jared, is it any closer to us now?"

For a moment there was no answer. Then the voice slid through the darkness, a sound like the hissing of a snake. It took Josh several moments to realize it was Jared's voice. "Yes. Much closer. It is not taking the stairs. I can feel it rising. It used to be below us but..."

Josh tried to lick his lips but there was no moisture in his mouth. "Jared, how do you know it's a demon?"

"I read minds, remember? I can't do much else, but Ms. Ryerson says I have potential. His mind is crazy. He's thinking all this really gross stuff. Way worse than anything Wisdom thinks of."

"So that's it? You can't really tell if it's a demon, but it just sort of feels like one?"

"Is there a difference?"

Another flurry of gunshots reverberated through the hallway. Then there was a long period of silence. Suddenly their footsteps were as loud as drums.

"Where are we going? Don't make me ask again."

"The kitchen. It should be two floors down, right off

the stairwell. We should be getting pretty close to the stairs if my memory's right."

"My, my, your memory is pretty good. The door is about twenty feet up on the left. How did you memorize the layout of this floor?"

Josh laughed. "Like I said, part of the wonder of growing up with a father like mine. He taught me you never know when you have to run. First thing I do wherever I go is figure out how to leave. How do you know where the door is? I thought you couldn't see in the dark?"

"I can't," she said. She put her right hand against his side, just above his waistline. He felt her nails against his abdomen, felt the light pressure of her thumb against his back as she leaned forward into him. "I have a good memory, too."

He walked forwards twenty feet, then started edging to the left. He kept his left arm outstretched and wriggled his fingers like tentacles searching for the wall on the other side of the hall. When they found the solid cool surface, he released his breath. 'Didn't realize I was holding it in,' he thought.

Garnet still had a hand on his side. He swallowed again. His heart beat loudly in his ears, making it hard to concentrate on the other sounds around him. He heard another burst of gunshots and a strange little twist of sound he thought was a scream.

'If I can hear the screams that means it's closer.' His fingers brushed a small bump of wood followed by a number of sharp corners bending backwards. A doorframe. "Okay, this part will be anything but fun. Just try not to fall."

He opened the door to the stairwell and a million scary movies flashed through his head. Only stupid people took the stairs when a monster approached. 'Let's hope I'm wrong about that.' He reached out through the darkness searching for the handrail. His fingers touched nothing but air.

Then…

"I've got the handrail," he said. He heard Jared sigh. He also heard a snap like someone cracking their knuckles. Step by step they went down the stairs. With no carpet to dampen sounds, each footstep rumbled like distant thunder. Josh looked all around him, desperate for some sign of light, but found nothing. When they hit the first landing Garnet gave a little yelp of surprise.

"One more floor to go,' he said. Now both sets of breathing behind him were short and fast. He found it hard to breathe, himself. It was not until they reached the door on the next landing that he realized how afraid he was that they would never make it out of the stairwell.

"We're here."

He opened the door to even more darkness. This floor reeked of sulfur and fresh blood. He walked along the left-hand wall until he hit an edge. He traced his fingertips around the curve of the doorframe until his knuckles hit the sharp corner of the door. If someone had closed the door at that moment his fingers would have been snapped off. The thought made him jerk his hand back. He reached out with the palm of his hand, felt the flat surface of the door and used it to guide him forward. When his fingers hit empty air again, he bent his hand around the outer edge of the door until he held it in his grasp.

"Hurry in here. I'll close the door." Two sets of footsteps passed by him. The only breathing he heard came from within the kitchen instead of the hallway. He used his right hand to turn the doorknob all the way to the right. Then he pressed the door closed and released the doorknob. It closed without a sound.

"Now what?"

"Find the silverware. Knives, forks, spoons, anything."

"You think a knife will stop this thing? The guards have guns."

Josh sighed. "You have trust issues, don't you? Just find the silverware first."

The hand left his side. Footsteps moved slowly away

from him.

"Is it safe to turn on a light?" Jared's voice was so soft it was barely audible.

"What do you mean, turn on the lights? The power is still out."

"Not that kind of light. Garnet, do your thing."

"Do I have to?" Her voice was no longer throaty or soft. It came through the darkness flat and icy. "Fine. Whatever."

Josh turned away as a flash of orange light appeared. After the long period in the dark, it was painful. He put the fire extinguisher down and rubbed his eyes with the balls of his palms until the pain subsided. He blinked several times more before being able to look back at the light. Flames danced around a square chopping block. Now it was just fuel for the fire.

"Couldn't you have done that before?" Halfway through the sentence, he remembered he was supposed to be whispering and lowered his voice.

"And what would I have set on fire, Josh? The carpet? Even now, it will be a miracle if we don't set off the fire alarms. Luckily, the counter's metal or we could end up setting the whole building on fire."

Now that there was a little light, Josh could look around the room. It felt sterile. Like the countertop, the cabinets, fridge and stoves were all stainless steel. He left the fire extinguisher by the door and rummaged through the drawers. It did not take him long to find what he was looking for.

"Got them." He grabbed handfuls of silverware. "Jared, help me out. Grab those butter knives and follow me."

"What are you doing?" Garnet ran her right hand under a stream of water in the sink. She hissed in pain as steam rose up from her hand where it contacted the water.

"I'm reaching, that's what I'm doing." He placed the forks and spoons in front of the door. "This thing, demon or not, can probably see in the dark. Otherwise he wouldn't have cut the power. Since none of us can, this should help us know where he is in the dark. If he walks through that door, he'll have to cross over the silverware to get to us. The silverware will make noise and – voila! - homemade radar. Even if he tries to sneak around it, we'll still hear something. That's right, Jared, put them just like that."

Garnet looked over at the block of fire, bared her teeth like she was hissing and shook her head. "This is sooo not what Wisdom would have done. It's not going to be that easy for me to set him on fire, you know?"

As Josh stood, his back cracked loudly. "I wasn't thinking of you burning him, Garnet. I didn't know you could do that. My plan is a little different. I learned a few things from my dad about fighting dirty. I know a few things about death."

***

"I'm serious, Josh," Tommy drew his knees up and hugged them close to his chest. "They're real, and if you don't get away from the closet they're going to get you first."

He stood beside the closet door while Tommy Delonki sat up in bed behind him. Tommy wore his Star Wars pajamas, the ones with C-3PO and R2-D2. He was only 12, but he was starting getting grey hairs. Josh watched as Tommy pulled the blankets up to his chest. He looked cold, shivering against the headboard even though it was mid-July and the temperature was well into the 80's.

Josh, also 12, felt goosebumps rise on his bare chest. He wore plaid Joe Boxer pajama bottoms. His mother had bought them for him the last time they'd gone to New York – a business trip for his father. He didn't understand why a mechanic needed to go on business trips at all. He thought they just fixed cars. Father said it was something about getting products. He could tell by the way his mother looked on the flight there and back she didn't believe him, either.

"Maybe," he said. Sweat trickled down armpits that had yet to grow any hair. "Or maybe I'll get them first."

***

"What is it?" Garnet moved away from the fire and placed her hands on his cheeks. They felt very warm – even the one that was damp from being run under the tap.

Josh shook his head and looked down at himself. Somehow he had ended up on the floor. He pushed Garnet's hands away and got to his feet.

"It's nothing. I just remembered something. Let's find the plates. We can put them on the floor, too."

***

On the 13th floor of a building in London, a thing of darkness walked. Wherever it walked, it stole the light. The name of this darkness was Paeder Ferris. He was dressed in a black leather jumpsuit with yellow trim along the collar and cuffs. It matched his motorcycle parked two streets over.

As he walked by the window, he caught his reflection in a wall of glass. Since he was a teenager, people had said he looked a little like Robert Redford. His hair was strawberry-blond and he had a well-chiseled face with freckles and deep blue eyes. He couldn't see the resemblance. When he looked at his reflection, all he saw was the same lines and curves as his brothers.

His brothers.

He turned away from the window and spat on the floor. The carpet and the cement underneath bubbled under his saliva.

Before entering the building, he had reached into the shadows and sent a blast of Discord throughout the high-rise. The anti-energy consumed all electricity and the light was gone. It hurt to expend that amount of power but he knew it was worth it. Nothing made humans more irrational than what they could not see. If they could see it, name it, it gave them a sense of power over it. In the dark, they had no power.

From behind a reception desk, two security guards shot at Paeder Ferris. Bullets bounced off his skin and ricocheted off the painted walls. Before his transformation, bullets would have killed him easily. Now he was one step closer to Eyeness. He was much harder to kill.

He leapt ten feet forward and slammed his fist into the head of the nearest guard. He hit him so hard across the chin his neck snapped back, broken instantly. Even as the body fell, Paeder grabbed the second man by the throat and lifted him off the ground. He held him there until he heard bones snap.

The guard's legs still twitched, but he was dead. Paeder sensed the life leaking out like air from a tire with a slow leak. When the legs stopped twitching, he dropped the corpse. He brought his hand up to his nose and smiled. He could smell the sweat and cologne of the dead man, but that was not what excited him. It was the scent of death.

He walked towards the elevator. He put his hands against the metal and used his new powers to dissolve the cohesive bonds that kept solid objects solid. The sensation danced over his skin like an orgasm. It continued to build until the metal turned to rust and flaked away. This was the power of decay, the third level of Eyeness. Most humans could not carry this power for long – their bodies gave out long before their will did – but Paeder did not care about that. He would survive long enough to retrieve the boy. He would drag the boy back by the hair if necessary. And once the Council was done with him, Josh Wilkinson would die.

He slammed the side of his fist into the rusty metal. It shattered like brittle ice. The actual car was somewhere above him. As long as he kept the power off, it was not going anywhere. He leapt into the shaft, grabbed the nearest set of wires and started to climb.

***

As soon as the plates and silverware were in place, Josh had Garnet dump a pot full of water over the burning knife block. The air was now thick with smoke, although it was too dark to see any of the black clouds. Josh and Garnet hid behind an industrial-sized steel fridge. Jared curled up in a nearby corner. Josh could hear the crinkle of the kid's jeans as he rocked back and forth.

Garnet peeked past the fridge. "My God. I can feel him now."

"Just stick to the plan." Josh put a hand on her bare arm and drew her back to their hiding spot.

"The demon is angry," Jared said. Jared smacked his head against the wall with a soft thud.

"Stop that," Garnet said. There was no heat in her voice, no sense of worry, either. But it was enough. Jared stopped.

The weight of the fire extinguisher grew heavy in Josh's hands but he didn't dare set it down.

"Are you sure it will come in here?" Garnet whispered close to his ear.

Josh nodded. "If there was any doubt before, the smell of smoke will solve that. Now hush. Let's not speak until..."

"It's gone," Jared said.

"What's gone?"

"The demon. I can't feel it anymore."

Josh rose to his feet, pins and needles shooting through his legs.

"Garnet?"

"I can't feel it either," she said. "One moment it was there, this pool of pestilence, moving through space. Then it was gone. I can't feel the taint anymore."

Josh shifted his weight and listened. "I can. It's coming."

Click.

Garnet gulped in air. Then there was absolute silence.

Josh held his breath and listened. His head buzzed, like a sudden hangover pounding in his skull.

Tap tap tap.

'That's the door being pushed all the way open,' he thought. Then he heard a series of clicks and ringing vibrations. 'A fork being thrown against a spoon and tumbling into a plate.'

Then nothing.

Silence.

Eventually, he detected a third pattern of breathing. Deep and solid. Despite his blindness, the sounds gave him a perfect visual of where the demon was.

'Almost there. Just a few more steps.'

***

Paeder couldn't help it. His eyes lit up and he fought not to burst out laughing.

'Utensils on the floor? This is the man that slaughtered my family?' After the forty or so armed guards, he felt like he had stumbled upon a child trying to catch their pet dog in a fancy mousetrap. The only thing that kept him focused was the memory of his mother's dead body, vacant eyes in a cold skull.

The Third Level of Eyeness also allowed him to see without light. He was in a kitchen big enough for a restaurant. Metal pots and pans hung from the ceiling over three of the islands. The walls were filled with cupboards.

'Reminds me of our place in the Laurentians,' he thought. He sniffed at the air. Smoke masked the stench of sweat and fear making it difficult to pin down locations.

'Hide all you want. I'll still find you.'

He crept forward, dropping to all fours. 'There. I can hear them breathing.' The sound came from the left. 'If I concentrate just a little harder…'

He heard something like wind in the air. He turned just in time to see the thing flying through the air. He caught it with both hands and called up the power of decay. It shot through his hands before he recognized what the object was. The area around his fingers melted, creating quick holes in the pressurized steel container. He did not have time to curse before the fire extinguisher exploded.

***

As soon as he threw the fire extinguisher, Josh moved. "Garnet, now!"

Behind him, Garnet held up one of Jared's sneakers and set it on fire. The flash of light was blinding but this time he was prepared for it. He closed his eyes and rushed to where he'd thrown the fire extinguisher.

The explosion took him by surprise. It threw him back several feet. Luckily, he was far enough away not to be hurt. The blast lasted only a second. Afterwards, there was an eternity of screams. The demon held hands over his foam-covered face, metal shards sticking out of its upper body.

Before the demon could focus beyond his pain, Josh kicked and shattered its kneecap. The demon fell, still holding its face. Josh slammed both his fists down on the back of its head. It hit the floor face-first; metal shards dug deeper into its body.

"It's not dead!" Jared screamed.

A bloodied hand reached out and grabbed Josh's ankle. It clawed at him, trying to drag him off his feet. But Josh was lucky. He leapt free of the hand and landed near a block of knives. He grabbed the two largest blades and spun around. That's when he caught his first good look at the face of the demon.

"You!" he said. When he'd heard there was a demon coming, he'd imagined horns and scales. He didn't expect to see one of the Redford twins.

The demon smiled back at him. "You killed me mumsy. I'm going to make you scream."

An oily tentacle darker than the shadows reached out from the demon's hands and grabbed Josh by the throat. Josh screamed. Searing pain burned into his neck as the tentacles tightened. He was vaguely aware of Garnet throwing something she'd set on fire, but it was hard to concentrate.

'Have to move or I'm dead,' he thought. He slid his fingers under the bottom edge of the tentacle and concentrated. Nothing happened. He focused harder, ignoring the howl of pain as the corrosive ropes burned his skin. Then his mind was clear. There was nothing in the world but silence.

In his mind's eye, the smoke and pain parted. A figure appeared dressed in a tuxedo woven from living maggots and writhing beetles. Wet intestines wrapped around its neck and waist, crafting a mockery of bowtie and cummerbund. But it was the face that struck Josh the most: the dull grey slate of a powered-down television cracked open in scales and oily boils, lips like wet tar and beautiful blue eyes that were far too familiar.

'Ah.' the creature said in his mind. 'Now there's my boy.'

Josh howled, filled with terror. His hands broke through the tentacle. He fell to the floor, gagging and struggling for breath. Something flew over his head – a flaming shoe. It hit the demon in the chest.

"Josh! Look out!"

He didn't have time to react to Garnet's warning. Something solid grabbed him by the throat again. With a grunt, he kicked out as hard as he could. Luckily, his foot connected with something and the grip around his neck broke free. He shook the blackness from his eyes in time to see the demon holding its left knee.

All the Redford twin's clothes and hair were on fire. Still, it would not fall.

'How the hell am I going to beat this thing?' Even as the thought came to mind, the demon pointed at him. Another tentacle of darkness shot out toward him.

"No." Josh held his hands out. As soon as he said the word, the tentacle stopped moving. It hung in the air, twitching, dripping shadows, but it did not move forward. Josh looked the demon in the eye.

"You killed my best friend. Tortured my girlfriend. Making me angry was the worst decision of your life." Something pulsed in his mind. Then it jumped forward and wrapped around the demon. With a violent jerk and a loud snap, the demon's head twisted clockwise and up. Then, wide-eyed, it fell.

Paeder Ferris was dead before he hit the floor.

Josh stared down at the body. 'What the hell have I done?'

***

The building came back to life with a series of whirls and hums. The kitchen overflowed with light. Josh blinked several times, forcing his eyes to adjust. Garnet came forward and knelt beside the Redford twin.

"He's dead," she said. "No more demon thoughts. Would you agree, Jared?"

Jared stood up from where he had been hiding – behind one of the islands – and nodded. He was crying. Somehow, he looked more frightened now than before the demon attack.

Garnet rose and stood in front of Josh. "That was pretty hard-core there, Mr. Wilkinson. I didn't know you were capable of that."

Josh shook his head. He could not look her in the eyes. "I'm not sure that was me."

Garnet raised her eyebrows. "Then who was it?"

Josh remembered the man in his mind, the creature in a living tuxedo. For a moment it felt like the creature had taken control of his body. "You wouldn't believe me. You'd think I was crazy."

"Whatever. It worked. We're alive. That's all that matters now. You knew him from somewhere, didn't you?"

"He's one of the psychos from Quebec, the ones Wisdom rescued me from."

"That's funny." Garnet examined the wounds around Josh's neck.

"Weird is an understatement." Josh stepped back away from her prying eyes and fingers. Then she gave him a look that froze him in place.

"No, not funny as in weird, funny as in ridiculous. You think Wisdom rescued you? That's flippin' hilarious."

"What do you mean?"

"Garnet, you should be nice to him. He might kill you, too."

"Hey! I'm not going to…"

"Just kidding." Jared broke out into a bright smile. He danced over to the demon's body and kicked it in the head.

Josh went pale. "You know, Jared, you're a very troubled kid. What do you mean, Garnet? He did rescue me. If it wasn't for him, those freaks would have killed me."

Garnet laughed, but there was no humor in it. "Honey, if it wasn't for Wisdom, freaks like that probably wouldn't exist. Don't get me wrong. I love the big guy — as much as you can love someone like that — but there's so much about him you don't know. There's even a bit I don't know about him. The parts I do know help me to realize he never rescues anyone. He might recruit you, but saving you was the last thing on his mind."

Jared kicked the demon in the head again. This time the skull flopped about on the broken neck with a series of crackles.

"Can you please stop that?"

"Come on! How often am I going to get to play with a dead demon? This is sooo cool."

Josh was not sure if he was going to throw up on or throw something at Jared. 'Have to be careful,' he thought. 'I might just kill him by accident.'

Jared smiled again, this time not so brightly. "Don't count on that, mister."

Josh blushed. 'Oh my god. I forgot he could read minds. Which means he's probably still reading my mind.'

With a snicker, Jared kicked the demon's head once more and then walked over to Josh.

"I told you he was a demon, didn't I?"

"Yeah. It's just, he doesn't look like a demon, does he?"

"He does on the inside. You know, you have a lot of weird things in your head, too. It's like you put parts of yourself into little boxes in your mind and thrown away the key. I could help you open those boxes."

"Another time."

"You can't always rely on what you see," Jared said. "Maybe this demon can change his appearance. Maybe he doesn't really look like this at all."

"That's a lot of maybes."

"Have you ever seen a demon before?"

Josh shivered. 'Who or what exactly was that thing in my head?'

"Oh yes," Jared said with a smile. "I guess you have."

Josh turned away. "I don't know what you're talking about."

"Not yet. But you will."

Chapter Twenty

David looked over the secret city below. Tall sand-colored spires rose on either side of dust-covered streets. Deep-cut stairs followed the outer wall of the canyon heading to the lower level. The stairs looked solid but the edges were cracked and worn. As they came closer to the city, he made out landmarks that made it more and more difficult to think of the Edimmu as simple winged monsters. Several open city squares lay covered with layers of dust. In one of them, seven forty-foot tall peacocks encircled a dry fountain. Dozens of smaller statues dotted the city: life-sized replicas of sleek humanoid figures with massive wingspans.

"I'm starting to envy the Edimmu," he said. "I'd love their wings right about now. At this rate it'll take hours to reach the city."

"You could always jump," Jessica said. She walked close to Elaine, but she was moving much more easily now. The wounds were scabbing over, the bruises fading. The speed of her healing unnerved David.

"Are you getting anything from Echo?" he asked for the third time.

Jessica turned to him, put her hands on her hips, and said nothing.

"I was just asking." David focused his eyes on his feet.

Below, mosaics of turquoise and onyx splayed across several of the larger buildings. One showed a reptilian face, forked tongue out to the side in what seemed to be a smile. The series of white figures to the side of the face reminded him of hieroglyphics. Another mosaic was troubling for another reason. It showed two small reptilian creatures without wings riding the back of what could only be a pterodactyl. Either the Edimmu had been around since the dinosaurs or the mosaic was an advertisement for a children's fantasy book. He wasn't sure which idea was more unsettling.

"Can we rest for a sec?" Todd sat down on the edge of step. He put a hand to his ribcage.

Elaine set her guns aside and sat cross-legged with her back to the outer wall. "Once we're down, we need to find shelter. There should be running water in some of the buildings. Echo told me the aqueducts are still sound."

"I'm hungry," Jessica paced back and forth along the steps. "What are we going to do for food?"

"Echo stored supplies down here last week, just in case. See that square with the dry fountain? There's a wooden crate near one of the peacocks. It's filled with dried goods and bottled water. She said there would be enough for 50 people to survive a few weeks. I'm hoping it doesn't come to that. Echo's still around somewhere. Even if she's not, Wisdom knows we're here. Someone will come for us."

'What if no one comes?' David thought. He looked over at Todd. He saw the same fear he felt echoed in the other man's eyes.

David cleared his throat. "How you holding up? I'm surprised you can even move after what they did to you."

"It's one of my EFHBs. PK. Psychokinesis. I can move things with my mind. I'm not as strong as Jessica, but it's enough to keep a kind of mental splinter around parts of my body. I've got three broken ribs, a shattered ankle, and a fractured shin. Plus, I think my arm is toast." He looked over at Jessica. "I feel bad for her. Her PK is different. It's better for heavy lifting but hard to manage for small jobs."

"I don't need your sympathy." Her voice was weak. She coughed and brushed away a loose strand of hair. The hair she pushed away fell stubbornly back into place. She brushed it away again, her eyes wet with tears. "I'll be fine."

***

An hour later they stepped off the last stair and entered the city. Walking through block after block of abandoned buildings unnerved David. The shadows, like the light, were dim and ill-defined but numerous. Each window was a square of darkness, each doorway a portal away from the light.

Though the buildings were made of stone, there was an organic quality he found disturbingly familiar. Several blocks into the city, he realized what they reminded him of: honeycombs. The buildings reminded him of the inner workings of a beehive. Everything felt connected. He could not even distinguish where the floor of the large cavern ended and the buildings began. Entire blocks of buildings seemed to have been carved out of the rock at the same time. The interconnectedness made the city feel like the skeleton of a giant.

"This place is massive," he said. "It's at least as large as Halifax back home. How is this possible?"

Todd stared up at the tall vacant buildings. "I don't know. There's enough housing here for hundreds of thousands of people. What I don't get is how they lived underground. What did they do for food?"

"I don't think people lived here," David said. "It was Edimmu. Can you imagine those things living in a place like this? I mean, look over there. Either I'm nuts or there's more of those glowing spheres, the same ones up in Echo's apartment. That means those things were advanced enough thousands of years ago to have electricity."

"And where the hell is all this light coming from?" Todd looked at the ceiling. "Those spheres are nowhere bright enough to light up the whole city."

"How is it we know nothing about them? How can a society just get erased from the history books?"

"You have heard about them," Elaine said. "They built these cities a long time ago, back when they were in control. There was a time when the people around here called them gods. The lizards taught them things – how to farm, write, forge steel. Stuff like that. They're all over the Bible. Of course, most of the stuff about them was taken out once the Canon was set."

Jessica squinted her eyes. "Are you talking about angels?"

When he didn't hear an answer, David looked over at Elaine. She was nodding. Then she stopped. "If you have questions, ask Wisdom. There are things I'm not at liberty to discuss with you Anomalies."

"Why do you talk to me like that? The way you call me an Anomaly makes it sound like I'm not even human. I told you, I'm not a monster. I am just as human as you are. I can just do stuff."

Elaine sniffed and shook her head. "Whatever gets you through the night."

"Goddamn it! Why do you all think I'm not human? I'm not the spawn of Satan! I have a mother and a father, you know."

Again, Elaine shook her head. When she finally spoke again, it was the last thing he expected to hear. "When Wisdom gets back, ask him about your parents. You don't know as much as you think."

Chapter Twenty-One

After they found the supplies, they settled into one of the abandoned houses. A cursory look at the provisions confirmed there was enough food and water to keep the four of them alive for months.

David found a corner and ate a quick meal of dried fruit and canned beans. The silence and the sore muscles began to work on him. Despite the dirt floors and the stale air in the ancient underground city, he felt exhausted. He leaned his head back. The second he touched the wall, his mind went somewhere else.

***

Once again he stood on the rooftop. He watched the Edimmu city burn, smoke rising to the stone ceiling. Inhuman screams rang out in all directions. A guttural whisper, both intangible and irresistible, filled the air. Something was in the shadows, swarming the city and killing Edimmu.

With a jerky abruptness, the vision changed. The flames died out, revealing a different horror. Lines of Edimmu, shackled and yoked together, marched in tight formation through the streets toward turbulent ovals of darkness. The ovals swirled like black holes; stripes of bright blue light clearly defined eddies and ridges within them. The Edimmu walked, heads lowered, into the black portal. They didn't reappear on the other side. They were simply gone. Soon the last of the Edimmu disappeared into the darkness.

And the streets of the city were empty.

David heard the whimper of the abandoned metropolis. It screamed for vengeance.

Then he was flying. His mind pulled off the roof and into the darkness. He stood before a mirror, seeing not himself but the body of an Edimmu. Then he flew into the mirror, through it to the other side.

He floated above cages and enclosed pens filled with Edimmu. All around the cages, vaguely-humanoid shapes moved. Many were masses of viscous pus, abscessed flesh and bleeding sores that bore no similarity at all to humans. Some had tentacles that flapped in the air. Others were hideously misshapen dwarves. At least one, in the distance appeared to be a mutated Tyrannosaurus Rex with vestigial wings. There were several thousands of them, hundreds of thousands stretching in every direction.

And at the middle of the place, just on the horizon, was a large body of black water. A Black Sea.

"It is called the Axeinus," a voice nearby said. David whirled to see who was talking to him. He nearly screamed, but was stunned into silence when he saw the source. An Edimmu. Age sat heavy upon the reptoid who, although hairless, gave the impression of being gray. He was dressed in flowing red robes that hid most of his body.

"This is where they held us," the Edimmu said. "After the fall of Atlantis, they were gone from the world for a time. When they returned, they sought a new work force. They found us. We remained their slaves for three hundred years. Then Propates found us. He rescued us. He's our savior. He could be your savior, too. If you stop fighting, we can teach you many things. If you continue to fight, you and the Anomalies will end up just as we did. Slaves to a dark power."

"I will not be a slave," David said.

The Edimmu reached out and touched David's face. "Child, you already are one."

***

David woke, leaping away from the wall.

'Was that real?' He stood, moving silently to not wake the others. Jessica and Todd had nodded off nearby. 'It felt stronger than last time. Clearer. If what I saw was real, maybe the Edimmu aren't the real enemy. Maybe what we need to be worried about are the creatures on the other side of the mirror. The things that live in the Axeinus.'

Elaine stood in the hallway looking out through a large open window. She scanned the empty streets, hands on the submachine gun. She didn't turn around as he approached, but when she spoke it was apparent she knew exactly where he was.

"You should still be sleeping. Your injuries are just as bad as the others'."

"I feel okay," David stopped beside her and looked out the window. "Looks like I heal fast, too. Besides, I don't sleep much. Never have. Too many bad dreams. Not the kind you talk about."

"Makes sense. Wisdom thinks one of your EFHBs is psychometry. It means you can feel things by touching them. This place must be wreaking havoc on you. Bad things happened here. What did you see?"

David shifted on his feet. "Edimmu. They were taken away, enslaved by shadowy monsters. It felt so real."

Elaine looked at him briefly out of the corner of her eye. She let her eyes drop down the front of his body until they reached his abdomen. She smiled.

David's face turned completely red. Suddenly, it was very hard for him to breathe. In the dim light, he found her suddenly beautiful. Involuntarily, he took a step closer to her.

Elaine went deathly pale. "Oh God." She turned away from David quickly, her voice dropping to a whisper. "Goddamn you, Wisdom. Please tell me I didn't..."

David frowned. "Didn't do what?" He wanted to tell her how beautiful she looked, how he envied her strength, but his instinct told him to stay quiet. He took another step toward her.

Elaine leaned against the wall, a genuine sparkle in her eyes. "Nothing," she said. "Forget I said anything. I should sleep." She turned from the window and slid her back down the wall until she was sitting on the floor. "Do me a favor? Just stay awake for the next little bit. Wake me the second you see or feel anything strange."

David stared down at her. She raised her head, smiled and winked her left eye.

'What the hell was that all about?' He shook his head and left Elaine. He heard a cough and a curse from the nearby room. He walked briskly down the hall and arrived in time to see Todd help Jessica to her feet. There was blood on her lower lip.

"I don't know about this." Todd looked at Jessica with wide wet eyes. His face was pale and, despite the cool air, he was sweating profusely.

"You don't have to 'know' anything. Besides, Ms. Ryerson put me in charge. That means you have to do what I say, right? So stop being a baby and just do it already."

"God! How did you get to be such a witch?" Todd grunted as he helped Jessica move to the center of the room. His voice, though still a sort of whisper, was much harsher now than it had been. "Ms. Ryerson put you in charge for like ten minutes. Elaine's here now. As far as I am concerned, that means she's in charge. Let's run it by her before...."

"We don't have time for that. I told you. Twice. I'm bleeding inside. If I don't stop it, all my blood is going to end up in my stomach or someplace like that. If I don't have any in my veins, I'll die, right? So you've got to close up my wounds with your PK. I'll mind-link with you, tell you what to do. It'll be that simple. I'd do it myself if I could, but you have way more control and finesse than me. Don't smile like that. It doesn't mean anything. Not really. And don't even say what you are thinking because I can tell what you're thinking and it's not something you should ever say to me. Ever."

David felt his eyes go wide. Any second now he expected her to say 'I'll tell my mother on you.'

"Don't you start, Mr. Ross," Jessica said. "I can hear your thoughts, too. Would you like me to tell Elaine you want to sleep with her?"

"Hey! I never said that."

"Don't worry," she said. "I won't say anything. Sadly, I think she wants to sleep with you, too. Adults are just ridiculous. Now if Todd here doesn't stop being so Todd-like and do what I'm telling him to do, I won't be able to say much of anything much longer."

Todd frowned. "What does that mean, 'so Todd-like'?"

Jessica coughed. More blood came to her lips. Todd became even paler. "You know, you're right, Todd," she said. "Maybe if you just whine enough, my internal bleeding will stop. Now get over here and help me get this shirt off."

Todd hesitated a moment longer, then walked over to Jessica. He slipped the tattered shirt over her dislocated shoulder and off her body. Seeing such serious wounds on such a small body reminded him of made-for-TV movies about child abuse. What kind of person was Wisdom that he could put someone so young in a position like this?

"Jesus," Todd said. "You're nothing but bruises. I'm afraid to touch you anywhere." He handed the torn shirt back to Jessica. She grabbed it like a towel in her left hand and used it to wipe sweat from her forehead.

"Is it the bruises or are you just afraid to get more blood on your delicate hands? Besides, who said anything about touching me? Keep your hands to yourself. Just hold them out. Yeah, that's right. Point them at me. It will help direct the power."

"What if I use too much power? I could snap something by mistake. This is too dangerous."

"It's not as dangerous as doing nothing. I'll let you know how much to use. We're mind-linking, remember?"

"At least lie down. What if you slip?"

"If I lie down you won't be able to move the bones the way you need to. You could end up pushing a bone down into the floor instead of back into place."

"Fine. Just don't blame me if this goes badly."

David felt a buzzing in his head, like a television turned on playing only static. He pressed the heels of his palms against his temples, trying to block out the sound. Black spots flew past his eyes and he felt nauseous.

"Go," Jessica, said. "Now just like in class, let me into your mental activity. Release that thought pattern. It's creating interference."

A moment later, the buzzing in David's head relaxed. He let his hands drop from his temples.

"That's better," Jessica said. "Can you feel me in your head now? Don't use words, just think, okay? You can feel my pain now, too, right? Let's start with that rib that's poking into something or other. No, I don't know what that organ is called. Does it matter? Just grab hold of it with your PK and put it back into place. Let me guide you."

David held his breath. There was a long period of silence. Then Jessica moaned. David caught her before she had dropped more than a few inches.

"Not. So. Hard."

Todd helped her back to her feet and they stared into each other's eyes. The buzzing returned and grew progressively louder in David's head. He felt like he was going to pass out soon, himself.

"What the hell are you doing?" David moaned.

"Not now." Todd stood, arms outstretched, fingertips hovering a few inches away from Jessica's skin.

Jessica clamped her hands over her mouth, stifling the scream. She was crying freely now. When her hands fell away, her teeth were bared and covered with blood.

"That hurt," she said.

"I did what you told me to," Todd said. His voice had the tonal quality of a dog that has been whipped.

"I know. It still hurt. Just one more. Please be quick. I think I'm going to pee my pants."

"I think you already did, sweetie. Hold on."

Jessica threw back her head, her mouth opened in a silent scream. Her eyes rolled back until all you could see was their whites. David grabbed her by the shoulders and helped keep her on her feet. The buzzing in his head was so loud now his vision blurred. He hoped, whatever Todd was doing, he got it finished quickly.

As suddenly as it began, the buzzing stopped. It left behind a very sharp headache. All of his muscles felt sore, as if he had run a marathon.

Jessica's legs finally gave out underneath her. David lowered her gently to the floor. Her lower lip trembled and her tiny limbs shook as she sobbed silently.

"What did you do to her?" David stroked Jessica's forehead. Her skin was almost too hot to touch and she was covered in oily sweat.

"I couldn't have done it on my own. She used me in a way. Used my power to lift a couple of bones back into place. Then she, or we I guess, fused the torn flesh together. It was kind of like pushing pieces of wet dough together until they form a whole piece. I felt everything she felt. I don't think, hell, I know there is no way I could have put up with it. Whatever I felt, she felt it a hundred times worse. But she never lost control of her power. Not once."

"That must be why Ms. Ryerson put her in charge."

They jumped at the voice. As David spun, lines of fire danced on his fingertips. Then he relaxed and the flames disappeared. She was only a few feet away, arms folded across her chest. The machine gun hung at her side. Her face seemed as cold and solid as the gun.

"That was a stupid risk." Elaine sighed, turned and walked back to wherever she had come from. "All that power you used, even I felt it. Any Edimmu within a few miles would have as well, let alone anything worse. Now get some sleep. I think we've all had enough excitement for one day."

Chapter Twenty-Two

Echo opened her eyes to the darkness. Surprisingly, she was still alive. It took her several moments to remember exactly what had happened. Memory hit her about the same time her eyes adjusted to the dark.

"I'm back on the island," she said aloud. She pushed herself up and looked around. "Damn you, Propates."

After sending Elaine away with the Anomalies, she had made her way to her bedroom. Propates was there, seated at her vanity, flipping through her most recent diary. When she entered the room, he looked up and smiled.

"Really charming the way you describe me in here, Andromeda. Sorry, sorry, I forgot. Echo. I had no idea you still held a torch for me. I thought we quenched that flame in Jerusalem."

"We did. Chalk it up to too much wine."

Propates closed the book and stared at the cover. "It doesn't have to end this way."

Echo flicked her wrist and her diary flew out of his hands. "You know there are about four hundred and fifty ways I hate you. Don't you think you should stop while you're ahead? You come in here, destroy another of my favorite homes, kill my servants and kidnap a bunch of kids I'm supposed to be taking care of, and now this? But reading my diary? You must have a death wish."

The shadows in the room swirled and collected in the corners with implications of something fluttering in their depths.

"I'm starting to think you're the one with the death wish." He rose to his feet and the shadows stretched out toward him. "I warned you to stay out of this. You chose differently. I didn't want to do this but I have no choice."

Echo prepared to respond but never got the chance. A bullet of shadow shot at her and sliced through her shoulder. Before she could scream in pain, another piece of darkness sliced through the air. Then another. And another. She turned in circles, trying to anticipate each new attack, failing each time. Within a minute, every inch of her skin was covered in blood. She opened a circle of light and prepared to jump.

"Tsk tsk," Propates said. "Not so fast. " He blew a kiss at the portal. Shadows poured out of the corners and recesses of the room, filling the portal, blocking her exit. "Can't let you get away this time, pet. Bad example and all. This should send the kind of message that even Wisdom can't ignore."

The bullets of shadow were larger now, foot-long jagged shards. They sliced through her skin like shears through rose petals. The pain grew to a numbing heat.

'Move quickly or die,' she thought. Then she couldn't think. In the end it was instinct and luck that saved her. A little trick, really. A simple thing. The underground tunnels were lined with a psycho-luminescent mineral that was the source of the ever-present light. It reacted to the presence of sentient life and hummed with soft light. Echo understood the reaction, if not the chemistry behind it. Her will provided the energy for the light, so she funneled as much as she dared into the ceiling. Bright light flashed from corner to corner, melting the shadow weapons in mid-air. Propates took a step toward her, cockiness replaced by fury. Before he could react, she opened a second circle of light below her and let her body fall.

Now on her island, Echo took several deep breaths and cleared her mind. Then, for the first time in a decade, she sobbed hysterically.

'He would have killed me,' she thought. After the fit passed, she walked to the bathroom, paying no attention to the bloody footprints she left behind her. She healed herself, closing the wounds. She didn't feel clean, however, until she showered off the blood. She stayed under the spray until the water ran cold. Then she wrapped a robe around her trembling muscles and walked to the kitchen.

The house was empty now. Annisa and Roma's bodies lay somewhere in the rubble back in Turkey. She rummaged through the cupboards for canned goods, allowing herself a moment of fantasy. Maybe they really were all dead. Maybe Elaine had failed and the Anomalies had fallen to the Edimmu. Maybe even Wisdom had got himself killed. Then she would be free.

As much as she would have liked to believe that, she knew it was not true. She felt it.

She ate a sparse meal of mushroom soup and chocolate ice cream and turned her mind to other things. Even from literally the other side of the world, she could feel Propates back in his squalid little Grecian encampment.

'Why didn't he follow me?' She scratched her chin and stared at the ceiling. 'Maybe he's giving me one last chance to stay out of this. If I was smart that's exactly what I'd do. But Elaine and the Anomalies are waiting for me to rescue them. This is the last thing I'm doing. Then I'm done.'

Leaving the dirty dishes in the sink, she opened another gateway.

"You owe me one for this, Wisdom."

***

David screamed at the flash of light and nearly pissed his pants again. It was not until Echo stepped through the portal that he started to breathe again.

"Where the hell have you been?" he said.

Echo raised her eyebrows and lifted her hand as if to smack him upside the head. Instead, she waved her hand at the portal. It disappeared as quickly as it had come.

"Way to show your gratitude, David." Elaine walked toward Echo. "Forgive the pretty body. He's an idiot. Glad to see you made it. We were worried."

"I'm sure you were. Let's get out of this dead city. The sooner I hand you back to Wisdom, the better. I want nothing more to do with this whole fiasco."

"What about the other Anomalies?" Todd grimaced as

some inner pain racked through his body. "We have to rescue them or something. We can't leave them with Propates."

"Not my concern," Echo said. "Not even on my radar. Wisdom created this mess. He can fix it."

"Wisdom had an errand to run," Elaine squared her shoulders. "I don't think we should take his not being here as a bad thing. I'm sure he'll show up as soon as he can. When he does, we'll make a plan to get them back."

"How do you know he's not back already?"

"Jessica says she can't feel him. And like I said, he expected to be away for quite some time."

"And I take it you're not at liberty to discuss his little mission, are you?" Echo bit her tongue and shook her head. "Typical. That man is never here when I need him. I don't know why I keep expecting that will change."

"You're more important to him than you realize, Echo." Elaine cleared her throat and put a hand on Echo's shoulder.

Echo's shoulders slumped and she sighed. "Let's get the four of you someplace safe. When Wisdom wants to find us, he will."

Echo flicked her wrist again and the portal reappeared. David let Jessica and Todd go first. He motioned for Elaine to follow them. She rolled her eyes and pointed him forward by jutting forth her chin.

On the other side of the portal, he closed his eyes to shake off the afterimages of bright light that stained his retinas. To his left, something roared. He opened his eyes and slowly realized what the sound was: ocean waves crashing against a beach.

Eyes wide, he walked past Todd and Jessica to the open-air windows. He took a deep breath of the salty air. Although Dartmouth never got this warm, the scent reminded him of home. Sweat poured freely down the back of his neck and ran in a steady drizzle from his armpits to his elbows.

"Glad to feel moisture again," he said. "I felt like I was drinking sand the whole time we were underground."

"Nice, isn't it?" Echo handed him a glass of ice with a little iced tea thrown in for color. He drank it down quickly, convinced it was the best iced tea he had ever tasted. Then he put the glass against his cheek. He could almost see steam rising up from where it caressed his hot flesh.

"It's paradise," he replied. She smiled in response and put a comforting hand on his elbow. Then she handed out drinks to the others. David turned back to watch the waves crash against the beach and listened to the conversations around him.

"What's wrong with him?" Echo's voice was throaty and solid, full of command. Jessica rattled off a list of various injuries. Several times Todd tried to speak for himself, saying that Jessica was the one who needed to be looked after, but she kept shushing him.

The windows looked out over a wooden porch to the high crescent moon and millions of stars. It was bright enough for him to see fairly far. At the right end of the porch, a staircase ran down to a ten-foot wide patch of grass. At the edge of the grass, greenery gave way to clean white sand. He looked up and down the beach. It went on as far as he could see to left and right. Off to the left he also saw a patch of forest with a thin strip of grass separating it from the sand. A breeze blew over his face and dried the perspiration on his cheek.

'I have no idea where in the world I am,' he thought. 'My life is so completely crazy. Earlier today I saw psychic surgery in an underground city built by reptilians. Now I'm standing at the edge of an unknown ocean. I barely know these people. Hell, I don't even know their last names. Home feels incredibly far away.'

He lifted the glass to his lips. The ice cubes were melting and he drank the build-up of water collecting in the glass. 'Strange to think I just left Dartmouth a few weeks ago. Wonder how Mom's doing. Is she even trying to look for me? Probably not. She probably hopes I disappear until the police close the case.'

His third murder.

It was easy to forget he was a killer. Sometimes he went an entire day without the thought popping into his head. Then a piece of an overheard conversation or a stray fragrance would take him back. He would smell the burning flesh; hear the screams of the gaggle of kids across the street. Worst of all was when he remembered the feeling, the satisfaction he felt as Dane Houghton rolled around on the grass trying to smother the fire that ate him alive.

Thinking back, David fought to keep his lips from curling back into the same smile he had worn as he had stared past the orange and blue flames to watch flesh and bone melt. At the time, he had not even known the boy's name. He had heard it on the television hours after the boy had stopped struggling.

***

Dane Houghton was nobody, not in David's life anyway. He was a 16-year-old high school student with a part-time job delivering newspapers.

At 19 David graduated high school and took a job washing dishes at a fish and chips restaurant. It was ludicrously hot as he walked home that day in late July. He had changed his shirt after work, but it was hopeless; everything about him reeked of wet garbage. His hair was thick from the oily air in the kitchen. A pungent film coated his face and neck. So when the kid walked by and told him to take a shower, David wasn't feeling particularly charitable.

It was tempting to think it was temporary insanity, brush it off as a psychotic break. Only, he seemed incapable of fooling himself. As comforting as it would have been to believe otherwise, David was fully cognizant of his actions and the consequences of what he planned to do. He knew it was wrong, but he didn't care. The voice of reason told him he should just ignore the thin brown-haired kid. After all,

David was the adult now. The most he should have done was tell the kid to screw off. Instead, he turned, slowly, and snapped his fingers.

Flame flashed over Dane's t-shirt and jeans. He waved his arms around, dropped his bundle of newspapers before any of them caught fire, and then threw himself on the ground. It was only then that David saw the group of kids getting off the bus. The kids who pointed and screamed. The bus driver got out and pushed all the children back on the bus. David barely paid attention to them. He kept his eyes on the burning body, the boy he set on fire.

The boy he killed for telling him to take a shower.

***

"I'm not a monster." He looked at the glass in his hands and set it down. He felt sick to his stomach. The smell of burning flesh was thick in his nostrils.

"Did you say something?"

He looked over his shoulder. Echo was just putting the phone back in the cradle. He had not heard her speaking on the phone. He realized he had been staring out at the sea for longer than he had intended. He walked over to one of the beige chairs in the living room and sat down before his legs gave out beneath him. "Nothing," he said. "Just talking to myself."

She shrugged her shoulders and walked out of the room.

***

He woke up to the smell of food. He didn't remember falling asleep in the chair. It wasn't like him to nod off like that, but he did feel better now.

Jessica and Todd were playing cards at a circular table between the living room and the kitchen. Both seemed stronger, somehow. It took several moments before David realized they were no longer covered in bruises. Jessica's shoulder bone was back inside the flesh. He felt the back of his head and looked over his own body. Except for the remnants of dried blood on his skin, none of his wounds were visible. It appeared Echo was a talented healer after all. Hearing muffled talking, he searched for the source. Elaine sat at a mahogany desk at the far end of the living room with a phone to one ear. She was writing notes with her right hand, her voice rising occasionally in angry tones. David stood up and walked over to his classmates.

"What's going on?"

Todd placed a seven of diamonds over a seven of clubs in a pile of cards on the table. "Crazy eights. Echo took off again. I think Elaine's calling Wisdom's offices around the world trying to track him down."

"I hate you!" Jessica kicked a leg of the table and picked up a card from the turned-over pile. "Shoot. I can't go. Are you happy?"

Todd smiled and laid down a three of diamonds. "Very happy. Do you want to play, David?"

"No thanks," he sat down at one of the other two chairs around the round table. "Isn't this kind of unfair? I mean, with you guys being psychic and all? Can't you tell what the other one is going to play?"

Jessica rolled her eyes and picked up another card. "It wouldn't be much fun if we did that, now, would it? Besides, all we would have to do is think of a whole bunch of cards we don't have and it would throw off the other person. Even if I tried to cheat, I know Todd well enough to realize he wouldn't think about the cards he really has in his hands."

"You know me that well, huh?" Todd laid down a two of diamonds. Jessica kicked the table leg again and picked up two more cards. "Echo rounded up a few servants somehow. A few of them are cooking supper for us. She said she'd be back by the time we're on dessert."

"Damn!"

They all looked away from the table and stared at Elaine. She had slammed a fist against the wooden desk so hard David was sure the desk was cracked somewhere. She was no longer on the phone. He was about to ask her a question when she got up from the desk and walked over to them.

"There was an attack at the London offices," Elaine said. She moved toward the remaining chair, then decided against it. She paced back and forth between the mahogany desk and the table. "Not an Edimmu, they say, but definitely not human. It killed twenty-seven guards and almost got Garnet, Jared and the new guy."

"What new guy?" Jessica put down the eight of clubs and mouthed the word 'Spades'. Her face broke out in a smug little smile. In response, Todd stuck his tongue out at her.

"Another Anomaly Wisdom picked up. That's not important right now. Where the hell is Echo?"

Todd shook his head and laid down a five of spades. Before his hand was fully withdrawn, Jessica laid down the Queen of Spades and started laughing. "Burn, baby!"

"Can you stop the damn card game?" Elaine stopped pacing and put her hands on her hips. "People died, remember? Garnet could be next if we don't get her out of there."

Todd raised his eyebrows and scratched his scalp. Then he started picking up a series of cards from the deck. "Garnet can take care of herself, remember? You said the same thing to me about two months ago when we had that conversation about her wardrobe."

Jessica put her cards down and looked back and forth between Todd and Elaine. "You had a conversation about the clothes she wears?"

"No, we didn't." Elaine pointed a finger at Todd. "We had no such conversation, understand? And I know she can take care of herself. This is different. People died. I should have been there instead of...whatever." She sat down at the fourth chair, resting her elbows on the table.. "I can't believe this is happening. I should have retired by now. Where the hell is Echo?"

She got up from the table and started pacing again.

A woman with light brown skin walked out of the kitchen. She was dressed in a blue blouse with a white skirt that hung to her knees. She was lightly tanned and blond. Seeing her reminded David of Annisa and Roma and what their absence meant.

"Supper is ready," the servant said. She glared at them, taking in the large patches of dried blood and dirt marks over their skin and clothes. "You may want to freshen up first. The bathroom is down the hall to the left." When she said "you may want to freshen up" she lowered her head and stared each of them squarely in the eyes. The way she said it did not sound like a suggestion. Even though he was not hungry and had no intention of eating, David was on his feet quickly. Jessica and Todd both laid their cards down and headed toward the bathrooms as well. Even Elaine stood in line to wash her face and hands.

David surprised himself by eating two servings of the turkey and mashed potatoes. It reminded him of happy times, Christmas and Thanksgivings before he knew he was different. Before his parents realized he was different. He drank a few glasses of white wine and ended up in a conversation with Todd about which Radiohead album was the best. Jessica asked for wine once. The servant, Courtney, put a glass of apple juice in front of her. Then she stood, arms crossed, waiting for Jessica to say something else. Jessica stared back, but only for a moment. Then she said, "Thank you," and took a sip from the apple juice.

Elaine barely looked up from her plate. David tried to involve her in the conversation. When she admitted she did not know who Radiohead was, he realized it was hopeless. No matter how hard he tried, though, he could not keep his eyes from straying over to her throughout the meal. He was glad she kept her eyes on her plate. He didn't want her to realize how often he stared at her.

When they finished talking about Radiohead, they talked movies. Not long after that, Courtney brought them each a plate of thick cherry cheesecake with hazelnut ice cream. As soon as she left the room, Jessica got up from her seat, walked over to Todd and picked up his 1/4 full wine glass. She lifted the glass to her lips and then froze when they all heard someone clear their throat. They turned to see Courtney standing in the doorway between the kitchen and the living room, arms crossed with one eyebrow raised. She stayed like that until Jessica, slowly, put the wine glass back in place and returned to her seat. Once Courtney disappeared into the kitchen, Todd and David broke out laughing. Elaine put her hand over her mouth, barely hiding the smile while she very studiously looked at the ceiling. Jessica did not look amused.

They were deep into a discussion about *The Lord of the Rings* when Echo walked in on them.

"Good," she said. "You look better. I've brought some company."

David stood as Garnet and Jared walked into the room. Behind them was someone he did not recognize, a blond man about his own age who walked with his hands in his pockets.

'That must be the new guy,' he thought.

"Hey, strangers." Garnet walked forward and put a hand on Elaine's shoulder. "You all look like hell. Where are the others?"

David's mouth fell open. It was like a mirror shattering, he thought. Just like that all the warmth and happiness fell into sharp shards and clattered noisily on the floor. Jessica dropped a forkful of cheesecake and got to her feet. She started to run but slowed herself, walking briskly out of the room and down to the bathroom.

"Oh," Garnet let the word out like a balloon deflating. "Little Amy. God." She spun and faced Echo. "Jesus, woman. You could have told us."

Echo shrugged her shoulders and sat down in Jessica's seat. "Wasn't my place. It was better for you to hear it from one of your own." She put the forkful of cheesecake in her mouth and spoke as she chewed on it. "Look, I hate to rush you and all, but you've got to decide where you want to go. Where you want to hide out until Wisdom resurfaces."

Garnet frowned. "Can't we stay here?"

"No," Echo ate another forkful of the cake and then pushed the plate away. "There's not enough room. And even if there was, I've been involved in this too long. I can't have the Council of Peacocks after me."

Garnet's face went red but she kept her silence.

Echo got up from the table. "Look, obviously you all have some talking to do. Catch each other up on what's been going on. I am going to make myself scarce but I'll be back again in the morning. Let me know then where you want to go and I'll drop you off. There's plenty of food and drink here. Be nice to Courtney, she's a doll really."

"Wait!" David stood up, his fork clattering against the plate. "You're really not going to help us? Those things could kill us. Don't you care?"

Echo waved her hand and a circle of light appeared. "I've already lost two homes because of this needless drama. Now I have to stay in this little shack until I can find a new home. I helped you because Wisdom asked me to. And as much as I hate to admit it, I owe him. But now it is too serious for me to stay in this little game. A suggestion, though? Elaine, I think it is time to stop with the whole secrecy thing. Normally, Wisdom would be upset with show and tell. Given the circumstances, I'm sure he'll understand."

She looked down at the plate of cheesecake as if deliberating. Then she picked up the plate and fork and walked over to the portal. "You all enjoy your evening. Do your best not to use any of your powers and I can pretty well guarantee the Edimmu won't track you here. You'll be safe for now. See you in the morning."

With that, she stepped into the portal and was gone.

David sat down slowly and stared at his plate. Once again he had lost his appetite.

***

For several minutes no one said anything, locked in their own heads. Then, Jessica walked back into the room. Her eyes were red, but she had her chin firmly out and her jaw set. She did not sit back at the table. Instead, she found a beige over-stuffed chair and sat with her arms crossed.

It was Elaine who broke the silence.

"Tell me what happened in London."

They all left the dining table and moved into the living room proper. Josh introduced himself, which led into the story of his kidnapping and how Wisdom had rescued him. Garnet took up the story at this point, using security jargon that only Elaine seemed to understand. She then told everyone about the attack in London and how they managed to escape it alive. When she finished, Todd and Elaine took turns relaying how Echo had rescued them during the initial Edimmu attack in Toronto and the events in the underground apartment. Neither of them talked at length about Bethany, Amy or any of the other Anomalies, saying only that they had been killed or stolen by shadows. David was thankful no one pressed for any more details.

Their stories finished, they all sank into silence, breathing air that sat heavily in their lungs. David wished he had not drunk the wine.

"So what now?" Josh said. "Does Wisdom have any secret hideouts? Some place we'll be safe?"

Elaine nodded. "He's got tons. Only problem is they *are* secret. I have no idea where they are. I only know of the offices he has around the world. We could go to any of them, but we'd have to assume that the Council knows all about them."

Josh leaned back. "So what exactly is this Council?"

"Yeah!" David leaned forward. "Echo's right about one thing. Stop playing around with the whole secret society crap. Let's lay it all on the line. What the hell is going on?"

Suddenly a crack of thunder shot through the room and the lights went out. David held his breath. There was a buzzing in his head, persistent but not painful this time.

Lightning flashed outside, slamming and slicing into the ocean. Garnet found some candles and lit them each by touching the wick. Wind blew in strongly off the ocean, making the flames flicker, casting strange shadows around the room. David wished she would put the candles out.

"That was just a coincidence, right?" Todd rubbed his hands together, twisting in his seat as if trying to get comfortable.

"Of course not," Jessica was on her feet now. "I know you can feel it, too, so let's stop pretending. Something is out there. I just don't know what it is."

She squinted her eyes and stared out at the lightning. In the candlelight, it was hard to make out the expression on her face. David stared at her. Lightning flashed again and he got a clear look at her face. It was frozen in horror.

"Oh my God! Wisdom!"

Even as she screamed, a dark shape flew in from the ocean and slammed against the side of the house. Jessica ran forward. Even though Todd tried to grab her and keep her back, she climbed out through the open window and dropped out of sight. Elaine followed, a blur of motion, and leapt headfirst out the window. Heart pounding in his throat, David walked with the others to the window and looked down. In the flashes of light he saw a body in mangled red clothes lying on the grass at the foot of the house. Jessica knelt at the body's head, stroking it while Elaine held two fingers against the man's neck.

"It can't be." Garnet put her hands against the side of her head. She looked like she was about to start screaming.

David looked at the body again. In the dark it was impossible to make out anything. He stared where he knew the head was and waited for the next flash of lightning. When it came, he recognized the features.

"David, come on!" Garnet yelled. "You have to help. Elaine is motioning us to go down. I don't think Wisdom's dead. Not yet anyway. Come on!"

Chapter Twenty-Three

"Is that the last of them?" Propates rubbed the back of his neck and cursed under his breath. A cloud was forming in his head. Since the Orpheans had invaded his bathroom, he couldn't shake the sensation he was being watched. Coupled with the annoyance of letting Echo slip through his fingers, his concentration was paying the price.

"Yes, sir," the acolyte said as he shut the door to the cell. They were moving from room to room in the subbasement of the Thessaloniki headquarters checking on the kidnapped Anomalies. Behind locked doors, drugs kept them sedated, nearly comatose. "We took 35 of them alive. We believe three are hiding somewhere in the old Edimmu city. Several were killed during retraction."

Propates sighed. "I would have preferred more but we have enough to move forward."

"This also proves Wisdom doesn't know what we're planning."

"Do you stuff your head with paper? Of course Wisdom knows what we're planning. He's traveling through time, idiot. He must have seen this coming."

"But if he saw it coming, if he knew you were going to take the Anomalies, why wasn't he there to stop you?"

"Now that is a good question." Propates closed his eyes and put a hand against the wall. A shiver ran through him – an echo at the bottom of his awareness. It called to him, willing him to go to the Vulture Antechamber. "Retraction was easy. Too easy, especially considering how much trouble Paeder faced trying to retract just one Anomaly. If you knew Wisdom like I do, you would realize he's not one to give up. He let me have these Anomalies for a reason. I just need to figure out what that reason is."

"Are we sending a team to retrieve the others?"

"No." Propates shook his head. "A storm is brewing out there, spreading all across the ether."

"Is it the Activation?" The acolyte said the word 'Activation' with reverence and fear.

"Of course not. That's still months away. But time moves quickly. Have the ceremonial chamber and the tattoo artists prepped within the hour. I want all these Anomalies taken through the first phase of Eyeness by this time tomorrow."

The acolyte nodded, bowed and scampered off. Propates steeled his nerves and headed for the Vulture Antechamber.

***

"We have to get him upstairs," Elaine said. "Spare room."

Josh nodded. "I know where it is." He grabbed Wisdom's ankles while Elaine took the shoulders. They carried him up wooden steps. Before they reached the top, Josh's hands and arms were covered in warm blood, his shirt smeared.

They set him down on the queen-sized bed in the spare room. Josh grimaced as Wisdom's blood splattered the light flowery sheets and pillowcases. Garnet pushed Josh aside and helped Elaine strip the remnants of the mangled suit from Wisdom's body. He looked away. In the dark it was difficult to tell the flaps of cloth from flaps of loose skin.

"Go," Elaine said over her shoulder.

He knew the remark was aimed at him. He left the room. The door closed firmly behind him. For a moment he stood completely still. His head buzzed with too many thoughts.

'Where will we go if Wisdom dies?' His chest constricted and his heart pounded so fiercely it was difficult to breathe. 'How long would it be before the Council of Peacocks and their Edimmu henchmen finally captured the rest of us? I don't think I could take being captured again.'

"Stop it," he whispered. He forced himself to take deep breaths, panting like a woman in labor. Josh pushed himself to his feet and steadied his nerves. Careful to avoid the red, wet smudges of blood on the steps, he walked downstairs and looked around the living room.

In the candlelight the group of strangers looked intimidating. He heard something dripping and realized it was him. Wisdom's blood fell from his hands and torso, creating tiny puddles around him. A quick look at the light beige furniture told him it was not safe to sit anywhere, at least not until after a thorough shower. Aware that everyone was watching him, he walked over to the only other person in the room he knew. Jared sat at a card table with an overweight brown-haired man and a prepubescent girl. His physical presence was a welcome moral support.

For the better part of an hour no one said anything. From time to time a maternal-looking blond woman entered from the kitchen with hors d'oeurves and glasses of iced tea. No one ate and most barely drank. Then the door to the spare room opened and Garnet walked down to the bottom of the stairs. Although she was not crying, her eyes were completely bloodshot and her lower lip trembled. The maternal servant, Courtney, walked over to Garnet and spoke in a low voice Josh could not hear. Garnet slowly nodded her head, then straightened her blouse and walked into the living room.

"He'll live," she said. "His wounds are healing remarkably quickly. He hasn't woken up yet. There's no way to tell when he will."

"Let's let him sleep tonight." This came from Elaine, who stood at the top of the stairs. Several people jumped as she spoke. Even Josh had not heard her approach. "He should be fine by then."

"What happened to him?" Jessica sat on the edge of a chair, her hands close to her mouth as if she was going to bite her nails. Then she looked at the hands, closed her mouth and put them firmly on the sides of the chair.

"I think that would be best left for him to say." Elaine rubbed the back of her neck, turned and headed back into the spare room.

***

David's eyes settled on Elaine as she appeared. He wanted her to look at him but she did not. She seemed to peruse everything in the room except him. Bags seemed to grow suddenly under her eyes, although it was more likely David had decided not to see them until that moment. He wanted to comfort her. The realization made him cringe.

'That's a joke,' he thought. 'Me comfort her? She's far more confident and powerful than I'll ever be.'

He shook his head and walked quickly to the window. He needed to feel the breeze against his skin. He crossed his arms and hung his head. He was not aware that he was crying until the tears hit his lips.

He felt a hand on his shoulder.

"It's okay. You've had a rough few days, haven't you?"

Garnet.

He wanted to open his eyes, to see a friendly face, but keeping his eyes closed was the only thing preventing his tears from flowing freely. Any hope he had of maintaining a degree of masculinity was gone now. Even Jessica, the child, had shown the grace to leave the room for her breakdown. Knowing he was outclassed by a 12-year-old was bad enough. Realizing that everyone was watching his breakdown made it all the worse.

Violently, he wiped his eyes with his palms.

"Thanks." He felt like sinking into the floor. He looked back out the window. The storm still sporadically lit up the waters in the distance, but the thunder seemed very far away. It did not seem to be raining, either on shore or where the lightning fell. Still, some summer storms were like that, even back home. Sometimes it was just the heat and the humidity in the air that brought the storms on. No reason to think it was anything different. Only, it felt different. Maybe something had caused the storm. Maybe, on some level, that something was Wisdom.

He shook his head and covered his eyes. 'I have no idea what's going on. I'm surrounded by members of a secret club, strangers who refuse to tell me what's really going on. Not that it would do me any good. I can't even deal with what little I know. I'm a murderer. A freak. Even if I leave Wisdom's circle of freaks, I can never go back home. I'm totally trapped.'

***

The Vulture Antechamber was dark, lit only by burning embers in incense braziers around the room. At first glance the chamber was deserted. Then Propates saw the whisper of a man hanging in the air.

The agent from away.

"Why are you here?" Propates disliked this man. He knew he was an alien, a creature from a planet far away. The fact that he so closely resembled a human disturbed him. It hinted at a common ancestry he could not explain. "Have you acquired the Miscellany?"

"No," the agent from away said. "But I know where it is now. I'm assembling a party to retrieve it. We leave within the week. But that's not why I'm here. I was contacted by the Djinnistani."

"What did he want?" Propates shifted on his feet.

"He was injured. He needs to retreat to the Kaz for a few days, but he wanted to pass along a message. He fought Wisdom and Wisdom won. Don't let your chin hit the floor, Propates. I need you to concentrate. Wisdom is more powerful than his father expected, which means he's probably more powerful than you suspect. The Djinnistani also wants you to know Wisdom claims he killed his father in the future. If that happens…."

Propates' headache was much worse now. He felt faint. "If that happens, all our plans might be for naught. I can't let that happen. I'm not going to let the world be destroyed simply because Wisdom doesn't know when to lie down and die."

Chapter Twenty-Four

Josh knew things were moving too quickly. He clenched and unclenched his hands repeatedly as he scanned the room. He did not know these people, did not know who to trust. God, he could not even tell which ones were human and which were things like Wisdom. He wished his father was there. He would know what to do.

The sudden emptiness in his chest made him realize it was the first time in almost a week that he had thought of his father and the rest of his family. Jan. How was she coping? Had she recovered from the horror of the Laurentians? What did she tell her parents? And what about Matt? Was the damage to his knees permanent? How was he dealing with Tonia's death?

But of all the questions that ran through his mind, the worst was: 'Will I ever find out one way or the other?'

By now, his father would have scores of CSIS agents looking for him. Nothing was more important than family to Richard Wilkinson. His father was a tall man with the well-groomed look of a Mormon. But behind his eyes, visible now that Josh knew what to look for, was a cold strength. They never talked about the work his father did, but from time to time Josh caught fragments of regret and rage coming off him in waves. Richard Wilkinson knew things about the world. He'd seen things other people were never forced to see. That knowledge was the reason he had trained Josh.

"I'm heading to the washroom," he told Elaine.

"I think Todd's in there." She watched him with a cold look that reminded him of his father. "I hear you took out a demon unarmed and by yourself?"

Josh swallowed hard. "Guess I'm just lucky."

Elaine nodded, a vacant look on her face. "There's more to you than meets the eye. I think we need to find out what that is. I know you don't remember how you killed the Edimmu, but that type of amnesia is a luxury we can no longer afford. Can't say I blame you. About the not wanting to remember thing. There are several things in my head I wish I could forget. Like my brother. He was like you, an Anomaly. The Council took him. It's how I met Wisdom. Long story. Point is, we need you to remember what happened. Talk to Jessica. She can help."

Josh asked himself what his father would do in a situation like this. There was not much doubt about that. "Sure. Let's see what she can get me to remember."

***

Echo accepted the bowl of noodle soup with a smile. The Chinese man in the white uniform of a waiter reached out his hand, smiled and bowed, under the delusion he'd been paid and tipped well. He wouldn't realize he was short for hours. By then Echo would have faded back into the crowds.

She came to New York partially to hide in the crowds, but mostly to be reminded what civilization felt like. This affair with Wisdom and his Anomalies seemed to take up her whole life. Here amongst the noise and the carefully regulated chaos of Chinatown, the secret war seemed a million miles away.

She was halfway into her noodle soup when she felt the presence. She kept her eyes on the bowl, hoping to hide the fact that she was aware. She scanned the restaurant casually, her eyes brushing over the tables filled with smiling patrons all engaged in quiet conversation. The air was filled with scents: garlic and fish sauce, ginger and deep-fried batter. But there was something underneath it all. Something dark and subtle. Despite the well-spaced lights around the restaurant, there were still puddles of shadows. One in particular stood out. Near the swinging door that led to the kitchen, the door to the broom closet stood slightly ajar. Dropping all pretence, Echo stood and started walking toward it. From the shadows, inside the closet something glistened. A flash of gold. Echo stopped mid-step and looked over her shoulder, judging how long it would take her to make her escape.

Then, as clear as a bell, she heard a voice whisper from deep within the closet: "Found her," it said. "Tell the Djinnistani."

Echo bolted for the front door of the restaurant. She pushed it open too quickly, too forcefully. It shattered in a rain of glass. She was barely aware of the destruction in her wake. She was too focused on trying to think of somewhere else she could run.

***

Josh sat in a beige armchair and watched the others swirl around him. The power was still out. Garnet and Todd rearranged the candles in the room, making Josh the center of the light. Jessica took a wooden chair from the card table and sat opposite him. She slipped the elastic out of her hair, unraveling her ponytail so her blond hair fell loose around her face.

"It might help if you take your shoes off," she said.

"Why?"

She shrugged. "Don't know, really. It just always seems to work better if the other person has their shoes off. Actually, it works best when they wear as little as possible, but I don't want to see you naked, so don't do that."

"Okay." Josh bent down, suppressed a grin, and took off his shoes. She was a strange little girl. "Should I keep my socks on?"

She shrugged again. "Doesn't matter. Just let me know when you're ready."

Any other time, Josh would have found the little girl precocious. Under the circumstances, he found her a little frightening. He left his socks on and placed his shoes to the right so they were out of his way. As he settled back in his seat, he became aware of all the eyes on him. Garnet and

Todd sat nearby on the beige sofa, watching him expectantly. Elaine stood near the foot of the stairs at the edge of the living room. She would not stray too far from Wisdom, but she kept her eyes on Josh with an unblinking stare.

'It's like they're all getting ready to watch a movie,' he thought.

He nodded. "I'm ready."

"Good." Jessica squared her shoulders and let her hands rest on her legs, palms up. Then she closed her eyes. "Now, this is not like hypnosis. I'm not going to count you down from ten or whatever those guys do. It's more like I step inside your head and we walk around together."

"Have you ever done this before?"

Jessica opened her eyes. "Of course I have. I do it all the time. Just 'cause I'm a 'precocious little girl' doesn't mean I'm a newbie. Now, any more questions or can we actually get started?"

Josh cleared his throat. When was he going to learn to watch his thoughts around these people?

"If you must know," Jessica said, closing her eyes again. "I used to do this all the time with my big brother. It was like a game for us. At first, I thought I was just a good guesser. Then I told him I knew what our uncle did to him at the cottage. We stopped playing after that." She stopped talking and Josh felt his head grow heavy and distant, like he had ingested too much cold medication. Something was happening. Then there was a vibration in his head, almost as if he could hear something: a distant noise.

"I feel something," he said. "Is that you?"

"You're fighting me," Jessica said. Josh watched the way her face was scrunching up and looked to Garnet for a clue. He didn't know how he could be fighting something he did not understand.

"Close your eyes, Josh," Garnet said. "It'll help. Think about whatever you're trying to remember. If you don't concentrate, your mind will fill up with random thoughts. That will make it more difficult. For both of you."

Josh nodded and closed his eyes. It really was like fighting someone. If your mind was on anything outside the fight, you had a better chance of losing. He took a deep breath and concentrated. He thought back to the bush party, focused on the memory until he could smell the smoke from the bonfire. He saw himself standing next to the keg, laughing with Brian, but he could not remember what they were laughing about. Then, the vibration in his head changed. It stopped being a faint rumble and became a clear ringing, like metal hitting crystal.

***

At the bush party, he stood next to Brian. They were checking out Moira McDonald, a cheerleader wearing a tight blue turtleneck. He started his third beer from the keg when he saw Tommy Delonki running.

***

"I knew." He said aloud as the thought ran through his head. "As soon as I saw him I knew they were there. I knew the Edimmu had come back for Tommy. They were going to kill him if I didn't stop them."

***

Tommy collapsed at his feet, as if he had reached a safe place. There were long bloody gouges along his legs and arms. A few people swarmed around Tommy. Most, the under-aged drinkers, ran for their cars. All this blood meant someone was going to call the cops. They were more worried their parents would find out about the drinking than whether Tommy was going to live or die.

"They came back for me," he said. "I told you they would."

Several of Tommy's teeth were missing. Several others hung by threads to his gums. Somehow, this seemed the worst of his injuries. Josh wiped tears from Tommy's eyes. Something inside him went very hot and solid.

He leaned close and whispered: "I warned them."

He stood, reaching into the bonfire to take out a burning log. He chose not to let his hand burn: a solid, conscious decision.

***

"How is that possible?" he asked.

"Don't fight it." Jessica's voice seemed clearer than his own. "Don't think. Just focus."

***

He walked into the woods. He didn't need to ask Tommy where they were. He could feel them. The stink and wrongness of the creatures pulled on him like magnetic North. They called themselves Edimmu. They wanted to do things with Tommy. They said he belongs to them. They said he has been promised.

Josh's memory changed. Dark trees and the smell of blood dissipated into a fog, only to be replaced by clean walls and the smell of a good dinner still lingering in the air.

He stood beside the closet door while Tommy Delonki sat up in the bed behind him. Tommy wore his Star Wars pajamas, the ones with C-3PO and R2-D2 repeated over and over against a blue background. Tommy pulled the blankets up to his chest. He looked cold, shivering against the headboard, even though it was mid-July, the temperature well into the 80's.

"I'm serious, Josh." Tommy drew his knees up, hugging them close to his chest. "They're real, and if you don't get away from the closet, they're going to get you."

Goosebumps rose over Josh's chest, but he didn't move. Sweat trickled down from his armpits, but he also felt something inside him get as strong as steel.

"Maybe," he said, "or maybe I'll get them."

He stood there staring at the door as Tommy turned off the light. Tommy cried into his pillow. Josh saw a flash of purple light under the closet door. It seemed familiar.

The thing inside him burned even hotter now, but he wasn't sweating. And he wasn't afraid, even though he knew he should be. He stepped in front of the closet. As it opened, he moved with it, hiding behind the door while the monsters from the closet came out.

The room looked so dark. Though some illumination came from the streetlights outside and a nightlight in the shape of the Death Star, everything seemed much darker with the closet door opened. He could just barely make out the shapes. There were three of them, but their bodies did not seem normal. He stared at them, bile rising. These were the things that made his best friend so scared. Even though they were much bigger than him, he made up his mind to hurt them.

He was about to yell at them when something strange happened.

Tommy never said what they did to him at night. He just said it was bad. Josh assumed it was a sex thing. That is what they taught in school: strangers can be bad and want to touch your private parts. This was much weirder. It was like they were playing doctor. One of them put a black shape that looked like a briefcase on the bed and took out a bunch of needles. The metal parts shone in the dark.

"He's not asleep," one of the things said. Josh thought the voice sounded familiar, too.

"No problem." Another one of the things put a hand over Tommy's body. Shadows deeper than darkness poured out of the hand and covered all of Tommy's body. There was a lot of screaming. The bed bounced up and down. Josh held his breath. With all this noise, Tommy's parents would surely come in to see what was going on.

But no one came.

Josh tried to step forward, but found he couldn't move. He looked down at his body. It seemed normal, but his muscles refused to respond. It reminded him of the time last Christmas when he had drunk a few of his dad's beers and fallen asleep on the floor. His body just would not listen to him.

'Move, I say!' His body always did what he told it to do, at least when he consciously told it to do something. It was why he was good at sports. As soon as he made up his mind, the sleepiness was gone from his body. Now he was really mad.

He slammed the closet door closed. The three creatures turned. Despite the darkness, he saw them very clearly. He saw the way their wings hung limp at their sides, the way their scaly skin gleamed under the nightlight. And he saw the way their eyes glowed red in the dark.

"You're bad men and you need to go away."

"Josh, what are you doing here?" one of the creatures said. "This isn't your concern."

Josh snapped his fingers and the lights came on. "He's my friend and you aren't going to hurt him anymore."

The Edimmu nearest Tommy finished taking blood while another knelt down beside Josh. It ruffled his hair and smiled. "I know you like him, but don't forget where you come from. Let us finish up and we won't have to tell your dad about this, okay?"

Josh slapped the Edimmu's hand away. The creature cried out in pain.

"Tell my father whatever you like, but you are not going to bother my friend again. Don't forget who I am!"

***

Josh opened his eyes.

Jessica stared at him.

Josh stood too quickly and his knees gave out beneath him. He fell forward limply, each slow breath he took the only thing he could really feel. His head was spinning. He felt as if a part of him was still outside his own body.

"What was it?" Garnet took a few steps toward him. She reached out her arms as if to help support him, but Josh shook his head and waved her away. "What did you see?"

"I don't ... Oh God. I don't know..." He looked up at

Garnet, took in her beauty, and for a moment her green eyes seemed the most solid thing in the world. "What the hell am I, Garnet?"

"Josh," Jessica said. Her voice was weak. When he looked back, her eyes were wide and rimmed with red. She looked completely terrified. "We've got to finish. I can feel you don't have very many blocks left."

Josh shook his head as he pushed himself back to his feet. He heard people shout but did not know why. Then he realized he was on the floor again. Todd and Garnet helped him get back up and led him back to the chair.

"Maybe it's best if we wait for Wisdom," Elaine said. She took a few steps toward Josh. He looked up and saw that her hands were placed lightly on the sub-machine gun.

"That can't be real," he said. "It can't be a real memory."

Josh didn't realize he was still shaking his head until Garnet rested the palm of her hand against his cheek. There was such tenderness in the touch the remnants of his dignity disappeared. He sobbed, confused and exhausted.

"Oh, Christ. That's how the creature touched me. The Edimmu. I knew it. It liked me. I...I think I might be going into shock. I can't feel my legs anymore. It knew my father."

Jessica slipped off her wooden chair, kneeling in front of him. She put a comforting hand on his knee. "I saw it, too, Josh. It was real. I don't understand it any more than you, but I can tell you it really happened. Who exactly is your father, Josh?"

Elaine pulled Jessica back and put her palm on Josh's forehead. "Enough. Look at him. Garnet, get some blankets. The linen closet is at the end of the hall by the spare room. Hurry. David, I need your help."

Josh felt David throw his arm over his shoulder, leading him off the chair to a couch. Josh stared at the floor, unable to concentrate on anything. He heard voices, but they made no sense. Everything was distant and secondary, like moving through a dream. His knees buckled and then Elaine was beside him, helping him. Then his head fell backwards and the world just stopped.

Chapter Twenty-Five

Josh stared at the ceiling with open vacant eyes.

Todd paced back and forth by the windows. "We can't just leave him like this."

Elaine rolled her head back, stretching out her neck. "Well, I can't let her play around in his head anymore. Look what she's done already?"

"Hey, you're the one who said we couldn't afford the luxury of amnesia, remember?" Todd spoke with uncharacteristic anger. "Well, Jessica has unlocked something poison in his head. If she doesn't get it all the way out, who knows what will happen."

"Christ. David, can you go wait outside the spare room? Let me know if Wisdom wakes."

David ran a hand through his hair and nodded.

Elaine looked around the room and grunted with annoyance. "Has anyone seen Jared? Jessica, can you look for him? When was the last time anyone saw him?"

Jessica closed her eyes. "He's fine. I can feel him down on the beach."

"What the hell is he doing wandering off?"

Jessica shrugged. "He's a total dork. Who knows why he does the things he does? I'll be right back." She walked out on the patio and headed down the wooden steps.

Elaine turned to Todd. "I made a mistake, Todd. What if he's somehow connected to the Edimmu? If he's our enemy…"

Todd backed away from her. "You can't shoot him, Elaine. Look at him! Does he look like a threat?"

"Looks can be deceiving. You don't look like a threat either, but I've seen what you can do. I'm not promising anything. I know you think I'm a hard ass but you don't know how dangerous the Edimmu are."

"I don't? Jesus. I was thrown around by a few of them this morning, remember? I lost my best friend." He stopped and gasped. Then he hung his head and continued in a very quiet voice. "I lost my best friend to them, watched three of them slaughter and abduct others I care for. I know they're dangerous. Whatever Josh is, whoever he knows, he's not one of them. I am psychic, you know. I can tell that much."

Elaine bit the corner of her lower lip. "I'm sorry, Todd, but you don't really have a clue. No matter what they did to you today, they represent something a whole lot worse than that. You say you can trust him, so we'll go with that for now. But if he or anyone else crosses Wisdom, you have to know I'll kill him. Like it or not, it may be the best thing."

Todd cocked his head to one side and rubbed his nose. "You know, Ms. Ryerson told us we're some kind of monster, all us Anomalies. Freaks. So how are we any different than him? Do you plan on killing us, too?"

Elaine stared back at him. The expression on her face drained the rest of the blood from Todd's face.

"Do whatever you want," she said as she left the room. "Just don't expect me to watch."

***

Hours later, Josh sat up, conscious again. Garnet was holding his hand, smiling down at him. Jessica ran over to him and stood beside her.

"How are you feeling?" Garnet realized she was still holding his hand and went slightly red. She slid her hand back to her lap.

"Like I was hit repeatedly with a tire iron." Josh laughed softly, unconvincingly, and put a hand to his head. "I just wish that was the worst of it. Truth is, I know we have to finish. We all need to find out what else I'm blocking. Jessica, can you do your magic while I'm lying down?"

Jessica nodded and sat on the edge of the couch by his feet.

"Good. That way I won't have far to fall if I faint."

Everyone smiled at that. No one laughed.

"Okay," Jessica closed her eyes. "The Edimmu acted like they knew your father. Why don't we start there? Start going through your memories of your father."

Josh closed his eyes and lay back down. It was easy to bring a picture of his father to mind.

***

The first moment: his dad in a three-piece suit walking beside him. Josh was six years old, riding a bike. His father held one of the handlebars to help keep him stable. This is how he saw his father: a tall, strong man, always smiling and with love in his eyes.

The second moment: the hotel room in Lebanon. Josh sat on the floor flipping through the channels on the television. His mother lay on one of the twin beds reading an Agatha Christie novel. His father shaved in the adjoining washroom. He was the type of guy women liked to look at: square jaw, blunt nose and high cheekbones. His hair was darker than Josh's. It could only be called blond in the summer when the sun brought out its highlights.

The room was small with no air conditioning. One of the windows was open. A slight breeze brought in the smell of spices from the restaurant across the street.

"You sure you don't want to go shopping?" His father's voice was deep. He raised his voice to be heard over the running water in the bathroom sink and the babble of voices from the television.

"I'm fine here, doll," Mother said. "Five hours of shopping is enough for one day. Just go to your little seminar thing. Josh and I will be fine here."

"I'm bored," Josh said.

"Kid, you're always bored." His father wiped the remnants of shaving cream from his face with a white towel.

"Am not. It just sucks here."

"Josh, you have a ton of books to read," his mother said. She didn't look up from the mystery novel, but Josh still had the impression that she was looking right at him.

"Let your father do his thing. When he gets back we can go out for supper, okay?"

Josh groaned and rolled his eyes. Maybe that's why he saw the flash of light out of the corner of his eyes. He got up on his knees and looked out the window. There it was again. Across the street on the rooftop, something shone, like a mirror reflecting the sun.

"What's that?" He got to feet and walked toward the window.

"What's what?" His mother flipped the page on her book. She still didn't look up.

"On the roof over there. It's like someone's sending signals with a mirror."

Then the memory slowed down: a videotape played frame by frame. Disjointed still images linked together in the illusion of movement. Every second was an independent moment in time. He saw his mother lift her eyes from the book and turn to the window. He saw his father run out of the bathroom, razor still in hand, eyes wide in disbelief. Then he saw someone move out of the shadows on the roof, a very large gun in hand.

***

Josh gasped and sat up.

Jessica stared back at him, shaking her head. "Josh, that can't be right."

"Oh, I think it is very right." He pushed her away from him and walked toward the stairs. His legs felt like rubber. With each step he worried he would lose his footing and trip over his own feet. But he couldn't let that happen. This wasn't the time for weakness. He was vaguely aware of people shouting behind him, but it seemed very far away. The only thing in his mind was the memory of that face on the rooftop and the gun pointed in his direction.

He kicked in the door to Wisdom's room. In a heartbeat, Elaine rose from where she sat on the bed, her submachine gun pointed at Josh's head. Her expression wavered from anger to relief and settled into worry. She cocked the gun and did not lower it.

"Back away, Josh," she said. The worry on her face escalated into anger.

"You shot my mother." Josh took a step forward.

Elaine repeatedly pulled the trigger of the gun. Josh saw the mounting horror on her face as each pull of the trigger had the same effect. Nothing. The gun refused to fire.

With his left hand, he pushed the weapon out of the way. With his right hand, he grabbed Elaine by the throat, lifting her off the ground.

"You shot my mother," he repeated. "Why?"

He stared up into her eyes as her face grew redder and redder. She was choking. The look in her eyes was definitely not fear for her life. Now there was only rage in her expression.

"Josh, let her down!" Todd was in the doorway behind him. "You're killing her."

Josh did not take his eyes away from her to acknowledge Todd. "I can still hear her screaming. The bullet nearly tore her arm off. And the way my father howled. We thought she was going to die."

"Josh, I won't warn you again!"

Josh flexed his shoulder muscles, his fingers digging a little deeper into Elaine's neck. Then there was a sharp pain in his chest followed by a blow to his nose. He dropped Elaine, his head swimming in bursts of heat. Before he could shake the pain away, something slammed into his head and he fell into a dark place.

***

"What the hell was that about?" Elaine rubbed at her neck. "Give me a reason why I'm not putting a bullet in his head."

If he were anyone except one of Wisdom's prized Anomalies, she would have. She was also furious with herself. She should have moved faster. No matter that the kid had somehow prevented her gun from working; it was no excuse for almost getting herself killed. Breaking out of a hold like that should have been second nature to her. What had stopped her from acting? Maybe this Josh was able to affect humans the same way he did the gun.

"You shot his mother." Jessica stepped past Todd and came into the room. She knelt down beside Josh's unconscious body and put a hand to the wound. Elaine had rammed the butt of her submachine gun into his skull. If she was lucky, the kid would have permanent brain damage; but she doubted it. Anomalies were pretty quick healers.

"What are you talking about? I don't even know the kid's mother."

Jessica brought her hands back. The fingertips were covered with blood. "I saw it. It was in Lebanon a few years ago. You were on the roof of this building. Your hair was a bit longer and a little blonder but it was you. I'm sure of it. You shot a rifle of some sort through a window into a hotel room."

"Oh." Elaine swallowed and kept rubbing her throat. She would have trouble eating for weeks now. "That's unexpected. It's also need-to-know."

"Enough with the *X-Files* cloak and dagger." Todd grabbed Elaine's arm and spun her around. "We've all had enough of this *'it's classified'* crap. What do you know about this guy? Why did you try to kill his mother?"

Elaine pulled her arm free. "You don't get to tell me when things are no longer classified. Only Wisdom can do that. I can tell you it was about five years ago, just before Wisdom started gathering most of you."

"I remember that trip to Lebanon," Garnet said from the doorway. "I'd been with Wisdom for about six months. You were supposed to kill the father, right?"

"Zip it, Garnet." Elaine's hand slipped to her gun.

"I don't think so," Garnet replied. "Todd, help me bring Josh back into the living room. Maybe you and Jessica can do your little healing trick on him and bring him around.

I think it's time to put together some of the pieces of this puzzle."

Chapter Twenty-Six

Technically, Wisdom was dead. He was just too pissed off to let his body realize it. Rage was his life-support machine; it forced his lungs to breathe, his heart to beat and his organs to heal. Like a sentient hologram, each particle of his body held the blueprint for the whole of his being. His willpower crafted tendons and tissue seemingly out of nothing. A mortal would have bled to death. Wisdom simply grew new blood from the heat and subtle, elemental fire that hung in the air around him. As his body fought to regenerate, his mind traveled back through his history and remembered.

***

"Don't fidget, dear," his mother said. "Little gentleman do not fidget."

"Who says I want to be a gentleman? I'm just a boy." He was six years old, walking through the candlelit corridors of a pyramid in Egypt. His dad, an Atlantean statesman, was part of a global initiative to construct a weather machine. They hoped to install crystalline devices in various structures around the world which would communicate through the magnetic fields of the planet. It would allow them to temper the massive hurricanes and tidal waves that had buffeted coastal regions of the world for the last ten years. Eventually, it would be controlled by a station in the foothills outside of Poseidus. Egypt was one of the primary focal points of the magnetic sub-web. According to the experts, one of the devices needed to be installed here. His father was solidifying the deal.

"All the same, stop fidgeting." His mother ruffled his hair and smiled. Her face was blurred by the spanning eons but her warmth rushed back to him easily. Her skin was a dark, rich blue, the color of the ocean at night. She was dressed in the style currently popular in the cities of Atlantis:

a one-piece pleated dress that hung below the ankles with a plunging neckline barely concealing her breasts. The only jewelry she wore was a commitment necklace: a living crystal choker that pulsed with energy. Because she loved his father, it glowed a healthy green with freckles of comforting red.

Just outside the door to council chamber, his dad talked with three Egyptians. A native of the north of Atlantis, his father had pale skin with a slightly yellow tinge reminiscent of the surface of the moon. He was dressed, like the Egyptians, in a simple robe that covered his torso and legs but left his arms bare. With a cursory movement over his shoulder, his father waved goodbye and walked into a brightly lit chamber filled with priests. Wisdom would never see him again.

"Is this going to take long?" He pouted and stared at the floor. "This place is boring."

His mother smiled. "It won't take too long. I promise."

"Yeah. You said that last time."

"Such a cute little gentleman you are." She bent down and kissed him on the forehead. "Why don't you wait over there in that little room? As soon as we're finished here I'll fly you home for supper. Anything you want. Okay?"

Begrudgingly, he smiled and watched her walk into the priests' chamber.

He waited.

His mother didn't return for hours but that wasn't unusual. The project was important and she believed he was safe. Egypt was nearly as civilized as Atlantis and he was surrounded by the priests and acolytes that ruled the country. But he got bored, as children will. At first, it was only his eyes that wandered. Then it was his feet.

He left the cul-de-sac and walked toward the chamber where his parents conducted their meeting. There were at least fifty people in the room. Judging by skin color alone, most were Egyptians but there were several other Atlanteans. In one corner sat three Edimmu in thick cloaks made of vulture feathers. One of them looked over and saw him standing in the doorway. She smiled; an old female with graying scales and deep eyes. Wisdom waved and smiled back. Back home in Poseidus, many of his teachers were Edimmu.

He listened to the speeches for a moment but they made him sleepy. All that talk about Ice Ages and solar storms. Adults can be so boring. Not far from the chamber was a thin hallway. The walls rose high above him giving the impression of a chasm between two cliffs. No child could resist investigating it.

The hallway ended in a small octagonal room. The ceiling was far above him, hidden in darkness. The only light came from small luminescent globes similar to the technology back home. A palpable hush hung over the area. Golden statues ringed the perimeter, some holding light globes, others holding weapons. One held what looked like a still-beating baboon heart. At the time, Wisdom did not recognize what the monstrosity was; he only recognized the fear it instilled in him. Against the eastern wall was an altar crafted from cold, bleak stone gilded with sections of gold and emeralds. But the thing that held him, the thing that he could not look away from was the diamond suspended in midair.

As a child of Atlantis, he'd seen the marvels of technology: the fences of solid light that protected cities from rampaging dinosaurs, silver disks mounted on walls that relayed pictures from around the world, airships called Pharocai in which they'd flown from Poseidus to the pyramids. Yet looking at the jewel suspended in space, he knew it wasn't science that held it in place. Even then he could feel the dark mystery of different forces and he knew it by name.

Magic.

"What are you doing down here?" He felt a hand on his shoulder. His mother's warmth and scent flowed over him but he could not turn away. "Little gentlemen don't snoop. Come away."

But he could not move. He had to touch the gem – this thing suspended by forces he could not yet understand but which sang in his bones. His mother's hands pulled him out of the room but he slid from her grasp and ran for the diamond. She cried out in warning but it was too late. He reached out and clutched the diamond in his hands.

Initially, he only felt the weight of it. It was twice the size of his childhood fist but seemed to have the weight of an entire planet within it. He marveled at how he could keep something so heavy in his hands. Then he noticed a sound. A hum. At first a hum, then a beating, like a slow heart. He turned to share the joy he'd discovered with his mother.

Then he saw the Djinn.

***

The diamond was a Calling Stone, similar to the one King Solomon would use centuries later to command an army of Djinn. This one only summoned one being: the creature he would learn to call father. His mother screamed for hours as the Djinn raped her. He set her body on fire but she did not die. The Djinn regenerated the parts of her body consumed by flame. Broken and paralyzed, she watched as her child was stolen and taken back through the diamond. They travelled through the jewel to the Kaz, the city at the edge of an emerald mountain range in the world of Djinnistan.

For four thousand years (give or take a decade), he lived in the Kaz. He grew to maturity a slave of the creature who had abducted him. The Djinn taught him just enough magic to survive the fiery environment of the elemental plane. On Earth, all matter is a combination of five basic elements – earth, air, fire, water and divine spirit – but in the Kaz everything solid was fire and spirit. As he learned to filter out oxygen from the toxic air, his body evolved into something that was no longer flesh and blood. His skin turned from blue to black. Once he reached 30, the Djinn stopped his body from aging. Although he would never be a true Djinn, he was something close.

As a slave, he wasn't allowed friends, nor could he find a mate and raise a family. The only relationship he had was with his father. Then, twenty years or so before he finally escaped, he stumbled upon another room he was not supposed to see. Unlike the chamber in Egypt, this room was not one of ceremony. It was a vault.

While scrubbing the floor in the foyer of his father's villa, his eyes strayed to the cascading molten stream that fell from the ceiling down a carefully crafted path to a lava pond. Sulfurous fumes rose from the sizable pond and small fish-like creatures swam through the lava. It was a pretty thing - a conversation piece for the Djinn's many visitors. It was the sort of thing you only really saw the first time; after that it blended into the background like a painting or plush carpet. Something on this day made him look at it with fresh eyes. His jaw dropped.

After thousands of years submersed in subtle fiery air, eating the flesh of animals suffused with magic and the taste of flame, he saw a new level to it. On the other side of the molten stream was a door. He stood up from where he knelt on the floor, dropped his scrub brush and moved to the edge of the pool. Yes, there was definitely a doorway there. The more he stared at it, the clearer it became. His eyes could see the tendrils of magic wrapped around the edge of the door, effectively locking it. The weave was complicated, far from anything his limited skills could open.

At least at first.

For months he studied the door while going through the motions of cleaning. Then, when he knew he had the skill to open the door, he waited until the Djinn had left for the Senate to conduct his affairs. Then he made his move. He waded through the lava pool, a feat that would have disintegrated a human in seconds. Bit by bit, he unfurled the magic tendrils from the door.

The room was filled with treasures from Earth: piles of gold coins and chalices, tubs and bowls of gems and bits of technology from Atlantis. There were a dozen swords, a few shields and suit of armor built of a material that he couldn't identify. The air was different in the vault, too. He breathed it in deeply and realized there was more to it than fire. There was water and earth in this air: the same atmosphere as on Earth. Breathing it in, he felt a strength return to him. Strength and anger.

He did not spend long in the room that first time, but he returned at every available moment. He never thought of stealing anything. What would he do with gold? It was worthless amongst the Djinn and, if he was caught with it, there would be no doubt of its source. He did not go to take. He went to look.

After a year or so of looking, he started to see something else in the room. In the presence of other elements, his mind saw more than one layer of reality. Thus, he slowly began to see the Akashic Realm. Engraved in this higher level of reality was every moment of history, every thought, and every experience in creation. Mystics call this engraving the Akashic Records. He saw what happened to his mother, where he really was now, and what had happened to his home world since he had left it. He saw the destruction of Atlantis and the second Stone Age of Earth. He watched the enslavement of the Edimmu and the rise of the Orpheans.

Over twenty years, he learned what it meant to be human. The more of it he saw, the more determined he was to be free again. Wisdom decided to do more than watch. The Akashic Records revealed that escape from Djinnistan was only possible through refractory surfaces – like gems. He studied and practiced for months until, one day, he succeeded.

***

The Djinn was at the Senate, brokering a trade treaty with the Marid, creatures from a water elemental plane, when Wisdom made his move. Inside the vault was an emerald brooch in the shape of a scarab. It was small enough to fit easily in his palm, but it was large enough to create a portal. He could not escape alone. He needed someone from Earth to ground him. So he focused his desire through the gem and found his benefactor in a young princess from China.

She lived in a walled city surrounded by guards and servants. Her father was away fighting some battle on the outskirts of his territory. She was a lonely child admiring a bevy of gifts from men who wanted her hand in marriage. One of those gifts was an emerald brooch – not the same style as the one Wisdom held in his hands, but close enough. He poured out lust through the gem and the princess responded. She lusted back. All it took then was a brief touch, her hand grazing the emerald, and Wisdom was free.

His body fell through cracks between dimensions. His flesh was ripped apart and reconstructed repeatedly. He landed on carpet as the princess screamed in shock.

"Nothing to fear from me." He smiled up at her. Though he did not speak Chinese, it was evident in her eyes that she understood what he had said. It was an element of his magic he would use for the rest of his life. Wisdom knew how to speak to everyone. He pushed himself to his feet. Then it was his turn to scream.

Rich oxygen hit his body, mingled with the elemental fire in his body. He burst into flame. A true Djinn could control the combustion, but he'd never learned how to temper the burn. The fire spread over his body but did not consume his flesh. Carpet and ceiling burst into flames. The princess tried to run, but the inferno snatched her. The fatty parts of her body melted like butter, muscles and bones charred beyond recognition. Two servants rushed into the room, drawn by the screams. When they saw the flames, they ran away just as quickly.

As the princess's room burned around him, pain overwhelmed all other sensations. Time hung still as he burned for three hours. Then, fear grew more powerful than pain. He felt a shimmering on the Akashic plane.

His father was near.

"Have to make a move," he whispered. If he did not gain control of the fire, his father would drag him back to the Kaz. He focused on the elemental water in the air and, slowly at first, stopped his skin from burning. He opened his eyes to the blackened destruction and flames around him. The scarab had not made the journey with him. It was, presumably, still back in his father's vault.

Something glistened in the light of an unseen sun, a sparkle of green. Wisdom walked past the burnt corpse of the princess and bent down. He picked up her emerald broach and held it up to his eye. Looking through the emerald he saw a set of eyes – not his own, but those of the Djinn.

"Run all you want," his father said. "When I want you, I'll find you."

He threw the emerald into the flames and ran as quickly as he could. On the outskirts of the walled city he saw it again: the emerald broach lay at his feet. Once again, he picked it up and threw it as far as he could. For two days, he walked toward a nearby mountain range. Everywhere he looked, there was the emerald broach. On the other side of the mountain range was a city. He slipped into an empty room at a local inn. There, waiting for him on the bed, was the emerald. No matter where he went for the next year, the emerald was there before him.

Eventually he stopped running from it. He picked it up and kept it with his possessions. There was no escaping his father.

At least not at the time.

***

Sometimes the Djinn tried to talk to him through the emerald but Wisdom never spoke back. He could think of no rational reason why he wasn't coming after him. If the Djinn knew where he was, why had he not come to reclaim his slave? After a century, he decided there was no rational reason because his father was not rational. He was an elemental creature, a force of will and fire that no human could ever understand.

After meeting Echo, Wisdom changed. There was something about her. Something remarkably human. She refused to submit to him, no matter what he did to her. Her obstinace reawakened his own desire to be free of the Calling Stone. He spent several centuries traveling the world to meet with magicians and shamans, anyone who claimed to know anything about magic. From some he learned little tricks. From most, he learned nothing at all. Most of the magic he knew now he had learned in the Kaz. It wasn't until the trip to Africa with Echo and Propates that he made any real progress.

***

"You look tired."

"I don't get tired, Andromeda." Wisdom glanced over at her as the caravan neared the edge of the village. Propates was several feet ahead lost in his own thoughts as usual. "It's one of the benefits of being me. You must be happy to be away from the Parthians. I think that cook was getting dangerously close to asking for your hand in marriage."

"I believe that's called changing the subject." She frowned and touched his chin. "Whether you get tired or not, you certainly look that way. Maybe it's time for a vacation."

"Vacations are for peasants," Wisdom sighed. "I'm far too important to sit around and do nothing."

She slapped him playfully across his cheek. "Welcome back to reality. All you do is kill people and feel sorry for yourself. Hardly that important in the grand scheme of things."

Wisdom smiled and said nothing else as they approached the village. Perhaps she was right. Maybe it was time to take a little break from the quest.

The tribe was called the Uzuu. They were one of the

many losers in the game of history. Very little was known about them in the modern era yet, over time, they grew to be a highly civilized culture. Their shaman was descended from a long line of demon fighters and claimed to know how to break the bonds of Calling Stones. Wisdom held very little hope, having heard the same promise from dozens of others.

As they entered the village they were met by five bare-chested men wielding short javelins as weapons. Draining them of their resistance and fear was an easy task for Wisdom. Before his horse came to a stop, the five men had lowered their weapons. Every one of them smiled up at him like he was an old friend. The man behind the warriors was a different matter. His skin was as dark as the other Uzuu's but his hair was long and gray. He wore a necklace constructed of human teeth and crystals.

Wisdom dismounted and bowed to the old man as a sign of reverence.

"You worked magic against my men," the shaman said. "Do not enter my home as a serpent or I will crush you underfoot. Are we agreed?'

Wisdom smirked and raised an eyebrow. "Agreed. I've lifted the spells. You saw the magic, didn't you? I could see it in your eyes. You followed the waves as I warped reality. Perhaps you will be the one to end the curse."

The shaman took a step closer as if to whisper in his ear. "I can break the link between the stones but the real curse is your father. I have no control over that."

Wisdom looked away in a failed attempt to hide his shock. "I told you nothing of my father when we spoke in the Dreaming. How do you know about him?"

"I am Mundugu. I know." Mundugu reached over and grabbed Wisdom's hand — a gesture of such bare sincerity that he did not flinch. "Many years I've walked between the worlds. You are not the only creature I have talked to. There are many in the world that can see like I do. We meet in the Dreaming from time to time. Your story is known to us. I know you've tried for many years to break the bond your father has on you. When we spoke in the Dreaming so many moons ago, I already knew you would come to me in time. I am just surprised it took this long."

Still holding his hand, Mundugu led him away from the caravan toward a mud and straw hut. Wisdom glanced behind him and signaled Andromeda to get things settled for the night.

Inside the hut, he was overcome with the sense of serenity. He shivered, the first time he felt a chill since his childhood in Atlantis. "Why is it so cold in here?"

Mundugu let go of his hand. "It is not cold. Not to humans. I do magic in this place. That means I need to put up barriers. Protection. What you feel is a shield to keep out evil things. You are an evil thing, aren't you, Wisdom?"

Wisdom did not answer. Instead he sat cross-legged on the floor just as Mundugu directed him. In the center of a hut was a black bowl filled with water. At the bottom of the bowl was a human tooth. Sun-bleached bones formed a protective circle around the bowl, pointing outwards like the rays of the sun. Mundugu sat opposite Wisdom and closed his eyes. Wisdom followed the cue and allowed himself time to center. When he opened his eyes, Mundugu was starting at him.

"Place the Calling Stone in the water."

Wisdom reached into the folds of his beige robes and pulled out the princess' brooch. Despite its age, it sill gleamed as if newly crafted. He dropped it in the water and waited.

Nothing happened.

"What now?" Wisdom looked up from the brooch and his eyes fell on Mundugu. The transformation in the man was disturbing and rapid. The instant the broach hit the water, the shaman started to change. The grey left his hair, replaced by luminous blond streaks that glowed in the dim light of the hut. His eyes were open in an unbroken stare and his lips mouthed silent words. Magic flowed in swirls of bright color streaming from each chakra of Mundugu's body to fill the air. Translucent serpents circled the outer perimeter of the hut at ever-increasing speeds. Then, in a blur of movement, they shot directly at the Calling Stone. The brooch cracked, snapping in two.

All light around him disappeared, replaced by a sudden darkness. Slowly, the veil of shadows dissipated like fog under the steadily-rising sun. When he could see again, Wisdom realized he was no longer in the hut. He was no longer on Earth. He was somewhere in-between. And he was not alone.

Standing before him was the Djinn. His father was dressed in blue and green armor encrusted with gems. His skin was sand-colored with a strong red tinge. Long black hair was drawn back in a ponytail and his eyes burned and flickered with flame. In one hand he held a massive six-foot-long molten sword. In the other he held Mundugu by the neck.

"This is becoming tiresome," his father said. He squeezed the hand holding Mundugu, snapping Mundugu's neck. "I have abided your ridiculous attempt to blend in with humanity for long enough. You are coming home with me. Now."

Wisdom swallowed. Hard. "This is my home. You always told me I would never be a true Djinn. I belong here with my people. I am not going back with you."

The Djinn tossed Mundugu's body away and put both hands on the sword. "I wasn't asking you, slave. I was telling you. Despite your birth, you are of the Djinn now. There is no place for you on this planet."

Wisdom clenched his fists. "I'm not your slave anymore."

The words were barely out of his lips before the sword was swinging. Wisdom spun away from the attack. He called up a teleportation disk. It was a common form of transportation in the Kaz. He jumped through the disk and appeared behind his father. He reached out for the elements and found an abundance of earth. He reached into the ground and giant spikes of metal shot up from the earth under his father's feet.

The Djinn was too fast for it. He sidestepped the attack and swung the sword at him again. Wisdom transmuted his body to sentient gas and seeped through the soil, diving through earth like it was water. He came up on the other side of his father and opened a portal. The other side of this portal was the vacuum of space above the planet Earth, causing an implosion in the area. The Djinn was sucked through the portal, but, before he was through, he grabbed Wisdom by the ankle.

They both emerged above the earth and started to fall. As they fell, the Djinn swung his sword and shot bolts of blue flame from his eyes. Wisdom managed to dodge each attack. He was so focused on his father that he didn't see how close the ground was. He smacked into the dirt, creating a sizable crater.

For a moment his father was eclipsed by a mass of noise and earth. Pain shot through his body as mangled bones tried to re-knit and flesh struggled to keep his innards where they belonged. Before he could recuperate, his father grabbed him by one leg and slammed him against a tree. Then against a boulder. Then, to finish it, he stabbed the six-foot sword through his chest.

"No one runs from me," his father said.

Wisdom coughed up blood, amazed that he wasn't dead. He tried to focus past the pain but it encompassed his entire world. Acting on instinct he transmuted to gaseous form again and sank into the earth. Only this time instead of returning to the surface for attack, he resurfaced miles away under cover of trees. Despite his tactic, his father was there waiting for him. Wisdom barely dodged the swing of the sword before he could open a portal. He teleported back to the Uzuu tribe.

The village was quiet. Too quiet. He looked around and saw everyone was gone. Maybe his father had stolen them away just as he had Mundugu. He tried to speak but found his throat uncooperative. Instead he reached out with his mind and looked for Andromeda.

Nothing.

He also noticed the brooch was gone. For the first time in hundreds of years, it had not followed him. He was free.

He stood on unsteady legs and began to walk for the jungle. The bond between him and his father was broken now. The Djinn would never again be able to use the emerald scarab to track Wisdom down. If he could find a place to hide, maybe he had a chance.

Above him, the clouds swirled purple and black. Thunder rumbled in the distance.

"I guess running is out of the question. I think I'm too predictable." His father must have guessed Wisdom would run to the only friends he had. Lightning flashed inches in front of him; the concussive backlash threw him back several feet. By the time he was on his feet, his father was standing before him.

"Hate me all you want. This is for your own good. Come away now before my limited patience is exhausted."

"I would rather die than go back to the Kaz with you."

The Djinn hung his head. "As you wish." He pointed the fiery sword at Wisdom, using the blade as a focal point for his magic. Though the sun was still in the sky, the sword seemed to steal all the light out of the air, turning the jungle into a twilight place. He shot a bolt of white light, brighter than anything a mortal eye could see. Wisdom didn't run, did not turn aside. Instead, he opened a portal directly in front of him. The fire sped through the portal like a spear and appeared on the other end of the spatial distortion – directly behind the Djinn's head. The magical attack staggered the Djinn, knocking him to his knees.

Wisdom saw his opportunity. He ran.

Bloodied and wounded, he stumbled back to the village, vaguely aware he wasn't alone. Propates was there.

"Run," he advised Propates. Then he was gone.

***

On occasion, Wisdom was very lucky. Africa was one of those times. Echo – or Andromeda, as she called herself then – was not a fighter by nature. She sensed the Djinn's presence just before he sucked Wisdom away. She hid in a nearby stream, waiting until she felt Wisdom's return. Then she opened a portal and transported them to the home of a druidess in England. It took nearly two months for Wisdom to recover from the battle, two months of being unable to hide his weakness and need. Echo saw his weakness and she did not laugh. She did not take advantage of him. She helped him heal.

He had never felt more ashamed in his life.

***

Wisdom recuperated in a shallow cave near a small waterfall. It was summertime in England and the shadows were pleasantly cool. The druidess was off performing a hand-fasting ceremony in a nearby oak grove. Andromeda wiped the perspiration from Wisdom's fevered brow and lifted the bowl of hot liquid to his mouth. He drank the medicinal broth, unable to tear his eyes away from her.

"Why do you stay?"

She smiled and put the bowl down. "Where would I go?"

"I'm serious." He reached out and touched her forearm. "The things I've done to you…to your family…to everyone. If you left me now I could not stop you. So why do you stay?"

She turned away and started to rise. Then she stopped and looked at the ground. "Like I said, where would I go? Everyone I loved is dead. All my family, my whole village – dead. Even Propates is gone now. This is the only life I know. You are the only life I know. So I stay."

"Do you forgive me?"

Andromeda turned to face him so quickly that for a moment Wisdom thought she was going to strike him. "Apparently your fever has made you delirious. I don't forgive you. I do not love you. And I never will. Never."

***

Wisdom opened his eyes. Instinctively he tried to sit up, but pain paralyzed him. A quick look at his surroundings confirmed he was at Echo's island home. He felt the fear filter out of him. Once again he had run from a fight with his father and Echo had saved him. No matter what words she used, her actions were transparent. She did love him, nearly as much as he loved her. It made everything else worthwhile.

A thought solidified in his mind and he caught his breath.

"Why couldn't I kill him?" He whispered the words. He needed to say them aloud, to give solidity to the fear and doubt now churning inside him. Experience told him he had the power and wiles to defeat his father. Somehow the old Djinn had defeated him. He needed to understand how that was possible. He replayed the battle in his head, going over every minute detail. Then it hit him.

His father had help.

***

Several days ago, he confronted his father in a forest clearing. The Djinn took a step forward, the heat of his body pushing Wisdom back.

"Something is coming, son. Something beyond anything you can handle. I'm here to take you back where you belong before the end-game starts. For once, live up to the name you've chosen and come with me."

"We've had this conversation before. You're not my father. You stole me. I still remember what you did to my mother. You raped her."

The Djinn sighed. "I apologized for that. What more can I say?"

"What more can you...? It's not something you can apologize for! It pretty much puts you in the bad guy column for all time."

The Djinn shook his head and sighed again. "Fine. Have it your way. I've tried, but you're still a disappointment. Weak and short-sighted. A complete waste of life. If you won't come home willingly, I will beat you into submission."

Wisdom called forth the fire inside. "Old man, that's not going to work anymore."

And the battle began.

This time, Wisdom struck first. Over the centuries he'd refined his control over the five elements. This time, when he reached out for elemental earth, it was not with clumsy hands – it was with the refined touch of an artist. Instead of stone spikes, he bent the forces of magnetism and gravity to his will. Lightning sparked through the air around his hands as he negated all inertia around his father. Humans seldom think about how quickly the Earth moves through space as it circles the sun. A native of the Kaz, a dimension without stars, the Djinn knew little about the higher astrophysics. The move caught his father unprepared. Freed from the protection of the planet, he stayed in place as the planet sped by him at over 67,000 mph. Within a heartbeat, he was thousands of miles away from the planet in the vacuum of space. An instant later, Wisdom was there.

The sudden change in location disoriented the Djinn. Wisdom took the opportunity to alter the inertia field once again, reversing the velocity so that the Djinn slammed into the nearest planet. His father smashed into the molten surface of Venus. The impact threw up lava and stone, polluting the atmosphere in a mushroom cloud. Wisdom waited and smiled.

His father flew up from Venus, quickly recovering from the initial shock. He had a sword in his hands now, the same sword he had once used to impale Wisdom. This time there was a difference. This time there was fear in the old Djinn's eyes.

"Didn't see that coming, did you?" Wisdom opened a portal behind him and stepped out of space. His father, caught in his rage, rushed through the portal after him and found himself on an elemental plane of water. Cool liquid crushed down on the Djinn, cooling the superheated gaseous form until it appeared nearly human. Born on Earth, Wisdom was not affected the same way. Humans, after all, are nearly 83% water. As his father struggled to rebuild his power, Wisdom opened another portal – this one directly behind the Djinn. Using elemental spirit, Akasha, Wisdom pushed his father out of the elemental plane high above the Gobi desert back on Earth. The Djinn fell quickly, his wet body pounding into the cold sand of the Chinese desert. Wisdom flew through the portal. Hovering in the air, he brought down bolt after bolt of lightning upon the Djinn.

In the distance, a portion of sand gleamed gold under the light of the lightning.

"I am not the weakling you believe me to be, Father." Wisdom touched down on the sand, reached down into the pits of the planet and called forth a pillar of crystal. Clear quartz shot up through the sand and impaled the Djinn. "Unlike you, I've grown over the years. I've learned. This is what you can accomplish by doing instead of just thinking."

The Djinn's body flickered, disappeared and reconstituted several feet away from the spear of quartz. "Tricks. You offer me tricks. You cannot possibly hope…"

"You're right. I don't hope. I know. I've already done this, remember? I'm going to kill you, kill you with my little 'tricks'." He reopened the portal to the plane of water, a rush of cool liquid spilling out over the desert. The carefully-constructed tsunami slammed against his father with a roar of sound. Pain contorting his face, the Djinn struggled to stay upright. Inch by inch, his body of solidified fire gave way to the deluge, steaming under the flow of water. Wisdom knew he had won.

Then something changed.

Pain evaporated, leaving an expression of rage and concentration. The Djinn pushed back against the tide, and the elemental water stuttered like the image from a faulty projector. The water's momentum slowed and then reversed.

Wisdom's eyes went wide as his weapon was snatched from his grasp and tossed aside. In an instant, the surge of water bled back into the portal and returned to the elemental plane.

"Didn't see that coming, did you?" His father smiled now, an expression of intense violence. "Where is your confidence now, boy?" The Djinn swung his fist, hurling a stream of superheated gases like plasma from the surface of the sun. Wisdom stumbled away from the attack. The move threw him off balance and he fell on his back. "Where is your bravado now? Maybe you thought this was going to be a fair fight. Well, you're right. It's not fair. I outclass you. Did you really expect to dispatch me like this? By the Heavens, I'm a Djinn. I'm older than this planet. And you? You are nothing but an aberration, a diversion, a toy of mine that has forgotten his place. Give up now. This is not a fight you can win."

At the taunting, Wisdom recovered. "Hello? Have you been watching this fight? That was you getting your ass kicked a moment ago. You know, the psychologists of this planet would have a lot to say about the way you carry on." Wisdom pushed himself to his feet and brushed sand off his shoulders. "I mean, the sword speaks volumes. Over-compensating much? And I have to wonder, are you like this with everyone, or is it just me? Do all the Djinn get together over coffee and talk about who's the biggest baddie of them all? Or maybe, and I'm just putting it out there, maybe the reason you kidnapped me all those years ago was because you realized how much of a disappointment you are. I'm guessing part of the reason you didn't let me associate with the other Djinn is because they all knew what I'm just starting to realize now. You're a loser. Just a big fat joke amongst the Djinn. Maybe you just wanted me around so you can point out my weaknesses as a diversion from your own inadequacies. It's kind of like picking up a dog from the pound just so you can kick it when you have a bad day. When you think about it that way, it actually makes you kind of pathetic."

The glare of hatred in the Djinn's eyes was answer enough. Distracted by the small victory, Wisdom did not see the slab of molten lava until it was inches away from his face. The impact hammered him into the ground, even as his body instinctively absorbed the heat and flames. Before he could recover, the Djinn grabbed him by the right arm, just above the elbow. He lifted Wisdom high over his head and slammed him against the ground.

"When we get back to the Kaz, Akushula, be prepared to eat those words. I'm trying to save your life. Whether you want it saved or not. I will not leave you here on this planet to face what's coming."

Over and over the Djinn slammed him against the ground. It was far from subtle, but it was effective. All Wisdom could do was wait for an opening. Finally, his father threw him high in the air. The Djinn's hands began to glow with subtle fire, but Wisdom took his moment. He called upon the power of Air, increasing the quantity of oxygen in the area around the Djinn. The gases responded to the flame and, for all intents and purposes, his father exploded. Pieces of the Djinn's body showered the desert.

Wisdom took the opportunity to run. Something very wrong had happened. The Djinn was an elemental. Under the treaties of authority, as a creature of fire, his father should not have been able to manipulate elemental water as he did with the tsunami. It was physically impossible. And yet the old bastard had done it. Bloodied and confused, Wisdom's consciousness leaked away like blood. His body flew on instinct to the one place, the one person he knew would make him safe. Then he collapsed.

***

"You almost had me there, old man," Wisdom whispered. Thinking back on the fight was all that it took to convince Wisdom his instincts were correct. Someone was helping the Djinn. And the only hint of it was a distant gleam of something under the lightning. "I'm not usually a betting man, but I'd put money on that 'thing' being a gold ring. Looks like the alien is no longer just a problem for Josh. He and I are about to have words, as soon as I am whole again."

Chapter Twenty-Seven

David stared out at the ocean without really seeing it. His ears were ringing, a sound that seemed to bypass his eardrums altogether to buzz inside his head. His short time with the Anomalies told him what that meant: power.

"That's the best I can do," Todd said from the couch. He let his bloodied hands drop away from Josh's head and slumped forward, his elbows resting against his knees.

"His skull wasn't cracked, really, but it was pretty close," Jessica said. She wiped sweat from her forehead. The two of them had once again combined their healing powers. Under normal circumstances, Jessica would barely feel the exertion; but these were hardly normal conditions. Despite her protests to the contrary, she was just a child and her little body could only deal with so much. "We stopped the bleeding and fused the bone."

"So why doesn't he wake up?" David moved away from the window and joined the others. His face was still pale and somber under his shock of red hair, his eyes moving too quickly.

Jessica looked up at David and narrowed her eyes. "Do I look like a doctor? I know nothing about head trauma. Maybe it's all been too much for him. All this stuff about his connection to the Edimmu and now it turns out Elaine shot his mother. Maybe his mind just shut down. Maybe it won't let him wake up until he's processed it all."

Sitting at the dining table, Garnet poured a glass of red wine – her third so far. "Well, I can't speak for Josh, but I can say this is all too much for me. I can't believe how 'full circle' this whole thing is. It's like we stepped into the third act of a trilogy without all the Jedi and hobbits."

Todd nodded. "Actually, you could kind of say we're like the Jedi. And, you know, Jessica is basically a hobbit."

Jessica kicked him in the shin and walked toward the bathroom.

Todd winced at the pain but kept smiling. He sat down at the table next to Garnet and leaned back in his chair. He folded his arms across his chest, the smile fading. "What can you tell us? Why did Wisdom want Josh's father killed?"

For a moment Garnet said nothing. Then, after a large swig of her wine, she spoke. "Elaine was right about one thing. It really should come from Wisdom. But seeing as how he's all coma-like and we're being chased by reptoids from the center of the earth, what the heck. Josh's father, well, he's not exactly what you would call an innocent bystander. If he's the one Elaine was told to kill in Lebanon, he works for the Canadian branch of an organization called Candleworks. They're a quasi-military group whose sole purpose is to catalogue and eliminate non-humans on Earth. You already know about the Edimmu. There are a surprising number of other species on the planet. This group, Candleworks, was investigating Wisdom. They caused him some inconveniences. He wanted to send a message."

"So," Todd said, slowly nodding. "Wisdom really isn't human, is he?"

Garnet looked at him over the rim of her wine glass. "Did you hit your head? Of course he isn't human. Hell, technically we're not even human. You know that. I don't know all the details. I was new at the time and Wisdom only gave me limited information. From what I gather, this group Candleworks was investigating the same kind of events Wisdom was. Meaning us. I think there was some sort of recruiting competition, like Candleworks wanted the Anomalies to work for them. Obviously, Wisdom wanted them for himself. I'm not sure exactly. That we'll have to ask the big guy."

"So if he's not human, what is he?" David bit his nails, his eyes darting quickly between Garnet and Todd.

Garnet took a sip of wine and held it in her mouth for a long time. She chewed the wine, a physical manifestation of the thoughts running through her mind.

"I don't know if there's a name for what he is. I know

he's very old. From what I've learned, he's from…somewhere else. Some people, mostly his enemies, have called him a demon, but I don't think he is. He's not inherently evil and he's not out to steal souls. But he's definitely not some sort of angelic presence here to save us from ourselves, either. I do know that there is no one else like him on this planet. That's part of the reason he has so many enemies. Most people that know about him want him to go away. A few others seem to think they can use him for their own purposes."

"Excellent," David said sarcastically. "Clear as mud. You should go into politics. What does all this have to do with me? With us?"

"Long story." Garnet took another drink of wine. "Wisdom's fed us a few different stories, about who we are and *why* we are. About a year after they're recruited, Newbies are told a story about evolution and how the human genome is affected by background radiation, forcing it to adapt. Stuff like that. It's all complete crap. Well, maybe not complete crap from a scientific standpoint, but it has nothing to do with us. About year three you hear a slightly different story. That's the one everyone here has heard."

"You mean that wasn't true, either?" Jessica came back into the room and stood in front of Garnet with her hands in her pockets. "That stuff about our parents?"

"What about our parents?" David had a flashback to something Elaine had said earlier. "Elaine said something about how I didn't know as much about my parents as I thought. Are you saying my parents did something to me?"

"No."

David jumped at the sound of Elaine's voice.

They all turned to look at her. She stood at the top of the stairway. The submachine gun was no longer strapped across her front.

"Elaine…" Garnet started to stand.

"Sit down, Garnet," she said. "I'll tell them. There are things even you don't know, so you might get it wrong. I'll tell you the truth. Wisdom might skin me alive if – no, when – he gets up, but I think you're right. We can't afford to play by the same rules anymore. David, your parents didn't do anything to you, not in the way you are thinking. The truth is the people you call your parents aren't really your true parents at all."

"What?" David felt something wash through his body. It was hard to breathe, but he could not pinpoint the emotion. "Of course they are. I..."

"If you want the truth, shut up and listen! Your mother did give birth to you, physically, but you weren't conceived like a normal child. Like a human child. Oh, I know that look. You're wondering how they could have kept something like that from you. The reason they kept it from you is because they have no idea. They have no clue that you are anything other than their child.

"This part Garnet knows already. There are forces in this world some would call demons. For all I know, that's exactly what they are. Some call them Nephilim, but it's doubtful they are the creatures from myth. Today, they're normally called Orpheans. How they got that name is a story for another day. They live in a dark twisted place called the Black Sea and they do not want to stay there. Their only pleasure in life is to screw with people's heads. Make them do bad things. But they like to do it in sneaky ways. See, if it's obvious that an external force created all the havoc on earth, people would rally together and fight them. Like they did in the Middle Ages. So they only appear for certain people. Usually, weak people. Crazy people. Sometimes they just drive them nuts, make them see and hear things that just drive them over the edge. And sometimes, thankfully not all that often, they step into the world and do secret things themselves.

"If each of you asked your parents, they would all have this one story in common. They would all remember a very vivid dream where they changed into monsters and had really incredible sex. If you don't believe me, ask them.

Although, being all parent-like, they might not want to discuss their sexual fantasies with you. What these demon-things do, the Orpheans, is kind of take possession of the human body and..."

"You have got to be kidding."

"No David, I'm not kidding. And don't interrupt me again. They slip into human bodies and take over. They do weird, violent, fetish-type stuff that is meant to be anything but pleasurable. It usually leaves the victims so physically messed up they can't have sex for months. Naturally, this type of sex with all the blood and decadence doesn't normally result in pregnancy. Every once in a while, though, accidents happen and – voila! We have an Anomaly."

"But," Jessica chewed the fingernail on her thumb, her eyes focused on something no one else could see. "But don't these things know they created children? And, if they did, wouldn't they keep in contact or something? Try to, I don't know, use them or take custody or something."

Elaine shook her head. "They can't exactly take custody. They're in a different dimension, remember? They're not really physical in the same way we are. And they can't take you back to where they come from for the same reason. As far as I understand it, they know what they've done and that's good enough for them. They've put a bit more chaos into the world. They probably figure having a bunch of kids running around that can kill at will and blow things up with their mind is about as evil as you can get. Truth to tell, God only knows what you guys would become if Wisdom just let you wander around on your own."

David laughed, his body shaking as he held his head. "This is too much. I mean, demons? There is no way that's the reason. I mean, there has to be another explanation. There just has to be. There's no such thing as demons anyway, so..."

"Listen up, pretty boy," Elaine said. "I don't really give a hoot if you believe me or not. What I've told you is the truth. You're all hybrids: part-demon, part-human. That's how you can do the things you can do. The reason you exist is to do evil things. That's the truth. Now you can choose to accept it or you can make up some other story that will help you sleep at night. It won't change a goddamn thing. Each one of you was born a monster, made for one thing and one thing only. Wisdom wants to help you, for reasons I cannot even begin to understand. If you let him, he'll show you a different way."

"What about me?" Everyone turned, surprised to hear Josh's voice. He sat up on the couch holding a hand to his head. His eyes were unfocused but looked in the direction of Elaine. "What about my father? My *human* father. Does he know what I am?"

Elaine shrugged. Then she shook her head. "I don't know. I don't see how he could, but working for Candleworks, maybe he figured it out."

Jessica walked back to the couch. "Josh, your father must have known something, right? Those Edimmu seemed to know him and all, but...Oh. Wait."

Jessica's face went lax and pale. She stared at Josh, her left eye twitching.

Josh stared at Jessica. The two held their stare for some time, as if they were holding their own silent conversation. It was Josh who finally spoke.

"Maybe the Edimmu were talking about my other father."

Jessica nodded. "The one who wasn't human."

"So these demons are in cahoots with the Edimmu?" Todd asked. "I thought you said they were two separate things."

"They are," Elaine said. "As far as I know, they have nothing to do with each other. The Edimmu are just sort of hired muscle the Council of Peacocks uses to do their dirty work."

Josh rubbed his head. "Maybe this Council of Peacocks is aligned with these demons in some way. And if you don't know what the connection is, either Wisdom didn't tell you or he has not figured it out yet."

Garnet walked over to Elaine. "Which is it? Is Wisdom keeping something this big from us?"

"Why don't you just ask me?"

Wisdom walked down the stairs. He wore a white sheet draped around his body in a quasi-toga. It left several of his bruises and cuts across his body very visible. Perhaps it was the hunched-over weary way in which he was standing, but he looked the very image of a gladiator.

"Wisdom!" Elaine rushed over to him, arms outstretched in an offer of support. Wisdom shook his head and waved her away.

"It's okay, Elaine. I'm fine. Believe it or not, I've been worse than this. Things are progressing faster than expected. I need to get you up to speed quickly. So ask me whatever you want. I'll tell you whatever you need to know. But as soon as that sun comes up, we're heading to Greece."

"Greece?" Elaine said the word as if it had never crossed her lips before.

"Yes, Greece. It's a country. In the Mediterranean. Maybe you've heard of it. And no, I don't know of any connection between the Council and the demons. I didn't think anybody on the planet knew about the Orpheans except Candleworks and the few I've told. If they are working together, something very bad must be in the works. Garnet, why don't you make us some coffee? Elaine, can you see if there are any decent clothes here I can put on? I'm far from modest, but parts of me are showing that seem to be making Jessica sick to her stomach."

Before either Elaine or Garnet could move, a circle of light appeared by the windows, bringing everyone to a standstill. When Echo stepped out of the circle, the temperature in the room seemed to drop ten degrees. There was a wild look in her eyes.

"Wisdom, we have to move," she said. "Your father is coming."

***

"When did I get that?" Josh couldn't stop staring at his hands. There was a small cylindrical bulge on his palm, like a piece of skin that had been pinched together and had not fallen back into place yet. He rubbed it, but it did not move. Was it a sign? Did the others have similar marks? He forced his head up to look at the others in the room. They all looked so normal. He couldn't pick out anything about them that screamed 'monster'. But they were demonspawn, things created for the sole purpose of increasing evil in the world.

He thought back to the creature who had come to him back in London: the one in the maggot suit. Was that thing an Orphean? If so, was that his father?

"Get what?"

Josh looked up and found Wisdom staring at him.

"It's probably nothing," he said. "Just this thing on my hand."

Wisdom glanced at Elaine. "Damn it. You said he'd been checked."

Elaine ran to Josh, grabbed his hand, and held it up to her face. "How the hell did we miss this? I swear I've never seen this before."

"It's probably been there since he was taken," Wisdom said. "We don't have time to deal with it now. Echo, close that portal already. You need to open another one. I'm still not strong enough."

"Where?" Echo took a few steps and then flipped her wrist. The portal flashed away, leaving only an afterimage on Josh's eye. "Where are we going?"

"Greece?" Elaine handed a towel to Echo.

"No," Wisdom said. "We can't risk it if Josh has a tracking device in him. We'll go to my offices in Hong Kong. I have certain devices set into the building there that will hide us from my father for a time. They should also block Josh's tracker until we can have it removed. I'm not ready for another round with him just yet, and I think one way or another our next meeting will be our last."

Echo straightened her blouse, smoothing out the

wrinkles. "I'm not exactly thrilled by this turn of events, Wisdom. You owe me a gazillion favors."

Wisdom laughed a strange strangled sound that was closer to a sob than a sound of amusement. "I'm just glad you're...It's good you're still alive. We can talk about repayment later."

"You think there will be a later?" Echo flipped her wrist again and a second circle of light splashed into the air with a hissing sound.

For just a moment, Wisdom faltered. An expression crossed his face; it was just a glimmer of fear and then it was gone.

Chapter Twenty-Eight

When they arrived in Hong Kong, it was already late afternoon. Echo's portal opened in a deserted boardroom filled with cold neon light and mahogany furniture. Wisdom walked straight to a phone on a nearby desk and made arrangements, while the Anomalies filed out of the portal. Moments later, he faded away in a flurry of security guards and a swirl of men and women in dark suits. Elaine and Echo went with him, leaving Garnet in charge of the rest. She slipped back into the role of authority quickly, telling everyone how to get to their rooms.

On his way to the quarters he'd been assigned, David kept his head down. He felt dirty surrounded by so many impeccably dressed people and the clean business sterility of the building. Although he was hesitant to be alone, as soon as the door clicked closed behind him he peeled off his bloodied and sweat-soiled clothes. He dropped the clothes in the wastebasket in the bathroom. Naked, he felt more civilized than he had in days. He walked over to the window and looked out over the city.

It reminded him of the movie *Blade Runner*. Everywhere he looked there was steel and glass and neon signs. Large billboards with television-like screens flashed pictures of smiling Chinese women and pop cans. People and cars filled the streets below like schools of fish swimming in different directions through narrow streams. He was not completely convinced that the little oval of light had not brought them forward in time. He half expected to see air ships moving between the impossibly-high skyscrapers. Toronto was a large city but, compared to this, it seemed intimate and backwater.

He walked to the edge of the bed and sat down. Alone. The silence was oppressive. Thoughts of demons and shadows bubbled over in his mind. Pushing those thoughts aside, he took a long hot shower. As the hot water pounded on him, he thought of the television show *Survivor.* He remembered watching a group of women relish a simple shower. At the time, it had seemed like a silly reward. Now he understood. There was something extremely civilized about taking a shower. The soft spicy scent of the soap and shampoo erased the dirt and the wildness of the past few days.

He dried himself off as he walked over to the closet. It was filled with designer clothes and tailored suits, names like Hugo Boss and Versace attached like cattle brands marking wealth. Normally he spurned designer clothes; they were pretentious wastes of money worn by silly people with no respect for their own wealth. Growing up, his family had never had extra money lying around to buy things like this. He opened the top drawer of a nearby dresser and removed a pair of underwear. As he slid them on, he had to admit they were more comfortable than the ones he got at Wal-Mart. Even the socks seemed different when he stepped into them. When he walked around the room, his feet felt cushioned as if he was not really touching the ground. He slid a pair of pants off a hanger and put on a grey high-necked sweater. Both were his size, which, while unnerving, was not completely unexpected.

As he finished dressing, he shook his head at the amount of money it must have taken to stock this room. He was sure his mother could have fed them for half a year on what it took to buy a few of the suits.

"Admit it," he said as he walked over to one of the full-length mirrors that hung on either side of the door leading to the bathroom. "You're eager to dress up like someone else." He wore black silk pants, the pleats hanging like something out of a catalogue, and a bulky loose-knit grey wool sweater that rose up his neck and gathered around his face, framing it. It was a very maritime sweater, reminding him of cold nights damp with the wind off the ocean and drinking pints of Moosehead in pubs. His skin was still pale, his hair was as red as ever, but he barely recognized himself. He felt like a movie star. "So that's it, eh? That's why people shell out all that money for these clothes. I guess I get it now."

Satisfied he was unrecognizable, he moved to the window and looked out into the city from the future. Thirty minutes or so later, there was a knock at the door.

"Come in."

Jessica walked into the room, her eyes focused loosely on the ground. She was dressed in a pair of blue jean overalls and a white t-shirt. Maybe it was just the way she moved, but David felt her change in clothing made her a different person, too. There was no sign of the smart-mouthed girl who believed it was natural for her to be the one in charge during a crisis. The way her cotton shirt hung against her chest that had not yet grown breasts, the way her ponytail bounced as she moved, she looked like a young Jody Foster.

"The last time I was in Hong Kong, Amy and I went for Dim Sum at this really cool restaurant." She leaned against the wall just to the left of the mirror and kept her eyes on the ground. "Mr. Wisdom took us there. He said it was a special treat for all the progress we had made in class. It seemed like the most important thing in the world back then, doing well in class. Now I just want to run home to my mother. Pretty pathetic, isn't it?"

"Jessica, pathetic is the last word I think of when I look at you. I am way more pathetic than you are. Look how you handled yourself against the Edimmu. You were like Ripley and Sarah Connor all wrapped into one little package. Meanwhile, I was the one crying like a loser. Terrified. You feel that way because you're human. And I mean that. Human. No matter what Elaine or Wisdom says, we're not monsters. Not if we don't let ourselves be."

Jessica nodded and looked out the window. "It might be easier, you know, if we let ourselves become monsters. I think that's why Ms. Ryerson tried to convince us we were. I am not psychic – not in the precognitive way, anyway. I don't really know what's going to happen to us in the next couple of days, but I think it's going to be pretty bad.

Wisdom is freaked. I can feel it in the way he moves. After he passes through a spot, the air radiates spots of black, like it's filled with anger and fear. If we were monsters, maybe it would be easier for us to, I don't know, get through it and all."

"But at what cost, eh?" David walked over to where she was standing and got down on his knees, forcing her to look into his eyes. "No matter how hard it gets, we can't let ourselves become something dark and scary. Listen, maybe our parents were demons and maybe we have a little monster inside of us. I don't know if I believe that, but let's just say it's true. I saw what you were like with Amy. There was nothing monstrous about that. You were a little girl. You still are a little girl. And if you feel like running away from all this crap, that's good. That's what a logical, sane person would do."

Jessica raised her head. "I think that was actually inspirational, Mr. Ross. You know, Amy liked you. I used to think you were a doorknob. Now I'm thinking she was right."

"Well ..."

David stopped as Jessica leaned over and kissed him on the cheek.

"Thank you," she said. "I'll see you tomorrow."

Jessica walked out of the room and David smiled, feeling good about himself for the first time in months.

***

Josh had been in his room for only a few minutes when Garnet was at his door with a stack of manila folders. She handed them to him, then bit her lip and looked over her shoulder. The look in her eyes made it clear she did not feel comfortable around him. She did not step into the room. Josh realized she wasn't alone. Two armed men in dark suits stood to either side of her.

"I can't see how they're going to do you any good, Josh," she said. "We don't even really know what your

EFHBs are. Makes it kind of difficult to develop them."

"All the same," he said, trying to be as charming as possible. "Thanks again."

Garnet kept eye contact with him for what seemed a very long time. Then shook her head and looked away. "Maybe you are a miracle worker," she said. "I wouldn't normally do this sort of thing, but God knows things have been very strange since you showed up."

Four hours later, Josh pushed himself away from the desk with a grunt and leaned back in the leather chair. Looking at the files before him made his head hurt. He had always considered himself a good student. He'd spent all of his high school years on the honor roll and carried his average over to university. He was in his second year of classes working toward a degree in electrical engineering. You did not make it past first year if you didn't know how to study.

Still, these files were way out of his area of expertise. There were dozens of exercises on how to access certain areas of your mind, control your biorhythms, and focus under extreme stress. A lot of the material seemed like complete *Star Trek* fiction: page after page dedicated to the energy fields of the body and how they interact with the global electromagnetic fields and sub-atomic structures. He found it hard to believe that a kid like that girl Jessica could comprehend any of it. According to Garnet, though, this was all pretty standard material that the other Anomalies were expected to learn in their first year. He could only imagine what the more advance material was.

"I need a break." He pushed away from the desk and walked into the bathroom. He went to the sink, turned the stainless steel faucet and splashed cold water onto his face. He repeated this several times until he could no longer feel the remnants of sweat on his skin. Then he dried off with one of the thick black towels piled on the countertop and turned to meet his reflection.

"Can I really get used to this?" Only when he said the

words out loud did he surrender to the notion that he would never go back to his old life. He had already registered for classes for the upcoming semester.

"I'm never going to make it back to class. I don't even know where things stand with me and Jan." Would she ever want to see him again? How would she react when he told her that even now she did not know all his secrets? Hell, even he did not know all his secrets.

He closed his eyes, thought back to that day he had snapped orders at those winged monsters. Since Jessica had helped him recover the memory, it was easy for him to remember every detail of it: the heat in his body, the anger he felt towards them, and the way they looked at him. They'd looked at him with warmth and affection because they knew his father. Because they respected and feared him.

But which father?

He opened his eyes and followed the lights of a helicopter as it circled a nearby building. There was only one way for him to find out. He would have to sit with Jessica one more time and see what else they could dig up.

"But not tonight." He turned away from the window and slipped under the covers on the bed. He left the lights on. When he thought about turning them off, the memory of those monsters flowing out of the shadows kept him from moving. It was a long time before he fell asleep.

***

"Are you mad?"

Wisdom looked over his shoulder. Echo sat up in bed, her head leaning against the headboard. She wore a piece of frilly pink lingerie. Wisdom could not decide if he liked it on her or not. Echo was far removed from the fragility the lingerie implied, but it was extremely flattering to her physique. He decided not to criticize. He finished taking off his shirt and started unbuckling his pants.

"No, I'm not angry at you," she answered. "No more than before. I am, however, curious."

"About that new one? Josh?" Wisdom walked over to a hook on the outside of his walk-in closet and took down a pair of flannel pajama bottoms.

"Yes, about that and about your father's sudden appearance. I've been around too long to believe in coincidence, Wisdom. This thing with the boy's father, it's not the sort of thing you usually overlook."

Wisdom rubbed his forehead, unable to meet her eyes. "No, it isn't. How could I not have seen Richard Wilkinson's son was an Anomaly? How could I miss the connection? I studied that family in depth for months before I ordered the hit. I don't like overlooking anything. In hindsight, I should have thought something was strange when Elaine missed. She never misses, you know. It's uncanny."

"The way you talk about her, Wisdom..." Echo crossed her arms and looked away. "Are you two...? I have to wonder if your relationship is entirely professional."

Dressed in the pajama bottoms, Wisdom slid onto the bed and drew Echo toward him. "I love Elaine like a child, Echo. A daughter. And I would be very surprised if anything I could do would make you jealous. I think we're both too old for that kind of foolishness."

"As old as you are, Wisdom, you should know something about women by now."

Wisdom cupped her face with his hand. "No one could ever take your place."

Echo leaned into his touch and closed her eyes. "What are you going to do about the boy, Wisdom? Are you planning a visit tonight in the Dreaming?"

Wisdom reached his free hand down between her thighs. "Assuming you don't wear me out, yes. If things go badly tomorrow, tonight may be our last night together. Are you finished talking now?"

Echo answered with a moan.

Chapter Twenty-Nine

Josh sat on a tiled floor, cross-legged. He played Jacks with Tommy Delonki, vaguely aware that something was not quite right. He stared at Tommy for quite some time before it hit him.

"You're dead," he said. Yet he saw Tommy, 12 years old, dressed in the *Star Wars* pajamas he wore that night when the Edimmu came for him. Josh was dressed in blue jeans and a black t-shirt but he was the right age: 20.

"I'm dreaming aren't I?"

Tommy smiled and bounced the pink ball against the tiled floor. In a single swoop he gathered up three jacks.

Josh looked around. They sat in the middle of the Eaton Center. The mall was deserted, even though the bright lights that shone through the glass ceiling showed it was the middle of the day. The Canadian Geese sculptures slowly flapped their wings, flying but going nowhere.

"You want to get away from it, don't you?" Tommy bounced the ball again and took four jacks.

"Get away from what?" Josh felt a chill against his chest. He looked down and saw he was naked to the waist. He wore only the pair of plaid Joe Boxer bottoms his mother had bought in New York, only they were now big enough for his adult body.

"Do you know why you're here?" Tommy threw the ball over his shoulder and it bounced away into the distance. With each bounce the light around them dimmed. By the time the ball stopped, there was almost no light coming down from above.

"What do you mean? In Toronto? I do not know. Didn't we come here on a school trip in grade 8?"

"Yep. We got to share a room. You, me and that Brian guy. I never liked him, you know. He used to call me a nerd. Made fun of me a lot. Do you remember what happened here?"

"Um…"

"Think, Josh. Don't you remember that guy you saw? The one that made you run back onto the bus? It was outside the ROM. Do you remember now?"

Suddenly the Eaton Center was gone. Josh stood beside Tommy on a street corner. Cars drove by at turtle speed and a cold wind blew his hair. On the opposite side of the street, a steady flow of people stalked up and down the sidewalk. Then his eyes fell on a figure standing as still as a monument. A tall dark man dressed in a red suit.

"Wisdom." Josh put a hand over his mouth, confused. The wind picked up. The cars and the other people disappeared. Suddenly it was just him, Tommy and Wisdom. "I saw him and I knew him. Knew what he was. And it scared me. That's why I ran back to the bus."

"How exactly did you know me?"

Josh looked to his left. There was Wisdom. This one was not dressed in red. He wore a long charcoal grey robe that swirled in and out of the shadows like oil in water. His forehead shone lightly, almost like a halo hung around his head. He seemed much more solid than anything else in the dream.

"How…?" He took a step toward the new Wisdom. The city slowly faded away until it was little more than mist.

"Jessica isn't the only one who can pop into people's heads, Josh. I thought it was time for us to have a little conversation, the kind best had away from the others."

"You tried to kill my father." Josh found he had a sword in his hand. It glowed like a lightsaber. Heat and strength ran through his body as he tightened his grip on the hilt.

Wisdom glanced at the sword but did not seem threatened by it. "I've killed a lot of people in my life, Josh, some for a lot less reason than I had to kill your father. I can apologize for it, if it would make you feel better. Sorry. Now can we focus on the matter at hand? How exactly did you know who I was? If I am reading the situation right, you were about 12 years old, right? That would place this little memory about four years before Lebanon. That would be about three years before I was aware of your father and how his little gang was getting in my way. I'm not used to being in the dark. So, how did you know me?"

Josh shook his head. He looked down at his hand. The sword was gone. "I don't know. There is so much I don't know. Can you help me remember? Like Jessica did?"

"That's why I'm here. Just make sure you're able to deal with whatever we find. I don't want to go through this and have you wake up in the middle of it because it is too scary. Are you ready?"

Josh looked back at the misty figure of Wisdom from his memory and nodded.

"Then follow me."

Wisdom pointed to the left, toward a red-painted wooden door with a shiny blood-red doorknob. He motioned Josh to open it. Josh looked down and saw that he was dressed in a set of black robes similar to the ones Wisdom wore. Everything seemed much more real than a dream. He could almost hear himself breathing. He walked over to the door, turned the knob and pushed. It opened to Tommy Delonki's room. He saw the scene Jessica had helped him remember. There was Tommy on the bed. Over by the closet was the 12-year-old version of himself pointing a finger up at the Edimmu. Nothing moved. It was like walking into a wax museum.

"Now this is different," Wisdom said. "The way they are looking at you. I haven't seen that expression on an Edimmu since I was a child. I'd almost think..."

"They loved me." Josh knelt down and studied the frozen face of his memory-self. "I felt it. They cared about me, like I was a nephew or something. How is this possible, Wisdom? How can a person block this much stuff out of their mind? Until a few days ago, I thought I knew everything there was to know about myself. Now it turns out it was all a huge lie."

"And how would you have gone about the day-to-day routine of your life if you knew all this? Would a 12-year-old boy really be able to focus on his schoolwork if he knew he was pals with the monsters that came out of the closet at night? It's one of the interesting things about the human mind: its capacity to dis-remember is almost as great as its ability to store things. Humans block out much more prosaic memories than this. Rape, murder, adultery. It's obvious, to me anyway, that you – or at least a part of you – decided not to remember certain aspects of your life because it did not fit in with what you thought your life should be. So let's not focus on the 'whys' or the 'hows' of you not remembering. For now, let's focus on the 'what'. Shall we see what's on the other side of that closet?"

Josh felt his head swim. The images around him became foggy and distorted in a blur of motion. Then they snapped back into place even more solid than before.

"Focus, now, Josh. I have a bit of control over what's going on here, but if you are going to lose it, we might as well stop right now. We haven't even seen the fun stuff yet."

"I can hardly wait." Josh maneuvered his body around the frozen memory of himself and the Edimmu and walked into the closet. Whatever he had expected, he found something else.

Instead of clothes hanging from hooks or toys scattered like landmines on the floor, he found an entrance to a cave. He stepped past the threshold and looked back at Tommy's room. It looked so bright and human compared to where he was now. The cavern floor was smooth and grey, covered with dirt and pebbles, but the walls were sharp and jagged. Stalagmites jutted down like teeth while the rocky wall reached out toward him like claws and barbed wire. The ceiling was only about 12 feet from the ground, and the cave was no more than 6 feet wide. It left him feeling claustrophobic, as if he was literally walking through an esophagus and into the belly of the beast.

"Well, I didn't expect us to get here so quickly."

Wisdom still stood at the threshold. He surveyed the cave, hands on hips.

"Where is here?"

"Nowhere on Earth." Wisdom stepped forward and motioned for Josh to walk with him. They moved away from the door, deeper into the cave. Josh had to duck several times to avoid the sharp teeth hanging from the ceiling. "Some call this place Axeinus. Others call it the Black Sea. You could call it a prison if you want. Close enough for our purposes. Remember Elaine telling you about the Orpheans, the demons that made you all Anomalies? This is where they live."

Josh felt a shiver run through him. The knowledge that he could feel something at all, even though this was supposed to be a dream, made him feel all the more vulnerable.

"But..."

"Yeah, I know. There's not supposed to be a connection between the Edimmu and the Orpheans. If anything, given their past, they should be mortal enemies, not in bed with each other. But what I'm most curious about is how you, a human, found your way here. We would only be here if you had a memory of this place, a dimension where no physical being should be able to go."

"What does that mean?"

"It means my father was right. I am an idiot. Someone changed the rules of the game and I know nothing about it."

For Josh, it felt like they wandered through the dark cave for hours. Like a normal dream, reality moved in a strange way. His movements felt doubly removed – more like watching stop action photos than a movie of himself. Each footstep was a moment in time placed side-by-side with the others without any sense of continuity. It was impossible for him to judge the distance they travelled. At times, Josh was certain they were spiraling downwards or walking sideways even though the path before them continued to move in a straight line.

Eventually the air in the cave grew brighter.

"There's something up ahead."

Wisdom nodded. "Let's hope it's an answer."

Abruptly, the cave ended. They stood on a cliff at the edge of a large cavernous valley. The ceiling rose high above Josh, disappearing into the shadows. The ground dropped sharply at least forty feet to the floor of a vast mechanized area that reminded Josh of a factory. The valley spread out as far as he could see in all directions. He also noticed they were no longer alone. Hundreds of workers moved about on the floor below. He was so overwhelmed by the numbers that it took him several moments to realize the workers were not human. Most of the creatures had horns, and a few had tails. Aside from the grey overalls they wore, the workers had almost nothing else in common. Some had blood-red skin while others looked like solid shadows, animated patches of night sky moving among the machines. There were also pockets of Edimmu, some in their angelic disguise – all blond hair and white-winged majesty – but the majority were in their natural reptilian form. Their black wings hung limp on their backs. Several flew or hovered near pipes that ran along the ceiling. Most of the valley floor was filled with conveyor belts and robotics, large metallic arms moving metal parts from one belt to another, streams of sparks where mechanical devices welded objects together. He followed the flow of the assembly line until his eyes fell on something that looked like flesh.

"What the hell is that?" Josh saw patches of red that glistened like raw meat covered in blood stretching for yards. At the edge of each patch was a row of metal rings and thick wires.

"You're looking at it too closely," Wisdom said. Something in the tone of his voice made Josh shiver. He glanced at Wisdom and saw the man's lower lip quiver slightly. "If you keep looking only at the parts, you'll never see the big picture. That's what Propates meant. I have been so stupid. Look higher up and take in the whole thing at once."

"The whole thing?" Josh let his eyes race to the top of the machine. It was several kilometers above him and it took his brain a moment to process what he was seeing. He covered his mouth. He was not sure if he was going to scream or laugh. "That's ... that's not possible."

At the top was a head. From this distance, it was hard to judge how big it was, but he guessed it was as large as a football stadium. Now that he acknowledged what it was, he could easily make out the flicker of eyelashes and the slight flare of the nostrils as it took in each breath. Even though this was a dream, he was absolutely certain that what he was seeing actually existed. At the same time, he knew there was no way it *could* exist. A gigantic ring of metal encircled its very-human looking head and another ran around its chin. Large metal spears jutted out of each of the head's temples. These were connected to tubes that ran down to various parts of the machinery below. There was no skin on the face. It glistened like a recent scab, blood glistening over blue veins and tender tissue. Josh shook his head, not wanting to believe what he was seeing. The whole area beneath it, all the way to the ground, was a humanoid body, also skinless and punctured with metal tubes. Small tumors protruded from various parts of its body, tumors that moved like dreaming eyes behind closed lids. Josh prayed the creature did not open its eyes.

"Unless I'm mistaken," Wisdom said, "that is Propates. The real one. I think I'm beginning to see what's going on here. This might be a good time for us to leave. Technically this is a dream but you never can tell how real things like this are. Shall we?"

Josh was about to leave when something caught his eye. Over by one of the machines was a figure he recognized: a man in a tuxedo of maggots and beetles, a man with eyes that were far too much like his own. Around the man were a number of Edimmu, their wings tight against their backs.

"Wisdom," Josh said. "I think that's my father."

Chapter Thirty

Wisdom stopped mid-step and followed Josh's eyes down to the floor.

"Well, well, well, this certainly is interesting."

"Do you know him?"

"We're acquainted," Wisdom said with a grimace. "Let's get out of here before he sees us."

Josh followed Wisdom's lead away from the edge of the valley and back into the cave. He waited to speak until the entrance to the factory was far behind them.

"Who is Propates? And what did you mean by 'the real one'?"

Wisdom shook his head and placed a finger to his lips with a soft shushing sound. He stopped at a flat part of the cave wall and laid the palm of his hand against the black stone. At his touch, stone faded away and another red door appeared. He turned the handle and pushed the door inwards. It opened to a bright sun-filled field filled with white and purple wildflowers and knee-high grass. Josh followed Wisdom out of the Axeinus. When he looked behind him, the door was nowhere to be seen. They were in a valley surrounded by tall white-capped mountains. There was no sign of humanity anywhere.

"That's better." Wisdom snapped his fingers and two plush red loveseats appeared. He sat on one and took a deep breath. "To make a very long and complex story short and simple, the Council of Peacocks is an organization started in Greece over two thousand years ago. They worshipped an all-seeing God with 100 eyes. They called him Argus Propates. They believed in the pursuit of knowledge without being bound by the restrictions of morality and social convention. Some people believe there are things humans have no business learning. I have to say I fall into that crowd. I can think of at least fifteen things I know myself that I don't think your average person should know."

"Isn't that kind of, I don't know, arrogant?" Josh looked down at his body and saw he was now dressed in a black trench coat. His mind must have created it to combat the slight chill he felt on the wind, even though he knew there really was no wind. "If you're capable of dealing with these things, what makes you think other people don't have the intellectual capacity to deal with them?"

"Well, you're right. It probably is arrogant, but you missed my point. I'm not saying humans don't have the intellectual capacity to deal with these little facts. Not everyone is a moron, after all. It's just, knowing certain things makes it difficult for the average human to go about and do the average human things he or she needs to do. Take those demons, for example. Just imagine Mrs. Peggy-Joe Housewife. She has a husband and two little children. How does she put her children to bed at night and tell them there are no monsters in the world, if she finds out that there really are monsters? How does she sleep at night knowing that any moment something could creep out of the shadows and take her children away? Should she really have that kind of knowledge? Or would it be better for her to really believe there are no monsters?"

"I don't see how it's any better for her not to know. Maybe if she knew, she could protect herself. Set up defenses against the demons."

"That's just it, Josh," Wisdom leaned forward. "There are no defenses against them. They come and go as they please. They choose their victims at random. Nobody out there can stop them. Peggy-Joe can't send the police after the demons, can she? You can't shoot things that aren't physical. It's like fighting fear with a shotgun. Knowledge may be a weapon but it has no power over the dark things that crawl out of the night."

"So what are you, Wisdom? Are you one of those dark things?"

Wisdom leaned back and looked at Josh for a long time. Then he lowered his eyes and chewed on his lips for a moment. "I might be. I can usually convince myself that I'm something more evolved than the Orpheans, but we're more alike than I care to admit. Once I was a boy, innocent and stupid. Then the creature I call father turned me into something else. I spent years doing very bad things. I have a set of standards I live by. I try to do as much good as I can in the world. Maybe that's enough." He nodded his head a few times. "I have to believe it's enough.

"Anyway, as I was saying, the Argusites were pursuers of knowledge. There were religious wars in those days just like there are today. They fell out of favor, went underground and stayed there. But their desire for learning wasn't stopped by dwindling membership and state sanctions against them. If anything, oppression fed their desire. They saw the roadblocks as a sign that the Powers-That-Be were trying to oppress them, prevent them from true knowledge. They hid out with the Yezidi, another spurned religious group. The surviving members of the Council met a former student of mine, a man called Propates. Not the one we saw back in those caves, mind you, just a man with enough power to be dangerous. He offered them knowledge, lots of it, and the things they learned changed them. You know how it is. Once you know certain things about the world, you can't look at anything the same way again.

"When you're a kid, you learn about pain by burning your hand on the stove. And you change. You learn to be cautious. You learn that the world can hurt you. Up to that point you have absolute faith in the world. It's not even that you feel invulnerable. You are innocent and pure because you have no concept of vulnerability. When you get older you find out that there are deviants in the world who steal children. You change again and learn not to talk to strangers. You start to realize your life could be destroyed in a single moment of someone else's psychosis. When you get even older you realize that it is not the strangers you have to be afraid of. It's your friends and relatives that can hurt you the most. You learn not to trust other people. Finally, you get to a stage in your life when you realize the biggest threat to your well-being is yourself. Now you can forget about trust altogether. Most people, if they're lucky, go through this stage and learn to believe in something else, something outside their Selves. Something bigger. Karma, destiny, God. They start to see the patterns in life. If they are not lucky, well, life starts to look an awful lot like Hell.

"The Argusites learned a whole set of thought patterns not conducive to daily life. They changed their name to the Council of Peacocks and they made themselves a plan. They decided to recreate the hundred eyes of Argus in the bodies of one hundred fully-realized humans, each with the power and knowledge these thought patterns bestow. They believe if they do this they can resurrect their dead god and start a new age on Earth. Blah blah blah – your typical religious zealot crap. The problem for them is that most human beings really can't handle the things they learn. Physically. No, I'm definitely not going to tell you what the patterns are. You're not like other humans, but I still don't think you could handle the crap they deal with. You see, the knowledge that Propates gives them sort of works in levels. You see one weave of the pattern and you have this eureka moment. Your mind, your body and your sense of your spirit go through this transformation. Then you're able to see another thread in the tapestry, you follow it until you can see the whole pattern and – voila! another eureka moment. On and on until you reach the point they call 'Eyeness', where you see and appreciate all the patterns of Creation. Seems like a waste of time to me. They spend their whole lives learning what they'll know instantly upon dying. So instead of enjoying the world around them, they waste their days in an impossible search. Well, whatever. To each his own."

"None of this explains why you're out to get them." Josh sat down, finally, on the other loveseat. Even though he was just dreaming, his feet were starting to hurt from being on them for so long. "What's so bad about resurrecting their god or the pursuit of higher knowledge? It just sounds like a

New Age cult."

Wisdom nodded. "Yeah, except for the whole stealing babies and human experimentation thing."

"The what?"

"Oh, I skipped that part, didn't I? I always do that. There's a lot more to the Council than just expanding their consciousness. They want to create a super-race, people that could survive the process of achieving Eyeness. Only problem, being a secret society, they don't exactly create a Facebook page and hand out flyers to attract new members. They prefer the Nazi approach. They steal children and teenagers and conduct genetic experiments on them. Sometimes it is surgery. Other times it's radiation. Either way, they always mix in their magic and certain brainwashing methods. Sometimes their experiments actually survive. I've seen far too many examples of their failures."

"So what does that make you? Are you some sort of, I don't know, police force or vigilante out there to stop threats to world peace?"

"Yeah, I know. Kind of hard to swallow, isn't it? Well, since we're being honest and all, I'll tell the real reason I started curtailing the actions of the Council. Boredom. Not very heroic, I know, but when you've been alive as long as I have, you need a reason to keep going. A *raison d'être*, as the French would say. It was either this or the aliens."

"The aliens? You mean those UFO things are real?!"

"Let's not get into that. Loooooong story. Whatever my reasons are, I've made it my personal mission for the last few centuries to be a thorn in the side of the Council. For a very long time I was able to do it in anonymity. I'd prevent a kidnapping here, reverse the damage done to the gene structure of a kid there. Then they found me out. That's when the Council started using the Edimmu. They'd come into contact with the Edimmu during their time with the Yezidi. You see, as far as the Yezidi are concerned, the Edimmu are angelic heralds from God. The Council just sees them as hired muscle. Whatever the truth is, I don't know.

Maybe they are angels of a sort. All I know is that they've been on this planet at least as long as humans and they are very, very different from the Orpheans. I just find it hard to believe an angel would hire himself out to the highest bidder."

"Wisdom…." Josh hesitated. "That creature down there, that thing, it was my father, wasn't it? The demon one. How do you know him?"

"A tedious story, really, but it all boils down to a poker game."

"A poker game?"

"That's what I said, isn't it? He's got this sort of vendetta against me because he lost his wife in a poker game."

"You won my mother in a poker game!"

"Well I doubt very much she's your mother. This was several thousand years ago and Ehpslab – that's his name, by the way – he's not exactly the most monogamous of demons. I'm sure your demon mother was someone else altogether."

"I think I'm going to be sick."

The air above grew darker, as if something had drifted in front of the sun. Josh looked up, but there were no clouds, nor any sun for that matter. "Did you do that?"

Wisdom shook his head and slowly rose to his feet. "I only have a little control of things here. This is your dream, after all. Shall we make one more stop before I let you get some sleep?"

Josh stood as well. He walked as Wisdom created another red door out of thin air.

"Back in the Axeinus," Josh began, "you said you thought you knew what was going on. Why do you think the Edimmu and the Orpheans are working together?"

Wisdom took several deep breaths and stared off into the distance. "That factory we saw is new. As long as I've known them, the Orpheans have been unorganized. Somehow they've managed to capture a powerful god and build an advanced manufacturing plant in a plane of existence without physicality. Maybe I'm getting too old for this. How could I not have seen this coming? No matter. The crux of it is, they are preparing for war. That factory was constructing an armory – body armor and weapons infused with the blood of a deity. The Edimmu, being solid as they are, must have helped them construct the factory. Something much bigger than I suspected is going on here. For that, I think we need to ask your father. The human one."

The door swung open even as Josh's jaw dropped. On the other side of the door was the kitchen back in his home in Ottawa. The walls and cupboards were painted a light yellow with a trim of white daisies. An apple pie sat on the counter and Josh knew instantly what he was seeing. As he followed Wisdom through the door, the kitchen began to fill with people.

"This is Thanksgiving," he said.

The people moved slightly faster than they should have. They were also incredibly silent, but they were clearly his family. There was Uncle Perry sipping his third martini, flirting with Cousin Rob's girlfriend. Josh's grandparents were helping his mother set the table while Jan did her best to look interested in whatever Uncle Kyle was saying. Seeing Jan, even if it was only a dream, brought a tear to his eye.

"Do you think you could have picked a busier memory to pop into?" Wisdom stepped out of the way of Aunt Janet, who was carrying a tray of crystal glasses out to the dining room.

"Don't look at me." Josh waved back at Jan, who had motioned for him to save her. "I don't know how this thing works. You're the one with the magic doors and everything."

"Well, can you make them go away now?"

Jan started walking over to Josh, her face brightly lit with an eager smile.

"How do I do that, Wisdom?"

Wisdom reluctantly accepted a glass of wine from a man Josh couldn't place. "Christ. Just remember what your kitchen was like after all these people went home."

Jan was inches away from him when she faded away. Her absence hit him like a stone. Like fog dissipating, all the people disappeared. It was dark in the kitchen now, and the apple pie was gone.

Wisdom walked over to the table and set the wine glass down. He snapped his fingers and the lights came on.

"That's better. Now, let's go find your father." Wisdom walked up the stairs to the second floor.

"Wait a minute." Josh tried to run after him, but he could not make his legs work properly. He moved very slowly, followed by a sudden burst of movement up the steps that almost sent him flying into Wisdom. "What does my father have to do with this? You can't think he knows anything about those demons, can you?"

Wisdom turned around as soon as he got to the top of the stairs. "Of course he knows about the demons, Josh. That's his job. The group he works with, Candleworks, their sole function is the study of nonhumans, like the Orpheans, and the search for ways to fight them."

"I thought you said there was no way to fight them."

"Are you going to hold me accountable for everything I say? Well, in that case I'll have to make sure I say less. There are ways to fight them, if you can find the right energy fields through magic or advanced science – half a dozen of one, six of the other – but it's not what your father knows about the Orpheans I'm most interested in. It's what he knows about the Council. Which door is their bedroom?"

Josh pointed at the first door on the right. "But, that's... I mean, it's just not possible."

Wisdom stopped, his hand on the doorknob, and spoke over his shoulder. "You say that a lot, you know. After the things you've seen recently I would think you would have a better appreciation of exactly what is possible."

"Point taken. It's just, my father couldn't keep that kind of stuff from me. From us. Hey, I have an idea. You said I have another father, right? A demon. He has to be the father those Edimmu knew. That makes sense, doesn't it?"

"Yesterday I'd have agreed one hundred percent. Ten minutes into your head and I knew differently. Those Edimmu knew you. They have interacted with you in the presence of your father. It's highly improbable they were talking about a non-material creature like Ehpslab. Like I said, things are getting very clear to me. I have a few questions for old Richard Wilkinson."

With that, he pushed the door open.

Josh looked in on his parents in bed. His mother was fast asleep, dressed in a flannel nightdress. Josh wanted to rush over and cover her so that Wisdom could not see the way her breasts rose and fell with each breath, but he fought the urge. It was not real, after all. This was just a dream. His father sat propped up in bed reading a thick white book by the small pool of light coming from the lamp on the night table. He wore the wire-framed glasses he had needed for reading since his last birthday. Richard Wilkinson did not look up as they walked into the room.

"Go ahead, Josh." Wisdom waved his hand forward.

"What?"

"You'll have to say something to your father or he's not going to see us. Once you get it going, I can take over."

"You're not going to hurt him, are you?"

Wisdom rolled his eyes. "Again, not real, remember? That is not really your father, just your memory of your father."

"Then how can he...?"

"Smart question. How can he provide information that you don't know if he's just a figment of your imagination? Don't know. Maybe he won't. Who can say what information you have tucked away in your head? Let's just think of him as a focal point to get the information we need and take it from there. Come on, ask away. I don't have all night, you know."

Josh looked back and forth from Wisdom to his father several times. Then, with a shrug, he took two steps toward the bed. "Dad? Hey Dad, can you see me?"

Richard Wilkinson looked up from his book. "Of course I can see you, son. What's the matter? Can't sleep? I told you not to have that last piece of pie. You just can't handle the sweets." When he started speaking, his voice was very faint, but as the words continued, they grew steadily louder until they reached a normal volume. There was still a strange quality to them, though, an echo as if his voice was reverberating around a very large room.

"It's not that, Dad." Josh looked back at Wisdom. "It's kind of serious. I need to know about the Council, Dad. The Council of Peacocks."

Richard put the book down and took off his reading glasses. "Maybe I should be the one asking what *you* know about the Council of Peacocks, Josh. Who have you been talking to?"

Josh looked over at Wisdom. His father still had not reacted to him. Somehow, Wisdom was invisible. "I talked with a man named Wisdom. More importantly, I talked with these things called Edimmu. Sometimes they look like humans with wings, but they're really more like lizard people. And they say they know you. I mean, I know they know you. That's how they know me. The only thing is I don't know how *you* know them. I don't know why they respect you, like you're their boss or...Oh."

Richard folded his hands together on his lap. "What is it you think you know, son? You think that maybe I'm a member of this Council of Peacocks and I've hired these Edimmus for some reason?"

"Dad, please..."

"No, don't hold anything back, son. I'm really curious now. What else do you think you know?"

Wisdom leaned forward and whispered into Josh's ear. "Ask him about Propates."

"Dad," Josh said after a moment. "I know about Propates. I saw the factory and the demons. I just don't know why. Tell me what's going on. What's the connection between the Orpheans, the Edimmu and this Council of Peacocks?"

His father lowered his head. A smile crossed his lips unlike any expression Josh had ever seen on his father's face. The light from the nearby lamp flickered and dimmed, the shadows bled forward, filling the room with animated darkness. It was just like back in Quebec. Suddenly, despite appearances, his father was really not his father anymore.

From behind Richard's face came a strange voice. "Wisdom, you should know better than pulling a stunt like this. I should fry the kid's brain just to teach you a lesson."

Wisdom squared his shoulders and squinted his eyes. "Propates, is that you, you little snake?"

"Careful with the name-calling, Wisdom. My patience is very thin nowadays." The image of Josh's father jumped, twisted and changed, as if someone had changed channels on a television. There was a different man in bed with his mother now, a man with shoulder-length black hair and dark, Mediterranean features. His eyes shone neon blue, like a fire was trapped in his skull. "You're making it very difficult for me to stay civil, you know."

"Civil?" Wisdom flicked back his cloak to free his arms, a motion that held such violence in it Josh thought instantly of blood flying from a bullet wound. "If you had any idea what I've been through recently, you would realize how incredibly civil I've been. I think you've forgotten who I am. But then, you seem to also forget who you are."

Propates snapped his fingers and the bedroom disappeared. He now stood, legs spread in a defiant stance, dressed in a double-breasted black suit with a neon orange tie. In his hands was a pitchfork, orange flames dancing along the tines. "I know exactly who I am, Wisdom. I'm your son. I am what you made me, just as you're what your father made you. Despite evidence to the contrary, I believe deep down you are a reasonable man. Let's call a truce, shall we?"

Wisdom gave a sort of short cough that sounded like

laughter. "That would be a 'No'. I've seen the future. It's time for me to stop you once and for all. So why don't you head home, get a good night's sleep. I'll see you tomorrow. Oh, and for the record, the pitchfork is a bit much."

Wisdom waved his hand before him, like he was wiping frost from a window and...

***

Josh sat up in bed, a scream of shock in his throat. He pressed his knuckles against his forehead. Whatever Wisdom had done, throwing him out of the dream like that, it left him with a killer headache. He sat there rubbing his head for a long time before he was able to lie back down.

No matter what he did, he couldn't force himself to go back to sleep.

***

Wisdom came back to his body with a jolt.

'How did he do that?" He wiped sweat from his forehead. "I never taught him how to walk in the Dreaming. When did he get that powerful?"

Only the sound of Echo's deep breaths prevented him from flying into a rage. He looked down at her body, saw the peaceful expression on her face and wondered if everything he had done would be enough. Could he stop Propates from killing her?

He slipped out of the covers and went to this closet. He grabbed the first suit his hands fell on and left the bedroom. Getting dressed in there might wake her. He would get dressed in his office upstairs. Then he would spend a few hours calming down. After that, he was going to shatter every bone in Propates' body.

Chapter Thirty-One

The sun had been up for some time. Josh stayed under the covers, unwilling to move. He found it hard to focus on anything. His joints ached from hours of twisting and tossing in bed. Still, it was warm under the sheets and his room looked cold. Pallid red light filtered in through the tinted windows and the shadows seemed far too solid for his liking. Something was going to happen today, something that would make the horror in the Laurentians pale in comparison. So he stayed in bed for a long time. He knew once he got up, events would start rolling toward an ending.

God only knew what kind of end was waiting for him.

Eventually he surrendered and threw back the covers. He knew they were no real protection from the things waiting for him. After last night, he realized there really was no place where he was beyond being touched by others. Not even in his dreams.

He walked to the bathroom, stripped and turned on the shower. He kept the water cold, hoping it would help him shake off the sleepiness under his skin. He stayed under the stream of water for about twenty minutes. Only when his teeth started chattering did he turn off the nozzle and step out. He dried off and wrapped a large white towel around his waist and went to the dressers to decide what to wear.

On top of one of the dressers was a jewelry box. He opened it and pursed his lips at what he found. There were dozens of gold and silver rings with different types of jeweled settings, at least ten different chains and four different watches. While his family had never lacked for money, they did not have the kind of wealth Jan's family had. Yet these pieces of jewelry spoke of wealth on a completely different scale. Josh was not the type to steal, but, if he was, he could probably pawn off one of the diamond-rimmed Rolexes and live comfortably for a year or two. There were two of them, one with a platinum wristband; the other had alternating rows of platinum and diamond studs.

"Is every room here equipped like this?" Just how rich was Wisdom, anyway?

He decided on a silver Movado watch. Though not a cheap watch, it was the least expensive he could choose. The thought of losing or damaging any of the other watches tied his stomach up in knots.

He was just slipping the watch on when he noticed a dark blur over his shoulder. He spun, expecting to see shadows and wings. Instead, his eyes focused on Jared. He started to relax, his face breaking into a smile. Then, slowly, the smile died. There was something about the look in the young boy's eyes, the way he stood. The way he repeatedly clenched and unclenched his fists.

The way the light slid away from him and shadows pooled around his feet.

***

David stood in front of the vending machine in the lunch room trying to decide between a chocolate bar and a bag of chips when the feeling hit him. He took a deep breath and looked around. The corridor outside the lunchroom was empty. It was still too early for most of the staff to be here. So far the only other sign of life he'd seen was Garnet. She was dressed in a form-fitting emerald-green suit. She smiled at him as she passed by, making a comment about meeting up with Wisdom.

'Something is wrong,' he thought. He turned his back on the vending machine and went to the doorway. He looked up and down the corridor but there was no sign of anyone. He shook his head and tried to get back to his hunger, but the feeling would not go away. It reminded him of the prom, back when he'd had the sudden impression of Ramona cheating on him in the parking lot. He walked back to the vending machine and decided on a chocolate bar. He bent down to retrieve it when Todd and Jessica rushed into the lunchroom.

"Where's the fire?" he asked as he unwrapped the Big Turk.

"Quiet!" Todd spoke in a whisper. His hair was uncombed and wild, and he was still dressed in a pair of blue silk pajamas. There was a nearly-identical pair in David's room.

David started to speak again, but Todd just raised his open hand in the universal signal for 'Wait'. A moment later a Chinese man in a dark blue suit passed by the doorway. He barely paused to look up at Todd. Jessica, also still dressed in her pajamas, bit her nails and paced back and forth. Todd watched the man disappear from view. Only then did he turn back to David and lower his hand.

"What the hell's going on?" David asked.

Jessica stopped pacing and looked up at him. "Can't you feel it? God, why do you have to be such a newbie? I wish Amy was here instead of you. I wouldn't have to explain everything to her."

"You know, where I come from they wait till after breakfast before they start insulting people. Why don't you....?"

"Quiet! Both of you." Todd pushed Jessica further into the lunchroom so their voices would not carry so far. "We're in enough trouble as it is. Last thing we need is for Wisdom to know I've been playing psychic detective. See, I woke up this morning and everything just felt, I don't know, wrong somehow. So I took a quick peek into Wisdom's mind."

"You did what?" David felt his mouth go dry and knew there was no way he was going to be able to eat the chocolate bar now. "You can do that?"

Jessica started pacing again. "Well, obviously he can do it or he wouldn't have just done it. Loser. Keep up, will you?"

"Again with the no-rude rule. In case you forgot, I'm not the heroic type. I am not above hitting little girls, you know."

"Please, keep quiet! Jessica, behave yourself. He

obviously has no idea what's going on."

"What *is* going on?" David found it hard to concentrate on the drama being played out before him. Something kept drawing his attention away. He found it hard to focus on anything.

Jessica cupped a hand to her mouth and whispered as if she did not want anyone to overhear. "Todd thinks Wisdom's gone crazy."

"I did not say that!" Todd realized how loud he was, moved to within a few feet of David and continued at a barely audible volume. "I didn't even think that. Remember, be careful what you think around here. Having said that, I can feel him, Wisdom. He's all over the place. His anger, actually I don't even think anger is the right word. It's like the kind of rage you see in caged tigers, when you just know they would rip you to shreds if it wasn't for the bars keeping them in."

"So how is that different from yesterday?"

Jessica walked over to him and punched him in the stomach. "Stop being stupid. Maybe we should have gone to Josh instead."

"Don't do that again." David resisted the urge to smack her upside the head, and then decided there was no reason to resist. He slapped the back of her head, not hard, but enough to set her ponytail swinging. "And if you want to go see blondie, be my guest. Let him be all heroic and noble."

Jessica, her face turning steadily red, raised her fist again. Todd grabbed her by the wrist and pulled her away from David. "We don't have time for this. I'm glad you two have bonded so well, but you can act like brother and sister later. We are going to see Josh, but you were on the way to him so we thought we'd come get you first."

"Come on, Todd, let's just leave the baby alone."

"Jessica, enough!" Todd's voice rose above a whisper again.

Behind them, someone cleared their throat.

***

Josh was confused. "Jared, what are you doing in here?"

Jared's upper lip twitched and the light in the room dimmed ever further. "I don't see what's so special about you. But Propates says you can't be allowed to stay here anymore. He says you're dangerous and I have to bring you in. You don't look so dangerous to me, though."

Josh licked his lips and backed up. He quickly searched the room, looking for a weapon. Then he saw it, exactly where it was last night. Now he just had to make his way over to it before....

Jared rolled his eyes. "Idiot. I am a mind reader, you know?" He looked over at the letter opener on a nearby desk. The sharp blade jumped into the air and flew toward Josh. Josh threw himself down and rolled back into the bathroom, losing the towel in the process. He got to his feet and closed the door just as Jared approached it. Luckily for him, he was able to get the lock in place before Jared could reach the handle.

Josh backed away from the door and stared at the handle. For a moment everything was completely still and silent. Then, with a small popping sound, the handle dropped off the door and landed on the tiled floor with a clink.

"If there was ever time for a miracle," Josh said, "this would be it."

***

"Mr. Ross?" The Chinese man had returned. He stood just outside the lunchroom and David was now fully aware of a small protrusion under his suit jacket that could only be a gun. David looked back at the other two. Jessica put a finger to her lips and Todd just shook his head.

"Answer him," Todd said.

"What?" David asked.

"Just answer him. I'll take care of the rest."

David turned back to the Chinese man and smiled. "Yes. I'm Mr. Ross. Can I help you?"

"I heard voices." The man's voice was dark with strength and menace. It left David feeling like he was back in school and being sent to the principal's office. The Chinese man slipped into the lunchroom and looked around. "Where are they?"

"Where are who?" David stared at Todd. He stood exactly where he had been, right hand pressed to his forehead, left hand held out before him, fingers stretched and palm pressed outwards. But the guard's eyes did not seem to land on him.

"I saw them when I passed by before. The other Anomalies. Where are they?"

David shrugged and tried to look innocent. He also tried to keep his eyes from straying to the other two. He had never been a very good liar. "Oh, them. They left. Don't know where they are now. Really. But there's no one else here, right? I mean, you're here and I'm here and we can see each other. You could see someone else if they were here and since there is no one you can't see them. That means there are no other people, or another person here. Are you sure you saw them before? Maybe it was shadows or…I'll just shut up now." Five words in, David realized he should have just shook his head and kept quiet. As it was, he just let his voice fade away before his rambling looked any more suspicious than it already had.

The man looked at David and slightly shook his head. Then he walked back out into the corridor and disappeared again. When he was gone, David let out a breath he was not aware he had been holding and wiped his forehead with a shaking hand.

"Don't do that to me again." He walked briskly away from the door and stood in front of Todd. "I don't think I've got a heart condition, but I'd rather not find out."

"Wow," Jessica said. "Nerves of steel. Can't wait to see you in the battlefield."

"Jessica!" Todd lowered his hands and sat on a nearby table. "Can't you go back to the way you were yesterday?

You were actually tolerable then."

"How did you do that?" David kept looking back at the door. He was sure the man would be back any second now. "It was like you were invisible to them."

Todd smiled. "It's easy once you know what to do. You just alter the way their brain interprets the signals the eyes send it. You make someone see something that isn't there or make them not see something that is there. Bethany used to be really good at doing it. I always told her the two of us could make a mint as international thieves. You know what she said? She said it was too dangerous. Irony is she'd still be alive if we had."

"We don't have time for this, Todd." Jessica crossed her arms over her chest and stared at the ceiling. "Wisdom's almost ready."

"Ready to do what?" David looked at her, but once again his eyes refused to stay focused on her. Something was distracting him.

"That's what we've been trying to tell you." Todd rubbed at his eyes and got to his feet. "From what I can read from the crap he's throwing off, Wisdom plans on attacking the Council of Peacocks. And he's going to use us as the weapons."

David raised his eyebrows and felt his mouth go dry. He kept looking at Todd, expecting him to say he was joking any minute now. When that did not happen, he lowered his eyebrows and felt the strength bleed out of his knees.

"I think you're right. I think Wisdom has gone crazy."

***

The door swung open slowly.

Josh backed up until his back struck the back wall. He licked his lips – too dry – and tried to focus. 'Think', he thought. 'I've faced Edimmu, escaped a slaughterhouse and broke a demon's neck. One little boy should be no problem.'

Only it was. Josh had no idea how he did the things he did. He had never called them up at will. They just happened. Miracles. He was just extremely lucky. Or was he? Back in the Laurentians, the chains fell out of the wall when he thought about them. The car drove on missing wheels because he wanted it to. The pitchfork stopped in mid-air when he willed it to stop. Back in high school, at the bush party when he killed Edimmu, he made a conscious decision for his hand not to burn. And when he was a child, hit by a bus, had he not thought, just the moment before impact, please don't hit me, please don't touch me? Was it really that simple? Did he just have to will something to have it happen?

The bathroom door hit the inside wall, bounced slightly and settled into place. Jared stood in the empty frame, smiling.

"Yeah, not so tough at all," he said. Jared looked over to the shower and the taps spun alive. Hot water spurted from the nozzle, filling the air with steam. Jared looked over to the sink and spun the hot water tap so hard it flew forward and struck the side of the shower.

"What are you doing?" Josh tried to back up but there was nowhere else to run.

"Calling them. Don't worry. You'll be home soon."

Josh found it hard to see now. The bathroom filled with steam impossibly fast. Jared was a blur of shadow that seemed miles away. A sound like the rapping of a lead pipe against ceramic tiles built from a distant echo to a loud ringing. Josh looked around for the source of the sound and noticed the mirrors. They were completely covered with mist except for a small vaguely circular patch that was dark, like a skylight looking up at a starless sky.

"You're calling the Edimmu?" Josh realized how naked and powerless he was and wondered if they would still look at him with love now that he had killed their kind.

"No," Jared answered, his voice faint, like a whisper from a dream. "Not them. I'm calling the others. Like I said, you're heading home. Back to your father, Ehpslab."

Josh looked at the circle of darkness. Strength drained

from every inch of his body. He saw now what was making the circle. A hand, covered in red blisters and pussing sores was wiping the mist away from the other side of the mirror.

"No!" Josh jumped up. He suddenly knew beyond a shadow of doubt that he could not allow the creature on the other side of the mirror to make that circle any larger. If it was big enough, something would come through into this world, something he knew he would not be strong enough to fight. He focused on the mirror and channeled his fear. With a sharp deafening crack the mirror shattered into hundreds of pieces. He could feel the glass wanting to shoot out in all directions, to fill the room with shrapnel, but he kept it in place. The glass settled gently around the base of the floor.

Josh clenched his fists and turned to the doorway. The mist had dissipated. He saw Jared clearly now, saw the expression of shock and fear dawning on the young boy's face. Then Josh pushed with the force of his will and Jared flew back twenty feet and hit the wall in the bedroom. Pictures fell to the carpeted floor, glass shattering. Jared slid down the wall, shook his head and then jumped quickly to his feet.

"I am so going to kill you," Jared said.

Before Josh could react, Jared stopped and slowly turned to look at something to his right. Someone was in the door to his quarters. He could feel them. Could feel her.

"Jessica," Josh said and ran out of the bathroom. He was just in time to see Jessica jump into the air. The air around her turn to puddles and eddies of darkness and quasi-solid shapes. Then the darkness shot out from her and hit Jared square in the chest. It twisted around his body like pythons, squeezing and crushing his body. Then, with a final sick wet crunch, Jared's body bent backwards at a ninety-degree angle, breaking his back. A second later the legs bent sideways at the knee. Two more wet crunching sounds. For a moment, Jared's body hung suspended in the air. Then it collapsed and was still. A thin stream of blood trickled out of his left eye.

"Oh my God," Josh fell to his knees. He could not take his eyes of the dead body. 'He was just a kid,' he thought. Then he looked over at Jessica. She stood in the doorway with Todd and David. No one seemed to notice that Josh was naked. They were all looking at Jared's corpse.

"Humph," Jessica said. "Never liked him that much, anyway."

***

Wisdom arrived several long minutes later. No one had called him. He had just felt the use of power and the coming of death. Wisdom spoke briefly with Garnet who had arrived alongside him, making arrangements for the removal of the body. Josh dressed in the bathroom but did not trust himself to speak yet. When he came out, Elaine was there questioning the other Anomalies. Everyone fell silent as they became aware of him. Josh stared at the spot where Jared had hit the wall, where Josh had thrown him with a power he did not understand. Then he sat in a chair and told everyone what had happened.

In the end, Wisdom shook his head and turned to Elaine. "This wasn't supposed to happen. You understand what I'm saying, Elaine?"

Just for a moment, Elaine's eyes went wide. Then she nodded. "Perhaps we should talk."

Wisdom nodded and left the room without another word. Elaine followed.

Jessica snuck to the door, looked up and down the hallway, then stepped back inside and closed the door.

"Okay they're gone," she said. "We can get back to business."

David blanched. "Jesus, Jessica. Can't you give us a few minutes?"

"No, I can't. We've already wasted enough time, thanks to Jared."

"What the hell did you do to him, Jessica? How is that

even possible?"

Jessica punched David in the arm. "Here we go again. Just deal. He's dead. Get over it."

David swung his hand toward Jessica, obviously trying to smack the back of her head. Jessica saw the movement and ducked out of the way.

"You know child abuse is against the law." Jessica put her hands on her hips. She could not have looked more like a child if she'd been trying.

"Not in this country. Now be civil."

Jessica cocked her head to one side. "You're lying. Child abuse is, like, illegal everywhere. Isn't it? He is lying, right, Todd?"

Todd exchanged a look with Josh that nearly sent him laughing out loud. He covered his mouth with his right hand, realizing any sign of amusement on his face would just send Jessica over the edge.

"Let's not find out." Todd said tactfully, stepping between the two of them. "Jessica does have a point, though. We did come here to tell you something, Josh. And I'm sure this thing with Jared just made everything that much worse. Wisdom is on the verge of a meltdown."

"I told you he thought Wisdom was crazy." Jessica stuck her tongue out at David.

"I did not say Wisdom was crazy. He's just not overly sane right now. He plans on attacking the Council of Peacocks and he's going to use us as weapons."

Josh put a hand on the dresser drawer for support and took a deep breath. "I was afraid of that."

For a moment, no one said anything. Jessica glared at him while David and Todd exchanged a long silent look.

Finally, Jessica spoke. "What do you mean, you were afraid of that? You *knew* this was going to happen? How could you?"

Josh rubbed his hands over his face. He looked over at his bed and realized he had been very right about this day. He should have stayed under the covers. "Have a seat and

I'll tell you. Wisdom came to me last night. Well, he came to my dream. Anyway, this is what happened."

Chapter Thirty-Two

By the time Josh finished telling the story of what had happened last night, everyone in the room was wide-eyed and speechless. David chewed on his nails, slowly shaking his head, while Todd just stared off into a corner. Jessica did her best to pretend his story didn't faze her. She nodded and rested the index and middle fingers of her right hand on her chin in a fairly good imitation of Katie Couric interviewing a celebrity. However, she cleared her throat far too often and kept tapping her left foot on the carpeted floor. She was nervous. Josh did not have to be psychic to see that.

"I had no idea Wisdom could do something like that." Todd rubbed his palms against his pants, his eyes still focused off in the distance.

"Let's be honest, Todd," Jessica said, clearing her throat again. "We don't really know what Wisdom is capable of. We've never known, not really."

"True. I mean, I knew he was powerful but to enter someone else's dream like that, make Josh see the things he saw?"

"It's like he's Freddy Krueger or something. Spooky." David spoke through his fingers, not bothering to take a break from his nail biting. "Here we are, all signed up to do whatever he wants us to, and we know nothing about him."

"Speak for yourself." Jessica flung her hand away from her chin, a smug expression forming over her face. She turned away from Josh and focused on David, the act setting her ponytail flopping behind her head. "We know lots about Wisdom."

"Like what?" David started pacing now, still chewing away. "He's a man with lots of secrets and a whole bunch of money and some sort of mysterious power that lets him do things no one should be able to do? Hell, that describes Donald Trump. What I mean is we don't know what he is. He could be the devil himself for all we know. Who's to say we're not on the wrong side? Maybe the Council of Peacocks are the good guys in this."

Josh leaned back on the bed and cupped his hands behind his head. "Don't think so. There is the whole making deals with bloodsucking reptilians and pussing demons. Not to mention how they keep trying to kill us."

"Maybe they should!" David let his hands drop away from his mouth and stood there, stiff, each breath he took heavy and pointed.

"Maybe they should kill us?" Todd turned away from the corner. Josh could not read the expression on Todd's face. There were bags under the heavy-set man's eyes Josh had not noticed before. Todd's eyes moved rapidly in the sockets, as if trying to take in every part of David all at once. "You think because we're part demon, maybe we deserve to be, what, exterminated? Like vermin or something? Is that what you're saying, David? Christ!"

"Why don't you just go back to your room?" Jessica said. "For that matter, why don't you just go back home?"

David made a sound that was part laugh, part cry. "That's just it. I can't go home. Wisdom knows that. See, I'm sort of wanted on murder charges. Kind of takes away some of my options. I've spent that last couple of days – hell, the last couple of months – trying to convince myself that I wasn't some sort of monster. Thing is, I really am a monster. Maybe it is because I have this demon blood inside me, or maybe it's just because I was born wrong somehow. I've done bad things. Hurt people."

"And your answer to guilt is a death-wish?" Todd's lips raised in a sneer. "Bathroom's over there. Take one of the mirror shards to your wrist and get happy. Suicide is stupid. Period. Way I see it, maybe I am quote-unquote evil. Maybe I am damned to hell just because of how I was born. But I think the way you live says a lot more about you than the way you were born. So you're wanted on murder charges and you feel guilty about it. Boo-hoo. Turn yourself in if you feel so bad about it. Do your time in jail, pay your debt to society and all that cliché crap. Killing yourself or letting someone else kill you is not going to bring anybody back to life, and it certainly won't make you feel any less guilty. You want to be a martyr, go ahead. Be my guest. But I don't think you can be a demon and a martyr at the same time."

Jessica cut in. "I think what he's trying to say is quit your whining, you big baby, and focus on the trouble you're in now."

"Actually," Todd's face went lax, "that's not quite what I was aiming for."

"Whatever. I'm starting to think that being an adult just means you use more words than you need and pretend you're thinking something other than what you are. We all know he's wussing out. What he really needs is a slap across his self-pitying face, not a tough-love pep talk. Let's forget he's here, okay? Let him sit in the corner and get all weepy-faced about how he's a bad man and all. We need to figure out what we're going to do."

"About what?" Josh sat up again and let his hands fall to his side.

"Hello?" Jessica slapped the bed with both hands. "You were listening, weren't you? Wisdom is going to take us into a battle with the Council. Does any of this ring a bell?"

Josh smiled. "Gee, Jessica. You sure are cute when you're not, you know, killing things."

Jessica bit her lip. Blood raced to her face. She looked like Elmer Fudd in a *Bugs Bunny* cartoon about to blow his top.

"Look, you guys do what you want. I have to go with Wisdom."

Todd lowered his head as if the weight of Josh's words had pushed down on him. "Say what? You're going with Wisdom into Hell. Josh, of any of us here, with the obvious exception of Mr. David gloomy-pants, you're the least capable of surviving something like this. You have no idea what your EFHBs are, let alone how to use them. The Council has Edimmu, not to mention enough mojo power to make Wisdom think twice about taking them on. And so what? You think 'Oh I know karate so I can take on this secret society'?'"

Josh chuckled, a genuine smile on his face. "I don't know karate. I know how to take care of myself, that's all. And I did use my whatever-you-call-it to throw Jared across the room. I think I'm getting a handle on the power, but that is beside the point. This is about family, Todd. My father. He's mixed up in something – got me mixed up in something – and I need to know what it is. No matter what anyone says, whatever the circumstances of how I was conceived, my father is not a demon. My father works for a branch of the CSIS, but it also looks like he works for the Council of Peacocks. My real father is very human – a human mixed up in some very weird stuff, to be sure – and I need to find out what he is keeping secret from me. And just so we're clear here, I may not be able to read minds or levitate books but I can take out a couple of guys with guns before they fire a shot. And let's not forget that I'm the only one here who has killed an Edimmu before. Until a few minutes ago, I thought I was the only one capable of killing a human being."

Josh stopped.

Jessica and Todd stared at each other, their faces overly relaxed as if their muscles were dead. Jessica's eyes twitched ever so slightly as if she was actually trying to see through Todd's eyes into his brain. Todd's eyes glistened as if they were covered in a layer of tears.

"What?" Josh went stiff. "What aren't you telling me?"

Jessica nodded and looked at the ground.

Todd took a breath and let it out slowly between pursed lips. He licked his lips before starting to speak. "That wasn't the first time Jessica killed someone, Josh. It's part of the training we get from Ms. Ryerson."

"She trains you to kill people?"

David stopped pacing.

Jessica nodded.

Todd went back to looking off into a corner.

"Great. The fun just keeps on coming." Josh covered his mouth with his right hand and leaned forward, thinking.

For several minutes the only sound in the room was that of people breathing. Finally, Jessica cleared her throat and spoke. "Maybe we shouldn't have said anything about it. It's ... well, I can't say it's not a big deal, because that's kind of...."

"Monstrous?" David started chewing on his fingernails again. "Is that the word you were looking for?"

Jessica shrugged. Then she shook her head. "I don't know. It was necessary, at least the way I see it. If we don't know how to kill with our powers we wouldn't really know how not to kill. It makes sense if you think about it. It's like, well, the only way you can really know how strong you are is to push yourself to your limits. It was hard for me." The way Jessica hung her head made it obvious she disliked saying anything was hard for her. "But I got through it. Which is more than I can say for Jared."

Josh shivered. "Didn't look to me like he had a hard time with the idea of killing."

"Really?" Jessica said. "Well, maybe you're not looking at it the right way. He could have snapped your spinal column when you were in the shower or caused a brain hemorrhage. Instead, he had to call someone else to do the dirty work. It's true what I said. I never really liked him. I think it was those beady black eyes of his. He looked like a seagull with sandy-brown hair. Anyway, he had a few tests and he just wasn't able to go through with it. He left them wounded, but he could never finish them off. He wanted so bad to get to the next level in class, to catch up with Amy and me, but Ms. Ryerson told him he would have to keep taking that test and pass it before he could go on."

Josh fixated on the image of Jared sneaking into the bathroom while he showered and snapping his neck using the power of his mind. He shivered again.

"Count me in as extremely grateful he wasn't as good a

student as you."

Jessica smiled with pride, and Josh felt even colder than before. He went to the closet, took out a sweater and hoped that would help.

"Okay, you guys do what you want," he said. "I'm off to see Wisdom."

"What?" Todd raced over and grabbed him by the shoulders. "Stop and think, man. He wants to send us off into some sort of war and here you are skipping off to the head of the line?"

"I think I answered that already. There's no sense hiding from what you can't escape." Josh walked toward the door, stopped and turned back to face them. "David, why don't you come with me?"

"Huh?" David went slightly pale, which made his freckles all the more apparent. "Why me?"

"Because you need it most of all."

"Need what?"

"To confront the beast inside."

***

"Maybe it won't be enough."

When he first travelled back through time, a calm sort of arrogance filled him. He knew what was going to happen, so he knew how to prevent it. He knew when the Edimmu would attack Toronto, knew they would slaughter or kidnap most of the Anomalies; but all of that was unimportant. All that mattered was keeping Echo alive. That and making sure Propates did not get to remake the world in his image. So Wisdom found Josh: a new Anomaly who could perhaps lead to a different string of events.

Unfortunately, not all of the new string was to his liking. Jared's betrayal had caught him completely off guard. Maybe it was pride that had blinded him to that threat the first time or maybe, just maybe....

"The threat wasn't there the first time."

Perhaps he had not given enough thought to just how

much influence this visitor from another world was having on the course of events. Ever since he felt the surge of power preceding Jared's death, Wisdom had been filled with a subtle and recurring emotion. Fear. If Wisdom wasn't the only one traveling through time, maybe all of his carefully calculated plans were worthless.

He was still lost in thought twenty minutes later when there was a knock at his door.

"Come in," Wisdom smiled and looked at the gilded clock on the wall. At least this was roughly on schedule.

Josh and David walked in the door and the smile on Wisdom's face faltered. 'It was supposed to be Jessica,' he thought. Maybe this was a good thing. Maybe Josh could bring about something Jessica had been unable to do.

"We know what you're planning," Josh said as soon as he sat down. "The reason Jessica and Todd were in my room was because they couldn't help but read your thoughts. How exactly do you plan on using us as weapons against the Council of Peacocks? David and I haven't even gone through your bloody training program."

"Though, from the sounds of it, I'm not sure I want to anymore." David squirmed in his seat. "You know, the whole kill-a-person, win-a-prize thing. It's a bit too *Hunger Games* for my taste."

Wisdom's smile twisted slightly. "So I left out a few details. You knew what you were getting into. Look, I'm sorry things worked out this way. I would have preferred to spoon-feed you some of the more delicate material. Despite what the Council of Peacocks thinks, it is not healthy for the human mind to take too much in at once. I could have lied to you. Hell, I could jump through your bones and scramble your brains until you don't know if you're skinning a man alive or knitting a sweater. But I won't."

"Thanks," David said. "That makes me feel a whole lot better."

"I could take the Council out on my own. Possibly. Of course, with my power I'm not so good with the whole calculated strikes. You don't know much about me. Barely anything at all, really. Suffice it to say I have more power at my disposal than almost anyone on the planet. I'm not expecting you to be all Navy Seal-like, nor am I expecting any mystical Neo-Matrix ninjas. I have a plan that will utilize the specific strengths each of you have. You are more powerful than you realize. If everything goes well, we'll be in and out in half an hour with Propates' head in a bag."

"And what if it goes badly?" David kept his eyes on the floor. No matter how he tried, he could not raise the courage to look Wisdom in the eyes.

Wisdom sighed. "Do you really need me to answer that question? If it does not go well, we all die. Or I may end up blasting Greece into space. Either case would be unfortunate."

"And what about your father? What if he shows up again?"

Wisdom took a deep breath and turned his full attention on Josh. The young man sank deep into the chair, pushed back by the force of his stare. "My father will show up. Count on that. Things will get messy, but I'll take care of that. Still, it might be best if you don't mention my father again."

"Wisdom?" David cleared his throat. "Who is your father? Is he a demon? Does that make you sort of like us?"

"You know, I'm fairly certain I just said 'don't mention my father again.' Now, go get something to eat. We'll be leaving soon."

***

While the building's custodians cleaned up the blood and shattered glass in his old room, Josh got settled in a new one. As hard as he liked to think he was, he couldn't bring himself to stay even one more hour in that room. Every time he looked at the dent in the wall, he thought of Jared. Thought of how he'd thrown him back with the power of his mind.

Until that moment, a small part of him had held onto the faint hope that he really wasn't like the rest of the freaks here. He'd forced himself to believe he was fundamentally different from the others. Anomalies. It was just another word for freak. Since the advent of comic books, every kid over the age of six dreamed of being a superhero; but there was no mistaking Josh for a superhero. He was not a savior. He was not the next step in human evolution. He was a half-demon bastard. He was created by evil to do evil things.

And now he could no longer deny it.

He looked out the window at the chaotic streets below. The streets were so crowded it looked like beetles swarming through metal canyons. He wondered how long it would take to lose himself in that crowd. How long before Wisdom found him? How long could he run from the Council of Peacocks and the knowledge that his father had lied to him his whole life?

"Not long at all." Saying the words aloud was enough to dismiss all notion of running. He had to find out what his father was doing with the Council of Peacocks.

He was about to turn away from the window when something caught his eye. A single Caucasian face in the throbbing mess of people. It seemed to look directly at Josh. A feeling trembled in his gut, the building of fear. Then he saw the gold ring on the man's left hand. There was a flash of light and Josh dropped to his knees.

Memory washed over him, more forceful than ever before.

***

"I can't control him anymore."

Josh was sixteen years old, standing at the top of the stairs eavesdropping on his father.

"The subject is not open for debate, Lucius." His dad spoke in a hushed voice, but the anger behind the words came across clearly. "He got into a fight at school today. Nearly tore the arm of a kid right out of the socket. By the time I got there, Josh was...I know I should have expected some differences. ... Yes, I know that, Lucius. I'm not an idiot. But I'm telling you, he's different. He's not like the other ones....Whatever. Stop being a prick. I'm bringing him to Propates tomorrow. There has to be something....Look, I don't care how it's done. I need to have control of this boy until the army's ready. Even with the technological help of our friend from away, without the muscle to...I am not ranting. And I'm telling you because you're putting too much importance on the half-breeds. There's only a hundred or so we know about. Even if we take half of them, Wisdom will...Humph. There's really that many? Doesn't matter. It's still not enough to...I don't care how much demon is in him. There's no way Josh could win that type of war."

For several minutes his father was silent. Josh didn't understand half of what his father was talking about. By demon, did his father mean Wisdom? Or was he talking about the Edimmu? Josh had seen the scaly reptoids only a few times in his life. Most of those times were not pleasant. They'd tortured and eventually killed one of his best friends. As a child, Josh vaguely remembered several trips with his father to a meeting place somewhere underground, a place filled with hundreds of Edimmu, some with wings, others in almost human form. He remembered a lot of grownup talk but he hadn't paid any attention to what they were actually saying at the time. Now he wished he had.

"Fine," his father continued. "I'll send him and his mother to Windsor. But this had better work, Lucius. There's too much at stake. With what's coming, we can't afford to have the half-breeds fall into Wisdom's hands....No, I don't care about that. We're going to remake the world, turn it back to what it should have been all along. I can't let my personal feelings get in the way. If Josh has to die, so be it."

***

Josh felt nauseous and his head was swimming and he

felt nauseous. How could his father do that? For the last several days he'd assumed the stranger with the gold ring worked for his demon father. Now that he had all his memories back – and this did, somehow, feel like the last of them – he saw his father for what he really was: a single-minded man on a mission with no concern for anyone hurt in the process. His father was a monster.

Getting back to his feet, Josh looked back out the window and searched for the man with the gold ring. He was nowhere to be found.

Chapter Thirty-Three

Wisdom watched Echo pour a drink, studying the moment. A picture in a scrapbook. He placed it beside the image of the first time he saw her: a young woman carrying water back from a stone well in a wood bucket. Back then, she wore the same drab clothes as the other village women but there was something about her that cried out to him. In the distance, snow-capped mountains rose to pale blue sky. In that moment, Echo appeared as distant and untouchable as those mountains. That's why he took her. Forcefully.

Centuries passed but he still saw her that way. Untouchable. No matter what he did, she was beyond his control. In those first years, he tried to force his way in. He used power to prevent her from leaving, controlling her mind and body. But she never submitted.

Years passed, centuries passed and old pains dimmed. Their relationship changed. While she never forgave him, he knew she had feelings for him. It wasn't until he'd lost her that he realized how much he loved her.

'And I'm going to lose you again,' he thought. 'No, not this time. This time it will be different. It has to be different.'

"Echo, please don't go."

She shook her head and downed her drink. "We've been over this. I'm going with you. Period. I want this to be over. I need it to be over so I can get back to my life. That won't happen until Propates and his puppet army are taken out of the picture. After that, I intend on spending a century developing a truly excellent wine collection and enjoying my accumulated wealth."

"But…."

"I'm serious. I don't feel safe anymore. Not when I'm away from you."

Wisdom fought the tears in his eyes. It wasn't the first time he had heard this speech. The last time he'd heard it, Echo ended up dead.

"Look," Echo said. "About last night...."

"Please. Don't." Wisdom went over to her. He used his eyes to caress her. "Just let it be what it was. There are so many things I could apologize for, things I probably *should* apologize for. But I believe I'm well past seeking redemption from anyone. I love you, Andromeda. You know that. And I can sense how complicated your emotions are toward me. Just... be careful today. I don't think I can handle losing you again."

Echo took a step back. "What do you mean 'again.'?"

Wisdom shook his head. "Slip of the tongue."

"Wisdom, you don't have slips of the tongue. What aren't you telling me?"

He reached out now and placed tender fingers on her left cheek. "In many ways I've lost you many times. In other ways I've never really had you. Maybe, if we get through this – once we get through this – maybe we can start over. I'm not asking you to forget the things I've done, but..."

Echo brushed his hand away. "No, you're right. I can't forget. Maybe we should just get this over with."

Nodding to himself, Wisdom sighed. Last time he had said different words but the result was the same: Echo rejected him and he could not blame her.

***

Propates hated darkness, which, considering what he could do, was extremely ironic. With the abilities at his disposal he could travel around the world by jumping into shadows. He could slip into people's minds and bring their nightmares to life. Still, Propates had spent far too many years huddled and frightened in underground places escaping one enemy or another. Wisdom, the Djinn, pagans, Christians, Jews, rival secret societies: all had tried to eradicate Propates and his followers at one point. During the decades of the Inquisition, membership in the Council of Peacocks dwindled and those that remained cut themselves off from the World Above. Then, around 1850, things had changed. Aristocrats and debutants fell in love with the occult and magic was reborn. The Council of Peacocks rose steadily out of the dark places. Now he was finally ready to leave the shadows forever.

He wandered around the ceremonial room, casually examining the equipment to making sure everything was in place. Six stone tables engraved with gold runes encircled a central dais. Beside each table lay a silver tray with several gleaming, metallic surgical instruments and six vials of specially prepared ink. Soon, the last of Wisdom's precious Anomalies would be strapped down and unconscious before him The process of Eyeness would begin. He would make the demons divine.

The air above the central dais shimmered. Suddenly the air rippled and tore open. A puddle of darkness spilled out like Indian ink in oil. Splashes of purple and mauve shot through the shifting black.

Propates went pale.

"I thought our negotiations had ended."

A voice came out of the darkness. "Balance has shifted again. The Judas was caught."

"What about Josh?"

Propates looked over his shoulder. Richard Wilkinson approached, wearing his ceremonial robes of turquoise peacock feathers. Every inch of his clothes bore an artificial eye looking out at the world.

"He's alive," the darkness said. "My son, the idiot, is bringing him to you. Soon."

Propates inhaled sharply. "But you said...."

"I promised you he won't interfere. I hold my bargains. I will see to him. See to the children. Carla and Sanchez are away on a mission for Asmodeus but the Orpheans have eyes everywhere. Remember your deal with them."

Inky blackness poured in reverse back through the tear in space. The air shimmered again and was still.

"Should I try to contact our friend from away?"

"No," Propates hung his head. He put both hands on

the table beside him, leaning against it for support. "Even if he would help us, which is doubtful, we want to avoid bloodshed. We need them for our plan to work. Half the Anomalies we took from Echo's compound died in the process of Eyeness. Let's not waste the remaining ones."

Richard hesitated for only a moment. "I'll double the guards." He exited the room, leaving Propates alone.

"So close," Propates said. "For the sake of our world, please let this work."

***

When she finished arranging for the removal of Jared's body, Garnet came back to her room and stared at the wall for fifteen minutes. The stink of death was still on her. Her mind ricocheted: an image of Jared laughing during *Mortal Kombat*. An image of his body, broken and bent – wide dead eyes and blood. She let down her hair and was brushing it when Jessica entered.

"What's up, Jess?"

"Ugh. You know I hate that name. It's not like I call you Gar. Please don't call me that. It sounds so … I don't know what it sounds like, but please don't call me that."

"Okay. What's up, Jessica?"

Jessica did not bother to speak. She stood in the doorway, hands held behind her back, staring straight forward. One of the reasons Wisdom employed Garnet as his secretary was the high level of proficiency she possessed over her empathic powers: it helped during business negotiations and weeding out disloyal employees. Images and sensations clicked on in her like a daydream. In the space of time it would have taken to speak the words 'I have a problem,' she knew all of Jessica's fear.

"Oh. It's time." She put down her hairbrush. Her stomach was in knots as she studied her face in the mirror. Suddenly she felt very old. "Don't worry. I'm serious. Don't worry about it. Wisdom is many things – ruthless, emotionally stunted and extremely impatient – but he's not stupid. He's invested a lot in you, in all of us. He's not going to throw that all away for nothing. He wouldn't take us into something he didn't think we could walk out of."

Jessica narrowed her eyes. "Are you sure?"

"Absolutely." Garnet straightened a few wrinkles in her dark grey pantsuit with strong, crisp movements. "Go on ahead. I'll meet you in Wisdom's office in a few minutes."

Garnet kept her composure until Jessica left the room. Then it slid off her like melting ice. No matter what she said, she couldn't honestly say Wisdom had their safety in mind. It was completely conceivable that he planned to use the Anomalies as fodder for the Council. Maybe he saw her and the others as a disposable distraction while he snuck in and did the real damage. That could have been his plan all along. Only time would tell.

She walked out of her room and headed toward the elevator, barely looking at the people she passed. All their petty thoughts irritated her.

***

Garnet was seventeen when she first met Wisdom. Just a skinny girl in frumpy clothes who was a little too tall. At fifteen, her telepathy erupted. She heard how others saw her. They felt sorry for her and called her a loser behind her back. At first she was angry. Then she decided to do something about it.

She shed her frumpy clothes for more flattering ones and took up Aikido to firm up her body. Boys looked at her differently. She knew when they were thinking about her, what they were thinking about her. She also learned just the right way to wink at them. Within a few months she went from frail to feral. Teenage boys, drunk with their hormones, became her playthings. At least until Jason Kupnicke.

Jason was a football player, a cliché from a wealthy family, with a girlfriend named Allison on the cheerleading squad. Garnet thought he'd be a challenge. In the end, he was all too easy. She whispered things to him in the library, things he wanted but could never bring himself to ask Allison to do. Garnet promised him all that and more.

After one kiss under the bleachers, he trembled at her touch. Conquest over, she moved on to other things. Jason did not.

One night Garnet woke up from a dream and knew that someone was watching her. Jason. She slid out of bed and went to the bedroom window. There he was, in the shadows by the backyard shed staring up at her bedroom window. He was imagining her body naked under his hands. He would do anything to be with her, whether she wanted it or not.

She backed away from the window, not sure what to do. She looked at her bookshelf, her eyes landing on Stephen King's Firestarter. She thought of the father, the one who could control people's minds. She wondered if she could do the same thing. She focused on Jason's shadow and pushed with her mind.

For a moment, nothing happened. Then she saw the flames engulf his hair and clothes. Jason threw himself down and rolled in the dry grass, trying to smother the fire out. Her father entered the room to see why she was screaming. Outside, the fire grew larger and larger, the dry grass devoured by flame until the whole backyard was a sea of flames. She heard Jason's last thought as he died. It was of her.

She didn't sleep for days.

A rumor went around school: Jason had set himself on fire in her backyard because he did not want to live without her. It became accepted reality. Teenagers kill themselves every day.

She did not go to the funeral.

People whispered behind her back. Pockets of girls in the hallway talked about her between classes, wondering what was so special about her that had turned Jason crazy. She tried to tune out their thoughts, but that was something she only learned to do under the tutelage of Ms. Ryerson.

Wave after wave of judgmental anger and jealousy struck her daily, mingled with an almost-incoherent flow of teenage sexual hunger.

Eventually she struck out again.

Despite the Aikido, she did not have the type of physique to pound someone's head in. What she did have was the ability to see into their deepest, darkest secret. So, when Allison McGraw called her a tramp in gym class, Garnet asked her why she lay in bed listening to her parents having sex and masturbated with the image of her father on top of her. Allison was so shocked she screamed and ran out of the gym. Hitting someone with something that personal, that secret, did not allow time for a rebuttal.

Allison never recovered. Garnet felt a shimmer of guilt when she saw the tired look in her eyes. But only a shimmer.

By the time she was seventeen, she was bored and alone. She quickly discovered that boys were better lovers in their imagination than they were in reality. Even the fear and jealousy directed at her became tedious. So many people had exactly the same thoughts, it felt like facing a collective of petty, insignificant insects.

Then she began using her power outside of school. That's what drew Wisdom to her.

Unlike Jason, she didn't come from a wealthy family. Everything she wanted was so expensive. She started with extortion: next-door neighbors and people she stumbled upon at the mall. When you can read minds, it's child's play to blackmail people, easy to know which ones have the money to keep their secrets hidden. It was also easy to break into their houses when you knew their security codes, where they kept the spare keys, and when they would be away from home. It was so simple she called these break-ins 'shopping.'

During one of those little shopping sprees, she stumbled upon a ten-page report that changed the way she looked at the world. The house belonged to a member of Candleworks who broke protocol and brought home sensitive documents. The report covered a murder that

Candleworks attributed to a crazed Sasquatch. If not for the full-colored pictures accompanying the report – the creature's corpse on an autopsy table and mangled human bodies – she would have laughed the whole thing off as fiction.

The photos forced her to see the truth. Some people would have run. Instead, it left her wanting to know more. Maybe she wasn't the only impossible thing in the world. If Big Foot existed, maybe she wasn't alone. Maybe there were others like her.

She staked the house for several days before. When the agent was home, she read his thoughts from a car across the street. She discovered Candlework's Vancouver location. On a Friday night, she told her parents she was going to the movies with friends and drove to a twenty-four-story building at 1169 Alexander. Outside, a sign proclaimed the company was Fault-Aid: Seismic Hazard Mitigation Experts. She parked across the street with a cup coffee while she scanned the building for random thoughts.

Then there was knock on the window.

She yelped, spilling coffee down her front. She felt like a mouse caught sneaking out of its home, too startled to even think of running. She looked at the man who knocked and realized something even as his smile filled her eyes. She had not heard him coming. She should have been able to hear his thoughts long before he'd approached the car. Wisdom's mind was closed to her.

***

She felt the tension long before she reached Wisdom's office. It was a workday, not long past noon, but the reception area and the outer offices were deserted. Wisdom had sent everyone home early.

Wisdom leaned against the window, looking like something from a fashion magazine in his expensive red suit framed by the backdrop of Hong Kong. All the wounds from his fight with his father were healed. Jessica sat in a chair against the wall to Garnet's left. She held a ceramic mug filled with still-steaming coffee and stared into the liquid. Garnet flinched, instinctively thinking Jessica was too young to be drinking coffee. Jessica looked over and stuck her tongue out at Garnet. Obviously, she'd heard the thought.

Todd, eyes red and face smudged with wet streaks, sat in one of the chairs next to Wisdom's desk. He kept shaking his head: small measured movements. He was cleaning invisible dirt from beneath his fingernails, his eyes refusing to focus on anyone else in the room. Elaine stood beside another of the chairs, her body stiff and distant. She was decked out in a black pantsuit that showed a surprising level of class. Garnet was used to seeing Wisdom's hired gun in leather trench coats and mud-soaked dark clothing. David sat in a third chair. Although sitting was not quite the right word for what he was doing. It seemed like his body had been bent in half. His head was in his hands, which in turn were almost lying on his knees. His body jerked in sharp spasms like a fish in lightning-soaked water.

Josh sat on the edge of Wisdom's desk, his body relaxed and, somehow, extremely present. Garnet gasped. 'I can't read his mind, either!' She looked at him, seeing nothing but his body. 'How?'

Keeping her eyes on him, Garnet walked into the room and closed the door behind her. Josh pushed himself off the desk and took a few steps toward her.

"Sorry I'm late," she said. "I'm ready when you are."

"Oh, Jesus. We're dead." David stood up and paced in short quick strides.

"Sit down, David." From the tone in Wisdom's voice, it was not the first time he'd said those words today. David sat down heavily.

Echo yawned and ran her fingers through her hair. "Seriously, Wisdom, do we have to bring the child? We could bring Ms. Ryerson instead. David can barely stand right now, let alone fight a horde of Edimmu."

"Thanks for making it easier, Echo." Wisdom walked away from the window and sat in his throne-like leather chair. "Current theatrics aside, I know what kind of strength lies in David. And to answer your implied question, Ms. Ryerson has her own assignment, one just as important as our own. We'll likely hear from her tomorrow."

"What's our plan?" Garnet walked further into the room and took her position at Wisdom's side. Each step added more pressure to her, as if she was diving deeper and deeper into an ocean. Fears and doubts swam by like fish. "How are we going to fight them?"

"How else?" David said. His voice was piercing. "Invasion. Brilliant plan, really. Wisdom is going to pop us over to Greece and we're going to invade their headquarters like we're some sort of Navy Seal ninjas."

"The Navy Seals don't have ninjas, David." Elaine shifted her weight. "And please lower your voice."

"Oh, you're afraid someone is going to hear about this insanity?"

"Not really, no. You're just really annoying me."

"Too bad, so sad for you. Did you want to go and shoot my mother, too?"

"Enough!" Wisdom snapped his fingers and bright light flashed through the room. Garnet screamed and covered her eyes. The room fell silent and she opened her eyes, her face flush red with embarrassment. Whatever Wisdom had done, it appeared to work. Now there was only one thought, one feeling in all their minds.

Whatever lay ahead, they were all much more afraid of Wisdom than fighting.

"Better." Wisdom straightened his tie and leaned forward on his desk. "I know you're all afraid. It's a natural reaction. Now get over it. Quickly. And David, if I hear one more whine, one more pretense of weakness, I will pull your brain out through your nose. We both know what you're capable of. I'm not sure if this little performance is for your benefit or mine, but it's extremely tiring. I know you haven't been trained, but I also know something else. No matter how hard you try to deny it, you like killing. You committed each murder not out of necessity or desperation, but out of desire. You wanted to see them dead. So stop your whining and deal. Feel guilty tomorrow after the Council's destroyed."

Everyone turned to watch David's reactions. It did not take long for Wisdom's words to have their intended impact.

David sighed, dejectedly, and hung his head. "When are we going?"

"Now."

Wisdom walked around the table to stand beside Echo. She reached over and grasped his hand. Wisdom placed his other hand against her cheek. A moment later, he flicked his wrist and a 6-foot wide oval of bright light appeared. Elaine stepped through the portal first.

"Come on, children," Wisdom said. "The sooner we get this over with, the sooner we can go back to ... whatever it is we'll be getting back to."

Jessica walked toward the portal, coffee cup still in hand. Todd and Josh waited until she disappeared before they made their move. David squared his shoulders and followed them. When it was just Garnet and Wisdom in the room, she walked over to him and smiled.

"I'll never forget the things you've done for me, Wisdom." She felt blood rush to her face. "I've never been good with, you know, these sort of things, but I just wanted to say something in case something, well...just in case."

Wisdom bent forward and kissed her on the forehead. On his face was a smile.

"You're going to be fine. Don't worry."

Then Wisdom stepped through the portal. Garnet felt the last of her strength fade away. Normally, it was hard to read Wisdom but, for that instant, he had been exceeding clear. And she knew he had just told her a lie.

Chapter Thirty-Four

Fifty feet beneath Thessaloniki, Wisdom stepped out of the portal onto concrete. 'Here we go,' he thought. He chose a different entrance spot this time, hoping it would not set off alarms. A quick scan of the area suggested it had worked: no loud sirens, no gunfire, no buzz of panic in the minds around him. It was a definite improvement. The first time he'd been through these events, he had dropped the Anomalies right in the Vulture Antechamber. Edimmu had swarmed them in seconds just as his father had made an appearance.

"Is this Greece?" David asked. "I expected the Mediterranean to be warmer than this."

"Are you brain dead?" Jessica shook her head. "Seriously. We're underground, dummy. Kind of hard for the sun to get down here."

Todd smiled. "It is also conceivable they have air conditioning. You know, being a building and not a beach."

"Smart ass," David said. He looked around. They were in a storage room lined with industrial-sized plastic containers of chemical cleaners, large open boxes of sponges and paper towels and various other supplies. The air smelled of ammonia and pine. "It's just not what I was expecting. Where are the big baddies?"

Wisdom pointed at a blue-green door to the left of a stack of brooms.

"Oh," Josh said.

At a motion from Wisdom, Elaine went to the door. She pressed her ear to the door and closed her eyes. Everyone held their breath. Then she stood, looked at Wisdom and shook her head. Wisdom nodded once, a sign for her to continue. She crouched down, un-holstered her pistol and opened the door. It opened smoothly to a brightly-lit stairwell. Everyone exhaled.

"Remember, Edimmu can sense your EFHBs,"

Wisdom whispered. "So can Propates. Avoid power usage until we engage the Council. If you need to communicate, talk before using telepathy. If you meet resistance, be creative. Move quick and quiet, but no PK and no fires until I give the word. The more we can take out before the alarm goes off, the easier the final battle will be. Understand?"

Everyone nodded except Echo. When Wisdom looked at her, she squared off her shoulders.

"Don't even think of taking that tone with me, Wisdom," she said. "I'm not a child."

Wisdom opened his mouth, then shook his head and turned away. He motioned Elaine to head down the stairs. She raised her gun and moved downwards. One by one, the Anomalies followed her. Wisdom took Josh aside.

"Let me know if you see your friend with the gold ring," he whispered.

For a moment Josh said nothing. Then, a fierce glow in his eyes, he nodded.

The stairwell was lit by bare fluorescent bulbs in the ceiling. The stairs themselves were well-worn stone with a thin layer of dust, implying this entrance had not been used for some time. The bottom of the stairwell was an open archway into darkness. Wisdom used a sliver of his own power to dampen the sound of their footsteps, so the descent was silent. They traveled downwards for almost five minutes before Garnet stopped.

"Hold it," she whispered. "Two men at the bottom. Humans. Must be Council members."

Elaine looked back at Wisdom. She mouthed the word 'mine' and moved forward. It was too bright to warrant creeping, so Elaine moved quickly, descending the staircase. Everyone else froze in place while she crouched at the foot of the stairs. She holstered her gun and drew out her custom-made blade. Faster than Josh's eyes could follow, she flung herself forward. Josh heard nothing, but moments later, Garnet sighed.

"Done. She took them out."

One by one, they left the stairs and gathered in the small reception area at the base. Wisdom knew this to be a secondary reception area, nowhere near the apartment complex Propates used. Instead, Wisdom's team was almost directly below the White Tower.

The reception area was banal. Colorful prints of peacocks with inspirational sayings were propped up on three of the four walls. Although there was a sign-in book, there were no magazines. Nor were there any armed guards. A set of elevators was embedded in a nearby wall. There was only one other exit from the reception area: a dark metal door with a large glass window that showed the area beyond. A quick glance revealed rough dirt walls, high ceilings and a turquoise carpet.

Josh walked in as Garnet dropped the first dead body behind a large metal desk. Jessica made a choking sound when Elaine pulled her knife from the man's skull. Echo moved to the other body, a twenty-something man with a broken neck.

"Get ready," Wisdom said. "Edimmu were once revered as bringers of dead souls to the afterlife. They will have felt these deaths."

"What kind of resistance are we expecting?" Garnet asked.

"There will be Edimmu – perhaps hundreds of them – and men with guns. Just in case we have to split up, I'm putting you in teams. Josh, you go with David and Elaine. Jessica, stick by me and Echo. Todd and Garnet, you two team up as well."

"What's our mission, Wisdom?" Jessica asked. "Search and destroy?"

Wisdom gave a toothy smile. "Heavy on the destroy. The Council is up to something. We may not be able to completely destroy them in one day, but I want to hurt them. In fact, we need to hurt them, damage them so much that they'll be too focused on rebuilding to follow through with whatever they have been planning. But, whatever you do, avoid contact with Propates. That means you too, Echo. Leave him to me. He's too powerful for you and I need to ask him some very specific questions before I kill him. Everyone and everything else is fair game."

The Anomalies gathered together in the groups Wisdom had assigned. Josh rubbed the tension from his neck muscles and forced himself to take deep breaths.

"Are you going to be okay?" Elaine asked as she wiped blood from her knife against the white robes of one of the dead men.

Josh nodded. "Just the jitters. This is a first for me – invasion."

"I thought you knew how to take care of yourself," David said with a look of grim satisfaction on his face."

"This is a little different than taking care of yourself now, isn't it?" Josh took a deep breath and looked behind him. Jessica adjusted the elastic keeping her hair in a ponytail while Todd mumbled something and crossed himself in prayer. "My dad never taught me this stuff. He taught me how to get out of bad situations, not how to throw myself into one. Back in Quebec, dealing with those psychos, that was easy. Self-preservation is a natural instinct."

"A proactive strike can be self-preservation," Elaine said, sheathing her knife.

"I'm sure that's the logic you used when you shot my mother. No, don't give me that look. I'm doing my best to put it behind me... at least for now. I may be new to this, but I know enough to realize we don't have time for vendettas. You and I can have a nice long conversation when this is all over."

Elaine smiled. "Fine by me. Looks like Wisdom is ready to head out. How about you, David? How are the nerves?"

David said nothing. He rubbed his sweaty palms off on his pants. Clenching his fists, he took two steps toward a closed door and grabbed the knob.

The lights went out.

David squealed. The sound, far too much like a pig

being butchered, threatened to drown the resolve he was just finding. He turned in a tight circle but it was no help. Everywhere he turned was only the pitch black void of absolute darkness.

"Wisdom, what is this?"

No answer.

His voice sounded very weak to his ears, as if his ears were blocked. Then he realized it was not his voice or his ears to blame. It was the darkness. It consumed his words, ate them like nourishment. In response it became all the more dark.

"Wisdom?"

This time there was a response.

A sound like the call of a crow mixed with a long squeal of tires.

***

Todd felt sticks of ice jabbing into his skin.

"Where the hell did David go?"

Everyone turned quickly, searching the reception area. David was gone.

"Where did he go? There wasn't even a flash of light, so it couldn't be one of those portals."

"Shh." Garnet moved to Todd and put a firm hand on his shoulder. "No need to yell. Remember, we're supposed to be sneaking in here."

"I think we can forget about the sneaking-in part." Echo crouched down, the fingertips of her right hand resting on the ground. "Somebody obviously knows we're here. Wisdom, can you…"

Her voice disappeared a moment before she did. Todd felt his face going limp as Echo slipped away. It was sudden, quiet, like the image from a projector after the plug was pulled. He took a step back, distancing himself from the others. His head shook in small spasms of denial. He was halfway through his second step when the darkness came to him. And he was gone.

***

Jessica pulled at her ponytail, her hands moving erratically. Josh worried she would pull her hair out but he didn't dare take a step toward her to stop her.

"Stay still," Josh said as he squared his shoulders. "The last three people to move disappeared.

Elaine leaned towards Wisdom. "Is this Propates? Can he do this sort of thing?"

Wisdom shook his head. "No. This smells more like my father. He's early. Earlier than expected, I mean. Josh, this settles it for me. Our friend with the gold ring is playing 'I spy'. Expect him to show up any time now."

"Do we stay on mission, Wisdom?" Elaine shifted her shotgun. Josh noticed for the first time that her forehead was glistening with sweat although the room was far from warm.

For a moment, Wisdom was silent. He took a deep breath and then the muscles in his jaw relaxed. "We don't run. The more times I try, the more I try to manipulate, the more complicated this thing gets. One way or another, this ends today. Change of plans. Elaine, take the others through that door and head left at the third intersection. It's a processing room, a place where the Council conducts their experiments. Don't worry about my father snatching you away. I've just altered your auras slightly. It should be enough to shield you from his eyes, at least for a little while. Smash as much equipment as possible and kill anyone that looks like a scientist. Scratch that. Kill anyone that gets in your way. If you see any of the captured Anomalies, try not to kill them. Just remember they may not be themselves anymore. Also remember, do not engage Propates. You see him, you run. I'm going to look for our mysterious friend and then it's off to deal with my father. Don't go any further than the processing room until you hear my signal. After that, get heavy with the death and destruction. Start down here and make your way up to the apartment complex. Try to stick together. You're stronger that way. If you get separated, stay with your teams."

Elaine shook her head. "Wisdom, you can't…"

Wisdom raised his left eyebrow.

"Oh, grow up," she spat. "You know, despite your age, you still act like every other man I've ever known. Always about the ego. I saw what happened the last time you fought your father. We all did. He's too powerful to take on alone. And remember, he's got help now. This is no time for macho bull crap."

Wisdom smiled. "You're quite the woman, Elaine Radiq. The whole reason I'm going after that man with the gold ring is to make sure my father is alone for our final conversation. That, and I have about a billion questions that need answers. There's something else going on here, something I know nothing about. I'm not comfortable with ignorance. Have a little faith in me. I'm not exactly walking into this blind."

Elaine stared at Wisdom, her lips set in a firm frown. After a moment, she nodded.

"Fine," she said. "What's the signal?"

Wisdom's face lit up, a shrewd smile spread across his face. "I think you'll recognize it when you hear it." Then, Wisdom opened a portal and was gone.

"Well, at least we're off to a good start," Josh said. He yelped a second later when Jessica punched him in his thigh. "Nice to see you haven't lost your sense of humor, Jessica."

"Excuse me for not laughing in the face of certain death."

"Hey, it always works for Spider-man." Josh ran his fingers through his blond hair. They came back damp. He shook the sweat free. "And since when do you lose faith in yourself? I thought you were supposed to be the baddest of the bad."

Jessica crossed her arms over her chest and frowned. "You know, you are nearly as annoying as David. I think I liked you better when you were shivering and twitching over your screwed-up family."

Josh smiled, nodding as she spoke. "Ah, there's the

little fighter we know and love. Maybe tomorrow we can go find a pet store and make fun of the puppies that can't get adopted."

Jessica's lips turned up slightly. "Yeah. Tomorrow. It helps to remember there just might be a tomorrow."

Elaine opened the dark metal door and led the way forward. The tunnel, carved roughly out of earth, measured at least fifteen feet wide and nearly twice as tall. It seemed to go on forever. Glowing crystal orbs, nearly identical to the ones in Echo's underground apartment, filled the space with a soft but pervasive light. The air smelled of fresh mud and earthworms even though the floor was covered in pristine tiles. The only sound was the soft click of their footsteps.

Josh felt his body tense, ready for a fight. Sweat dripped down his forehead, nearly blinding him as it slid into his eyes. By the time they reached the first intersection, he was panting.

Elaine held up a hand, signaling them all to stop.

Silence.

Josh strained his ears, listening for a sign of whatever Elaine had heard. There it was – the mumble of distant voices. Jessica bit the side of her left index finger to keep her teeth from chattering. Garnet looked down at her and smiled weakly. Jessica threw her hand forcefully to her side and squared her shoulders. Elaine knelt down, lifted her Mariner shotgun and braced for fire.

Then the lights flickered. An invisible power hissed through the air and the glowing orbs dimmed. Darkness poured out over the floor, seeping like sewer water through the cracks in the wall. Shadows dripped from the ceiling, filling the air. Josh ignored it. His attention was focused on five tall figures ahead of them.

He bit into his lower lip as they turned a corner and walked slowly and deliberately toward the Anomalies.

As the shadows grew, the approaching figures spread their wings.

Chapter Thirty-Five

David was alone in a dark place. His sense of balance faltered. Tiny slithering things crawled over his skin, but he knew they were not really there.

'Stop it, stop it, stop it, stop it! Is this where the crazy people go?' As the thought echoed in his mind, he found he was no longer alone. He opened his eyes and saw a young man in a light blue t-shirt and faded jeans. His hair was nearly the same shade of red as David's, his eyes luminous yellow like candlelight from a jack-o'-lantern. All over his body, orange and blue flames danced without consuming flesh. Dane Houghton, his third murder.

"Still haven't taken that shower, have you?" Dane had a smile on his pale face.

"Go away!" David screamed as loud as he could. The sound hit his ears muffled and distant, like someone else's voice in a neighboring room.

"Or what? You'll kill me? That only works once, even for a monster like you."

David closed his eyes and covered his face with his forearms. "Not real! Not real!"

Even with his eyes closed, there was no escaping. David could feel the heat from the flames more than ever. Flames crackled and he listened to sizzling sounds like bacon on the grill.

"What's the matter, David? Can't deal with what you are? A monster. That's what you are. Monster. Deny it all you want. Avoid it as long as you can. You can run away to Toronto, Hong Kong or Greece. It won't change what you are."

"No."

"A loser." The air grew hotter.

"Get away from me."

"A murderer."

David felt pain on his arms and face. The crackling of

the flames seemed very close to his head now, as if Dane was leaning down.

"I. Am. Not." David shook his head. The smell of burning hair and fat hit his nostrils like a hammer. He knew it was human flesh.

"Of course you are. Three strikes, you're out, bud. It's time you just admit what you are. You, David Ross, are a cold-blooded murderer and a monster to boot. I mean, you set me on fire for saying you smelled bad. Over-reaction, much? Made you see a part of yourself you don't want to deal with. Well, you are dirty, Mr. Ross, filthy dirty, and no amount of showers or running away is going to change that. It might best for everyone if you just stayed in this little corner of hell."

"Hell?" David opened his eyes and let his hands fall down to his side. Only a few inches away from his face was a burning cadaver, raw flesh over off-white bone. The only thing human about it now was the way the eyes glistened with hatred. "You just took one step too far. You're right about one thing, though. I have been a loser. All this time wasted feeling sorry for myself. No more. If I'm damned for what I am, so be it. You think this is hell? Let me show you what HELL REALLY IS!"

David backhanded the burning skull. As the corpse fell to its knees, David stretched his arms out above his head. Thin streams of white and blue flame cascaded from his palms, twisting in the air like whirlpools, and swam in curved lines toward Dane. Even though the body was already on fire, the wave of flame that came from David created a new level of consumption. Within seconds, the whole body had been consumed, little but pale ashes left in the shape of a skeleton.

Then the darkness returned.

David felt the grin that had settled on his face slip away. He lowered his arms and stared at his palms. For a moment he felt absolutely nothing. Then he remembered. He thought back on each of the lives he had taken and remembered how much he had enjoyed it. Murder and destruction came to him easily. It was the after-effects he had the difficulty with.

"I really am a monster, aren't I?"

"Yes."

David's eyes went wide at the voice. It was grating and ephemeral, not in the least bit human. If ice and stone could speak, it would sound like this.

"Who are you?"

From out of the darkness came another figure.

***

Todd opened his eyes and found himself speechless. He was back in Alaska at the oil company work yard. Dozens of trucks, doors open, burned. Oily black smoke rose from orange flames. Charred bodies lay everywhere, still smoking.

He looked down at his hands.

They were covered in blood.

'It wasn't like this,' he thought. 'It wasn't this bad.'

"Of course it was."

Todd turned quickly at the voice. Even though he recognized it, he refused to admit what his eyes were seeing.

"Bethany," he said. "You're dead."

"Not in this place." Her slightly-wrinkled face broke open in a smile. She was dressed in a loose grey gown. Her hair flowed impossibly long behind her in a gentle wind that Todd could not feel.

"I have to get out of here, Beth. Wisdom needs me. Wisdom...."

"Wisdom can suck my arse." Her hands slid slowly down her dress until they reached the hem. "Or even better, maybe you can." With a deliberation that was uncomfortably seductive, Bethany pulled the gown up over her body until she was naked to the neck. Todd wanted to turn away from her grey pubic hair and wide hips but found himself stuck. He started to shake as she turned around and bent over.

Todd took a step forward.

"Come on, Toddy." Bethany reached behind her and

spread her butt cheeks. "I know you want this as much as I do." Then something gushed out of her behind – a dark green liquid shot through with gold flecks. Todd screamed but found himself still walking forward. When he was next to Bethany, he knelt down. The green liquid splashed into his face. He opened his mouth to scream and it poured into him.

'Not like this, not like this, not like this.' Something inside him started to gurgle, then things blurred and the darkness returned.

***

Echo looked down at herself.

"What the hell?" She found herself in a frilly hoop skirt, her torso choked by a corset. Her hair was done up in an impossible mockery of the style of the Southern states during the War of Independence. She was in a ballroom, immaculately decorated in rococo gaudiness. Dozens of crystal chandeliers shone candlelight down on a ghostly orchestra and delicate phantom women. Transparent shades of men in British uniforms drifted between marble pillars that went on as far as she could see.

"Wisdom, is this your idea of a joke?"

The sky darkened. "Wisdom isn't here, little Andromeda. Or should I call you Echo?"

She looked around and saw nothing but ghosts. Even though she had never met the owner of that voice, she knew who it was.

"Oh my. I…"

"Silence."

Echo licked her lips and looked around for some sign of help.

"Like I said, little Echo, my son is not here. This little conversation is just between the two of us."

"What do you want with me?"

The sky darkened even more.

"It's unnatural. You. Wisdom. The others. You

shouldn't exist. I've allowed you to go on for a time because it amused me. But I've been told that I can't allow you to exist any longer."

"Told by whom? I thought you were like...."

"The end of the chain?" The temperature dropped and everywhere she looked, Echo saw the world taking on more shades of blue. It was as if the air itself was freezing. "Is that what Wisdom told you or did you just think of that one by yourself? I'm still accountable to my superiors. Nothing of the Djinn can be on Earth much longer. It is too dangerous. Tell me, child, what is it about you that makes you so special? Why is Wisdom going to all this trouble just to...?"

The voice stopped.

"To do what?" Echo stared up at the sky, not sure she wanted the answer.

"Of all the nerve," the voice answered. "The boy has gone crazy."

"The boy?" Echo swallowed. "Wisdom? What is he...?"

"Leave me. I'll deal with you later."

Everything around Echo whirled and melted together like a fresh oil painting submerged in boiling water. Before she could react, the sensations stopped. She was back in the storage room.

"What the hell?"

Echo turned at the voice. Todd, his face and chest covered in green goo, stood next to David. The others were gone. She looked down at herself and saw she was back in her pantsuit.

"I think Wisdom just bought us some time," she said. "Let's put it to good use."

Chapter Thirty-Six

It took a moment for his eyes to adjust to the dark, but Wisdom knew immediately he was in the right place. He was back in the forest where the stranger had transported Josh and his cousin to another world.

The air smelled different now. Without the influence of his father to cover up the natural scents, Wisdom sensed within seconds what had never occurred to him before.

"There's a doorway here." With an exertion of will, he altered his perception. Not only could he see perfectly well in the dark now, he could also make out lines of energy and force beyond human sight. Many of the lines were magnetic in nature. Like veins of the planet, they pulsed and flowed with life. But there was another system here too, a subtle network of power he had seen in few places on Earth. "That's why the stranger chose this place. The walls between worlds are thin here."

There are many ways you can spend your life, especially if you are immortal. Wisdom had spent his life amassing every kind of power. In a civilized world, the greatest source of power is information. Aside from military strategies and the secret world of finance, over his long life Wisdom had learned quite a bit about the nature of things. He had learned most of it only after coming back to Earth. Whatever knowledge the Djinn had, he never bothered teaching it to Wisdom.

Parts he had gathered from the Akashic Records; others by talking with mystics and scholars around the world. He knew that, for the most part, solidity was an illusion. True reality was made up of energy. Thought patterns and the collective consciousness of all living things maintained the illusion of reality.

Like pressure points in a human body, certain locations were naturally weak. A small exertion of pressure in the right spot could split open the whole thing. Others, like

Stonehenge or the Vulture Antechamber, were manufactured weak points: piercings like a badly healed break.

Wisdom followed the lines of energy through the woods. To his eyes they looked like interchanging webs of mauve and navy blue lights. The scent of the stranger was strongest where the light of the web was brightest.

He walked further into the woods through knee-high grass. The trees, lush and green, filled the sky above with healthy leaves and branches. The air was warm and humid but a cool breeze blew shadows under the trees.

He saw the opening long before he reached it. The mauve and blue streams of lights converged on one spot. "It's like my portals," he whispered to himself. "It's a rupture in time and space, but it spreads out nearly a kilometer in all directions. And it's permanent. Lines of force anchored it like the roots of a tree. Judging by the thickness of the lines, this doorway's not new. It must be centuries old."

He approached the center of the door and ran his fingers along the surface. Nothing happened, which confirmed his knowledge of this type of portal. Mere contact was not enough to travel through it. It would require an exertion of will.

"Here goes," he said. He channeled his willpower down through his arms and out through his fingertips. The portal and its roots responded immediately. They swirled. Wisdom stood back to watch the change. The colors intensified and the air under the trees became slightly cooler. Wisdom touched the surface again and his hand disappeared. He quickly withdrew it and centered himself. "Here's hoping he's nearby. I'd hate to have to search the entire planet."

He stepped through the portal and noticed the difference immediately. The trees on the other side were taller, their leaves and bark different from any tree he had ever seen. The quality of light changed, too. The forest in Windsor had been dark, deep in the middle of night. Here the sun shone, its light more orange than anywhere on Earth.

One thing this place had in common with the other forest was a complete lack of animal life. The only thing that moved in the trees and underbrush was the wind.

He did not have to go far before he heard the roar of the waterfall. It was louder than Niagara Falls; it distracted him. He did not notice the figure until it spoke.

"You're not supposed to be here," it said.

Wisdom whirled around quickly and snapped an elemental barrier around him. His fingers erupted in fire, but he held it in check. He focused on the stranger before him. He was here to talk, not to fight.

It was obviously the same man Josh had described. Long, dark grey hair hung down his back in a ponytail. His features were sharp and somehow birdlike. His nose was long and sharp, cheekbones high and severe. Upon closer inspection, Wisdom noticed the pale green tinge to the skin and the vestigial gills at the base of the man's neck. He was barefoot and topless, wearing only loose raw-hide pants. His chest was covered in scars. Strangest of all was the man's left arm. Just below the elbow, a ridge of thick scar tissue separated two skin tones. Above the scar, the skin was the same pale green as the rest of the man's body. Beneath it, the skin was as white as new-fallen snow. His forearm also seemed to glow with an internal light. The hand ended in long, thin fingers completely unlike the fingers on the man's other hand. Wisdom spent a long time looking at the fingers of his left hand, especially the one adorned with a gold ring.

"If you know anything about me, this visit shouldn't be a surprise. Or did you really believe you could keep screwing around with my life and I'd just stand by and let you?"

The man chuckled and shook his head. "I wasn't screwing with your life, Wisdom. Not any more than you screw with the life of an ant when you water your garden. Whatever happens to you is of no consequence to me."

Wisdom looked at the ground. "Oh, of course. That must be why you helped my father kick my ass a few days ago. That makes complete and utter sense...in the way of not making any sense at all. Whatever you may have heard, I'm not an idiot. You have something to gain or you wouldn't be involved. Or do you expect me to think you are some sort of dispassionate saint?"

"At one point, some would have called me a saint." The stranger blinked. "Not anymore. I do have something to gain, Wisdom, but not from you. I really couldn't care less if you live or die, but the people I am working with do. They want you off Earth. It will be better for their plans. I'm just trying to assist them."

"Why? Oh, don't give me that look. I'm not in the mood for diplomacy. This planet, you call it Maghe Sihre, right? Well, since this is not my home, I don't really care what happens here. See that sun up there? I can open a portal right now that would blanket this whole area in molten plasma. Actually, I can do that a few times. It won't take long before this whole planet isn't what you'd call inhabitable. From the way you just went three shades paler, I'm guessing that's something you would like to see not happen. So stop the silent act before I lose the last bit of patience I have left."

For several minutes, the stranger glared at him with his pale blue eyes. Wisdom could almost hear the man's internal conversation; he knew the man was going to be reasonable.

"So much like your father," the man said, finally. "So much power and so little regard for it. Fine, Wisdom. I'll tell you what I can. It's too late for you to do anything about it, anyway. My name is Gaysun Defksquar and…"

"I'm not really looking for a biography, here, my friend." Wisdom pointed a flaming finger at the man. "Give me the condensed version, the one without all the unnecessary back-story. You probably already know this, but I am on a tight deadline."

Defksquar smiled. "Ah, your legendary charm. Fine. The condensed version. I have something I need to get rid of. The Council of Peacocks has agreed to take it. End of story."

Wisdom rolled his eyes. "Okay, you can be a little more back-storyish than that. What exactly do you have to get rid of? Why did the Council agree to take it? And what does all of this have to do with my father? Please remember I'm not stupid. Try lying and see what happens to all these pretty trees."

"I underestimated you, Wisdom. If I knew you were going to be this annoying, I would have killed you when your father beat you down. The exact nature of the device I want to get rid of isn't really important. Some call it technology, others call it magic. What it does is the important thing. Think of it as a sophisticated terra-forming machine. It alters the reality subnet of a planet, reshaping it in the image of the person who activates it. My world is at war. Both sides want it. I don't trust either side to use it properly, so I'm getting rid of it."

Wisdom trained his senses on the man, analyzing his facial expression and auric emanations. "You're telling the truth. And I can see why the Council would want something like that. They can reshape the world to make it whatever they want. I wouldn't mind one of those myself. So why not just give it to me?"

"Well, for one thing I've already made a deal. And second, I don't have it yet. I'm actually in the middle of an expedition right now to recover it."

"So it's somewhere in these woods?"

Defksquar shook his head, his eyes burning brightly in amusement. "Nowhere near here. You're not the only person who can teleport, Wisdom. As for the deal with your father, well, that's complicated. I don't really know how the Council is going to alter the world, but I do know they are going to weaken the boundaries between dimensions. I believe this has something to do with creating an alliance."

Something in Wisdom went cold. "They want to release the Orpheans from the Axeinus."

"Yes. Something like that. Only, what they planned will not stop there. It's going to weaken all the barriers."

"Including the one between Earth and the Kaz." Wisdom let the fire on his fingertips go out. "Now it all makes sense. He wants the Kaz to stay isolated. He figures if there are no remnants of the Djinn on this planet when the Council uses this device, the barrier will stay strong and he gets to remain the isolationist. If I'm still on the planet when the device is activated, more Djinn will be created."

"Like you said. You're not stupid."

Wisdom opened his mouth to say something, then clamped his jaw shut. Several moments later, he tried again. "I can't let this happen. I'm going to have to kill you to stop it from happening. You know that. And yet I don't see you exactly shaking in your boots. Why is that?"

Gaysun smiled again, this time showing his slightly-yellowed teeth. "Because of the nature of the Foramen you just used. That's what we call these portals between the worlds. Physically traveling through the Foramen sends ripples throughout the world. That's why I don't travel to your world physically. I always send my astral form so the players on this planet stay in the dark about what I have planned. When you came here, it sent signals all over your home world. You won't be alone for long. In fact, your father should be here right about..."

"Now."

Before Wisdom could look over his shoulder, a bolt of fire and earth slammed into him. He flew forty feet in the air before smashing through several trees. Dazed and in pain, he barely managed to get a shield up to block the follow-up attack. He looked around for a sign of Defksquar but he was long gone. The only ones in the forest were Wisdom and his father.

"Sloppy old man." Wisdom got to his feet. "You lost the element of surprise. You also lost the ally that helped you win the last time we fought. Now you're all alone and I'm beyond exasperated. Make peace with the Eternal Fire. We're ending this."

***

Jessica jumped into the air and screamed. Pinkish-white lightning spun around her body in jagged lines and then shot out at the approaching Edimmu. Like the wrath of Zeus, it sliced through the air. For a moment, it seemed that electricity was the only thing in the world. One of the creatures was consumed instantly.

After that, things moved very quickly.

Elaine shot an Edimmu in the head. Garnet cupped her hands and focused on the black, oily wings. One by one, the Edimmus flared, screaming as their wings erupted in flame. Still they approached.

'We're going to have to do better than this.' Josh looked down at his fists and made a conscious decision. 'Make my hands as hard as steel', he thought. 'I've decided not to be wounded by these bastards.' As the thought solidified in his mind, energy crackled all around his body, inches from his skin. His aura hardened, creating a suit of psychic armor. He jumped into the middle of the Edimmu.

Claws scraped at him but bounced off the armor. He struck out again and again, cracking bones and stabbing into their reptilian flesh. He was vaguely aware of Jessica screaming again, bolts of lighting and flame flashing all around him. One Edimmu, back a bit from the fray, stuck one hand in a pool of shadows and pointed the other hand directly at Josh. With shocking speed, nickel-sized particles of darkness shot out from that hand and struck Josh square in the chest. He flew backwards and hit the wall. He fell limply to the ground, his armor flickering.

'Can't. Let. It. Fall.' he thought. He focused his will. Once again the energy solidified. He stood and looked for a place to re-enter the fight. Elaine shot again and the last of the Edimmu fell. The lights stopped flickering and the shadows retreated.

Silence filled the corridors. Jessica was breathing hard, her face pale and clammy.

Josh looked over at Garnet. "Was that it?"

Garnet shook her head. "Not even close."

Josh looked down the hall again. This time the stream of Edimmu went on forever. There had to be at least a hundred of them.

Chapter Thirty-Seven

"Where are the others?" David asked.

Todd shook his head and wiped his mouth with the back of his hand. "That was...wow...sooo unbelievably wrong. Please tell me I get to kill whoever did that to me."

Echo went to the top of the stairwell and looked down. "I'm thinking no. That was Wisdom's father. He's not going to be killed by the likes of us. Come on, we have to catch up with the others."

Off to the left, the air shimmered and pulsed. A dark blur flew out of an oily patch of shadow and slammed into the rough wooden shelves. Wood splintered and bottles flew in all directions. Echo drew a deep breath and prepared to lash out. Then the dark blur stood and Echo relaxed. Wisdom shook the dust off his suit.

"What the hell?" Todd took a step back and stared at the patch of still-shimmering air to the left.

"Wisdom," Echo went to him and put a hand to his head. "Do you need....?"

"Please, Echo. Show a little faith." Wisdom smiled, showing just a touch of teeth. Then he walked back to the patch of darkness and stepped into it. After he disappeared, the air stopped its shaking and the darkness receded.

***

"What do we do?" Garnet asked.

Elaine threw her shotgun aside and grabbed her sub-machine gun. "We do like Wisdom said. Kill everything."

"But what about...?"

"No buts, Garnet. Wisdom said you three were strong enough for this."

Something in the way she said that made Josh uneasy.

"What do you mean 'us three'? What about the others? Did he know we'd get separated?"

Before she could answer, the Edimmu attacked. They

poured over the Anomalies like a wave: black oily feathers and glistening green scales. Josh saw razor sharp claws everywhere he looked. They raked at him but could not penetrate the psychic armor. Jessica was not so lucky. Even as she shot bolt after bolt of pinkish-white lighting, Edimmu slashed at her arm, pummeled her face and pushed her down. Garnet screamed, burned by her own flame. In the close quarters even as she set one Edimmu on fire, the flames spread. Elaine gave up using her machine gun and struck out repeatedly with her dagger.

'How can we be strong enough for this?' Josh pushed out with his mind, throwing body after body aside telekinetically even as he struck out with his fists. There seemed to be no end to them.

Then a voice called out: "Enough!"

A familiar voice.

The Edimmu retreated until they formed a tight circle around the four of them. Elaine bled from several parts of her body. Jessica was also bleeding. Garnet's face was red and blistering, her hands smoking. Josh ignored them. His full attention was now on the man who stood in front of him.

"Dad?"

Richard Wilkinson, dressed in a long robe of blue-green peacock feathers, stood just inside the Circle of Edimmu. He smiled and Josh felt his willpower dissipate. The shield around him weakened as he stared into his father's eyes.

"Have to say, I'm quite impressed, son. I had no idea you were this powerful."

"You knew, didn't you?" The shield around him weakened even further. Josh swallowed hard. "You knew what I really was."

Richard Wilkinson laughed. "Of course I knew. Kind of part of the agreement, you might say. Oh, don't look at me like that. It was strictly business."

"How can you say that?"

"Because it's the truth. You see, Josh, something big is

coming. Something much larger than anything you can imagine. The Orpheans are always looking for new things to play with and the Council needs an ally for the days ahead. Years ago, all the members of the Council of Peacocks surrendered our bodies and our wives to them. I was one of the lucky few to have a son. It's partly why I rose through the ranks of the Council so quickly. That and the fact I work for Candleworks, which gave me access to all sorts of information the Council found useful."

"Does Mother know?"

Richard shrugged. "Of course not. She's about as clueless as a brick. Helps for an easy marriage. I think you realize your little invasion has failed. Give up before anyone else gets hurt."

Josh felt sick. He knew the man before him better than anyone else in his life; yet it turned out he did not know him at all. Year after year of lies, and now this callous betrayal.

"A father is supposed to protect his son," he said. "Wisdom was right about you after all."

"I thought I taught you better than that. Never listen to the advice of vain men, my son, and he's about as vain as you can get. He actually thinks he's protecting the world with all his little games and intrigues. You know what Wisdom is? He's a joke. The Council of Peacocks, on the other hand, we can change the world. And now that we have you, we *will* change the world."

"Father," Josh said as he clenched his fists and strengthened his psychic shield. "You don't have me yet."

***

Echo heard the fighting long before they reached the bottom of the stairs. Then everything went deathly silent.

"The others?" David asked.

Todd squinted for a moment. "They're fine. Still alive but in trouble. We should get to them as fast as...."

A spear of shadow shot out at Todd and struck him in the temple. He fell to the ground, his body convulsing.

Echo spun, looking for the attacker. Before she could react, another spear of darkness shot forward. It stabbed her in the gut, threw her back against a wall and pinned her there. David raised his hands but, before he could ignite anything, three Edimmu flew out of the shadows and knocked him to the ground. Then, another figure stepped out of the shadows.

Echo went pale.

"Propates," she said.

He looked her up and down, then backhanded her.

"Why couldn't you stay out of this?" he said. He hit her again and her head bounced off the wall. "Why are you making me do this?"

"No!" David erupted, pale blue flame shot out from his body in all directions, instantly consuming the Edimmu. He rose on trembling knees and directed the full force of his flame at him. Propates waved his hand and the fire deflected off an invisible barrier.

"You know, you demonspawn are getting a tad tiresome. Why don't you go to sleep?"

David scowled, took a step forward, then fell.

He was snoring before he hit the ground.

"Now, my dear," Propates said as he turned to face Echo. "Let's get back to you."

***

Richard Wilkinson knew what was coming a moment before it happened. He didn't have enough time to react. Josh used his mind to grab one of the dead Edimmu and hurled it at his father, throwing him far outside the circle. Following his lead, Garnet struck out with the full force of her flames. Thick curtains of flame rained down in concentric circles all around them as she set the very air on fire. Edimmu screamed as their bodies burned. Elaine picked up her sub-machine gun again and fired out through the flames, not caring what she hit. Jessica did likewise, flinging bolt after bolt of lightning at unseen foes.

"I don't know how much longer I can keep this up," Jessica said. Her nose was bleeding and her eyes were bloodshot.

"We have to push on," Elaine shouted over the roar of the fire and her weapon. "Wisdom is counting on us to destroy the processing room."

Then the ground started to shake. What started as a low rumble built steadily into a full-fledged earthquake. Walls cracked, the floor twisted and broke. Josh struggled to stay on his feet as a voice filled the corridors.

"Time has come."

This was their signal.

The voice of Wisdom.

***

The earthquake knocked Propates back several feet, which gave Echo just enough room and leverage to kick out at him. Her foot struck him in the lower ribs and he doubled over. She grabbed the quasi-solid shadow spear in her gut and yanked it out. It dissipated as soon as it was free. Moving as quickly as she dared with a stomach wound, Echo clasped her hands together and brought them down hard to the back of Propates' head. He fell the rest of the way to the ground.

'Time to leave,' she thought. Wisdom was right about her being no match for Propates. Her long life had taught her sometimes it was better to jump into a fight and other times it was better to run from one. This was definitely a running situation. She opened a portal of light and ran toward it. She saw Todd rising to his feet, disoriented. She motioned for him to follow her and he started to move. Then, next to her portal of light, the air shimmered and rippled. A second portal of light appeared and Wisdom stepped through.

"Echo!" Wisdom's face glowed with a smile wider than she'd ever seen on his face. "I did it."

"Did what? Killed your father?"

"Oh, well, that too. But I…Oh God, I'm just glad you're alive."

Relief like nothing she had ever known rushed through her. Echo ran into his arms. They kissed. For a moment, she forgot all the centuries of violence. She pulled away and looked up into his eyes.

Then Wisdom took a slow step back.

"What's wrong?"

The color bled from his face. He grew paler with every moment.

"What is it, Wisdom? You're scaring me."

Wisdom stared at her, looked down at her chest. Tears fell down his face.

"Too late," he said.

Echo followed his eyes down to her chest. She saw the spear of darkness that pierced her chest.

"I don't feel any pain," she said, her voice weak. She looked back at Wisdom for answers.

Then she died.

Wisdom watched the body as it fell before him, grief and rage warring within him. Then rage won and he looked back at the man who, once again, had killed Echo.

"He told me, you know." Propates brushed dust off the edges of his colorful robe. "Your father. He told me you jumped back in time just to save her. What I don't get is why? You never loved her like I did. She was just a toy to you. We all were."

"She was my salvation." Wisdom took a half step forward then stopped. He could not trust the strength of his legs. "Do you know the myth of Andromeda? She was the daughter of vanity. Her mother, Cassiopeia, was full of pride. She believed she was more beautiful than the sea nymphs. So the gods demanded recompense. Poseidon forced her to give up her beautiful virgin daughter to a sea monster. Then along comes Perseus, her knight. He saved her from the beast. I guess I thought that if I could save her, maybe I could be her Perseus. Instead, I'm just the monster."

"You're pathetic." Propates shook his head and stared at Echo's body. "She wasn't a princess who needed saving. She was a person and you were never good enough for her. Maybe if…"

"Die."

Wisdom focused his rage and all the futility. Propates' body twisted and flopped until it seemed a two-dimensional image, bent paper in a three-dimensional world. Liquid shadow the consistency of oil bled wherever a bend appeared. Wherever the shadow-blood hit ground, it bubbled and ate through concrete and dirt like sugar under water. When Wisdom tired of the torture, he opened a portal and flung Propates through it.

He fell to his knees and cried silently for a long time. Afraid to move, everyone simply watched him until he rose again to his feet.

"Where did you send him?"

Wisdom shrugged and stared down at Echo's body. "The center of the sun. It's a faster death than he deserved but I want to make sure he's dead."

Todd's eyes went wide. A rush of footsteps came from the stairs. He turned toward the sound, ready for a fight. He relaxed as Josh and Elaine entered the storage room. A moment later, Garnet appeared. She carried Jessica in her arms.

"Is she….?" he asked, rushing toward them.

"She's just tired." Garnet lowered her to the ground. Then her eyes fell on Echo and she moaned. "Oh, my God. What happened?"

Elaine knelt beside Echo. After a moment she stood and shook her head. "You could try again, Wisdom."

Josh looked back and forth between Elaine and Wisdom. "What do you mean, you can try again?"

Surprisingly, Wisdom smiled. "That's just the thing, Elaine. I have tried again. I've tried over and over. This was the fifteenth time I travelled back through time to save her. She dies a little different every time. But she always ends up dead."

Josh rubbed the back of his neck. "You traveled through time? Then, couldn't you have stopped this? If you went back to the beginning, you could have saved Brian. You could have stopped me from ever going to Quebec. You could have..."

"Josh..." Garnet put a warning hand on his arm but Josh shook her away.

"This is the first time you've been a part of this, Josh," Wisdom answered. "Maybe if I tried again I could do those things. Maybe not. That's beside the point. I'm finished."

"Wisdom...." Elaine said.

"I've made up my mind. You're right about one thing, Josh. You can change things when you travel through time. The first time I made the trip, it was mostly out of pride. Propates won, killed Echo, and turned you all into killing machines. It was insulting. I went back several months, had Ms. Ryerson increase the training on the Anomalies. I saved them all from being killed by the Edimmu and killed Propates in his sleep. My father came by and killed Echo while we celebrated. Each time after that I did things a little different. Each time I lost Echo I realized a little more how much she meant to me. It became the only important thing. I found my odds were better if I weakened my father instead of saving the Anomalies from the Edimmu. With all my power I can't be in two places at once. No matter what choices I make, all paths end the same. Echo dies."

"What if you, I mean, couldn't you just kill Propates and your father at the same time?"

Wisdom rolled his eyes. "Gee, why didn't I think of that? Why does everyone think I'm stupid? Of course I thought about killing them both at the same time."

Josh gulped. "I just mean... if you can travel back through time, isn't anything pretty much possible?"

"Apparently not. Because, like I said, I can't be in two places at the same time. I can't even be in two times at once, which I guess is actually the same thing. There can only be one of any given thing in at a certain time. I don't claim to know everything about time travel, but I know the way those portals work. When you step through, it destroys your original body. All that transfers through the circle of light is your consciousness and a stream of energy that reconstitutes into a new version of your body. It's the consciousness that's the key. Your consciousness exists outside of time and space. I can't create another one. That's why I can't be in two places at once. It's why I can't kill Propates and my father at the same time."

Now Garnet knelt beside Echo. "Did she know?"

"No." Wisdom's voice cracked. "Not this time. Things were harder on her the times I told her. No matter what I said, she wouldn't run away. Once I even forced her. Kidnapped her. I wiped her memory and moved to New Zealand. My father found us eventually. That's why this has to be the last time. I hoped finding Josh would change things. But in the end...." Wisdom shook his head, smirking at a private joke. "It looks like even Wisdom can't change destiny."

For what seemed an eternity, no one said anything. Then Wisdom opened a portal directly under Echo and her body disappeared. Only then did he turn back to the Anomalies. "Did you destroy the processing room?"

Josh looked back at Elaine and then spoke. "No. We couldn't get to it. Too many Edimmu. After your signal, Jessica felt out where you were. Josh collapsed the ceiling of the tunnel but the Edimmu will be here soon. We came to regroup."

Wisdom nodded slowly. "That was smart. We should move quickly. While we're regrouping, so are they. I know you're all wounded but we have to keep going. I found out what the Council has planned. It's worse than I could have ever expected. We have to put them down once and for all. Not to be melodramatic and all, but the fate of the world may be in our hands. Let's try not to screw it up."

Epilogue

Josh looked across the coffee table at his mother and watched her sense of reality steadily crack. She wore a flowery summer dress that seemed both whimsical and formal. It was totally inappropriate for this conversation. She had just come back from church when he'd arrived with Wisdom and the others. Two hours later, he finished bringing her up to speed. She took it all very well. In fact, Josh was surprised at how easy it was for her to believe even the strangest parts of the story.

"I should have known," she said. "Not all of it, because how could anyone know? But there were signs. I knew your father kept things from me. I just convinced myself it was because of his job. The job with the government. Still, when you disappeared like that and he didn't make a big deal out of it, I knew something was wrong." She looked past Josh out the front window. "Do you think your father is dead?"

Josh shook his head, tears welling in his eyes. For a moment he was too choked up to speak. Then he cleared his throat. "No. I don't think he's dead. When we went back to destroy the processing room, we saw a lot of Edimmu. But most of the Council got away. We think they felt Propates die. Wisdom says even the first stage of Eyeness makes you sensitive to things like that. By the time we got to the processing room, there was no one left. We smashed the equipment. Wisdom transported a bunch of files and computers back to his offices. He's having people look them over for clues now. By the time we made it out of the underground tunnels and into the apartment complex, everything else had been cleared out. We don't know where the Council went but we'll find them. They took the other Anomalies with them, too. I'm pretty sure Dad is still alive. I think I might feel it if he was dead."

His mother nodded. "Me, too. God forgive me, but I think it might be better if he was dead."

Josh took a sip of tea and tried to think of something to say. Nothing he could think of seemed appropriate. The silence dragged on for minutes. Finally, his mother spoke.

"Have you seen Jan?"

Josh paled and set his tea down. "I don't think that's a good idea. I love her, but she deserves a normal life. That's something I'm never going to have. Like I told you, I have to go back with them, Mom."

"Is this Wisdom forcing you?" She looked at the ceiling. Wisdom and the Anomalies were searching the house to see if Richard had left clues around that might lead to other Council headquarters.

"Nobody's forcing me to do anything. I just made a decision, that's all. Since Echo died, Wisdom has been different. He's not keeping anything secret from us anymore. I know what's coming. And once again, no, I'm not going to tell you what it is. The less you know about that the better. Dad may try to contact you."

Mrs. Wilkinson nodded, a faraway look in her eyes.

There was another long period of silence.

"Do you think it was all a lie?"

Josh looked up at his mother. "All of what?"

"Do you think your father ever loved us? Loved me? Was it all a lie to cover up what he really was?"

Josh thought of a dozen different comforting phrases but said none of them.

"I guess that's just one of the questions I'll have to ask him when I find him." He looked up to see Wisdom coming downstairs with a stack of file folders in hand. "Guess it's time to go. Wisdom, can you give us a moment?"

Wisdom nodded and went back upstairs.

Josh went to his mother and kissed her on the cheek and embraced her for a long time. Then he walked upstairs to his old room. The others were there, still covered in blood and soot. The same blank expression played out on all their faces.

"I wish I could tell you the worst was over," Wisdom

said. "But if we don't find the Council and stop them, it is all going to get a whole lot harder. We have to find out more about Defksquar and his terra-forming device. We have to track down the Council of Peacocks and stop the Orpheans from coming back to Earth. All in all, I'd say we have a pretty full schedule."

Wisdom opened a portal and the Anomalies walked through it. As Josh looked at the portal, he wondered what he would do if he could step back in time. Would he try and save Brian's life? Maybe it would be safer to ruin the friendship before it began. Would he stop Jan from being tortured or break up with her years before so she would never be in that position?

The one thing he was sure of, the one thing he knew absolutely, was that if he could travel back through time, he would have told his father to stand in front of that window back in Lebanon. He knew he could never kill his father the way Wisdom had apparently killed his own. He also knew if Richard had died that day Josh would never have found out what a monster the man really was. And maybe, sometimes, not knowing is the greatest gift in the world.

Josh stepped through the portal of light and left his home behind.

***

"I so hate my job"," Amelia Ryerson, former instructor of the Anomalies, said for the fifteenth time in as many minutes. She felt vulnerable, even though she used her abilities to become invisible, cloaked from the perception of the people around her. It was the middle of the business day. Well-dressed people filled the lobby of the Manhattan building. Most were so busy with their own lives that they would not have paid attention to her anyway. Still, Wisdom had been explicit about her mission: no one could see her, not even civilians.

Finally, she saw her target: a man with dark, short-cropped hair that was just beginning to grey. She watched as he walked out of the elevator and headed out the front door surrounded by bodyguards. His name was Lucius Vitalli and, aside from being a successful entrepreneur, he was also a member of the Council of Peacocks. When Wisdom had removed the Anomalies to Hong Kong, he'd given her a different mission: follow Lucius and report on his doings.

Lucius looked shaken. Though more than one hundred feet away, with her enhanced vision she saw every detail of his suit. She had watched him long enough to know the way he moved, the way he breathed. Today, he walked with a limp. He was badly injured.

'What the hell is he doing in public?' she thought. Normally, Lucius stayed away from the crowds. He was a rich and reclusive man with a reason to be wary of paparazzi. Only something important would put him near possible cameras. Weeks ago, Lucius had had a very public meeting here in New York with Otto Siegmar and Paavo Rothschild, a move that was also out of character. Wisdom knew nothing about what they were planning. Ms. Ryerson was there to find out.

Running faster than the human eye could follow, Ms. Ryerson followed him outside to his limo. She assumed he was heading back to his penthouse apartment, but she followed him closely, anyway. Whatever he was up to, she would find out sooner or later.

***

It was dark in Windsor as Travis Froese took out the garbage. Despite the heat, he shivered as he looked around him. For days now, he could not shake the feeling that he was being watched. A survey of the shadows convinced him he was alone; no one was outside at this time of night.

Out of the corner of his eye, he saw something. For just a moment, he could have sworn he saw a glint of gold coming from the garage across the street. Something about the brief glimpse seemed familiar but he could not link it to a specific memory. He stared at the spot for a moment, but the gleam did not reappear. He rubbed the goosebumps from his arms and headed back past the car parked in his driveway and went inside.

From under his car, two sets of voices began to laugh quietly.

"I told you he would come here," the first voice said. It was raspy and weak but held a fierce masculinity. "The alien is so predictable."

"I don't know about that, Sanchez," the second voice said. It was also raspy and weak but sensual and feminine. "I don't know if anyone saw this coming."

"Get serious, Carla. It's not like you have to be an evil genius to have a backup plan. He's obviously been planning this for a while. Josh might have been his first choice, but the young Mr. Wilkinson is so firmly in Wisdom's camp now that he's far from useable. Makes sense he would start focusing on Plan B."

"Thanks for proving my point, Sanchez. I don't think this is his Plan B. I think the whole thing with Josh was just misdirection. We've all been so focused on Josh that no one has been paying attention to his cousin, Mr. Froese. If you want my opinion, I think using Travis was his plan all along."

From the shadows, Sanchez gasped. Then he laughed. "You know what, Carla? I think you might be right."

"And the Council has no idea."

More laughter.

"Well isn't this just rich. I can't wait to see what happens next."

THE END

Coming in June 2014 – Beyond the Black Sea
Second Installment in the Activation Series

Acknowledgements

Last year, if you'd asked me, I would have told you writing was a lonely, solitary activity. Now I know better.

First, a thank you to my beta readers: James Marentette, Rob Welch, Bronwyn Cair, Stephanie Parent, Craig McGray and Carey Heywood.

To Charles Ekeke, a special thanks for being my harshest critic. You forced me to look at some of the largest weak spots in Council of Peacocks and make them stronger.

To Christie Stratos for spot-on line edits and constant encouragement. You pointed out weaknesses in the story and inconsistencies between scenes. This type of error is much harder to spot and more important to the reader's enjoyment.

I also need to thank Linda Johannesson for her thorough, in-depth proofreading. You were worth every dime and then some. You found things no one else did. You also helped immensely by improving Australian slang and finding all my Canadianisms.

A huge thank you to Mary Jeddore Blakney who did the edits for this second edition. Jae, you are the best proofreader I've ever met. You found tons of grammar errors and typos that slipped through in the first edition. Every author should be lucky enough to receive the type of tough love you give.

Lastly, a huge thanks to Travis Luedke who did line edits twice. You made me look at every word of every sentence on every page. You told me when my jokes weren't funny, when my exposition was too wordy, and when my dialogue needed more 'umph.' You've also been my largest supporter. There is no way I'll ever be able to repay your kindness.

Joseph Murphy was born and raised in Ontario, Canada. He earned his geekdom at an early age. He read X-Men comics from at the age of 8 and it only went downhill from there.

As a teenager he wrote short stories and wanted to be the next Stephen King. Instead of horror, however, he kept writing fantasy stories. After surviving high school as a goth with a purple mohawk, he studied English and Creative Writing at the University of Windsor.

When not writing, Joseph works as Lead Accounting instructor at Everest College. He also lectures to other businesses on outside-the-box marketing. He lives in Windsor, ON (right across the stream from Detroit, Michigan) with his husband, two cats, and shy-but-friendly ghost.

www.ingramcontent.com/pod-product-compliance
Lightning Source LLC
Chambersburg PA
CBHW070906260626
47162CB00007B/2573